Andromache: Stealing Tomorrow

Jennifer South

A novel of the Trojan Empire

I.

It was summertime and I had escaped.

The air was hot, a weight that pressed down with physical force, and my hair, not content to be curly, not content to be straight, had become a bird's nest. It had not rained as it should have for this time of the year, and the grass under my bare feet was dry; I could feel it crunch even more then I could hear it. The birds had fallen lazy in the heat, and, far off, I could hear when my father's oxen lowed, painting pictures in my head of their huge bulks lowered and resting in the still shade, calling to each other so they did not have to get up and walk the distance to touch. Today, the usually reassuring sound gave me shivers.

It was my overactive imagination. I had learned to hide it, but it was always there in me. Like my curiosity it lived just under the surface of my skin, waiting to burst to life when most inappropriate and cause me to do things that would bring me trouble. The far off sounds of the cattle reminded me that we were playing a game of Minotaur, and I was one of the hunted Athenians. In my mind, the lazy call became something darker and the grove of trees around me became great stone pillars and long dark halls that led forever inward like a dying spider's legs. Even in the heat I shivered, enjoying the scare even as my steps became quicker. One of my brothers was back there, somewhere behind me, playing the part of the bull-headed son of Crete as he hunted down friends

1

and siblings.

Even as a child, I did not miss the humor of one of my brothers 'playing' at being bull-headed.

We had the whole olive grove as our maze to hide ourselves in, though I knew most of my age mates would congregate near the old olive press and its outbuildings. I let them have the cool stone and shadow, knowing my safety lay in being where no one would think to look for me. It would mean a long time alone with nothing to entertain me but myself but it would give me secret pride to be able to walk into the hall once the sun had set and see my brother's sullen face. It irked the hunters that they could never find their little sister, but they never thought to look in the out of the way places that I found to hide in. They enjoyed lording their superiority over me in so many other areas. It was my little bit of revenge to have this at least. The ability to confound their much vaunted hunting skills.

I was a child and, with a child's mind, I chaffed against the restraints others would put on me just because I was born a girl.

In the distance I heard one of the girls shriek and knew my brother had found his first victim. I guessed it was probably Crythaliss, who never hid from my brothers as well as she should. It made me smile. She could keep her silly boys. I wanted to win.

I passed the beekeeper's hut, and almost thought of stopping there. Even if my brother did to bother check, Orease would hide me. I liked Orease. He was a magician. Who else could lull the bees into letting him take their honeycombs and walk away without a single sting? My mother used the honey in her magic sometimes, too, and that was just extra proof to my mind. Everyone knew my mother was a sorceress. That was why she was allowed to do what she wanted undisturbed and why no one stopped her when she called me into her dark rooms and I did not come out for days.

I wiped a hand across my forehead and kept walking. It felt good to be walking again. Orease would have to wait. I wanted to be outside, in the sun and fresh air. It helped drive away the thoughts of my mother and her secret dark room that even my father did not know of.

The grove circled a hill and I scrambled up it, taking the hard way instead of the winding path because climbing straight up was actually faster even if it took more effort. I liked the challenge, besides, and the way my body ached a little by the time I was to the top. I leaned against a tree and rested for a while, the fabric of my dress clinging to my back with sweat. Maybe I would go down to one of the little rivers and swim to cool off. It would be cheating, but if no one saw me, and we all knew my brothers could never find me anyway, did it still count? I was just looking back over the grove from my new viewpoint when I heard the sound of someone coming up the path behind me. Startled, I wasted a second debating what to do. If it was one

3

of the male servants or soldiers, they would surely tell my brother where I was if they saw me. If it was one of the maidservants or slaves, they'd be glad to have an excuse to stop their work and keep me company. I decided discretion was the better part of it and, as quietly as I was able, clambered up into the tree I had been leaning against so recently, quietly promising the nymph in it that I meant no harm and would sing her a very good song if she would but help hide me with her branches.

The tree was too slim for me to find a branch thick enough to sit on but I was a skinny girl myself, and so I stood, wrapping my arms around the thinning trunk, cheek pressed against her bark, and listened. For a short time there was no sound, and then I heard footfalls over loose soil and felt a little thrill. It was too early for my brother to be hunting this far afield but there was still the thought of being hidden from someone else without them even knowing it that made me smile. I was too young yet to realize that there were times you did not want to see what someone did when they thought they were in secret.

The occasional sound of passage drew closer and, for fun, I tried to figure out who it was coming. The steps were too heavy to be Saffo, my father's newest concubine and too light to be my, as far as I was concerned, outgrown nursemaid. It was not Orease because there were no flowers up here, and he was never interested in anything that was not bees. The fact was, it could have been dozens of people I knew coming this way. I knew that. I enjoyed the challenge of trying to figure out the puzzle though, shifting on my branch to see better.

In fact, it was no one I could have predicted.

My brows drew down over my eyes in a move my nurse would have assured me would cause wrinkles, and I frowned slightly as a man came into view, calmly meandering his way through the grove. His hair was dark and curly and he was wearing strange clothing. He was dressed like a shepherd but he moved like one of my brothers. I had never seen him before. Aware, in only the vaguest of ways, that strange men were to be avoided, I stayed still against my tree and watched him with, easily, more curiosity than fear. I thought, at the time, that I already knew what the face of fear was. And it was not young and beardless and male.

He paused to the right of my tree and shaded his eyes with a hand, looking out from our vantage point over my father's lands. The hill was not so tall as Mount Ida, but it was still enough of a rise to that I knew he would see the rest of the olive grove. Orease's small hut and the hives behind it. The oil press and the ruins of the old one that an improper sacrifice to Demeter had caused to be abandoned. The track for my brother's chariot races and the stables. The tip of one of our grain fields and finally, taking up most of the limited horizon, my father's house.

King Eetion's palace.

The stranger watched the land in front of

him and I watched him. He was sweaty just as I was. The path came up the back of the hill I had climbed the front of and I wondered if he had driven a cart or if he had been walking. I wondered where he would have been walking from. Our nearest neighbors were Hippoplacia and Killa to the East, but Fair Days would not begin until after harvest in the fall. There was very little to trade at this time of year. He could not be a messenger because it was a death sentence to be taking this much time to stop and admire a view if there was a message to be delivered. And he had not come from the sea, which would have placed him on the other side of the house and so my brief hope that he was something as exciting as a sea raider died quickly to my logic as well. As disheveled looking as he was, I knew he was no god in disguise. He was a new puzzle for me and I turned him over again and again in my head looking for the answer.

"I'm debating whether to acknowledge you or not."

The voice was mild with an odd accent and it took me a moment before I realized he must be addressing me, for he didn't move from where he stood looking out over the landscape. But how could he be talking to me if I hadn't made a sound to give myself away?

"In the olive tree. You must be up there for a reason and I'm trying to decide if it's a reason I should interrupt or not."

Now I scowled, dropping the puzzle of who

he was to deal with what concerned me more.

"How did you find me?" I asked and he finally turned his head so that I could see all of his face. He was darkly tanned and he had very dark eyes under low, straight brows. His nose was too big for his face. When he smiled though, it didn't matter. And he smiled as he spotted me.

"You're casting a shadow. And you don't look like a tree branch."

Still frowning, I looked at the tree's shadow myself. I saw that, indeed, if you were looking, there was my own shadow inside the tree's porous one, making an odd straightness against the otherwise twisting trunk.

"Oh." I was a bit crestfallen, but it only lasted a minute. I could appreciate his cleverness. I supposed my brothers never looked at shadows. Thinking about it, I couldn't see them standing still long enough for it. With a nod, because he had found me fairly, I slipped down the tree a bit until I reached the lower branches and knelt down on one of them to peer at him. "How did you know to look?" I asked and watched the surprise at my question move across his face before his lips turned upward and he shrugged.

"I always look," he answered, and I nodded again. With a child's mind, it made sense to me. How was I to know until much later what a strange trait it was to have, especially in a man?

"That's fair," I agreed. "What are you doing here?"

He chuckled then, a quiet sound, but it wasn't scary the way some chuckles were. Again he shrugged and I noticed he had wide shoulders. So he was no messenger or runner.

"I got lost. A bit. I'm exploring."

My eyes widened and I smiled. Exploring. That was fun. It was going to see just because you were curious and no one ever chided the great heroes or poets for curiosity like that. I wondered if he would let me go exploring with him and then realized that not only would Nurse explode if I even suggested such a thing, but that people who went exploring wouldn't want to be bothered with little girls. It was disappointing but I decided it just meant I would have to go exploring on my own.

"What are you exploring for?" I asked and he chuckled again, fuller this time.

"What a lot of questions you have."

"You answer them," I pointed out, because as far as I was concerned that gave me every right to ask more. He frowned in mock thought and nodded.

"I do," he agreed after a moment and then answered: "I don't want to see things on a map. I want to see them with my own eyes. So that when someone says Poseidon has touched his trident to the coast of Pedasus or that raiders have been spotted near Chrysa, I can see in my head what they're talking about instead of trying to understand it by looking at a map."

It made sense to me.

"You're a warrior," I stated, and he smiled in surprise but it only made sense to me. Traders were interested in maps and places too but not in raiders or earthquakes. Poets wanted stories about heroes, not bandits. So he must be a warrior. It pleased me that I had surprised him with my deduction. I liked surprising people by being cleverer than they thought a girl my age should be. A thought struck me then and I asked excitedly:

"Are you a mercenary?"

He actually laughed at that, though, I think looking back, he laughed more at how excited I was at the concept than at the inadvertent insult.

"Now I wish I was." He was still smiling, and it made me realize he must not be much older than some of my brothers. He did not look young until he smiled. "And I'm more than a warrior," his voice changed as he said it and his face did too, shifting so that it was softer and he still looked young but in a different way. I felt suddenly, without understanding why, bad for calling him a warrior, even though it was all my brothers wanted to be called these days. I leaned down from my tree and kissed his forehead the way my nurse did to make me feel better.

"I'm sorry," I told him honestly. "You can be a beekeeper, too, if you want."

His face changed again, and I forgot his nose was too big. He had the nicest eyes I had ever seen.

"Do you often go around kissing strangers

9

and offering them positions of service?" He was teasing me but it was in the nice way, not the cruel one, and I liked the way it made me feel.

"Only when they find my hiding place," I offered with a smile. Vaguely, for the first time, aware of the way words could be a game too. It was - an odd feeling, a bit like a puzzle too. "Where are you from?"

"Ilium." He moved a hand in a direction that was away from the sea. "Where am I?"

I grinned.

"Thebe. King Eetion's home. You're in his olive grove. That's his house." It was my turn to gesture. "Are you really from Troy? How did you get this far?"

The sound of his laughter reflected in his eyes and I thought they looked beautiful.

"I'm really from Troy," he said, using the city's Achaean name as I had. "And I drove. I left my chariot in the shade at the foot of the path. Do you think King Eetion would give me welcome if I showed up without announcement?"

Even if it were not for the unbreakable sacredness of guest and host, my father still would have welcomed a visitor. It had been over a month since the last ship had sailed up the coast, and a new face always brought new news and stories. Especially one from far off Ilium!

"Oh yes," I was very sure about it as I answered. "He will keep you up all night talking about what you've seen."

"Good. Because I need a bath," he grinned and then he found my face with his eyes. "But you didn't ask me a question. So I can't ask you mine now."

"Oh." I gave it some thought, then rested my cheek against the trunk of my tree. "What is your name?"

His eyes flickered in surprise, and he shook his head.

"Now I have two questions to ask to your one." But he was smiling. "My name is Hector. And I was going to ask if you would come down out of your tree."

I did come out of the tree, though there was a brief debate about it inside me. If I came down, my brothers might spot me and that would count as finding me. If they didn't and I got back to the palace, that would be cheating and I wouldn't win. If I didn't come down though, then Hector would go to the palace himself and I would miss the chance at a chariot ride and getting answers to my questions about far off Ilium.

"Not a nymph then," he teased as I dropped out of the tree and landed on my feet.

"No." I thought it was a funny assumption, but I did lean in and press my lips to the tree's warm bark, silently promising to come back with the song for her as soon as I could. Then I looked back at the stranger.

"But we can't stay in the olive grove too long," I instructed, still set on, if not winning anymore, at least not losing.

"All right," he agreed, starting down the dirt packed path and I was pleased by his understanding of how important it was. As I fell into step next to him, half skipping, even with my stork legs, to keep up, he asked:

"Why?"

"We're playing Minotaur," I explained the importance. "I'm one of the Athenians."

"Ah." He nodded brows down. Obviously, he was well aware of the importance of not being caught by the Minotaur. "Then why don't I pretend to be Theseus?"

I laughed, both at the thought of him trouncing one of my brothers, hero to their monster, and also because he slanted me a look from the sides of his dark eyes that was laughing and said it was all right for me to laugh as well.

"That's not the way it's played," I chided him. "Besides, I'm not Ariadne."

"No," he agreed and his face changed. "I wouldn't leave you alone on an empty island."

The way he said it made me feel suddenly awkward and I looked down at my dirty feet. It wasn't that I was unloved... just - unimportant. I didn't mind when my brothers forgot to include me in one of their games or the other girls forgot to tell me sometimes when they went out for picnics or wash chores. I wasn't good and I wasn't bad. I just was. Sometimes important things came up and I was forgotten. I had never before felt as if it was important not to be.

"Quiet?" my companion teased me and I looked up to see he was watching me with a smile in his dark eyes. It made me smile back.

"I don't always chatter like a magpie!" I protested.

"But I like magpies," he insisted, then returned to his teasing. "So if you're not a nymph and not a magpie, what should I call you?"

"Most everyone calls me Egret, but my real name is - oh!" and I broke off because we had reached bottom of the hill. "They're beautiful!"

"Oh-They're-Beautiful. No wonder everyone calls you Egret instead," he said but there was pride in his voice as he stepped up to the two horses that had lifted their heads at his approach and whickered.

"No," I admonished. "My name is Andromache. Your *horses* are beautiful."

And they were, as only horses from Ilium could be. My father had a matched set in his own stables that had been a gift from King Priam and, even though they were aged now, they were still the most magnificent animals in our country. These two were a mismatched pair, a gray and a spotted brown, but they were both tall and broad-chested with beautiful long legs and great warm eyes in their wide heads. Hector walked over to them and they tossed their heads and stretched out their noses toward him so that he could pet each of them in turn.

"Yes, they are. But don't tell them; they're horrible when they're full of themselves." Hector offered his hand to me. "Come and meet them. Andromache."

Hesitant, I took his larger hand and he drew me over. Chariot horses were fierce and barely tamed. They trampled men down at a command and knew no fear. Hector was reassuringly larger than I was though, and he obviously had no fear of them. I felt safe with his support and was soon offering my hand for the horses to snort over.

"I wish I had something to give them. A sliver of fruit or grain," I lamented and he chuckled, hand warm where it resting on my thin shoulder.

"They're spoiled enough," he mocked his horses with the same gentle teasing he'd given me and they glowed under it too. "This is Epimenides because he's a lazy brute and the brown is Marsyas because he likes to whistle."

I had forgotten I was supposed to be afraid of them by then and looked at the brown horse.

"Horses can't whistle," I protested, and in answer Hector blew out between his teeth, creating an odd, toneless whistling. Marsyas immediately picked it up, almost silent but there. I laughed, delighted, and pressed a kiss to the horse's wide forehead.

"He does whistle! How clever!"

Hector chuckled.

"Now he'll never stop," he teased. "Come. We'll go to the palace and ask for shelter for the night. He can't show off when he's working."

I gave Marsyas' soft nose one last stroke, then followed Hector to the back of his chariot. It was a small, comfortable wicker one and, short of a small bag that probably held provisions, empty but for a bow and quiver of well wrapped arrows. I clambered up into it easily, well acquainted with this kind of light chariot. Sometimes my father would let me ride in his when he was going out hunting or to some of the farther fields. I had even, once or twice, been brave enough to climb up into his larger bronze plate war chariot that was housed unused in the stables. Hector stepped up into it as well, unlacing the reins from their hold.

"You did that so quickly I feel I should ask if you drive," he said and I noticed he did not start the horses forward but instead held the reins slack in his hands and waited. Wide eyed, I turned my head to look up at him, wishing, suddenly, fiercely, that I could. Instead, I was forced to shake my head.

"No," I admitted. "I'm just a girl. I'm not supposed to drive." I explained it as if he would not have known that already. I looked at the leather plait reins in his big hands. "I wish I had been born a boy." An often thought and one that was not mine alone but belonged to the whole family. They wanted a boy because another boy would have been useful. I wished it for simpler reasons. My mother had no interest in my brothers. She said their blood burned too fast. Hector watched me silently for a minute and then he took my hands in his. He wove my fingers through the reins so I was holding them properly, as I had seen both my father and his chariot driver do.

"Horses respond to your voice as much as the touch of the rein," he said, "so you must be firm in both your grip and your tone when you do this." He closed his hands over mine and flicked the reins with a commanding "Hah!" The horses started forward immediately and I could feel the power of them through the leather in my hands. It was amazing and I laughed.

My companion gave a soft, humming sound of approval, hands over mine so he could guide the horses and I could both see and feel how he was doing it. After a minute he said: "My sister Cassandra also wishes she was a boy. My mother often tells her that it is better to be a woman because at least women are allowed to use their brains to make decisions."

Thinking of my own brothers, it made me smile. It was true. Thinking rationally didn't much factor into why they did the things they did.

"But boys get to *do* things," I disagreed after a moment. "Girls are just supposed to sit around and look pretty." So I'd been told often enough and with enough exasperation. The stranger behind me made a thoughtful noise and adjusted the reins slightly so the horses set their feet toward the middle of the path. After a minute, he stated:

"Don't underestimate the power of women, Andromache. Men do it all the time and suffer for it. A woman can make a man forget the blood on his hands and the weight on his soul, make him hurry to be home at the end of every day. Or she can make his life miserable." It was the first time someone had named the lack I felt in my own life and my own future. Power. Even so much of what my mother did was a bid for power, for control of the world around her. I had always been powerless and had always expected to stay that way. Except – Hector said otherwise. I had never heard a man speak about women that way and I rolled it over and over in my head, knowing that it was important… and that somehow, it would be more important the older I got. Hector finished. "Men can control a woman's body but it's women that have the power to control souls."

I thought about it as the trees of the grove went past us and the horses kept up their comfortable walk, Hector's hands on mine sure on the reins. Finally, I tipped my head back to look directly up at him since he was standing behind me.

"You're not hurrying home," I said quietly and watched his lips move, sadness and humor.

"I'm not married, Andromache."

I thought about it a minute, watching the road again. He said it oddly, not at all the way my brothers talked about marriage. He talked about women much nicer than my brothers did too. I liked the thought of having power over a man's soul. It reminded me of the kittens I was forever sneaking into my room. Nurse always took them away when she found them but I enjoyed sleeping with them against my chest and listening to them purr when they were happy. I liked taking care of them. I'd never thought about men's soul really, much less that they might need taking care of. I thought I liked the idea though. It certainly made me feel better about that distant, vague dread that was marriage. It might not be glorious but most glorious things seemed to center around killing and I'd never wanted to do that. Taking care of someone's soul though, seemed important.

"Hector?" I asked after a moment, tipping my head back again to look up at him. He tipped his face down in answer even though, since he was really the one driving, he kept his eyes on the horses. He made his humming noise to show he was listening. "Why aren't you married?" I asked and surprised a laugh out of him. His dark eyes looked down at me for a moment, smiling again.

"How old do you think I am?" he asked.

"My cousin just got betrothed. She's eleven summers," I stated factually.

The short, thoughtful hum of his and then he shook his head.

"I am a bit older than that," he admitted wryly. "I just don't have much to offer a woman." His shoulders shrugged casually but I saw it bothered him by the way his eyes narrowed as they watched the road ahead of us, as if he'd been stung or cut. "Besides, men usually have to make a name for themselves first. We don't marry as early as you girls do."

I fidgeted a bit at that. He didn't say anything I didn't already know, except about his status in life. I didn't like the way his voice sounded when he said he didn't have much to give a woman though. He was nice and friendly and answered my questions. He didn't tease me meanly and he let me drive... after a fashion.

"Well, I think you're very nice." I said it in my best grown up voice just so he would take me seriously. "I would marry you."

He laughed at that but I didn't get the impression he was laughing at me.

"Your father might have something to say about that," he teased, but his hands tightened into a pleasant squeeze on mine and it made me feel warm inside again. "Now," he said it in the tone of someone with a wicked idea, "shall we see how fast my lazy horses can pull this basket?"

If he had been looking for me to say no, he never should have asked.

We arrived in front of the palace, if possible, even more dusty and sweat streaked and disheveled than we had previously been. He showed me how he turned the horses as he braced with his legs and called them to a very competent stop in the outer most courtyard, dramatically spraying sand from the bronze rimmed wheels.

Much to their credit, and to my dismay, the servants descended upon us at once along with one of my oldest brothers. Hector was *my* discovery, one I'd been rather proud of, but my brother immediately took over and I was hauled away by several of the maid servants before I could even protest. It wasn't fair at all and I was sullen in response to their rebukes about the state of my hair and clothes. Nurse was even worse and upbraided me ruthlessly about my unladylike appearance and behavior.

"I did not gallivant!" I protested finally as I stood in the bathing area. She poured cold water over my head.

"You're an unmarried woman and your father will soon be receiving suitors for your hand. Princes don't want a wild woman that cavorts with strange men."

"I didn't cavort either," I told her, not entirely sure what cavorting was but from her tone quite sure I hadn't done it. "He was lost and I brought him home."

"Like some wild dog," she disparaged. "It's a good thing he's a nobody or the rumors he could spread about you, looking like a rat's nest and acting like an inn keeper's daughter."

"I always look like a wild rat," I snapped back at her since it was her favorite comparison of me. "And he's nice. I'm glad he's not one of those princes that always come to compete against my brothers during Fair Season."

She dumped another pitcher of water over me halfway through my derisive remark about boring and self-important princes and I tried not to give her the satisfaction of sputtering. The cold water had felt good at first but now it had stolen all my hoarded body heat and I was getting cold. I hated cold more than anything else, even more than wet or hot. I shivered and Nurse was immediately contrite. Which, unfair though it was, was the reason I had shivered...

"You little dear." She hefted herself down off the stool she'd started having to stand on to pour my baths over my head and wrapped me in a thick towel. "You have no idea what men are really like. They only pretend to be nice to make you trust them."

I couldn't exactly protest that, remembering all too well some of my father's friends that pretended to be sweet to me and then made belittling comments about me when they thought I was out of earshot. It made the tips of my ears burn and I pressed my lips tightly together. Maybe Hector was laughing with my brothers about me right now. I went back over what I'd said, while Nurse tried to dry my hair and thought, now, how stupid and childish I must have sounded to him. My brothers made fun of me often enough so I could easily hear their laughter in my imagination. Inwardly, it made me cringe in embarrassment and I shut my eyes, pretending it was because Nurse was pulling my hair as she tried to comb the tangles out of it. I was suddenly very glad I had been dragged away right away by the slaves. Sometimes people didn't wait until I was out of the room to start their jokes and I was sure I wouldn't have wanted to hear Hector's comments about me. I'd been looking forward to dinner but now my stomach hurt.

"There, there," Nurse awkwardly stroked my half-combed hair. "I'm sure you were a very good hostess until your brother arrived." She went back to pulling the comb through my hair. "Though I don't know what we would have done if he'd been a raider and taken you for ransom."

I sniffed, pretending it was because of the water still dripping down my face at random intervals. I knew very well what they would have done because my brothers had teased me about it often enough. They would have left me there. Nurse knew it too. It wasn't that Thebe didn't have wealth. It was just that it was better spent on things that didn't involve gawky awkward daughters who didn't do what they were supposed to often enough. It wasn't all bad. I wasn't adverse to the idea of being a sea raider.

"The Lady wishes to see her daughter."

Nurse jumped and I froze at the voice, invisible shivers running through the muscles buried deep in my back. The scar on my shoulder throbbed painfully and I didn't turn around, knowing the liquid poison voice of my mother's maidservant anywhere. My stomach, which had been hurting, suddenly felt very cold and very empty. Nurse's hands tightened painfully in my hair.

"But she's not dressed. I haven't even combed her hair out," she protested and I was

22

grateful for her attempt to buy me at least a little time. Threnody shook her head; I could hear the chiming of the tiny silver bells she wore in her dark hair.

"The Lady wishes to see her daughter."

It was all that needed to be said. Chest shaking painfully inside, I wet my lips and nodded.

"I'm coming," I answered, voice flat because I was too scared to give it any other inflection. Wrapping the towel around me as if it was Jason's Golden Fleece and could afford me some protection, I turned to my mother's dusky servant. Nurse's large hands fluttered helplessly in the air in the side of my vision.

"It's not my fault she looks this way. I was trying to make her presentable. It's her own fault for running so wild."

"I will be sure to tell the Lady you're not responsible for her daughter," Threnody intoned solemnly and I knew she was mocking Nurse without inflection or word. I didn't even try to take the comb or find clothes. Mother would find something wrong with me no matter what I did if she wanted. With a last nod to Nurse, not trusting my voice, I started toward my mother's servant and fell into silent step behind her as she departed. Inside me my heart raced like a little bird's.

I had just finished one of my lessons with my mother two days ago. I was just now starting to feel better and I'd been able to go outside for the first time just today. Usually mother didn't want me again so soon after a lesson and my throat and mouth were dry over why she might be calling me. Threnody gave no indication but I had long ago stopped expecting one. My mother could be in a foaming rage and Threnody would look the same as she did when my mother was all soft, wordless songs and smiles. I thought I understood why.

One so often changed into the other...

II.

We passed through the women's apartments and then into the darker hallways beyond. The queen's chambers. All the windows had been sealed long ago, and all the walkways walled in. No light but what she chose to bring with her was allowed into my mother's realm and I was very careful not to stumble as my eyes adjusted to the darkness. Once you were in Mother's rooms, she saw everything, whether she was present or not. It would not be the first time I was punished for being clumsy when no one should have seen me being so. Grace was very important to Mother, so I had made it a point to make it very important to me too.

I hesitated in the outer chamber, but Threnody kept walking. Panic skittered on tiny sharp claws through my chest but I followed her into the room beyond. Hesitating only made things worse. I knew that much. The inner chamber was as barren as it had been on my last visit with only a single ornate, cushionless bench in the middle of its carefully scrubbed stone floor and two doorways led off from it, both covered in identical long hanging drapes. I knew what lay behind them both though and there was a terrible urge to run. I didn't have to be the least bit intelligent though to know what running would mean once I was caught. My teeth were starting to hurt and so was my jaw, I had my mouth shut so tightly. My mother was not in the inner chamber. Which meant she was waiting behind the curtain. Which meant she didn't want to talk tonight.

Threnody paused in the middle of the room, just to draw the moment out, I was sure. I knew I should hate her but there was very little room for any emotion inside me but what was already taken up by my mother at the moment. And then Threnody turned and pushed aside the curtain to my mother's bedchamber.

I hesitated again but this time it was in surprise and then I remembered and scurried forward to follow my mother's slave into the room. It was brightly lit with oil lamps and rare tapers, and I came to a stop once I was inside, blinking against the sudden excess of light against my sensitive eyes. The room was almost too warm with all the flickering fire and lack of air but my shoulders stayed hunched inside my towel. My stomach still felt cold.

"My precious," my mother rose from the stool she'd been sitting on and swept toward me. I locked my knees to keep from pulling back and she enveloped me in her cool arms, smelling like sweet flowers. I didn't have to return the gesture; she never cared either way, and I was still terrified by what new trick this was. My eyes were wide over her slim, pale shoulder but all I could see where the dancing flames.

Everyone said I took after my mother. Everyone.

"You look like a wet little cat," my mother chided but there was affection in her voice. I didn't dare relax. She might just be enjoying herself before she -- before we started my lessons.

"I'm sorry," I remembered to mumble. Terror was no excuse not to answer her. She laughed and patted my head absently. I shut my eyes so I wouldn't cringe.

"It's that nurse of yours. She has no elegance in her at all. That's what your father gets for hiring country dregs. I shudder to think of how much worse you would have turned out if I'd let her nurse you as a babe."

I should have staunchly defended Nurse. I knew it and hated myself inside for not being brave enough. Instead I just stood there. I would stand there all day and night if she wanted me to. This was the one place in all the worlds I did not dare ask questions for fear of the answers.

"Take off the towel. I want to look at you," my mother instructed and, suddenly embarrassed the way I never was in front of Nurse or the other maids, I let my protective 'fleece' drop, my eyes fixed straight ahead because Mother hated it when a woman dropped her eyes to the floor. Even when she put those liquid drops that burned in my eyes and gave me night sight, I wasn't allowed to look down. I kept my hands limp at my sides as mother walked around me.

"Too bony. Not enough fat on her. No chest. And so tall. Like a little boy instead of a girl." She shook her head and placed her hands on her hips, coming to a stop in front of me. I didn't mind. It wasn't her voice I was scared of and I already knew I was built like a boy. Everyone said it and what a shame it was that I didn't live up to the promise of my mother's beauty. Because my mother was beautiful. Utterly, breathtakingly beautiful. She had pale, pure skin the color of foaming cream and dark, rich hair that gleamed and almost touched the backs of her knees. It scared me, deep inside, that when people said I was just like her they weren't talking about looks, but rather what was inside. My mother's long finger prodded my ribs suddenly and I almost jumped, stopping myself just in time so that it was only a wince. She saw it and laughed again. The sound of her laughter was the reason I knew not all laughter was well ment. Then she caught my hand in hers. Her strong fingers pressed at the same spot on my palm and dug down between the bones and tendons on the top of my hand to almost join. It was one of her warning punishments and I took the pain silently as I could not always take some of her others, panic inside me kicking up another notch because I did not understand what was going on.

"Pay attention, little boy. We're making the future tonight. And you will be exactly what I want you to be. I will be inside you and if you do anything I wouldn't approve of I will take little bites out of your heart until you can't breathe right anymore. Do you believe me?"

Blinking, I nodded. She never asked if I understood, only if I believed. And I did. With every fiber of my being, I believed whatever my mother told me. Too much of it had proven true for me to doubt. Her grip, like two bones rubbing together, eased on my hand and she rubbed absently at the spot. Almost as if she would wipe it away but whether it was the mark or her touch on my skin, I never knew.

The next few hours were - confusing. My mother's mood seemed generous and I trusted that less than anything. I was given another washing, but this time it was in a great brass bath with legs carved like lion feet. The water was so hot it made my skin turn pink and Threnody scrubbed me mercilessly with a rough stone. Then I was rubbed down with oils and my mother dropped something that burned onto my shoulders, deploring the freckles that had bloomed there from my time in the sun. She made Threnody do most of the work and would not touch the winding scar on my shoulder blade.

I felt like a doll, one of those silly things Nurse had given me when I was younger. I'd been disappointed to find out all it was good for was dressing and carrying around. Now all I was fit for was dressing and moving around and I did it docilely. Moving as I was told, standing or sitting as I was told without question or hesitation. I can only maintain terror so long and it had faded into distrust and unease. I was bound in a dress I had never seen before. Threnody did something painful to my hair but my mother made approving noises over it. They put kohl around my eyes with a brush that was so fine I could hardly see the hairs on it and rubbed stain into my lips. Mother refused it for my cheeks, saying that I had too much sun as it was and it would only make those horrible freckles stand out more. My shoulders still burned from what she had done to the freckles there and I was glad she obviously was getting me ready for public spectacle just so that she would not do the same to my nose and cheeks.

"Remember," my mother instructed her servant. "She needs to look young and virginal. But on just the peak of being old enough to bed a man. She's not a Hittite whore. She's valuable."

It was the first time I'd heard I was valuable but it hardly brought me pleasure. I doubted meat at the market, hanging on one of its hooks, thought itself valuable. I didn't dare show it but I was beginning to breathe again. Mother was putting a lot of effort into me today. I thought that might, if I was very good and very lucky, mean that I would be safe. Finally, Threnody was done and my mother circled me, reminding me of a panther with a goat and my throat tightened painfully again. She frowned.

"Such a waste of flesh," she declared finally, tiredly, and I didn't even dare press my lips together in response, fearful I might smudge the stain and call down her anger, instead of just her disgust. I could almost see my freedom from a night of pain and I was going to do nothing to jeopardize it. Then she stood in front of me and cupped my face with her hands, long nails slipping into place under my jaw as she tipped my head so I was looking up at her.

"Now you are going to eat with your father and his guest tonight. You will not talk, you will not ask your stupid questions, you will not laugh that obnoxious donkey laugh of yours. You will answer when you're spoken to with the answers a good daughter and a true princess would give and you will not do anything that you would not do if I were standing right behind you. Because I am going to be there, even though no one will see me, and I will know. Do you believe me?"

Terrified again, I nodded, eyes fixed on her pale ones. I would do something wrong tonight. It didn't matter how good I was or how little I did. I would still do something tonight that would displease my mother. And she would hurt me for it. I knew it as sure as I knew there would be air when I inhaled or that night would fall and there was nothing I could do to change that outcome. All I could hope to do was mute it, even just a little.

"Good." Her nails in my skin tightened slightly and then relaxed and she patted my cheek the same way she would slap it but with less force. "Now go wait in the other room until Threnody comes to lead you down to dinner. Looking at you is making me sick."

I nodded and went, careful to keep my steps calm and unhurried, careful to glide instead of walk.

I made it out the door and onto the little wooden bench with its grimacing carved faces, settling down on the very edge of it and not daring to even breathe. The dress I was wearing was unfamiliar and I suppose it would have been beautiful under different circumstances. It was purest Siodonian purple shot through with electrum pins that fastened it close and gave me the illusion of having a shape. The combs in my hair were set tight against my scalp and they hurt. The sandals my feet were in were a size too small and the new leather rubbed. My shoulders still burned. And still - for the moment - I knew I had gotten off very lightly. I very pointedly did not even look at the second curtain out of that room, sure that if I did something would move behind it in the dark and come to drag me into the second room. Even though it was the first time I had been there, I hadn't even paid enough attention to the make up of my mother's room to tell what kind of bed she slept in or what her wardrobe would have looked like. I hadn't dared take my eyes off her except when it had been to stare at flickering oil flame. My curiosity failed me utterly when I was with my mother. I had learned long ago that any answers I found wouldn't be ones I wanted.

I should have been delighted, or after Nurse's words, embarrassed, that I was going to be allowed to have dinner with my guest but Hector and the memory of this morning was very far away in my mother's rooms. I couldn't even remember what he looked like and it didn't seem that important.

It was the horses that finally gave me a distraction from my thoughts. I could remember his horses and their huge faces and their liquid dark eyes and it made something inside me relax. Outwardly I knew better, even in a seemingly empty room than to show anything but I could remember Marsyas whistling and the nice horsy way they smelled and how it felt to hold the reins and feel them moving though the leather. It was a nice way to keep my mind occupied while I sat straight backed in my uncomfortable dress and missed mid-meal. I'd gotten very good at being unmoving in these rooms however and it was second nature to me now. In my mind I was elsewhere, dreaming about driving my own chariot and going wherever I wanted to go. I visited Egypt and challenged the great Pharaoh to a race, then rode with the Amazons in the far north. When Threnody finally appeared in front of me I stood and let her lead me wherever she wanted, her presence driving away the imagined feel of thundering hooves and the jar of rolling metal wheels over plains of tall grass. I held the small peace those thoughts had given me tightly to my heart though. It was not often I was allowed to escape into my dreams while in my mother's dark hall and I knew the cherish the moments when I was. What little inward calm I'd found though was scattered and lost entirely when I stepped through an arch and found myself blinking in the bright glare of torchlight. Somehow, in a roundabout way I'd been unaware of before, we'd come to the main hall. Threnody said nothing. She didn't need to. She simply turned and was gone and I found myself dry mouthed again at the growing awareness of my mother's hidden eyes watching me already.

I had sat at feasts with my father rarely but often enough that they were usually something I looked forward to. I was always forgotten during them and so I got to stay as long as I wanted, eat anything I wanted and listen to the stories they told when they forgot I was around. I loved the stories most of all. Especially my huge father's roaring stories full of laughter and energy. I loved the sound of my father's great voice. It was booming merrily across the hall now as servants scurried to set things in place and my brothers straggled in. Usually I would have run over to my father, homing in on that great voice like a hunting hound, and thrown myself in his arms and asked about anything, anything at all, just to have him concentrate on me while he answered. But I was dressed strangely and I smelled strangely and my hair was strange. My mother would not approve of my running or hugging or asking questions. But I, oh so badly, wanted to be in my father's arms, even for just a minute. He was far outside of my realm of women and children, belonging to the realm of men and warriors, more a shadow on the edges of my life than a solid fixture. Yet he had never raised his hand to me the way he had every right to as my father and he never sent me away when I crept in close to be by his side. Even at that age I knew I confused him, that he had no idea what to do with me. It did not matter. I adored him beyond everyone else in all the world because he was my hero. Because my mother would not touch me or even look at me when he was nearby. Even temporarily, his presence was the only thing that thwarted her when it came to me. Torn, I stood at the edge of the room and was only vaguely aware of it when the whispering started.

Enoch, the head steward caught it before I did in fact and I only noticed him because I was watching my father so intently. King Eetion's shaggy head turned and he glowered down at the smaller man as Enoch came up next to him to murmur near his ear, before my father's eyes turned to glower in my general direction. I wanted to sink into the floor then, knowing I looked like a dressed up monkey on display but my father's vague glance focused on me and the puzzlement moved across his face followed by surprise. And then he was grinning widely, wide teeth very white in his dark face. His long, long strides took him across the room and in a moment, I was in his huge arms, lifted off my aching feet and held so tightly that the breath went out of me. Tears stung my eyes and I wrapped my arms around him as far and as tightly as I could and held on desperately to that safety.

"Well, well," even set toward soft, my father's voice still boomed and I felt it rumbling from his chest to mine. "My little she-pup. I hardly recognized you. Is that perfume I smell?"

"I don't know," I answered, fighting down being as hysterically happy to be in his arms as I had the panic at being first summoned to my mother's rooms. He laughed at my answer. Lost and scared in my new Mother assigned role, I wanted him to hold me forever that way but he dropped me back down to my sandaled feet.

"You did a good job, bringing that young man here," he told me, and something in my chest rose wonderfully. "Your brothers are all jealous you got to ride in his chariot," he confided in me with a wink and then someone called his name and he turned away and I was forgotten. I went back to being lost.

"Sit by me?" a voice near my shoulder asked. I looked up to see my stranger from this morning. His dark hair was curling slightly, still damp from his bath, and he was dressed in much nicer clothes, even if they were still a simple design, unembroidered and simply hemmed. He had a cuff of hammered silver on each of his wrists. When I didn't answer right away, he added: "I'm tired of talking about dogs and horses. You found me first, it's only fair."

Egret would have known how to answer. She would have been full of questions. But I wasn't her tonight. I wasn't sure who I was, under both my mother's threatening instructions and the unfamiliar way my body had been changed. Hector dipped his head and his dark eyes under his dark hair came even with mine. For a minute he was very quiet as he searched behind the oils and powders and paints. I watched him back mutely, waiting for.. what? I didn't know. Then his thumb brushed my cheek and I jumped a little, touch from a stranger unexpected.

"It's all right," he told me softly and his voice low and soothing. "It's just me."

It should have been a strange thing to say. I hardly knew him and so he couldn't be reassuring by being himself. Yet... he had been kind to me, answered my questions and paid attention. He had let me into his world without expecting anything in return. Looking at his dark eyes, I was reminded of the gentle way he'd treated his horses. How his laughter and his teasing had been something that felt shared with me instead of directed at me. He made me feel safe, I realized. Not safe from my mother the way my father did but safe to be whoever I wanted to be and it would be all right with him. As if whatever happened between us would be all right.

"Do you talk to your horses that way?" I blurted before I thought about it and watched his eyes widen.

"Sometimes," he admitted, sounding embarrassed but his eyes were laughing. Somehow I found I could still smile.

"I feel better then," I told him – and realized I meant it.

"Come sit with me," he asked again and I

nodded, taking the arm he offered and resting my own hand over it.

I hadn't expected to enjoy the dinner at all and, at first, I didn't. I was so aware of my mother's judgment over everything that I did, that I did as little as possible to make all my mistakes as small as possible. It was very hard to concentrate on being proper and elegant and graceful and wise and dignified and calm and serene. Hard enough for someone like me under normal circumstances. Impossible, surrounded by my rowdy brothers and father and my father's men. I had gotten quite a few surprised looks at the beginning from some of the regulars at my father's table. It was hard not to squirm under the scrutiny. I knew I looked like one of my father's boar hounds with a silken bow around its rough neck but I could not even sink low into my seat because my mother's training insisted I sit tall and straight backed and ignore it. Once the fourth and fifth bowl of wine made the rounds, most of the watchers had forgotten about me though and the mood of the feast was so infectious I began to forget my orders.

Father and my brothers were at their finest. They laughed and told their stories and joked roughly. Hector was quieter, but he held his own when it came to stories about his travels. He had a knack for inserting the punch line of a dry joke or observation into the story at the perfect moment. It seemed he had done and seen a great deal for his age and I was very proud of him, my discovery. It was hardly as if I'd created him from scratch, but I *had* found him first and brought him home. It felt as if I'd done something worth praise in doing so. Hector was a good bench partner too and I was grateful for that. I didn't know how I would have explained slopped gravy or spilled honey on my dress to my mother afterward. She hardly would have cared if it was my seatmate's fault.

The night wound on pleasantly, while the stories became more glorious and sentimental as father and his warriors reminisced about the men they had fought against and beside in their younger years. Everything took on heroic proportions, and it was easy for me to imagine my father, a giant with a flaming red beard, defeating far-off princes and battling ferocious storms on the deck of a rolling ship. I was very proud of him and very proud to be his daughter.

Hector didn't talk to me very much. It would have been hard to, over the voices of my siblings anyway. He nudged the choice pieces of meat onto my plate however along with sweets and bits of fruit. I don't think anyone noticed. Sometimes I didn't even notice until I looked down and realized there was something new on my plate. The silent attention warmed me as much as the sips I took of the wine or the fires from the braziers. By the end of the night, growing drowsy on a full stomach and the safety and warmth of the room, I might have ended up snuggled against Hector's side, the way I usually ended feast nights against my father or one of his older soldier's sides. The dress and the headache from the hair was a constant nagging reminder though that tonight I wasn't supposed to be a little girl.

In fact, I still wasn't sure what I was supposed to be. So far I hadn't been expected to do much more then eat and listen and I would have done that anyway, albeit a bit less self-consciously. I couldn't tell whether I was pleasing my mother or not, but I couldn't think of what else she might want me to do. As the night went on, I couldn't seem to hold back my true nature, finding it slipping out more and more. I got especially bad about it once I realized that Hector liked to listen to my aside comments that I usually only made for my own amusement. He would tilt his head down slightly toward me and chuckle and I did not feel like he was humoring me, especially when he would add his own observations in his low voice to me as well.

When the screams started, I, at first, thought they were just an extension of the night. My father's men often got overeager with the slave girls after the wine had been flowing a while. Hector's head came up though from where it had been leaned close to listen to me and he frowned toward the far arches. I tipped my head and listened as well -- and realized there were mingled male voices woven in with the women's screams and that none of them were the sounds of male revelry I was used to.

"Father," I reached across Hector to grab at my father's thick wrist and my father's hand closed like a trap over mine even as he thumped his other fist hard enough onto the table to set everything jarring. It caught everyone's attention. In the sudden silence that followed, the sounds from outside wailed louder and more aggressive.

King Eetion was like a great bear as he released my hand and rose to his full height.

"Weapons!" he called and his voice was like Zeus' itself to me. The men, even Hector, were all on their feet before his bellow had even finished and there was a mad scrabble. I stayed where I was, frozen like a mouse. I knew I didn't belong in the hall of sudden warriors but I didn't know where else to go. I did know, with absolute surety, that I needed to stay out of the way. But how when I was in the middle of everything? Even as I thought it, the doors at the far end of the hall burst open and some of my father's soldiers that had drawn the short straws and had to stand guard duty tonight were forced backward into the hall. Serving women screamed and fled to the opposite end of the room, while the men, some of them still weaponless, surged forward in the opposite direction from the fleeing servants. I thought I would hide under the table and crawl to the far end of the hall away from everything but hesitated. It would surely ruin my mother's dress. And there was nothing, not death, not the brutality of strangers, that I feared more than my mother's punishment.

"Andromache!" It was Hector's voice, yelling near my ear and he hauled me off the bench and to my feet. I saw that he had a sword in his hand, blade unsheathed and the bronze caught the firelight from the torches and ran it like blood down the length of it. He shook me and my eyes flew up, snapping out of my frozen moment, caught and held by his darker ones. I had never seen a man's eyes look that way that Hector's eyes looked then. "Where do those doorways lead?" he demanded, jerk of his chin indicating the separate archways that lined the great hall. I shook my head. His face tightened but I wasn't shaking my head in denial. I was trying to think and the movement helped me past the numbness that wanted to set in and freeze me in place.

"To the kitchen in the north corner," I yelled over the increasing noise of chaos. "The others lead to antechambers!"

"Can you get the shutters in the antechambers locked? Any of them that have windows to outside?" He was asking me to do more than huddle with the rest of the women and I nodded quickly, finding my mind again in having something to focus it on. His lips moved ever so slightly upward.

"Eetion's daughter," he called me in the noise and then: "When they are locked take the women and slaves and go out the way of the kitchens. Stay away from the stables and any treasure house your father might have. If anything happens, I want you to go where we first met. I'll find you there. Do you understand me?"

"Yes." I nodded again. We had been raided two summers ago but I had been out with Diones and the sheep and hadn't realized it until I'd come back late in the evening to see wounded men and hear wailing women.

"Go!" his voice had command in it and I reacted instantly, moving even as my mind raced to keep up with what was needed. There were three doors on this side and four on the other. Several of the antechambers had outside windows. The room was quickly filling with fighting men. I realize I should have been scared but all I could seem to focus on was the need to get the windows shut. I would never get all the shutters locked that Hector wanted shut on my own. I didn't question why the storm shutters needed to be locked or what would happen if they were not locked. I just knew it was my job to see them locked.

Reaching out I grabbed the nearest woman. Sharia, one of the cooks.

"We need to lock those windows!" I shouted it at her. She was panicked and crying and did not hear me. I found myself, or whatever it was I was supposed to be tonight, grabbing her face, just as my mother had caught mine. Her eyes blinked, wide and frightened, but focused on mine when my nails bit into her skin and I pulled her eyes level with mine.

"We must lock the windows to this room!" My voice matched my actions. An adult. Whatever I was that night, it was a creature of strength. "You will help me!" I was losing precious time explaining but I lost it anyway. "You will take Zoe and Demetria and you will lock the two windows on that side of the hall. Now!" I snapped it and somewhere in all the chaos and noise and panic of battle there was a small quiet circle that my voice rang through. I had never felt anything like it and when Sharia nodded I found myself fiercely kissing her forehead and letting her go. Spinning, she caught the two women I had named that were cowering on the floor behind her and took them with her, moving fast and close against the wall.

"Enoch!" I called my father's steward to me. The battle crowded the front of the hall but it also tangled there, a maelstrom of men and tables and benches, giving the rest of the hall a short space of sanity. Already the invasion was beginning to spread though, raiders pushing in, combat beginning to splinter into individual fights. My father's steward was herding shocked slaves and servants toward the door to the kitchens but he heard my call even over the chaos of the room. He came. I wondered later why anyone was even listening to me but in the moment it was too important that they simply did. "We have to lock those shutters," I pointed even as I dragged at his arm. He looked confused, but again, without even questioning why or why he was listening to me, someone did what I told them to. Between the two of us we darted forward and managed to pull the shutters closed and slide the heavy bolts home across them. We were lucky. Most halls would have only had curtains for their windows. We were too close to the coast though and when the storms blew in, it was important to be able to shut them outside. The last shutter jumped under my hands just as I threw the bolt and I jumped back with a stifled noise. Outside was pitch black to my light accustomed eyes and I had been too intent on pulling shutters closed to waste time looking outside. Only when I felt a body impact with the wood under my hands did it occur to me that we weren't locking people in, we were locking people out. I turned, gathered up my skirt and ran, Enoch close behind.

I had been so focused on what I was doing that I had been aware of the fighting and yet not aware that it was moving in the same world I was. Running now, staying close to the side of the room and dodging around the results of the violence, I could not seem to notice anything but the war around me. I could not tell who was winning, who was losing, or even who was dying. The hall was full of the sounds of cries and screams, the smell of blood and vomit. My sandaled feet slipped in a puddle of something and I threw myself heavily against the wall. Suddenly desperate, willing to do almost anything to keep myself from ending up in that sticky warm liquid, to see it on my hands and covering my dress. That need went so much deeper than the fact it was my mother's dress.

We reached the back of the hall but the fighting had pushed back right on our heels and I was terrified by how little space we had. Without a word I pulled open the flimsy door to the hall that led to the kitchen and then to the granaries. It all lay in the opposite direction from the sea and the direction the intruders had burst into our hall from and I whispered a general prayer to any god that was listening that the entire passage was still safe.

"Go! All the way to end!" I pushed the nearest woman through and it was all a rush after that. I watched faces as they fled past and was relieved to see Sharia, Demetria and Zoe fleeing past. Enoch ran past. And then, suddenly, there was no one left. I turned my head to see a room of heaving bodies. I recognized no one. Not even men I knew must belong to my father for I had never seen faces like that before. Even my father, so easy to spot by his very height as he stood in the middle of the room, was unrecognizable to me, blood spattered and smiling such a terrible smile. It flashed through my mind that the entire world had ended and all that was left on it were monsters. And it didn't matter how far or how long we ran, because they would always find us.

"Andromache, go!"

Hector. The shout from the room had me jerking in a breath and I turned on my heel and fled myself as if Cerberus himself was at my very heels. This was a new kind of terror to me.

No one had waited for me and the torches in the empty hall flickered fretfully. I prayed as I ran but they were strange, desperate prayers. I had no idea which god to pray to for something like this. My family honored the gods when it was called for but relied on only themselves when there was need. I did not feel big enough to rely upon myself over something this overwhelming. Artemis ended up with my prayer but only because she was the goddess of all things small and hunted - and we all knew how little their prayers were answered.

I darted out into the kitchen, half expecting some huge monster with a bloody sword to come sweeping down on me. All that was there however, were huddled servants and slaves, glassy eyed with terror.

"Princess!" My hands were caught. I looked up in surprise to see Sharia. "What do we do now?" she asked me and I realized with a great hole tearing open in my stomach that she was not the only one looking at me that way. How could they look at me that way? I was just a child.

"Has someone gone to find the guards?" I asked. I had not idea how many raiders there were or how much they had spread out but my father had a good number of fighting men. If they knew, they would come.

"Enoch went," Nikias volunteered. I nodded, glad I was at least thinking along the lines that others must have thought. I looked around at the pale, huddled faces. I was not sure we should stay here but I had no idea if it was safer making a run to somewhere else. So far there were no noises following me down the hall. We were safe – but for how long?

"Is anyone hurt?" I asked. There were a few and someone had brought one of my father's men with a bad looking gash across his head and was only semi-conscious with them when they had fled. My small group had already been taking care of the bandaging of our wounded though and so I just nodded again, wishing someone would show up and tell me what to do. I looked back down the hall I had just run through, wondering if the sound of fighting really was starting to fade or if I was just imagining it. Cautious, I untangled my hands from where Sharia was still holding them so tightly and made my way over to the outside door. Our kitchen was set low in the ground, partially because it was one of the oldest parts of this palace, here long before most of the other buildings began to go up and also because it helped keep things cool. I listened at the great wooden door and then cautiously slipped it open a crack, just enough to see out of.

It was a dark night. So dark. My eyes adjusted slowly, letting me see. I could see the far wall. See the grain barn to the side and half forgotten. I watched for movement but everything was still and dark on this side of the palace. If we ran, we would probably make it to the granary... and once we were there we could huddle there the way we were here. I pressed my lips together. If my father - if my father lost this fight, the raiders would come for us. It would not matter if we were in the granary or the kitchen, they would find us and take us away. If we left the kitchen and another party of raiders came in this way, they would go through and into the main hall and my father would be surrounded. There was no way we could stop armed men.

"We stay here," I decided and to my horror the others in the room nodded and started to settle in. Not a single one of them disagreed or questioned me. What if I'm wrong? I wanted to shout at them. Why isn't anyone afraid I'm wrong and making a stupid decision? If anyone was, they didn't say anything. My head ached terribly and I reached up and started pulling the combs out of my hair, surprised to see they were ivory and abalone. I rubbed at where my scalp felt pulled, exhaled and leaned against the side of the doorway so I could still peer out through the crack in the door.

"Here." I found a cup of water pressed into my hand and I drank it gratefully, suddenly tired. My feet ached.

"Someone should go just a little way down the hall and listen," I heard myself saying after a minute. "Just so we have some warning."

And again, no one questioned me. Instead two of our women slipped quietly down the hall just far enough so that we could still see them and crouched down on the floor. The rest of the group was silent. Waiting. We were all waiting.

The night moved on. It seemed very long to me but the feast had seemed very short. I knew my grasp of time's movement was not very good. After a while one of the slaves came down from the hallway to tell us that the sound of fighting had died down into silence. They looked at me, too. I should have done something. I knew it. But I was very tired and very scared. I was not so scared for myself any more but I was very scared that I would make a bad decision and someone would get hurt. Or worse. So I just shook my head and everyone stayed where they were. If the raiders had won we would find out soon enough and if they had not - well, we would find out soon enough too. I stayed on my feet, watching out the cracked door and the people around me settled back down into their quiet murmured conversations and waiting. This was not the first raid for some of them. Some of them had become the slaves they were now on similar raids in their own home countries. I knew it but it had never been real to me before.

A figure moved in the darkness outside and I stiffened before widening my eyes and looking slightly to the side of the form so that it was more distinct in my night vision. Its limping steps and familiar form revealed themselves to be Enoch and it was all I could to do keep from throwing the door open and crying his name. I was still worried about what else was in the darkness though and so I waited until he was to the door before I pulled it quickly open and he tumbled in.

His old face looked even older to me, streaked with dirt and blood. He had a wicked looking cut along his cheek. He smiled tiredly at me though when he saw my worried face and patted my hand as I helped him to sit down.

"It's all right, my lady. Your father has driven the Achaeans off. Your brothers are pursuing them back toward their ships. We're safe."

I felt suddenly very weak and small and I almost would have climbed up into his lap to press close if I was not so used to him being aloof and giving me disapproving looks. I wanted my father very, very badly. I wanted someone else to come and take over very, very badly and Enoch was sipping the drink someone had pressed into his hands and doing nothing. It was not until much later that I realized he had called me 'my lady' for the first time that night.

Both of the girls that had hidden down the hall now came rushing back to say someone was coming and I think we all forgot to breathe. I stood very, very still as we all began to hear the sounds of several men coming down the flickering pathway, eyes feeling huge in my face. Enoch said we had won. What if the raiders from the hall did not know that yet?

And then I heard my father's voice, calling my name with its great booming demand and I forgot that my feet hurt and that I was supposed to be pretending to be an adult and that anyone else was in the room. I launched myself in the direction of that one perfect, safe, protecting sound like an arrow from a bow and he had barely finished ducking to clear the doorway into the kitchen before I had thrown both of my arms around him and was holding on desperately.

"My girl. My little girl." He picked me up and held me bone-crushingly against him. I could not breathe but it did not matter. He was damp with sweat and dirt and blood and he smelled like it too. None of that mattered. "I heard you locked the raiders out. What a good girl."

I should have corrected him. I should have told him it was Hector's idea but I was too busy pressing as close against him as I could. It was not often he held me but when he did I always felt beyond fear. He made the rest of the world go away.

My father started barking orders and Enoch sprang back to life. Soon the steward was organizing places for the wounded and parties to go out and check the damage as well as they could by moonlight. Groups of father's men went out to make sure there were no Achaeans left hiding anywhere around. My father carried me, forgotten, in his arms until he finally came to a stop and remembered to set me on the ground but he kept a huge hand on one of my shoulders and I did not even care that because of what mother had done earlier, it hurt. I wished I could stay there forever.

Despite his touch, I thought he'd forgotten me as he spoke to soldiers and runners brought him news. Suddenly though, just as one of his men turned to leave, he looked down at me with his great shaggy head. He smiled and it was wide and white.

"I like that boy you brought home with you," he told me, and I blinked, having forgotten Hector in the face of my father's presence. "He fights like a man. And he's got a good head for strategy. He'll make a fine king one day."

"Hector's a king?" I asked, peering around the side of my father to look automatically for him. My father chuckled, a great round, rolling thing.

"There's only one Hector of Troy even if he didn't come out and say it. Priam's oldest son. He'll be king of Ilium one day. If he lives long enough."

"My Hector?" I asked in surprise, eager to forget the fading fear of the night in favor of this new puzzle. My father looked down at me, clinging to his side and his face changed. I saw it go soft and a little sad and for the first time his eyes really focused on me and only me. One of his big hands stroked gently down my hair.

"You look more like your mother every day," he told me and I frowned at him. Wondering why he thought so when my mother was beautiful and controlled and I was obviously neither.

"No, I don't," I disagreed with him. He laughed and the look left his face.

"Not when you scowl like that," he told me, already starting to look around the main courtyard that we'd ended up in, beckoning one of my waiting brothers over to discuss sending runners to outlying settlements on our banks. "You look sweeter when you scowl."

Which made no sense to me either but now

that he'd brought him back to my attention I looked around for my dinner companion.

"Where is Hector?" I asked when my brother paused in his run down of homes in that area. My father shrugged.

"Over in the stables checking on his horses last I heard," he answered and I looked up at him again and then toward the stables. They weren't so very far from where we were, easily within eyesight and the courtyard was full of light and our soldiers. I pressed my lips together for a minute.

"I think I will go see him," I said and my father looked down at me in surprise at the interruption, then nodded. I wasn't usually bold enough to interrupt but tonight – tonight nothing about me seem usual to me. And something in me wanted to see Hector's face.

"Don't go beyond the stables. We haven't finished sweeping for strays yet," he instructed and I nodded seriously. I wasn't about to get into trouble by carelessness on my part. Tonight the outside world had come to Thebes with an ugly face and I thought it would be a long time before I wanted to face it again. Instead, I turned and caught up my skirt to run to the stables. Hector was the good face of the outside world and I wanted to remember that tonight in my sleep.

I paused only when I got to the stables. They smelled like the great hall. Like blood and death and its interior seemed very dark with only the shielded lanterns we used for its interior. I should have at least pretended to be brave but I was all out of bravery by then and instead I wrapped my arms around myself, suddenly realizing how cold I was and called softly into the interior.

"Hector?"

It was quiet for a moment and I glanced back to see my father's form across the torch lit courtyard talking with one of his men. I did not have it in me to go into the dark stable alone, not when I could imagine too easily what was waiting in there. Then a form moved in the darkness of the stable's interior as I looked back into that gloom and I heard Hector's voice asking:

"Andromache?"

"Yes," I managed something like a smile but still couldn't bring my feet to move forward into that darkness. Hector came out to me instead. His hair was plastered in erratic curls against his head and the side of his face. There were dark smudges of drying blood on his arms where they was bare and there was a cut through his tunic's chest and right at the tip of one of his dark eyebrows. He was wearing his sword now, sheathed and in a baldric that hung from his shoulder and across his chest. He looked older. His eyes were very dark.

He frowned and his eyes swept over me. I realized what a mess I was between the loose hair and the smudged paint on my face and whatever stains had soaked from my father's clothes into mine. I looked away, suddenly embarrassed.

"You're all right?" he touched my chin and I

looked up at him. Grateful.

"Yes," I answered and he smiled. It was tired and I was reminded with a bolt of insight how he had, just this afternoon, told me how a woman could make a man forget the blood on his hands.

"Good. You might have just saved us all, sealing the windows when you did. It was very brave. I'm grateful."

"It was so no one could sneak in behind you, wasn't it?" I asked and he looked both surprised and then pleased.

"It was exactly that. You have to think of everything that can go wrong and then prepare for it. If I was the enemy I'd come at the hall from different sides. Just a few men would have been enough to change things if they'd gotten behind us."

I nodded, having thought of that if not in that detail or complete understanding.

"Father's very proud of me," I confessed. "But it was your idea."

"And you carried it through. We made a good team tonight. I fought and you kept everyone that couldn't fight safe. You'll take good care of your house once you're married."

I shrugged under the praise. Tonight I had pretended to be an adult and Hector was telling me that I'd acted like one. It was embarrassing but in a different way than I was used to.

"Are Marsyas and Epimenides all right?" I asked, both to change the subject and because I suddenly remembered them and the worry came immediately on its heels. Hector's smile was there again, quiet and sad.

"They're fine. Epimenides has a gash on his foreleg but it's not deep. I think he'll be all right. They're warhorses, Andromache. They're trained to defend themselves when people they don't know try to take them."

"Oh." The reason I smelled blood in the stable suddenly became much clearer and I felt silly and a little weak in my legs too. I don't know what Hector saw but he stepped forward and scooped me up in his arms. I wasn't used to being carried this way but it felt safe and I was suddenly very shaky inside.

"Come along, little one," Hector's voice was the same soothing one he'd used at the beginning of dinner. "You've had a very long night. Let's find your nurse. It's time for a warm bath and bed."

I wasn't looking forward to my usual dousing at Nurse's hands but the thought of my soft warm bed suddenly sounded like Elysium. Content, I snuggled close against Hector, wishing, wistfully, that he was my big brother instead of Cassandra's.

Hector carried me into the palace and down the hallway, following my murmured instructions to find my room. I expected Nurse to be there, but the room was empty and dark and the night breeze blew in through the open shutters. Hector hesitated in the middle of my room.

"This is yours?" he asked and I nodded against him.

"I have it all to myself," I answered, softly proud.

"There isn't an anteroom or anything else?" he asked and I shook my head. Extra room for me would have been a waste. I already filled my own room with too much clutter. Nurse was forever telling me so. Still holding me, Hector continued to hesitate.

"Is the bath near here?"

"Close," I answered. "Just down the hall, farther along. It's got fish tiled into its floor." Hector nodded.

"All right," he set me gently on my feet and kept an arm around me while I steadied. I was suddenly so tired I could barely keep my eyes open. "I'll get someone to fetch your nurse."

I nodded against him. Frowning, he looked around my room.

"I don't like leaving you alone."

"I'm usually alone," I reassured him. His frown deepened but he nodded and walked over to pull my shutters closed and bolt them against the night. Then he turned and looked at me where he'd left me standing in the middle of the room and his face softened. Coming back over he knelt down in front of me, which actually made me just a little taller than him. He took my hands in his larger ones and I remembered the way it felt to drive his chariot.

"I'm going to be gone in the morning," he told me and I nodded but it felt as if my heart had fallen into my stomach. I liked his company. He gave me one of those soft, sad smiles. "I need to go home and tell my father about this."

"King Priam," I supplied.

"King Priam," he agreed. "It's important. Will you remember what I said about what a woman can do to a man?"

Puzzled, I nodded in turn, feeling very serious even if I wasn't sure why or what that had to do with anything that had happened tonight.

"Good." His smile was still soft but not so sad now. "One day, you'll have your own house. I would like to see you there, if you'll let me in."

"Only if you bring your whistling horse," I instructed him and saw the softness in his smile as he gave it to me.

"I'll be sure to remember," he promised and then he stood up. "I'm glad I met you Andromache, Egret of Thebe. You're a very smart, very brave girl."

It made me glow inside and I felt ten feet taller in that moment as I looked up at him. I felt like I really was as brave and smart as he thought I was.

"I'm glad I met you too, Hector of Ilium," I told him in return. "You're nice."

"That's a description I can treasure all my life," he told me. His hands gave mine that familiar pleasant squeeze and then he was walking toward the door. He paused at it and looked back at me. "Bolt the door when I leave. I'll send someone to look for your nurse."

With that, he let himself out but I didn't lock the door immediately. For what seemed a very long time I simply stood where he'd set me and watched the shut door. Finally, I roused myself enough to bolt the door and then I struggled out of my dress and crawled into bed. Nurse would wake me up with her pounding but first I wanted to fall asleep while the feeling in my chest still felt safe and warm. Sleep took me before I could even worry about my mother's opinion on my performance that night.

III.

Less then a month later I met Bithia for the first time.

Nurse had not come the night of the raid, and when I woke very late the next morning I found myself stiff and sticky with dried blood and matted face paint. I bathed myself as best I could and dressed in one of my usual dresses. I left my feet bare because they were blistered from the sandals of the night before. Nurse would have chided me over both the lack of shoes and the sloth of sleeping so late - but she was not there to do so.

When I went into the kitchen to see if there was anything to eat, I found out why.

They had found my nursemaid in the gardens. Her body had been lying in the thyme patch and had bled out. They said she hadn't struggled. If you listened to the soldiers, they said the raiders had killed her. She was certainly not the only person to fall to Achaean blades. If you listened to the servants, however, they said the wound was not from a sword and the blade that had killed my nurse had not been wielded by a man.

I stood over her where they had laid her out with the others killed during the raid and looked down at her round face. Death had given it an eerie slackness and she looked much heavier than I remembered as the flesh sagged down from her cheeks and throat. I remember thinking, even then, that she was so much paler than anyone else laid out for burial.

The soldiers received a soldier's funeral with pyres and rites of fire but Nurse and the other slaves were buried out in one of the fallow fields. No one who had died was important enough to disturb the covering over the royal tomb.

I felt - cold. Inside. From the moment I saw her body through the day when she was buried and after too, because - there was no empty ache inside me for Nurse. I missed her. I must have loved her. I did not feel the desire to throw myself on her grave or weep or claw at myself in sorrow however. I didn't even have any words to say over her or even an amateurish dirge to sing. It made me feel as if I were ungrateful and - perhaps - not as human as I should be. Everyone knew how the heroes and gods doted on their caregivers and yet, though I missed her presence, it was more in the way I would miss a habit than in the way I should miss someone that had devoted their life to taking care of me.

At first I was afraid that the others would see it and realize how ungrateful and heartless I really was so I hid it as best I could. After a few days however, I realized - no one cared. In fact, other than the dying gossip and the complaints about the lack of hands to help with the workload, no one really seemed to miss the servants that had died. Somehow it seemed worse that they were forgotten than it did that I could not cry for them. So I started laying flowers over the mound that had been raised over them. Not every day. But when I picked flowers, I picked flowers for them too. I always loved to gather flowers and now, when I filled my hands with hyacinths and violets and wild roses, I left half on the mound that was quickly growing over with grass. I might not be able to mourn them but I could easily remember them. It seemed someone should.

Without Nurse to chide me, I went where I wanted and did as I liked even more than I had before. Sometimes I would not even return from the surrounding fields and forests until very late after dinner. I felt a difference in me and I did not know what it was, just that I was freer. It was as if unseen threads that had bound my ankles were not there anymore and now I could boldly do as I liked without waiting to see if anyone called out behind me to draw me back.

The servants in the kitchen grew used to my odd hours and to my surprise, they always made sure there was something for me to eat when I returned. It was embarrassing but it was an embarrassment that felt like the one I had felt when Hector had called me brave. It was strangely pleasing and warming instead of shaming.

My new freedom lasted less than a month though. It ended quite abruptly late one afternoon as I was coming back into my room. My hands were full of flowers again for now I decorated my room as I saw fit, and there was a kitten tucked in the crook of my arm, drowsy with the milk we'd stolen from one of the cows. I went into my room and even before my feet finished crossing the threshold,

I knew it was no longer my room. It did not feel right anymore. The smile was dying on my lips long before I even saw the beautiful girl sitting straight backed and patient on the new stool in the very center of my room and the yellow crocus I had been holding fell out of my hands and scattered across the unadorned floor.

She looked at me with heavily lidded eyes and immediately I was aware of my wild hair and the smudges on my skin. Of the stained dress I was wearing and my dirty feet that the hem, too short, didn't serve to cover. I wasn't even wearing sandals because there was no one to tell me to. In contrast, she sat cool and beautiful on her seat and one of her slim eyebrows, like an elegant wing, lifted at my arrival.

I had never seen her before in my life.

The kitten in the crock of my arm woke up enough to stretch and I shifted it to hold it close to my chest. Faintly, in the very air it seemed, I smelled my mother.

It was very quiet between us for a very long time. I had no questions because I knew whatever I asked I would not want the answers to. Finally she spoke and it was like swallowing honey, thick and rich and golden.

"Aren't you going to ask who I am?"

My jaw set stubbornly and I shook my head.

"I am Bithia," she supplied anyway. "Your new maidservant. I am to serve to you now."

"I don't want a maid," it skipped out from

between my lips before I could think to stop it and I do not think it was so much because I did not want a maid, as it was that I did not want *her*. Everything inside me, with no foundation or fairness, told me so.

"Ah, but you need one," she answered calmly. Still not moving. "Every proper lady needs maids."

I laughed. I did not mean to but it came coughing out of me and I shook my head. Shifting the kitten more comfortably in my arms.

"I'm not a lady," I answered, much more sure about that and where I stood in this world. Her eyebrow arched again and she looked me, very slowly, from toe to head top, but I did not know her and so the obvious mockery in her dark eyes meant nothing to me.

"I can see," she agreed dryly. "But that must change now. I'm to instruct you in a lady's habits."

"Why?" I asked petulantly, leaning down to let the kitten loose into my room and start gathering my flowers. If I ignored her as much as possible maybe she would go away. I certainly didn't need her. Even if the servants were suddenly starting to call me 'my lady' when they addressed me, it hardly made it true. In a few months they'd go back to 'Egret' and everything would go back to the way it was. Bithia folded perfect, polished hands in her lap.

"Do you know why the raiders came?" she asked and I shrugged as I straightened, no longer intimidated by her elegance. She looked very soft and I decided that that made her weak. I didn't have to be intimidated by anyone weak no matter how much they outshone me in beauty. If I could not win the contest, I would simply not play it.

"Gold, slaves, maybe horses or supplies" I answered, walking over to put the golden flowers into one of the pitchers I had dug out of an old supply room. Blue monkeys danced cheerfully around its red sides. Bithia shook her head and her hair, like the rivulets of a river, whispered against her shoulders. Where my hair was neither red nor brown but a mix of both, hers was like polished mahogany.

"Theseus of Athens has recently taken Helen of Sparta, King Tyndareus' only daughter. He's demanding a ransom of more than her weight in gold for her return. And her family will pay it too."

And, just like that, for the first time but hardly the last, Helen the Swan's Daughter intruded upon my life. Unlike heroines in good stories however, I felt no flicker of foreknowledge or unease at the name.

I scowled and sat down on my bed, starting to unwind the cloth I had wrapped around my calves to keep them from getting scratched while exploring through the woods.

"I am not Helen," I said, having no idea how laughable the idea would be to anyone that had ever seen her. "My father wouldn't pay two sickly cows for me." I exaggerated. He would pay two sickly cows for me I was sure but I wasn't the pillar of wealth she seemed to be implying. I was a daughter in a family of sons and I wasn't even pretty enough to have much potential in marriage. Nurse had explained it the last time one of my brothers had married. We were already closely tied with the other ruling families in the area through trade and my brothers' own marriages. I would marry one of the minor princes from nearby but it would hardly be as if my future husband's family wouldn't already be allied with my father even before that.

Bithia sighed. It was an adult sound that said I was being stupid and it rankled me, despite the fact I had decided not to care what she thought.

"Andromache, you are the only daughter of the king of Thebe. Do you have any idea what your worth on the marriage market is?"

"Not much," I dismissed it, tossing the wrappings in a corner. The kitten that had been hiding under an overturned basket made a quick skitter for them. It made me smile.

Bithia stood up suddenly and put her hands on her slimly rounded hips.

"You are the only daughter of a great king who rules over a mighty fighting force. Your father's stores, thanks to both his fighting skills and his hoarding, are impressive enough to buy you the place of a high priestess in a temple or endower your future husband with enough gold and oxen to finance a small war. In another year or two, kings from this side of the ocean and the other will start remembering that your father has a daughter and they will start sending their sons. I am here to make sure that when they come they find a lady of pleasure and not a wild little animal."

I cocked an eye at her. Even then I wondered if I should have been more receptive to her, knew that I was not being fair. Little did I know at that time just how much Helen's kingly ransom had changed the world when it came to daughters and their value. But she was a stranger in my world, meddling in things I thought she didn't understand. Couldn't understand.

"That's a wild little rat," I told her and tucked my legs up under me on the bed, reaching out to catch one of the ribbons of cloth to tease the kitten with. I was thinking of naming him Nemea, after the famous lion. The strange girl could talk all she wanted. She didn't have the force in her to make me do anything I didn't want to.

"I am your mother's idea," she stated. I froze.

Mother. My mother. I had not seen her since the night of the raid, though she was quite obviously still alive for there was no royal mourning. I had been sick for three days afterward, sure she was going to send Threnody for me and give me my punishment for my behavior that night. I had managed to scrub the dress clean of the blood and sweat and dirt, but the sandals had been impossible to save and I had hidden them under a pile of old clothes in one of the storage rooms, hoping she would not ask after them. The retribution that I had been expecting never came, however. Threnody never came. And I had - as I always did - hoped...

"She insists it is time you became a lady, so she had me brought from Rhodes. She says I am to teach you elegance and refinement or else she will be very disappointed in you."

It seized me cold in my stomach and my throat closed over. Ignored, the kitten amused itself with the cloth. My hands felt numb.

"Mother wants this?" I asked. My world suddenly seemed very small. I watched it narrow before my eyes.

"Of course," Bithia replied, satisfied with herself. "She wants a daughter she can be proud of when the sons of kings come looking."

My long journeys out into the fields and woods after that were curtailed. I could say that I embraced my new lessons but that would be a horrible lie and no one that knew me would have believed it anyway. I didn't like Bithia. I didn't like the idea of what she thought I should be. And I didn't like having to give up so much of my freedom, even more than when Nurse had been alive. I went through the motions, but only enough to keep myself out of trouble. Or so I thought.

Until the night I woke up to find my mother leaning over me while I slept.

She was not pleased with me.

Very not pleased with me.

She kept me for several days, I think, and

when she finally let me find my way back to the sunlight and the fresh air, I was already sick with the chills. Somehow, I found my way back to my room. Then the vomiting and fever took me and I didn't remember anything else for a long time.

When I finally did rise to the surface of the oily water I had sunk under in my mind, my first thought was that I would have to clean up after myself now. Nurse had always done it for me in the past, her face a frozen mask to hide the fear. We never spoke of what happened to me or the condition I was returned in after my mother saw me. There was no one here this time to make things clean and pretend nothing had happened though. Nemea was purring, his little paws were kneading against my chest. Weak, I raised a hand and ran it over his soft fur. The tips of my fingers still felt numb and tingled slightly at the pressure but his fur was unbelievably soft, softer than anything I had ever felt in all my life. I whispered his name.

"Andromache." Nemea's voice was a great deal higher than I'd imagined, even for a kitten, hissing it softly at me. I wasn't going to open my eyes because I knew from experience they would shoot needles into the back of my head. My eyes always took the longest to heal. Them and the scratches... I slowly felt my way up Nemea's back with my fingertips until I could rest them on top of his head.

"What?" I asked him softly.

"I was scared. I couldn't find you. What

happened?"

I wet my lips. My mouth tasted terrible and felt very dry. Nemea hadn't been around long. I suppose I did have to explain. I just didn't have much energy. Luckily for me, the answer didn't take much.

"Mother," I sighed it, tired to even being saying the word after begging with it for so long. She had been particularly furious with me this time. And then I sank back under the oil in my mind and did not have to think about it again for a very long time.

I woke up again much later, weak and very logy, as if my body had too much liquid in it and all my limbs were too heavy. My mouth tasted terrible and my throat hurt it was so dry. It felt as if my eyelids were crusted shut and I didn't even try to open them. Instead, I wondered how much I could get done without actually seeing anything.

"Andromache?"

Nemea's warm weight settle onto my chest and the edges of my mouth shifted upward. With a little effort I managed to raise my hand and stroke down his soft back. He purred under my touch and I thought he seemed bigger than I remembered.

"Nemea," I whispered his name and the purring increased. I sighed out, feeling better. My body still hurt and where my mother's nails had gouged me was alarmingly numb still but I didn't feel sick with fevers anymore. My stomach hurt but I knew from experience it was hunger. I still felt horribly unclean, both from the dried sweat and from what – from what had happened in my mother's rooms. I felt as if it had soaked into my skin, like a foul oil. I swallowed even though there was no liquid in my mouth and whispered:

"Oh, Nemea. I need a bath."

Nemea was crying but it wasn't the sounds of a cat's crying that I recognized. Instead, it sounded quiet and muffled, like a person. I knew because I had so often cried like that when I was younger, hopeless, scared and confused. I felt Nemea's weight lifted off of me and strong arms slipped under my back and helped me sit up. I blacked out immediately, even with my eyes closed and the dark world around me spun wildly but I braced myself on the frame of my bed and sat very still, waiting for it to settle again. The arms were still around me and Nemea was rubbing against one of my braced wrists. Blurry, my mind connected the two and my imagination lost its grip on the image of Nemea talking.

I was just too weak and tired to care.

I managed to gain my feet, even though my body protested like an old crone's and then slowly, with those arms still around me, I shuffled into the hallway. I knew my way by heart and the hands and steady arms guided me. The crying had stopped but the voice I'd thought was Nemea's did not talk to me either. I was glad of it. I already had too much to deal with in simply making my body move one foot in front of the other.

The simple shift I had been in was stripped off of me, and I was grateful for the help. The tiles under my feet were cool against my soles, which still burned. I was led into the long bath and I inhaled sharply against its mild warmth. I could have drowned and been quite content with that but the arms wouldn't let me and they supported me in the half-weight of the water. I let my body relax and my mind gratefully washed blank and thoughtless again. I don't know how long I stayed that way. I could have wrinkled up like a dried date and not minded. As much as the warmth and water took my strength from me I was at least left a clean hollow afterward. I could pretend I could almost feel my mother's touch slowly soaking out of my skin to dissipate, if not harmlessly, at least milder in the water.

"Bithia?" I said her name softly because my throat still hurt and I did not open my eyes. My mind was still mine enough to have worked out who had been my kitten's voice.

"Yes, my lady?" she answered and her voice was shaky. My lips shifted upward slightly, not in pleasure but in understanding.

"It's all right. You won't get in trouble for this. Everyone knows."

It seemed very important to me, who had just spent so long trapped in terror and the uncertainty of where the anger would come at me next, to make sure she didn't feel the same way. I was surprised when she made a little choking noise and pressed her face into my shoulder. In the water the way I was, I was sure my wet skin would ruin her carefully painted face.

"I'm sorry," she was crying but it was a quiet, hopeless sound that didn't expect comfort or acknowledgement. "I'm so sorry. I didn't know. I didn't. I'm sorry."

Gingerly, because my joints were still protesting movement, I raised my good arm and awkwardly felt about until I could rest it over her shoulders. How could she have known? Maybe I should have warned her, at least a little. It couldn't be pleasant to wake up with the person you were supposed to be taking care of missing and be worried that you would be held responsible. I felt suddenly and horribly guilty for all the mean thoughts I had had toward her.

"It's all right," I promised her again. "It's over for now. You won't get in trouble. Not for any of this. I promise."

"Why doesn't anyone do something? Why doesn't your father stop her?"

If my eyes hadn't been sealed shut, I might have blinked. As it was, I simply frowned even if it pulled muscles near my mouth a little. As someone that was supposed to teach me how to be a lady and wife, Bithia of all people should already know the answer to that.

"I'm a daughter. Not a son. It's my mother's right to punish me. Not my father's. He is not allowed to interfere in womanly matters."

And... I think he is afraid of her, I whispered only in the silence of my own mind. My father was strong, a warrior, and yet he was only mortal and my mother's magic was so much more. Not for the first time I wondered if I was the ransom that earned her inattention for the rest of the family.

"What was she punishing you for?" Bithia asked, voice broken and horrified. And I felt tired. So soul deep tired.

"Everything. Nothing. I am her one disappointment. I should have been a son. That I exist deserves punishment enough."

I might be young but I had finally understood that at least this last time. It did not matter what reason my mother brought me into her dark rooms for. By the end of a session, neither of us could remember it anyway. It had been like a light springing to life in my mind this last time. My mother didn't care what I did. It was simply that I was. It didn't make sense to me -- being hated for simply existing. I wanted to be hated for something I had done. But this last time, she had leaned over me and her hair, wet with sweat, like thin snakes around her breathtakingly beautiful face, had fallen onto my skin and she had called me her curse. She said that my birth had driven her from the light.

I didn't understand but I finally knew - she would never forgive me. She would never learn to love me. Nothing I did or didn't do would change what I was to her.

Bithia was quiet for a long time after that.

Her face left my shoulder, but she continued to hold me upright in the water. After a time, her voice came back to me. Steadier now.

"You should not answer every question so honestly," she told me quietly. "There are people that would use it against you."

"Where?" I croaked. We were all brutally honest here. There was a great deal we never said but everyone still knew. I could ask any question at all, and often did, and be sure of an honest answer even if there was impatience that went with it. As for myself, there was nothing I had worth hiding from anyone else. My mother had taught me the futility of trying to lie.

"When you marry," Bithia supplied. "Your husband will take you to live with his family. They will look for weapons to use against you, for ways to control you and through you, your husband. Every thing you say will be measured and weighted and given sharp edges so that it can be turned back on you. You must learn to measure what you say, half the response you would give and then cover the true meaning with rose oil so that it cannot be found."

I thought about it a moment. It was a good distraction from the dark whispers still in my own mind. She spoke with absolute surety, as if she had experience.

"That sounds miserable."

"It will save your life and the lives of the ones you love many times over. More than enough to pay for the misery."

****

Things were different between us after that. I still chaffed under her lessons. So many of them made no sense to me at all. So much more of what she was teaching me now dealt with mind sets though and different ways to see people and what they did. I realized as I learned that there were entire layers of things happening in my home that I had never known of. Bithia taught me to watch the way people moved, to listen to how they said things as much was to what they said, or didn't say.

I practiced it mostly on the servants and slaves. While my brothers and father and most of the soldiers were as straight forward as a charging boar, the men and women that served in our house were much more subtle. They had to be. I watched their courtships and fights and jostling for position, all done silently and unnoticed by the rest of us. It opened my eyes to great moving stories and I spent more and more time down in the kitchens or helping in the stables or simply out in one of the main courtyards.

Slowly, I started to join them.

It was a bit awkward at first. I was a noble after all and they were constrained around me but I was also not really that different for, unlike my father and brothers, or even my father's men, I lived very closely to the way the servants did though I'd never realized it until now. They were used to my presence coming and going without needing their attention. I learned from watching which of the older servants were respected and then I went to them with simple questions about a job they were doing or an easily resolved situation or just to ask them for a story. Being young and needing their help broke down the barriers between us. I learned to play knucklebones and dice and to cheat magnificently at both. I heard all the gossip. I was taught every single one of the herbs, wild and raised from both the cook and the bonesetter, so different from the uses my mother had for them. Sometimes, late at night, I would sit in the kitchen or the servants' quarters and listen to them sing and tell their stories. Strangely, I felt as if I belonged there so much more than in my father's great hall. It was true I was neither slave nor servant, but I was closer to them than the only noble woman I knew of.

It did bother me though. Did it count as real, if I had set out to earn their trust and friendship instead of simply being the kind of person that deserved it instead?

My lessons weren't only from the servants. Bithia was teaching me, impossibly, to be a lady. It was not enough for her that I simply mimicked the motions and acted like one. No. She insisted I actually *be* royalty. Since I was trying so hard to simply blend in with the servants and my family didn't treat me as such, the only time I had to be a lady was in Bithia's presence but while in her presence I was not allowed any alternative. At first I still shifted uncomfortably under the instruction until Bithia realized that if she made it a challenge or a contest for me, I was a fiercely determined student. There was something about working very hard and achieving a goal set for me that made something inside me expand. I even found I enjoyed the challenge simply for itself, not even for its completion. Bithia said it was an outshoot of my natural curiosity but I remembered Hector calling me 'Eetion's daughter' so many long months ago and I secretly liked to think it was for that reason I enjoyed the lessons so. Now that I enjoyed her instructions, and now that she had learned how to give them to me so I would, Bithia and I fell into a friendship. It was the first real friend I had ever had and, as much as I was aware that she might simply being doing what I had done to the servants, it still didn't taint my pleasure at my first true friendship.

Like a dry fleece laid out in the rain, my life became a pattern of soaking in what was offered to me and hunting, always, for more.

And then, one rainy day at the end of winter, my father came to see me.

I was sitting in the storeroom next to my own bedroom. Bithia and I, with the laughing help of some servants, had cleaned it out this winter and then gone raiding the other forgotten storage rooms around the palace for things to fill it with. Bithia called it my weaving room and my huge loom, awkward and ancient, did take up a great deal of it. A crippled older soldier had helped me replace all its joints in it over the long, boring winter and

Bithia had taught me how to weave, insisting that true ladies passed long hours doing just such an exercise. Strangely, I took to weaving like a fish to water, and I found that its steady, monotonous rhythm brought me great peace and comfort. I had an eye for color and pattern I knew I had not inherited from my father and my work grew more ambitious. When my father ducked awkwardly into the room one late afternoon, I was busy weaving the fourth of Heracles great trials into the border of a wall hanging.

I felt him while he was still in the hall. My father's presence always rang through me like a hammer against a bronze plate, and my mother's lessons had honed my ability to sense other people nearby. I paused in my work and looked up moments before he pushed aside the curtain we'd hung over the door to keep out the draft. Zoe's music on the flute faltered and Bithia looked up from the reading she was scowling over. Reading was the one lesson I could return to her. My mother had taught me to read several languages long ago and now it was my turn to pass that knowledge on to my friend.

"Father," I put down my shuttle, delighted to see him and he held out his arms. I was in them in a heartbeat and pressed bone crushingly against his chest by his embrace. It was the most wonderful feeling in the world to me.

"Quite a nest you've made for yourself, little bird" my father said and I glowed under his praise.

It was a small space but I had been pleased with it. There were thick carpets on the floor against the cold and one of my own beginning weavings hung on the wall. I had polished the wood of my loom until it shone and we had dragged in unused benches and covered them with cushions and pillows. The little brass brazier in the corner helped keep the room warm. My father shook his head with a smile that grew sad as he looked down at me.

"When did you grow up?" he asked softly and I was torn between pride and disappointment in myself that I had. I offered a weak smile and his large hand rubbed roughly up and down my back as he shook his head again.

"Well, you are. And it's just in time. I'm taking most of your brothers and sailing to Achaian lands."

"After the raiders," I watched the surprise move across his face. I caught Bithia's look from the corner of my eyes - men weren't supposed to like women that understood politics - but I could not help showing off a little bit for my father. He grinned down at me.

"Sharp little mind in that pointed face of yours," he approved and I glowed even more. My father didn't think of me as a woman and so he didn't think badly of me for knowing what was going on in the world around me. "We can't let them think they can get away with raiding without retribution."

And they had wealth. And we needed slaves

to replace the ones we'd lost. And, frankly, my father and brothers were getting restless for a fight and several of the younger ones wanted the chance to become true warriors. While raids weren't war, their kills and spoils counted toward a man's credit. This however, I kept to myself. It unglorified the situation.

"Are you going alone?" I asked. He shook his head with a slight frown.

"Hippoplacia wants to join us. The raiders got the drop on him before they hit us. He's got a son..." his voice trailed and he looked speculatively down at me. I blinked back up at him and couldn't think of anything to say. He shrugged awkwardly.

"Well, little matter right now. We'll deal with that when the time comes. I want you to be in charge of the household while we're away. Enoch is getting old and it's time you took your place as mistress here. Gods know your mother won't do it" he grumbled the last and it was the first time I had heard he speak of her at all. Both of them pretended the other didn't exist and they certainly never moved in the same parts of the house.

"I will." I wrapped my hands in the wide sleeves of his tunic. "I will take care of everything while you're gone. And when you come back we'll have a huge feast and you can tell us all your glorious new stories."

He laughed then and picked me off my feet.

"You're a good girl," he told me and remembered to drop me back down and let go before he turned and left. The drape swayed at his passage and I watched it, surprised with how quickly my life had changed. Just like that, I was suddenly left in charge of the household.

"It's about time," Bithia said, settling back down onto the stool she'd risen from when my father had entered.

"Lady of the house," Zoe intoned it with enough awe to make me feel both pleased and slightly panicked.

"Do you think I can do this?" I asked, suddenly nervous. Less than a year ago I had been that long used proverbial 'wild little animal'. Zoe chuckled and went back to her flute.

"If you don't worry yourself so badly over it you get sick, I think you'll do fine," Bithia told me and I sank back down onto my bench in front of my loom, reassured, even if not entirely sure I believed it. Nemea, already lord of my rooms, leaped lightly up to land in my lap and purred as I ran my long fingers along his back. Which helped almost more than Bithia's words.

Later that night, when only Bithia and I were in my bedroom and I was enduring the face cleaning ritual I still didn't see the point behind, Bithia told me:

"Being a leader is mostly about looking like you know what's going on. Leaders are figureheads. They're there to look good and make people feel good about themselves. You're already well liked in the slave and servant quarters so they won't play sloppy just to test you when your father's gone. Just be around. Most houses operate best when the servants are allowed to run it themselves anyway."

I nodded at her advice and it helped me steady myself for what was ahead. I wouldn't be alone in my new duties. Not anymore.

IV.

I stood on the shore and watched when my father's ships sailed the next day. My brother Podes stood next to me and grumbled that he had not been able to go too but the wound on his leg he'd gotten in the last boar hunt kept him at home.

There had been a young prince among the soldiers from Hippoplacia that had come to join my father's raiding party. I didn't know if he was the one my father had mentioned or not but he watched me with eyes like chips of sea glass and said nothing to me at all. His attention had made me self-conscious and uncomfortable and I had ignored him as best I could. I hadn't been the only one to notice the scrutiny though. One of my father's older soldiers had been standing nearby, watching the neighboring soldiers as they boarded their ship and he winked at me. Under the sound of the snap of sail and the rattle of metal armor being loaded, he'd told me with a grin that they'd "see if the young prince had the makings of a man to him or not" for me. The way those sea glass eyes from Hippoplacia had watched me suddenly took on new meaning and my thoughts, which had been making a list of the proper sacrifices to the proper gods for my family's safety and success while they were away, tripped over themselves. I must have looked dumbstruck the way I felt because my father's soldier had just chuckled cheerfully at my expression and boarded my father's main ship. I had intentionally turned away from the Hippoplacia ship and its glass eyes and concentrated on my father's two ships instead.

Raiding was not exactly a way of life for us. My father sometimes went years without anything but a practice sword in his massive hands. My brothers raised cattle. Something was going on in the Achaean homeland however, and the wars there kept spilling across the ocean to us here. My father was going to make a point but he was also going because a man with his house on fire often didn't have time to stop others from taking things from it while it burned. Several of my brothers were unblooded. There was glory and gold and women to be won. If it were a war, my family would have even been able to keep the armor of his dead opponents, which itself was often worth a small ransom. Strangely, I felt no fear for my father though I knew I should. To me though, he was immortal and nothing would ever fell him. When he strode across the shore to give last minute instructions to my brother and me as the low hulled boats were pushed into the water, I was more worried about disappointing him when he did come back than the possibility of him not coming back. My life has been full of learning that good men die as easily as bad ones but blessedly for me at the time, that knowledge was still far away. I clung to him when he hugged me but I let him go without foreboding and watched his giant form as he waded out to his own ship and hauled himself aboard. The colored sails dropped to catch the breeze and the oars rattled out to dip into the water, the newly repainted eyes on the bows watchful and protective. All too soon the ships were gone from the small harbor. As selfish as it was, my fears were more for myself than my departing brothers and father. What if something went wrong with the crops or the cattle? What if we had guests and I made a disaster of the laws of hospitality? What if I accidently burned the house down while they were away?

They had brought a cart for me to ride home in along with the rest of the women that had come with me to say their goodbyes. My family was not overly fond of wives but there were quite a few comfort women for the soldiers and concubines for my brothers and some of them had come to see their men off. At the last minute though, I skipped away from the offered cart for the return ride and instead climbed into my brother's light chariot. He and I had been left in charge of the house now and I thought that the ride back would be a good time to talk. He gave me a humoring look but didn't protest. I had woken late last night and laid in bed listening to the preparations and celebrations and a thought had occurred to me. I wanted to talk it over with my brother but I knew I would have to do it carefully. As siblings we ignored each other often and fumbled through interaction when it was necessary. We moved in different worlds that rarely overlapped and I suspected that the realm of women was as foreign to them as the realm of men was to me. Perhaps more so, because at least I was allowed at the edges of theirs while I doubted any of them cared for weaving rooms. Podes and I were going to have to work together now though and I wanted to make sure I didn't mess up my first attempt at it.

We rode for a distance in silence and I held the railing and watched the way my brother handled the reins and the horses ahead of us, trying to think of how to phrase my thoughts to him.

"Podes," I began and he snorted.

"Yes," he answered and it was such an emphatic 'yes' that it didn't sound as if he were just agreeing that was his name.

"Yes, what?" I asked and he looked down at me. We were all tall in my family but Podes was taller than most and still growing. His wildly curling hair only added to that height. He sighed as if he were making a large concession to me.

"Yes, I will teach you how to drive a chariot. Just because it will get me away from the healers."

"...oh!" It was a surprise and I blinked, mind blanking. It was so far from what I'd been thinking that I didn't even have an answer for it.

"You think I don't pay attention but I've seen the way your eyes go greedy whenever you watch a chariot go by. Your spending more time in the stables was just a dead giveaway what you were angling for. But just like mother you can't come out and honestly ask for anything."

As far as I knew he was blindly wrong about

most of what he'd assumed about me but the accusation about mother stung. It was my greatest fear, that I would become her -- that I was already too much like her -- but I knew better than to show it. No one respected weakness in my family, myself included.

"Mother doesn't need to ask for anything," I reminded him calmly, surprised because a year ago I would never have been that clear headed. He made a face and I knew it had hit home with him too. Our mother's unilateral authority and self-governing grated against all of my brothers and their natural assumption that men were the rulers and women the servants. For all my father appeared to rule the house, he had no power over mother. Mother said that the only power any man had over a woman with blood like hers was what she foolish might choose to give him.

"But thank you for teaching me," I added quickly, realizing that in provoking him I was not only not going to be able to talk about what I had in my mind but he might revoke his offer of teaching me to drive. It didn't cost me much pride at all. "I've been dreaming of chariots for such a long time now."

It must have soothed his own pride because he rolled his eyes.

"Women," he used the word dismissively, but because I used 'men' the same way, I didn't protest it or take it to heart.

I was quiet for a while, thinking of which

tact to take. Finally, I shivered in the early spring sunshine and asked:

"Aren't you scared?"

"Of what?" he asked roughly, as if I'd insulted him by even implying anything could scare him. He also said it so quickly that I wondered for the first time if he too was as worried about making mistakes as I was. It made me feel better about him. Holding the railing of the swaying chariot with one hand I used the other to rub imaginary goosebumps from my braced arm and looked out into the thin forest that lined the dirt path we traveled on.

"Father's not the only one raiding, surely," I said as I continued watching the trees. "What if someone decides to raid us while most of our fighters are away?" It was what I would have done, if I were a man and interested in easy bounty. If I had thought of it, maybe I wasn't the only one. If Hector could think to guard against hidden attacks... so would I. "It scares me," I added for good measure. My brother made a derogatory noise.

"You're a woman. Everything scares you. There's nothing to worry about."

I looked over at him.

"I'm glad you're here," I told him. It wasn't a lie. I certainly couldn't fight men with armed swords. It was just - a well-placed truth. I could almost see his chest swell.

"You take care of the women and the house," he said it as if it was a small thing. "I'll have the rest of our men prepared."

"But how will you know if anyone's coming?" I asked and he shook his head dismissively.

"I'll station some scouts at the high points. They can keep watch and signal if anyone's coming by water. No one would be stupid enough to come by land. The shepherds would tell us long before they reached us."

"That's very clever," I nodded and, for a minute, I thought I had pushed too far with the sharp look he gave me but whatever he saw on my face, he nodded confidently. Magnanimously, he added: "I'll teach you to drive every other day. It'll give you something to think about other than womanish fears."

"Thank you," I answered softly and looked back out at the forest with its bright slanting sunlight and its flitting birds. Trying not to smile. It hadn't cost me anything but a bit of tongue biting and now I knew the people under my care would be protected while my father was away. Both not saying what I wanted and getting it were new experiences to me. I realized it wasn't exactly an honest approach but it worked and that seemed more important.

Later that night, I confided in Bithia about convincing my brother to be on guard while my father was away. From the look on her face, I think it was the first time she realized that maybe I was paying attention to her lessons for more than just curiosity's sake.

Since I was the the lady of the house, I found that I now had the perfect excuse to ask questions about everything that was done - and to get involved in it too. I found I understood things better if I got to actually do them and so I spent more time out in the gardens and down in the animal pens and in the stables and the kitchens and the work shops and the metal smiths. I even joined the women cleaning clothes down at the stream. It was a wonderful time for me. I could go anywhere I liked without worrying about whether I should be there or not and no one minded. At first I think the servants were as nervous with the new arrangement as I was. We were all feeling out our new placements in this arrangement. In truth, there wasn't any difference in their work with me watching as opposed to anyone else though and so soon the household and I fell back into most of our old patterns. If anything I was simply called me 'my lady' exclusively now and I often found that what I had need of, from a cup of cool water while I was out in the fields to my favorite types of food during quickly grabbed meals was always, somehow, provided. I felt - cared for. It was an odd feeling.

I was out in the fields, learning about the sowing of grain and watching with fascination as the huge oxen plowed forward while the foreman explained why some fields were plowed while others were only furrowed when Zoe came running across the newly turned dirt toward me.

"Andromache!" Whatever her news was it was something that excited her because she called me by name instead of title. That lack probably should have bothered me but instead it was nice to hear my own name and it made me smile. 'My Lady' was nice, something I could be proud to be called, but it was shared with a hundred other women up and down the coast. Andromache was mine alone and it made me feel as if they were noticing me and not just the space I filled when they used it. "Andromache, there are strangers coming up the trade road!"

I remembered what my brother had said about the unlikelihood of raiders traveling over land but it still sent a shiver through me. To give myself time to clear my head in case I needed to act quickly, I waited until she was in front of me to ask:

"How many?"

"Two," she answered, eyes bright with excitement, not fear. "One huge chariot drawn by four horses! There are two women in a wagon next to it!"

Two did not sound very threatening. Raiders rarely brought women with them on raids. Which meant – guests?

"Thank you, Midious," I told the foreman and then I hiked my skirt up to leave my ankles free and started running back toward the house. I could have had them hitch up a cart for me but I had found that running helped clear my mind to think. Zoe, already winded from running out to the fields and fell in somewhere behind me. I had found that I could easily outrun most people thanks to the long legs that had once given me my Egret name.

I burst into the inner courtyard and already saw there was activity. We were going to receive guests! It was my first time and I was both thrilled and horrified by the thought. Hospitality was sacred. Even the gods who ignored so much, paid attention to the rules of hospitality. Houses were judged on their ability to carry out the proper forms and duties to visitors. If I did well with these guests, I would earn pride for my family name. If I did poorly... Aware of my dusty clothes and dirty feet, I hurried toward the house and my room.

"Artemesia, mix up some honey wine. Make it very light. Bring someone to carry a shade for the ladies. Euthimius, make sure the stable hands are ready to take the horses and have the stalls cleaned. Someone make sure Enoch knows what's going on so he can greet them when they arrive." I was inside by that time and moving quickly toward my room but a trail of servants still followed me for instructions. "Demetria, you're in charge of setting up the side courtyard for them to rest in and the guest rooms for them to use. See if you can find flowers for the pots. Oh!" I whirled and the slave on my heels almost collided with me. "Nikias" I recognized him by his bead woven hair before his face even registered and I smiled. He'd won the impromptu races the slaves had held several days ago. Perfect. "Please go tell Podes that we have guests." My brother was away at one of the watchtowers near the coast and I did not know if news would reach him or not. I did not want to be accused of being careless or seeking my own glory over my family's. Then I spun away and made it into my bedroom, where Bithia had already drawn a bath in the small basin we'd managed to squeeze into the space. I gave her a smile, pleased and nervous and she smiled confidently back.

"This is the last time your family is referred to as barbaric," she said, going through my dresses for something appropriate. "By the end of tonight whoever it is will be singing your praises and by the end of the month people will wonder they ever thought the House of Thebe on Cillia was roughshod."

I wiggled out of my work clothes and slipped into the bath with an exhale. It was true. Our family did not lack hospitality but we were a house of men. Thebe was not known for its delicacy. Put like that, some of the weight of acting properly as hostess was lifted from my shoulders.

Soon I was dressed in pale lavender with Bithia's clever fingers braiding my hair. The servants had told me that the guests were priests from Chrysa and that they had been received and settled comfortably into their rooms. I was just starting to look forward to the situation when Threnody arrived. For a moment, as she stood in my doorway, dusky and dark and exotic with the silver bells in her hair, my mind refused to make sense of her form. I had heard nothing from my mother since my father had left. In a way, I'd forgotten about her, the way you put out of your mind the monster hiding in the woods once you were safely home. Nemea jumped up onto the small tabletop we had cluttered with what little make-ups and oils I had and hissed at her.

"The Lady wishes to see her daughter," she intoned calmly and I felt the muscles in my lower back starting to shiver deep against the bone. My hands, toying with the polished wood of one of my hair combs, froze.

"Not tonight," Bithia hissed at the woman in the doorway and Threnody's face, without moving, managed to give the impression of raising an arched eyebrow at my maid.

"The Lady wishes to see her daughter," the dark woman repeated.

"We have guests!" Bithia snarled it at her, voice still low, as if whispering would keep my mother from finding out about this rebellion. "The name of this house is at stake. She can't go to *lessons* tonight!"

Threnody simply looked calmly at her, then turned those empty eyes on me.

"She wishes you to come now," she spoke irrevocably.

My mouth was dry and I pressed my lips together. I was supposed to greet our guests in the main hall in less than a few moments. My mother would see to it that I was not fit to do that. It was so clear in my mind, it was astonishing. It would have been a premonition but it was more. Because, without being able to put it into words, I understood what my mother was doing.

She wanted me to fail this.

I raised my chin.

"Tell her I will come later. I have guests to attend to right now."

For the first time in my life I saw emotion move across Threnody's dark face.

"She said you would come now," she stated.

"Tell my mother I am sorry, but I cannot come just now. I will come later." There would be no escaping my mother. But putting it off, I knew that the punishment would be worse, so much worse. I was shaking with terror inside, fighting the urge to do as I was told and follow Threnody immediately.

Except I wouldn't. I couldn't. The guests had already been told to expect me. Refusing them now would be the height of insult. This wasn't just about my mother and I and her games in the dark anymore. It was about the reputation of my father's house and Thebe.

The woman in the door stared at me, not believing what I was saying any more than I did. But then she turned suddenly and was gone. It was all I could do not to run after her and beg her not to tell my mother. To tell her that I would go, right then, with her. But I did not. Bithia touched my shoulder with a hand that shook.

"Oh, gods..." it escaped her and it was like feeling a chill wind across both our backs. I agreed with her but I did not think there was a god in this world that would listen to my prayers tonight.

My hands were surprisingly steady as I picked up Nemea. I inhaled and my back straightened even more.

"Come," I said, but whether it was to my cat or my maid, I didn't know. "We have guests to greet."

They were more than simply priests from the island of Chrysa. It was the high priest of Phoebus Apollo's temple there as well as his wife and daughter. I was stunned by the unexpected honored and Bithia murmured under her breath to me that it was a good omen that my first guests would be servants of the god of light. All I could think of was that the god of light could keep his omen and make my mother vanish instead.

The priest's name was Chryses and his daughter was Chryseis. She was just a year older than me. She was bright and bubbly and my friend immediately. Whether I was aware of it yet or not. She did most of the talking in fact and her parents and their servants seemed content to let her.

Since it was so close to the end of the day, we moved into the main hall after the greeting in the small side courtyard. My father's spot at the main table was left empty but I sat on the newly cushioned bench to its side and the priest sat next to me while his daughter and wife sat across from us.

Some of my father's older soldiers joined us for the meal to give the priest other men to talk to but it turned out he was more than content to engage the women in conversation too. I asked Zoe to bring her flute and Artemesia played the cither to give the air a lightness as the evening fell. The cooks tried several newer recipes that were more than simply the roasted meat my father preferred, cakes of grain and honey, a basting for the meat that held herbs I thought I recognized from our gardens, something with berries and mint in it. The gathering was only small, the meal informal compared to a real feast, but I was pleased beyond measure with the smooth way it flowed and kept shooting the servants grateful looks when I thought no one was watching.

"So you run this entire household? All by yourself?" Chryseis asked with her bright eyes huge in her heart-shaped face, curls bouncing around her shoulder in seemingly never ending excitement. "That's amazing! Everything's so beautiful!"

I glowed under her praise though I tried not to show it. Modesty was a virtue but I still couldn't quite stop my proud smile at her words.

"My older brother is here too. He is sorry he could not greet you himself tonight but he's watching our shores right now," I supplied. Chryses nodded his silvering head.

"A wise man," he stated. "The Achaeans grow restless amongst themselves."

"My father said the same," I agreed. Chryses shook his head and gave me a smile. He had kind eyes, I decided but they were sharp with intelligence too and I suspected they could cut when they wanted to.

"They don't like Troy's restrictions on the goods they get from the Euxine Sea and beyond. Everything that would come from the north must pass Troy's ports at the Hellespont. The tariff the merchants are forced to pay makes Ilium rich and drives up the price of everything the Achaeans import."

Paying attention in the kitchens I now knew the price and rarity of some of the spices that we bought or traded for during the autumn fairs. Dreams of their far off homes had filled some of the long winter nights with warmth and color for me.

"What kind of imports?" I asked, curious because spice could not be the only thing.

"Tin and copper. Spices. Exotic hides. Foreign gold and silver. Rare stones and gems. Grains. Horses. Even stranger animals. Women." Chryses did not seem to mind answering my questions at all and as he took a drink of his wine, he looked at me over the rim of his goblet. "All the things men could find for themselves in their own homeland but that simply aren't exotic enough unless they come from somewhere else."

"Except for the amber," Chryseis inserted cheerfully, thrusting her arm across the table and wiggling her wrist so the golden bracelet on it caught the torchlight. "We don't have amber here. They say it's sacred to the gods."

It was hard not to smile with Chryseis. Everything she said seemed to end in a thrilled exclamation. Genuinely curious, I shifted so I could lean over and look at the offered bracelet. It was set with what I at first thought were drops of honey but when she kept wiggling her arm, I touched the drops and found them quite solid and warm. Amber.

"They're like trapped sunlight," she told me eagerly. "It's said they wash up on the shore of a hidden inland sea and only the pure of heart can gather them. Look, this one has a little bug trapped in it. I often wonder if he's still alive and just waiting for the rock to split so he can come out."

I looked at the wonder of the tiny insect caught in a perfect moment inside the golden stone she indicated and her father laughed.

"And so we go from politics to jewelry. I should have known better then to travel with women." But he was teasing. I could tell because the women with him denied it cheerfully and poked fun at him for always talking about policies and places and boring every host that they stayed with. I however hadn't been bored. His short insight into the larger world had me fascinated.

After that, talk did not turn back to Ilium and Achaia and I was not such a bad host I would force it that way. The meal passed long and peaceful. I basked in the feeling. Eventually the parents retired with their servants for and the older soldiers left for their barracks with winks and nods of approval in my direction. Bubbly Chryseis wanted to stay up, however, and I was certainly not going to be sleeping anyway. In fact, I didn't intend to be anywhere alone at all tonight.

We moved out into one of the open verandas. Torches were soon brought out for us and the young girls among the servants joined us as well. Together, we sat around on the cushions and thrown blankets and ate sweets until we were full to bursting. And we talked. I had never just sat and talked to girls my age before and I had no skill in it at all but Chryseis had more than enough for all of us put together and we watched the stars wheel overhead and she shared gossip that she had picked up in her travels and funny stories about her home and in return we teased about my brothers and spoke of the raid of last year in hushed whispers. Of course, talk turned to men and our thoughts about future marriages but again, I had nothing to offer and Chryseis cheerfully teased me about my complete lack of attention to that area of my life. Then she told us her own hopes and they were so huge and obviously made grandiose that soon we were all laughing over them. Toward sunrise, the talk whispered down to simple things and the servants started to move around the house, preparing for the day. Chryseis and her family would travel on once the sun was high enough and I realized, quite unexpectedly, that I would miss her. I, who had not missed father or brothers or dead nursemaid, would miss this bright, laughing, passing girl.

We joined her father as he greeted Phoebus in his rising chariot and Chryses' voice was strong and pure as he sang the song and poured the libation. Afterward, we broke fast together and I made sure they were supplied with more food for the journey. Just before they left, I scooped up Nemea on sudden impulse and ran over to Chryseis.

"Will you take him?" I asked. They had already met during the long night's talk and he had charmed her with his rumbling purr and his regal name. Her clear eyes flew wide. I pressed my face into his soft fur and felt my throat closing over. I, who could not even mourn my own nurse...

I don't know what she saw in my eyes but she held out her arms and I quickly placed him in them. I saw his great golden eyes looking mildly puzzled at me, unaware of what I did, and I bit my lips to keep from saying anything, sure my voice would break if I did.

"I'll take good care of him," Chryseis promised solemnly. I was surprised to hear her voice was serious. I could only swallow and nod. Face suddenly brightening, she quickly unfastened her golden honey stoned bracelet and pressed it into my hands.

"Now we're friends," she held my closed hand in hers. "We always have to be friends now. Always and always." She gave me a smile and pressed a kiss to each of my cheeks. Then her parents were calling her indulgently and, holding my Nemea close to her chest, she climbed into the wagon next to her mother. I watched them leave and did not realize there were tears on my cheeks until Bithia touched them.

"You love Nemea. Why did you do that?" she asked and I just shook my head, feeling my heart breaking apart in my chest. Impulsive, I hugged her.

"Thank the servants for me. This was wonderful," I whispered against her ear, pressing the bracelet into her hand. I drew back and wiped my cheeks, forcing myself to steady inside. I had one last thing to do and suddenly I simply wanted it done and over with.

"Watch out for Threnody," I told Bithia and saw understanding fill her eyes. I had sent one of my heart's pieces to safety in Chryseis' arms. My other stood in front of me, still in danger simply because I loved her.

"Now?" she asked, voice choking. I gave her a sickly smile and could think of nothing to say. Instead, I kissed her forehead.

"Remember what I said about Threnody," I repeated firmly and then I turned and walked back into the house. Starting down the well-worn path to my mother's darkened lair, I wondered if Persephone would have understood my descent from the bright land of the living to the darkness below.

It would not have mattered if she had. Gods did not care about mortal pains and there was no one to save me from what would soon be mine.

Threnody was there to hold aside the curtain to my mother's second room when I arrived. In that waiting dark, the air was already heavy with the scent of foul things burning in preparation on my mother's squat three legged brazier.

V.

Father's raiding was successful.

He returned to us in the late summer just as the fields were beginning to show the first hint of ripening gold in their green heads of grain and the birds were beginning to grow restless, preparing for their autumn travels. I was in one of the storehouses with Enoch, going over what we had left from the previous year and deciding how much we could sell and how much we should store. I had taken to following the older man almost everywhere when I had full days to myself. Enoch's eyesight was failing, though he took pains never to show it, and he seemed to welcome my company and my questions. Whereas before he had been a somber, distant figurehead in my life, since the raid things had changed. I wasn't sure if it was my own changes or some of his own but, while I still found myself in slight awe of his austere dignity, he was not so distant now but had rather become one of my most patient teachers.

Somewhere along the way during my father's absence, I had stopped being merely called the lady of the house and actually become it. It was an odd thing and harder still to explain. Just that the men and women that served my house looked to me first now. When they were sick or hurt it was my heart that ached and I felt joy their joy as if it were mind when they were happy. I had never had anyone belong to me before, not even Bithia, who truly belonged to herself. The servants and slaves of

Eetion's house though, somehow, by the end of that summer, they belonged to me. I think, I, in a way, belonged to them too. Something had changed while my father was away and I was as aware of it as I was unable to place my finger on exactly when it had happened or how it had come about.

"Father's back!" Podes' smile was huge in his lean face as he burst into the storeroom Enoch and I were in and he actually picked me up by my waist, swinging me around in his enthusiasm. We were actually beginning to like each other a bit, he and I. It helped, no doubt, that he was so often far afield but when he returned I treated him as lord of the house and always made sure there was a cool drink and a warm bath waiting for him. He took it as his due but I knew in a house of so many brothers, it was not often he was singled out and taken care of. Things between us had improved even more when he had lured in and then routed a small band of raiders that had been sailing along our coast. Even if they had been a small, scruffy group, it still gave him something to brag about to father when he came back. We had already decided to keep my chariot lessons from the others. Father would laugh but we both knew that my brothers wouldn't approve and Podes would have the worse of it for daring to teach me.

I caught at his wrists when he dropped me back onto my feet to steady myself against the sudden lurching of the room. "Nikias spotted the sails. They're definitely father's!"

His words penetrated the haze of figures and measurements that had been taking up most of my head and my heart soared high as my smile grew to match my brother's.

"Father's back?" I said it just for the joy of feeling the words in my own mouth and impulsively hugged my brother. "When will he get here? Can we beat him to the docks?" I was halfway out the door when my brother caught my wrist and pulled me back. His face was surprisingly thoughtful.

"I'll meet him at the docks, Egret," he told me and I just blinked blankly back at him. For just a moment, his face softened. "Stay here. Get everything ready. Show father what you've done with his house when he comes." My brows started to come down and I don't know what he saw on my face but he looked at me almost sadly. "Andromache, men don't appreciate what's given freely to them. Make him wonder why you aren't waiting for him at the docks. Then surprise him with a real welcome when he comes to you. The uncertainty and the wait will make him appreciate it more when he sees you."

I didn't understand it at all. I would have wanted the ones I loved to run to meet me if I had been gone a long time. I certainly wouldn't have wanted to have to wait even longer to see them. Podes sighed.

"He's a man. Trust me on this. Men lose interest in things that come easily to them."

Confused, I still nodded and my brother

gave my shoulder a clap that sent me staggering before he rushed out the door. I could hear him calling for several of the house guards as he went. Vaguely lost, I looked over at Enoch.

"It's true, princess," he said. "When you run your own house remember to never make anything too easy or too expected for your husband or sons. Once they start to expect it all the time they stop noticing. And then they will stop appreciating you. When they stop appreciating you, you are not longer important to them."

My chin jerked slightly to the side and my brows were still down.

"That doesn't seem very kind. Or honest."

He shrugged.

"And still it is the only way to catch what you want. By never being caught."

I exhaled, not liking the new thought. Why would you play games about how much you loved someone or what you would do for them?

I still stayed at the house as my brother had told me to.

By the time my father arrived, I was reconciled to the idea - or at least parts of it. Staying behind did give me time to organize the welcome returning warriors deserved. I opened up the great hall as well as the rooms of my returning family to air out, had the floors swept of clean. Sheep were being slaughtered for a feast and all the slaves and servants were dressed in fresh clothes that didn't show the wear of the day we'd already worked through most of. There hadn't been time for much decorating but there were garlands for the eves and all the bronze had been polished to shine. I was proud of what the household and I had managed to do while he was away and it was a good chance to show it off a bit.

I dressed as the lady of the house too, which meant a veil and sandals, as well as a dress that didn't have dirt stains at the knees from kneeling next to servants in the gardens or inspecting the undersides of last year's barrels for durability. By the time I saw the chariots and the carts loaded high I was both nervous and excited.

"Remember," Bithia instructed from the side of her mouth as she stood next to me. It was a habit she'd picked up and used to give me last moment reminders when, in fact, since we were the only ones standing there, whispering it secretly was completely unnecessary. "You're a woman now. You want him to see the change."

I certainly didn't feel like a woman, but I did feel different. I had changed and - I thought I liked what I'd become. So when my father jumped down from his chariot, I waited until he'd taken off his helmet and a stable hand had caught the reins, to shyly step forward and offer him the first welcome cup of mixed wine in greeting. He took it from my hands but didn't drink it right away. Instead, he looked down at me.

"Is that my little bird?" he asked, lifting the edge of my veil. I felt as if I must be glowing.

"Welcome home," I said and he started to laugh. It was a wonderful rolling sound. He tipped the drink in offering to the gods and then drank the rest. It was my own mix of wine and water and herbs and honey and he drank it all without pause. Then he tossed the cup to the nearest servant and put his arm around my slim shoulders.

"Just like a grown-up," he teased me and my breath bubbled happily in my chest. It wasn't the breath-squeezing hug I was used to but with my ribs just healed from my mother's punishment for my rebellion and the pride in his eyes, it was just as good to me. "Where's the food?" he asked. "We're famished and it will take all night to tell the stories."

Something changed that night and it was wonderful. I was still forgotten but in a good way. I stood behind my father's chair and saw to the running of a great feast. The mixed wine flowed and the food came on great wide plates. And the stories - the men were in their glory. I heard about their raids and Podes told of his own defeat of the sea raiders and if he embellished a bit, I knew that my other brothers and father did too. Everything glowed like the warm honey stoned bracelet I wore on my wrist and I wanted it to never end.

Father had raided the Achaean coast. It was a constant back and forth struggle, sometimes more vicious than others, between our two people with a wide ocean between us to keep it from lasting longer than a season or two. It was done for glory

111

and for the spoils.. Each of my brothers took turns bragging about their deeds and their conquests, who they had fought and what they had done. I watched their faces change as they did, realizing, as little as I had known them before, I knew them even less when they spoke of killing. Killing was a necessity and a way of life. I understood that but for the first time, I could judge clearly what I had only seen in confusion during the raid last year. I saw Ares in their faces and heard his distant roar in their voices.

Once the meal had begun to die down and the drinking had started in earnest, my father had the spoils brought out and displayed. One of the raids had broken open a seaside storage house just before it was due to empty itself into a ship and the heaps of gold and silver and fine cloth astonished me. There were treasures of ivory and abalone in delicate carved bowls, marble jars of fragrant oils or incense, carvings of cedar and polished oak, some old and darkened with age and touch, others fresh and sharp edged. Cured hides piled on top of each other as well as furs and fleece. There were bowls of painted red and black clay, polished to shine and countless rings and bracelets and necklaces, earrings and hair clips and dress fastenings. There was even a small box of tiny pearls and I knew that there were also flasks of wine and oil, sacks of grain, sheaves of flax. Father laughed me over to him and at his gesture, one of the servants brought me a small, golden diadem that curled and branched like a young grape vine. I had never seen such delicate and perfectly detailed work before and my father's face softened behind its rosy haze from the wine.

"For you," he told me. "For keeping the house so well when I was gone. For being young and beautiful."

I gave him a look and he chuckled at me.

"Take it anyway," he told me. "It makes me happy to see your face when you look at it. Besides," he gestured with a wide hand. "You're looking at your dowry."

For the first time that night I was utterly lost and I could only gape at him. He actually looked embarrassed.

"Well, they were after you, weren't they? It's only right they should pay for your marriage."

I looked back at the glittering heap and my mouth felt dry. I, who had once thought I wasn't worth two sick cows. For my marriage? My mind hadn't even begun to fathom that one day I would leave my father's house for some stranger's, much less thought about what I would bring with me. Marriage was inevitable but… it had always seemed so far away. Lying in front of me was the statement that it was not as distant as I'd always believed. I didn't know what lost my mental balance faster, in fact. That all of that was what my father deemed me worth – or that it meant he was thinking of one day giving me away. I couldn't even find the proper emotion to respond with. My father chuckled and awkwardly patted my shoulder.

"Did you really think I'd forgotten you, little girl?"

"For me?" I managed and my father gave my shoulder a surprisingly gentle squeeze.

"You're better than Hippoplacia too," he told me. Then he turned to call for more wine even though I knew his cup was still half full and I was left with my own thoughts. My long fingers moving with slow hesitation against the twining wires of the diadem.

****

Harvest came upon us shortly after that. I had always known time flew during harvest and my brothers and father put their shoulders to the work of gathering in the grain and slaughtering the animals for salting and smoking right next to the slaves and servants. Running the house now, it was not only my duty to make sure everyone had food and drink ready in the fields but also that there was enough space to put everything we gathered in and that careful track was kept of it all. The wine and olive presses were always busy and the slaves that we had taken from Achaia quickly melted into our household with the heavy workload no one could be allowed to shirk. I still watched them. Firstly, because they had not yet settled into the hidden tides of our household and secondly, because I was honestly curious. Some of them had once been free themselves, just as surely as I was, and now they served us. If the raid had been successful last year, I would be as they were now, though my parentage would have earned me a little reprieve in the work load. It was a heavy thought, and even though Bithia dismissed it with a flick of her wrist, I could not help but watch their faces when they thought no one was paying attention, trying to understand.

"It's nothing," Bithia told me one evening when I mentioned it to her as she rubbed olive oil into my hair.

"But they had families," I protested, squinting at the feel of this new 'beauty routine'. "Lives. They don't even speak our language."

"They will learn," Bithia said it calmly as she twisted my thick hair into a knot. "It is just the way of things. What is the good of protesting it? Their protectors failed them and they pay the price for it. They're not important enough for their ruling class to ransom back. At least your family treats them well. Your father is not given to cruelty and your brothers always see that their women are cared for and any offspring are treated well."

"What about you?" I asked her and she again made a dismissive gesture before placing pins to hold my hair in place with an easy abandon that always made me nervous. I, perhaps, should have picked a different time to ask.

"My father sold me off to the meat market when I was hardly old enough to walk. I was lucky enough to be bought by an old merchant. He was gentler than the seller had been. He taught me about men and his wife was old enough and indulgent enough that she enjoyed pretending he'd bought me for her. She taught me about being a lady and what a lady required. When the merchant died, the sons fought over who should get me and so the lady of the house put me up for sale while they were away to avoid problems. That was when a trader acting for your family bought me and brought me here."

I blinked at her in the warped bronze reflection of my mirror, stunned and at a loss for words or even questions. My Bithia? I'd known she'd come from somewhere. Why hadn't I ever asked? Instead of soothing me, her emotionless, dismissive recitation of her history did the opposite. Everything she didn't say screamed louder to me and the fact she had hardened herself against it, and others in the same situation, did too. I had learned long ago that my Bithia was not cruel, but she was practical to the point of being stone when necessary. When had she learned to be that way? Young and young from the sound of it. When I tried to turn my head to look at her, her strong hands gently keep he facing forward so that I wouldn't drip oil down my shoulders.

"You're such an innocent," she said softly, but it wasn't unkind. "Just because this small world is all you've ever known you think it's the way things are everywhere. I was born a girl to poor parents. They could hope for nothing from me. I would have lived my life scraping in the dirt and prey to every wandering warrior and thug that passed our hovel. Instead I am well fed and warm and safe from all men because I belong to you. And you are a terrible mistress. You let me do anything I want."

It pulled a small smile out of me even though my heart was still aching, because I could easily see the arch look on her face without even looking and her actions said she did not want my thoughts or hurt when it came to her past.

"That is because I'm afraid to try to stop you," I told her and she laughed at me.

"Being a slave is hard for a man because it hurts their pride. And it can be a very dangerous thing for a woman. I could be in the hands of a man that enjoyed hurting me. I could have a mistress that was jealous of me and used me cruelly. Instead I have you and you love me." She pressed a kiss to my forehead and then made a face and wiped the oil from her lips.

"Do you - do you ever wish you were free?" I asked and she shrugged. Her voice was very quiet in the evening air.

"What would I do? This world has no place for women without protectors. In many ways, you are already more of a slave here than I am."

****

When the last of the harvest was safely stored away for the winter, it was time to trade our excess goods. It was my favorite time of year. Everyone was pleased and content with their work and my father decided we should go to Ilium. Podes grumbled, but insisted I ride in his chariot anyway, while Bithia followed with a large number of the house servants in the carts that were full of not only what we would trade but also what my family would need for comfort. We sent goods every year by way of trader to the Great Fair held on the plains in front of vast Ilium but this year my father had decided that the family would accompany our oxen, oils and wines. It was simply good politics to make an appearance from time to time. I was thrilled. It was a two day trip past the base of Mount Ida and I had never been so far outside of my family's lands, or from the fear of my mother's sudden summons, in all my life.

The first night we stayed at the summer home of one of our neighbors, a small but comfortable home tucked away in the foothills of looming Ida. The family we stayed with were going to Ilium as well. It was easily the largest fair this side of the ocean and families and trade came from much farther away than our few days of travel to attend it. I found myself with a new companion, a girl a year younger than me who managed to act as if she were ages older. Her name was Briseis and she had a tinkling laugh that could draw a man's attention no matter what he was doing. She used it unmercifully on my brothers and for the first time in my life I watched them become awkward around a woman. It was an education. I watched her in open curiosity throughout our welcome dinner at her parents' house.

"What?" she asked me finally, sounding annoyed and I shook my head.

"How do you do that?" I asked, and when she gave me a blank look, I gestured to my twin brothers. "You're sitting all the way across the table from Hermolaos and Hermokrates and yet you manage to get their attention whenever you want to by laughing."

One edge of her pouted mouth curved upward and she looked closely at me over the plate of food that was set between us with a smirk.

"You really mean that, don't you?" she asked and I nodded. I wouldn't have asked if I hadn't meant it. I truly was curious. I'd never known my brothers to pay attention to a woman's laughter before.

She simply proved my point by laughing again and I watched their heads jerk.

"It must have been horrible growing up with only boys." She plucked a candied date from the bowl in front of her and even though she was facing me I saw her eyes slide to the side and watch my brothers as she ate it - which seemed to take a great deal more effort than I used to eat fruit. "It's amazing you aren't running around in bared legs with short hair."

"I don't get to run as much as I used to." I knew she was mocking me but how could the opinion of someone I didn't know have much influence on the way I saw myself? She, however, was a creature I'd never seen before. Even Saffo, my father's well-established concubine, didn't imbue everything she did with the – the only mental

119

comparison my mind would give me was the smell of heated fragranced oil. It made me vaguely uncomfortable the way her mockery couldn't, as if somehow I was missing out on something very important about being a woman and yet I had no clue what it was.

"Oh, you're funny," she laughed yet again as if we were having the most fun and I was aware of heads turning. Only her father seemed oblivious. "So dry. You must use humor to entertain your admirers."

I was just about to correct her on her assumption that I had admirers, when Bithia, standing behind me to fill my wine cup, jostled me hard with one of her hips. I looked up at her and she shot me one of her 'you're making a fool of yourself' looks. Since I usually got those looks when I was asking questions, I ignored her.

Instead, I looked back at the girl next to me.

"Is changing the subject back to me part of it too?" I asked and she shot me a surprised, confusedly annoyed look.

"What?" she asked and I pointed. She was yet another puzzle to me and I was determined to work it out and understand.

"I asked you a question about yourself and you turned around and talked about me. Twice. Is that part of being attractive to men too?"

"Well, they certainly don't care about you," she said with a roll of her eyes and her voice said she was quite knowledgeable on that fact. Again, I felt as if I were missing something basic someone should have explained to me years ago. I hadn't previously thought I'd missed that much by not having a mother that taught me the basics of being a woman.

"Not just you" Briseis clarified. "Any woman. They only want women that make them feel good about themselves." Her voice was very mature and a bit bitter when she said it and then her painted eyes flew wide and she looked more closely at me as if she'd just told me a secret she shouldn't. I looked in confusion back at her because I hadn't caught any dark confession if that was what she was supposed to have given. "You're very strange," she told me, sounding puzzled and I coughed a laugh, losing my intent mental puzzling.

"I suppose I am," I agreed. She rested her perfectly smooth chin in her henna painted hand and looked at me with smoky gray eyes. Thoughtful.

"You know, you'd be truly pretty if you gained some weight. Your bone structure is very elegant."

I didn't know about bone structure but I wouldn't have minded a bit more weight. I ate. It was just that my body had decided to spend all that food on giving me unnecessary height instead of anything resembling feminine curves. It was something that I was beginning to notice, and be bothered by, more and more.

"You've got full lips and very large eyes. If your face was rounder it would hid the point of your chin," the girl continued and I really did laugh at that.

"You're doing it again," I told her. "Talking about me."

Her lips curved at their edges and her face tipped to the side slightly.

"I suppose I am," she agreed with a realer smile. She looked closely at me. "You really do want to learn about how to deal with men?" she asked me seriously and Bithia cleared her throat behind me. I ignored her.

"Yes," I nodded. "I want to know how you do the things you do."

"Hm." Briseis sat back on her bench with a little noise and looked speculatively at me. Then she smiled and it was beautiful. To me, it seemed more beautiful than the laughter or the way she used her eyes. "All right. I'll teach you. We're going to be traveling together anyway and we'll probably set up tents near each other too. I'll ask father if you can ride with us tomorrow."

****

"I can't believe you," Bithia hissed it at me the next day as I helped her repack what little we'd taken out of my trunk. "If you wanted lessons on how to be a whore, you could have just asked me."

I gave a snorting laugh and looked at her from the sides of my eyes.

"Are you insulting yourself?" I asked and she gave me a glare.

"That woman is nothing but a tease. She'll

get herself in trouble. Ladies don't act that way. Whores do. Noblemen don't marry whores."

"They do if they're very good whores." It earned me another glare. Truly though - what was the line between ladies like Medea and Ariadne and someone like Briseis? I was learning to look at the old legends with a different eye these days. I was learning to look at them from the women's point of view. Both those women, so close to my mother in the ancient skills, had won their men with a look. And lost them with one too.

"Men will think you are like her if you stay in her company," Bithia warned me and I shrugged as I stuffed my bedroll into the case and then tied the ornately carved lid shut while Bithia sat on it. Once again - strangers - why should their opinion matter to me?

"Fine," Bithia gave up and stalked to the door of the guest room to gesture in the slave that would carry my luggage to my family's cart. "But don't believe everything she says. There are better ways to bind a man to you than to wiggle when you walk and giggle when he talks."

"But the wiggling does seem to help," I pointed out just to annoy her and her narrow eyes were my only answer.

In all honesty, I was not that interested in earning the looks of men or their attention. It hardly mattered what I did. I would be married to someone because they liked my father or my father's lands, not because I did or didn't wiggle when I moved.

The way people bent to Briseis was fascinating to me though, in the same way Orease's beekeeping intrigued me. It was like a special magic only certain people could work.

Briseis was apparently serious about my lessons too because she began from almost the moment I climbed into the cart next to her. I think that was when I began to like her. She could have ignored my curiosity or kept her secrets to herself. Instead she was willing to spread out this new puzzle in front of me and share. Having seen my brother's concubines hoard their every advantage from each other, I took it as the gift it was.

"What do you see? Behind us?" She began my lessons with a question.

I lifted my veil to look better as the cart started off with a lurch.

"I see Hermolaos and Hermokrates jostling to ride closest. I see one of the soldiers stealing a last kiss from the woman he bedded last night before he leaves. I see your mother standing in the doorway and waving a blue scarf. I see the goose boy chasing the dog that's chasing a gander that got loose. And one of your chimneys isn't cleared enough. The smoke's coming out funny."

"Boys," Briseis corrected me. "All you see are boys."

"Well, I see several men too," I clarified and when she laughed, it was bright but there was a sharp, painful edge hiding under it.

"No, you don't," she shook her head and it

set the gold coins at the edge of her veil tinkling merrily. "Real men don't exist. They're all boys. Some of them are just in bigger bodies. But they all think just like they did when they were little."

I wasn't sure about that but I had to admit in fairness.

"Hermolaos and Hermokrates certainly are acting like children."

"I love having men fight over me," she told me cheerfully. "It saves me so much energy. Instead of concentrating on both of them, I let them concentrate on each other and all I have to do is sit back and enjoy it."

"But you haven't talked to either of them."

"You really are sweet," she leaned back against one of the cushions and shut her eyes. "I don't have to talk to them. Men don't want a woman that talks. Men want a woman that thinks they're a hero. All I have to do is look the littlest bit interested and they'll fall over each other to make sure I realize why I should be interested."

I thought it over as I dangled my legs over the back of the cart. My brothers and the soldiers weren't the most interesting view but the scenery on either side was beautiful in the new dawn light and it gave my eyes something to watch while I rolled her words over in my mind, comparing it to what I already knew.

"It's because they want what they can't have," I finally supplied and Briseis sat up a bit and looked curiously at me.

"I thought you didn't know anything about men."

"I don't." It was no pride lost to admit it. Tipping my head back, I watched the canopy of branches passing overhead, still thinking. "I was just told once that people don't appreciate what comes easily to them."

She made a noise that might have been a cut off snort, as if she'd caught herself before she could do anything so unladylike.

"Who does?" She leaned back again.

I do, I thought, but didn't say it. I loved the delicate diadem my father had given me 'just because'. I loved Bithia and she never drew away from me or made me wonder if she loved me back. I had loved Nemea. I had loved the driving lessons Podes had given me, again 'just because'. It didn't make sense to me that people would love things for *not* being there for them. Shouldn't they appreciate the ones they did have already more?

"Why are people like that?" I wondered out loud and Briseis shifted against her cushion with a shrug.

"Even sweetened dates taste bland after eating enough of them."

I supposed she was right. I remembered getting sick once eating the huge honeycomb Orease had given me when I was younger, but - wasn't love supposed to be more like meat and bread than honey? Filling and solid instead of sweet and passing?

I swung my heels thoughtfully.

"How do you know how much of the 'sweetened date' to offer someone?" I asked.

"Actually, you only pretend you're going to offer it. It's much more effective than actually offering. You're the single shiny trinket that only one of the boys can have. The trick is to make them all think they've got a chance at having you, even if none of them do."

"It sounds complicated," I complained and she opened her eyes to peer at me.

"You have no idea," she agreed and then she propped herself up on an elbow to look at me very seriously. I thought her eyes darkened like low clouds far on the horizon. "It's all about knowing how to read someone. Then you know just how far you can tease them before you get into trouble."

VI.

The trip to Ilium's plain took all day and it was just as well. It was only toward the end of it that I could start to look at things from Briseis' view. It was an enlightening mindset to find myself in even if I wasn't exactly comfortable with it and was actually grateful that I would never have a reason to need to use it. It seemed complex and shifty and - to me - it seemed a bit cruel. Yet, I had seen it work.

I stood with Briseis in the cart once we arrived and listened to her point out different Houses and families to me as our servants put up the tents. Living closer to Ilium than my family did, she saw more people pass through her homeland than I did in mine and she could guess quite a few of them from gossip too. I soaked all the information in, awed at how huge the land was here and also by the overwhelming amount of people. Surely, my entire country didn't hold as many people as were gathered under the shadows of great Troy's walls to buy and sell and trade their goods.

And Troy -- bright Ilium -- I had never imagined anything could be so massive. Its towering walls gleamed in the setting sun and seemed to stretch on forever. Huge gates rose along the length of the wall that I could see curving off into the distance and the thick doors set in them were covered with brass. Horse drawn chariots raced around its circumference and I thought I saw people on top of the walls, bright bits of color against a slowly darkening sky. It was hard not to believe that Poseidon had built them.

"Think your friend is in there?" Podes had appeared by the side of my cart and he too was looking up at the great walls in the distance. His awe was tinged with hunger but who hadn't heard of the heroes of Troy? It was the place that seemed to birth them.

"My friend?" I blinked down at my brother and he laughed.

"Prince Hector. Do you think he's there now?"

"Prince Hector? Hector Horse-breaker?" Briseis was looking at me with something like the light in my brother's eyes when he looked at Ilium. "You know the crown prince of Troy?"

All of the titles bothered me for some reason. To me, he was simply 'Hector' even though I knew he had more rights to the titles than I had to call him by name without them. Still, he was Hector before he was Prince or Horse-breaker in my head. I moved my hands with a jerk.

"He visited us once." I felt, strangely, as if I was defending him, though from what I wasn't sure. Both my brother and Briseis had spoken of him with respect.

Briseis gave me a speculative look.

"You really are full of surprises, Andromache of Thebe. Don't you know he's the one man on this entire continent that every woman is pining for?"

"That's silly," I protested. Not sure why it was silly, just that it was.

"He's the crown prince of Troy," Briseis told me firmly, putting her hands on her hips. "Whoever he marries will be a crown princess. And one lucky wife will end up queen of Ilium."

I frowned and looked back at the walls.

"How many women will he marry?" I asked. She shrugged.

"Who knows? Who even knows how many wives and concubines and asides his father has? Old King Priam has at least fifty sons that are legitimate and who knows how many more that aren't."

"Fifty?" I blinked. And I had thought that my seven brothers were a large number. Something inside me felt very sad for my long ago Hector. I had seen how my own brothers competed for attention and praise, friends and yet rivals too. I couldn't begin to fathom was living with that must be like with fifty.

"It's good to be king," Podes stated dryly and shrugged. "If he comes to see you, tell him I've got faster horses this time. He owes me a chance to win back my wager."

I watched my brother's wide back as he left and wondered why he'd really come over. I was learning that he didn't do things as randomly as he at first seemed. Briseis was watching me and the light in her eyes made me uncomfortable.

"I only knew him one day," I defended and she nodded.

"Of course," she agreed. "Boys are silly with the conclusions they leap too." She patted my hand as Bithia came over to hustle me off to the tent our servants had finished setting up. "But we're friends now, aren't we? We'll have to spend time wandering the fair together. If Prince Hector does stop by, bring him over to meet me too. I'd love to hear about his latest adventures."

I only stopped myself from pressing my lips together at the very last moment. I had never seen her eyes so hungry and sharp before. It reminded me of my mother and that sudden realization both felt unfair to Briseis – and yet sent a shiver down my back and made me feel strangely as if I would rather she never see Hector.

"I will remember you," I nodded and slipped easily off the cart to join Bithia. I did not have to turn around to know that Briseis watched me all the way back to my tent from her unmoving spot on her family's travel cart. The spot between my shoulder blades itched enough to prove it.

****

"Bithia?"

She was combing out my hair and made an inquiring noise. We had settled into the family tent and were fixing the damage traveling had done to my appearance. I watched her face in the warped bronze of the small mirror. After a minute, she looked up from what she was doing and raised an elegant eyebrow.

"That whore's been filling your head with

nonsense, hasn't she? What's the question this time?" she asked me. I shook my head.

"Nothing about Briseis. She just elaborated on what you already told me about men only wanting what they can't have." I toyed absently with one of the small jars that held something that was supposed to smooth my skin. It had a little elephant carved in its soft stone top and I had never noticed how appropriate the comparison might be -

"Well?" Bithia interrupted my thoughts and I shrugged. She put down the comb and knelt next to me, resting her lovely olive hands on my knee. "What is it, Andromache?" Her voice was softer and maybe a bit worried. I moved my shoulder again, a half effort at a shrug this time.

"If I wanted to find out if someone was here - just for myself... And I didn't want them to know I was looking for them - ?"

Bithia's smile was slow and knowing.

"Is it a boy? A soldier that marched through your father's land or a shepherd who traded with your family before I arrived?"

I felt suddenly stupid and refused to look up from the small jar in my hands.

"It's foolishness," I answered her, feeling the tips of my ears burning. "He wouldn't even remember me. I just - "

"I know. You just want to know if he's here or not." Bithia smiled at me and I gave her a grateful look.

"Yes."

"So, tell me who this mysterious man is."

I didn't know whether she'd laugh at me or simply roll her eyes but if I didn't ask, I'd never find out.

"It's Hector." I let the name sit between us while she waited for the rest and then she realized that the name alone was all the information she would need.

"Hector?" she asked. "Hector of Troy? That Hector?"

I resisted the urge to fidget uncomfortably on my stool.

"He stayed with us. Once. A little over a year ago." Had it been only a year? It seemed much farther away than that. Lifetimes. I had not thought of him in so long. Just small times, wondering what he would do in my situation to keep the people under his protection safe or how different his words about women were compared to what others said. Yet, suddenly realizing that he might be close again, I felt nervous and confused – and eager and hopeful. He had no reason to remember me, but I remembered him. And the thought of seeing him again, even if it was only from a distance, made my stomach feel warm and full in a way I couldn't explain. It didn't make sense – but I wanted it all the same. Just knowing he was nearby would be enough to let me feel that feeling again.

"My," Bithia blinked several times. "You really do make friends with everyone." She frowned in thought and nodded. "All right. It should be easy enough to do." She looked up at me and started to smile. "I'll just play the country bumpkin and be awed with all the legends I've heard of Troy. The way servants gossip it shouldn't be hard to work the subject around to your Hector."

The laugh exhaled out of me.

"It would be nice," I admitted. "Just to hear about him."

****

The next morning started early. The rising sun shining through the tent walls and the light doze that had been all I had managed thanks to my various siblings and father snoring all night long made it easy. So did the excitement. I had not forgotten what I'd asked Bithia to do but it was hardly the only thing on my mind. I must have been practically vibrating with energy, as she helped me prepare myself for the day. I was hardly the only one to feel that way too. Fairs were so much more than buying and selling. There would be competitions of all kinds and entertainment as well. My father would spend most of the time meeting with other kings to talk about all the things kings talked about. I had promised Enoch I would go with him for the household shopping. It was mostly because I wanted to learn what we would, and could, buy but also because he had been here often enough before that I could be sure he could show me everything I would want to see. Bithia debated briefly over whether to send a shade with me or not but I dissuaded her with a scowl. I'd bowed to her insistence that I start wearing a veil when I was outside, even though it obscured my vision a bit. I was not about to let her start sneaking a shade into my life.

Just before the family scattered to the four winds, my father dropped a purse into my hands. I looked up at him in surprise, thinking that he usually gave Enoch the household money to carry.

"For you," he told me. "To buy yourself something nice." He looked a bit awkward about it and I wasn't sure how I should react either. He gave me a crooked smile. "Don't spend it all on makeup. Buy some food and put some meat on your bones too." My face brightened as I threw my arms around him in a tight hug.

"Thank you," I grinned and he grinned back. Then he was striding off to talk to one of my brothers and I was looking at Enoch, who simply smiled quietly and then started out of our small camp and into the fair itself.

It was a good thing I was wearing my veil. If I hadn't been better trained I would have spent the entire time walking around with my mouth hanging open and at least the vague opacity of the veil hid my huge eyes. I'd never seen such variety and even in the common things I was used to, I'd never seen such quantity. And the people! There were so many people! All of them were different. There were dark Nubians and honey-and-milk Egyptians and light-haired Achaeans. The colors and styles of dress were astounding and the different accents and languages all wove together like a many-toned river. I could have sat in one spot and just watched people for days. Of course, I was saved from that by Enoch who confidently wove his way around stalls and booths and stages -- and crowds and crowds of people. It seemed he knew all the traders by name and they knew him in return. I was introduced to more of them than I could remember and I had always thought myself good with names. As the morning passed, our servants carried more and more, making trips back to our camp to empty their loads and returning only to have their arms filled again and still there was a great deal that Enoch simply had set aside for us to be delivered to our camp later. Everyone was more than glad to answer my questions about anything to do with their trade that I could think of. By the time we stopped for a meal and something to drink at one of the canopied areas by midday, I felt as if I had learned more in the past few hours than I had in the past year and I had thought I had learned a great deal in the past year.

Enoch was smiling proudly at me.

"You do make an impression," his quiet voice made me feel good inside and I smiled at him.

"There's so much to see."

"We still have several days. Not only is there a great deal we can find here that we can't find at the local fairs but we will get better prices on our goods that we brought to sell too. Miltiades is quite happy with the offers he's already received on our cattle."

Most of our trade goods had come with us but the cattle had been sent on ahead earlier. No one wanted to travel with cattle and they were slow travelers. They had already been penned in nearby fields set aside for just that purpose and to give buyers the chance to look over them. Poor animals. They would not be going home to their familiar pastures after this and no doubt quite a few of them would find themselves as dinner before the end of the winter.

"Your brothers will want to trade for Trojan steeds too." He looked at me and gently rested a hand over mine on the table. "And your father is starting to look for a husband for you."

My eyes blinked wide and I could only stare at him. So soon?

"Helen of Sparta's abduction has gotten quite a few fathers thinking about their daughters and sons in a new way. The prince from Hippoplacia was beginning to make marriage offers before he proved to be such a disappointment on the raid."

It was unusual for Enoch to speak so much and he never gave away my father's secrets. Yet he was telling me this? I met his eyes and gave him a weak smile. He wanted me to be forewarned to spare me the shock when the time came for me to leave my own house.

"Thank you," I told him and I meant it with deep sincerity. I could adjust to marriage in my mind but I would need time to do it. He was giving me that time. It was a precious gift. He nodded and stood up, our meal finished.

"Let me walk you back to the camp, my lady?" he asked me formally. "I'm sure Bithia is waiting to sweep you into the fair on her own errands."

It would have been awkward to acknowledge just how much his forewarning had meant to both of us and so we silently pretended there was nothing to acknowledge. Instead, we made our way back to the camp together and the silence was comfortable. It had been a full morning and the sun was now high in the vast vaulted sky. As crowded as the fair was, it was easy for me to forget how far the horizons all stretched here. When we moved away from it and toward my family's camp however, the plain again stretched on forever with the glinting blue of the sea behind us and Ilium's mighty walls before us. That vast horizon on one side held freedom but it was also the unknown, empty and yet full of life. I wondered if my someday marriage would be like the plains and ocean – or like a walled in city.

"Take a nap," Enoch suggested and gave me a quiet smile. "The tent will be empty and quiet and even a short sleep will refresh you for the rest of the day."

Given how little I'd slept the past few nights, it didn't sound like a bad idea, especially since we would be here for several days and I would have time for everything. I thanked him and ducked into the tent, greeting the guards at its entrance as I passed and then gave a sigh and took off my veil. The interior of the cream colored tent was much cooler and the murmur from the fair was pleasantly muted, like waves lapping on a shore. Bithia greeted me with a cup of well-watered grape juice and I took it gratefully, settling down on a low bench while I sipped it. She slipped down to sit next to me.

"I've been busy," she began and I chuckled into my cup. She ignored it and continued. "And Hector, crown prince of Ilium isn't here." I looked at her from the corners of my eyes, feeling disappointed but not surprised. "There are raiders trying to set up a base off the Propontis, near the Sanger River. He's taken a contingent of his father's men to drive them off."

It made sense, politically. The Euxine Sea fed into the smaller Propontis before it passed the narrow mouth of the Hellespont and finally became a part of the Great Sea. Troy's trade, as well as its allies on that side, depended on the ships that passed through that area to reach their trading allies.

"Everyone's very confident in him," Bithia continued. "Apparently he's already proven himself to be an impressive defender, just as his name says. There's already talk he'll be made warlord of his father's entire army when he comes back."

"My father said he was a good fighter," I remarked absently and Bithia looked at me with curiosity, but I was remembering the way his dark eyes had looked when he had come to me in the middle of battle and his face afterward in the stables.

"You'll have to tell me that story some time," she stated when I didn't offer more. Then her face brightened. "I do have good news. While I was wandering around I met one of Chryseis' maids. She's here with her father. When she found out you were here too, she almost jumped out of her shoes she was so excited. I told her you were busy today with shopping for the household but she asked me to beg you to come visit her in their camp tomorrow."

That did make me smile and I nodded.

"I think that would be wonderful," I agreed. The thought of the other girl's bright moods and bubbling spirit caught at my own heart and made me suddenly fiercely glad she was here. Things were very simple with Chryseis. I suddenly thought I needed that in my life.

"Good then." Bithia nodded and began to help me out of my overdress. "Because that Briseis also sent her maid over asking after your company as well."

I was very good the first day of the fair. I did take a nap but then I joined my father for the rest of the day. He was surprised to see me but he let me stay. I listened silently as he talked to various kings and rulers, soaking in this more political side of things with eager ears. I do not think it hurt anything that the fathers of my potential suitors saw me sitting serene and quiet and obedient either but that suited me, because I watched them too. I would be living in one of their houses one day and I wanted to know them before that.

My father did not spend the entire day simply talking. He also looked at horses and together we watched several of my brothers compete in different wrestling and running matches. Father was very proud of his sons and I was too. They were my brothers, after all. Even if we didn't always get along, I still wanted them to win. My father and I did not talk much but then we rarely did. It was more than enough for me to be able to be by his side. I was careful not to be a nuisance and to only ask my questions when it didn't interrupt anything else. Toward the end of the day, he brought me to the metal smiths' section of the fair and together we watched the way the plates of bronze were beaten out and formed into breastplates and greaves. Everything was done in layers. I saw leather covering a single bronze sheet to make a single breast plate and one breast plate that shown brightly in the fire made of four equal leaves of pure bronze. Father and I stood for a very long time in front of those devices of both war and protection.

Near sunset, father took me down to the harbor and we walked among the sailors and their beached boats, watching still more ships arriving with good for the fair. Father greeted several of the merchants and introduced me but for the most part we simply walked and watched. I had never been out of our homeland with my father before and I was surprised to see how much he simply watched things. As I so often silently watched...

On the way back to camp, while we walked along the Skamander River, I took his large, leathery hand in mine. His thick fingers closed around my slimmer ones and he said nothing. Neither did I. But it was a slow, meandering route we took back to our camp.

****

The next morning I was woken out of my light doze when someone literally pounced on me.

"Get up! Get up!" The sunny, cheerful voice was impossible to not recognize and I squinted one of my eyes open to peer darkly at the dignified, noble daughter of one of Phoebus' high priests as she bounced on my bed, and, because I was in it, on me as well. "You promised all day to me! And you're wasting it!" Chryseis sat back on her knees and crossed her arms, giving me a mockingly fierce glare. I returned a more honest one and she laughed and clapped her hands together. "Oh! You're ever so much better at looking dangerous than I am! Get up, get up, get up!"

"I didn't promise you the day." I shut my eye and tried to burrow back under the covers but she lifted the pillow I was trying to hide under off my head and grinned at me. I could tell even with my eyes closed.

"Come on, silly. You're going to miss

sunrise!"

She was clearly ignoring the fact I never promised her any time at all but I still had to give up my battle with not smiling. She was far too hard to resist. Chryseis saw it and my fate was sealed.

"Come on!" she squeaked. "Up and off! There's so much to do!"

"You get off," I told her but I was laughing by then and I sat up. She gave me a smile that was easily brighter than any sunrise.

"I knew I'd see you again," she told me confidently as she scrambled off the bed and, strangely, it made me feel like crying. We'd only met briefly a season ago and yet it felt as if I'd known her so much longer and been without her so much longer as well. I swallowed it down and climbed out of bed. Bithia, looking amused, was waiting for me and immediately started helping me get ready for another day.

"How's Nemea?" I asked as I pulled on a dress of pale blue.

"Horrible," Chryseis stated with glee. "He bosses around all the other cats and thinks he's related to Phoebus Apollo. Half the priests actually believe him!"

I laughed at that even if it hurt my heart too. I did miss him but he was safe where he was. That was what truly mattered.

"You can buy him some ribbons!" Chryseis put one of my veils on her own head and looked at herself in the bronze mirror. "I'll take them home to him and he'll know they're from you!"

That helped me and I grinned at her. It didn't take long for Bithia gave up trying to do anything more than a simple braid with my hair since I wouldn't sit still for her.

"I've got so much planned for us today!" Chryseis never needed contributions to a conversation to keep it going. "There's so much to see! And buy!" She took off my veil and spun back to where I was to catch at my hands. "Aren't you ready yet?"

"Yes" I told her, picking up the veil for myself. "Do you mind if we bring company?"
****

We must have been an odd combination: Chryseis with her pure innocence and her exuberant chatter; me, silent until the questions started, and Briseis with her dark attraction and teasing laugh. As I'd expected, Chryseis immediately befriended the other girl who, once she realized Chryseis was no more interested in being a challenge to her net of men than I was, stopped resisting her overtures and was soon laughing just as honestly as the rest of us. No one could resist Chryseis.

We spent the morning shopping. Or rather, looking at a great deal and buying very little. There was always another stall or booth further along that might offer something we hadn't seen yet. It was frivolous and exhausting but I had never had so much fun before. We cajoled each other into being wrapped in fine linens and even more exotic fabrics.

We held jewelry up to our ears and throats that came from dozens of different coasts and cities. We exclaimed over the ivory from Egypt and the painted Cretan vases. I looked longingly at the cedar furniture from the lands of the Philistine and Habiru kingdoms. Briseis dragged us from one scent stall to another, pouring over the exotic spices and skin creams and 'miracle' potions that would keep our youth. In the end we bought very little but I did buy Nemea his ribbons.

"I want to see the monument!" Chryseis was holding my arm and pulling. Briseis rolled her eyes.

"It's noon. I'm hungry," she complained and Chryseis wrinkled her nose at her cheerfully, still not letting go of my arm.

"We can eat later!" she protested.

"We can see the monument later too." Briseis shot me a look. "Andromache, tell her so."

I smiled and shrugged, helpless in the face of the sad, over-dramatically trembling lower lip Chryseis was giving me. Briseis saw it and protested.

"That's cheating! No influencing Andromache like that!"

I laughed quietly and then exhaled with a grin.

"All right. Why don't we do this?" I tried to find the middle ground between what they both wanted. "We can buy food at one of the booths and then, take it up to the monument and eat it there?

How does that sound?"

Chryseis beamed and let go of me long enough to clap her hands. Briseis shook her head with a wry smile, grey eyes laughing.

"It sounds like we're lucky you weren't born a man or you'd have wheedled your way into the position as some king's advisor and all the rest of our countries wouldn't stand a chance."

"Flattery," I chided.

"Food!" Chryseis, now that she had a goal that let her get what she wanted, was single minded and determined. Laughing, we linked arms and found a booth that sold something that each of us could enjoy.

Our servants were with us, invisible but always present, and Bithia had quickly taken charge of them. They each carried a basket for our purchases and so we stowed the food and I watched, bemused, as Chryseis climbed up on a tabletop to get her bearings so we could go to her landmark.

"Pity the man that gets his hands on her and tries to tame that spirit," Briseis commented next to my ear but she said it admiringly.

"She could stop an entire army," I agreed affectionately.

"I see it!" Chryseis was pointing and cheerful. "I see it!"

"Is she all right?" a voice near my shoulder asked and I turned my head in surprise to look up at a young man that looked vaguely familiar. It was obvious he'd been the one to ask the question and he currently was watching Chryseis verbally haranguing one of the men that had wolfishly called something to her. I shrugged.

"That's a good question. But she's not in danger, no."

"She might be *a* danger," Briseis added dryly, and I knew she was sizing the man next to me up from the corners of her eyes. He was young but leaning toward tall and slim, with dark hair and light eyes. His dress was simple but the make of it and the embroidery told me he was very rich. Chryseis swooped down from her perch and wrapped both her arms around my arm that Briseis had not already claimed.

"Why are we still here?" she asked. "Come on!"

Over my own laugh, I heard the stranger behind me ask:

"What exactly is the cause for all the excitement?"

Briseis rolled her eyes, but Chryseis was delighted to tell someone else what she'd already told us.

"The Monument of Ilus. It's the tower over the ashes of one of Troy's old kings! They keep a mariner's light on top it and they say you can see forever from it."

"Ah." Our questioner nodded. "The view from the top of it is worth seeing. Do you mind if I come too?"

We'd been trailed by and lost men all day

thanks to Briseis, so I wasn't surprised when another one volunteered. At least this one wasn't just skulking around behind us for half a day or more before finally wandering off. Briseis gave him a knowing smile under her kohl colored eyelids and Chryseis shrugged and looked at me. I gave her a look back that was the equivalent of a shrug. We had more than enough in our group between the three of us and the servants. We were hardly unchaperoned. I wondered, since he had spotted Chryseis first, whether it was Briseis he was interested in.

"Where are you from?" I asked him. He gave me a silently laughing smile and when he answered, I understood why.

"Ilium.".

"Really?" Chryseis was interested now. I could almost see her mind assigning him the role of our guide whether he intentionally volunteered for it or not.

"I think we have enough food for everyone," I told him. "Please come."

"I'd like that."

I passed through my mind briefly to wonder at how easily he joined us. Perhaps he'd been following us for longer than I'd realized and waiting for his opportunity. Usually that kind of plotting would have bothered me, but I was with Briseis and was getting used to men doing similar things for the chance to try to attract her attention.

Our new guide played his role well, pointing

out bits of interesting information over things we'd already passed and never realized. He was more than happy to answer questions and I was soon dominating the conversation with mine, my two friends snickering about it good-naturedly. We stopped by the horse pens on our way out of the fair so Chryseis could tell her father's steward where we were off to. I rested my arms on the fresh cut wood of the railing and looked at the yearlings going about their horsy business. Our guide imitated my move.

"Ilium has the best horses in the world," he stated. From anyone else it would have been bragging but he simply stated it as fact it was. "We've spent decades refining the perfect horse. I can't tell you how many different breeds we've mixed. It's all some of our people can talk about," he admitted with a quiet smile.

"I met a Trojan horse once." I watched a colt playfully nipping at the sack of grain over stable worker's shoulder. "He whistled."

The man next to me nodded.

"Marsyas."

I looked over at him in surprise, both that he knew the horse and that he was the first person I had talked to that *didn't* seem surprised that I might know Hector. He looked blankly at me and then broke into a grin.

"Hector's horse. It's the only one in all the world that whistles. It's a problem, a defect, with the roof of the horse's mouth when he was born.

Hector wanted him anyway. I don't know how he realized Marsyas could whistle but once he realized the horse could, he taught him to do it in response to his own whistle. Now the damn thing won't stop whenever it wants attention."

I had to laugh at that.

"You know Hector too." At his surprise, I explained: "You call him Hector and not Prince Hector."

He looked slightly embarrassed and quickly looked away at the horses.

"He's my brother," he answered with a grimace. He looked back at me. "Please don't tell the others. I'm enjoying being anonymous today."

I could only imagine how Briseis would deepen her 'attack' if she realized he was royal.

"You're safe," I smiled. "But you must tell me your name in payment."

"I'm Helenus. And I trust your hands," he mock solemnly intoned one of the lines of protection and protector that was given at weddings. I knew it must be a joke and yet it still bounced hollow and unsettling in my chest thanks to Enoch's earlier warning about my coming future. I couldn't take the words lightly as I was sure he intended them. Chryseis bounded over to us before I had to answer.

"We can go!" she announced, as if we had been waiting breathlessly for her permission. Somehow, Briseis, even out of hearing range, broke off her practice charming of one of the nearby merchants to waltz over to join us. I gave her a look and she just laughed, slipping her arm through mine and not incidentally ending up between me and our guide. I didn't mind because that meant that Chryseis automatically rotated to my free arm and latched on again.

"Lead on," Briseis cheerful instructed the young man. "I hear the tower has a lovely view. And I'm starting to get hungry."
****

The Monument of Ilus did have a beautiful view. We climbed to the top while the servants set up our lunch. Chryseis immediately let go of me to rush over to the very edge and look out over the landscape laid out almost at her feet. A bit more carefully, I joined her.

"Oh! It is beautiful!"

I had to agree with Chryseis' sentiment, right down to the amount of emotion she put behind the words. The plain of Troy spread out before us, colored with tents and small booths, hundreds of people from a hundred different lands, animals and merchandise... it was a living weaving of every color and texture, constantly moving and alive with life. It was breathtaking but for me it was the sight of the harbor and than the ocean beyond, vast and forever and so blue it made my heart hurt that wedged itself deepest inside my chest. That tear inside me that whispered a longing for freedom and a wider world than the one I would be allowed to have. I wanted more than just a few well-worn memories of Illium and the world beyond in my future.

"You can see forever from here!" Chryseis exclaimed. Briseis, behind us, laughed softly.

"Isn't it telling that you two look out at the ocean instead of back at Ilium?"

With a surprised laugh of my own, I turned around. She was right. We could just as easily see Ilium as we could the Great Sea beyond if we would only turn around. Our guide was smiling a private inward smile and I caught his speculative look at me. He looked back to Chryseis before I could puzzle out what it meant.

"Don't you want to go in?" Briseis gestured toward the grand city beyond, distracting me. From here we could see the inside of the city better, spread out almost like childrens' toys. There were hanging gardens down some of the interior walls and, on the outsides of some of the buildings cheerful tiles and frescos created stories and lively scenes. Its streets too were full of a moving river of people and animals and my imagination gave me the whispered echoes of their voices on the wind. It was a city of color and life. Surprisingly, Chryseis that shook her head.

"No," she answered cheerfully. "I like being out here much more!"

"Really?" Briseis arched an elegant eyebrow. "But I heard Chrysa has a magnificent city built entirely around the temple to Apollo that stands twice as high as any other building in its center."

"It's all stairs," Chryseis bemoaned the fact over-dramatically, complete with arm motions for emphasis. "Everything's stairs. We've got the world's thickest calf muscles. Nothing goes in a straight line. It's back and forth, back and forth."

I pressed my lips together to mute my laughter at her performance and from the triumphant look she flashed, I knew it had been her purpose.

"I like flat much better," she finished with a bright grin.

"Do you think you can manage one more set of stairs, brave Chryseis, and join us on the flat ground for lunch?" I asked and she chirped back:

"Anything for you, noble Andromache."

I caught our guide looking thoughtfully at Chryseis as we went back down the stairs. Of all of us, she had the most leniency. Marriage did not have to be in her future. She could follow in her father's footsteps and follow the god instead. I thought the flexibility in her future gave her the freedom that she was so easy with.

The servants had set up our lunch by the time we reached the bottom and joined us while we ate, sitting in their own circle and exchanging their own murmured conversation. Our conversation was dominated by Briseis' flirtation and our guide's witty response to it. His answers were quick and clever but, watching, it seemed to me, that if Briseis was a thought, he had something more occupying his mind. Finally, Chryseis asked about the history of the monument and that opened the door for me to ask about the history of Ilium itself.

The great city, he told us, had been built and rebuilt more times than anyone remembered. Legend had that the walls had been built by both Poseidon and Apollo, and were unbreachable. Looking at them, I could believe the second part at least. As for gods doing actual manual labor... I had never heard of them stooping to that before. Gods were notorious for not getting their hands dirty, not for building things by the sweat of their brow. I didn't mention it. Chryseis might not have shared my much more Theban sentiment and our guide might be offended. Even more threatening, one of the gods might have been listening.

I wanted to ask about the politics but Briseis interrupted me with how boring a conversation that was going to be and instead turned the topic to fashion. Which lead to talk of parties. Which lead to talk of songs and stories that were making the rounds. With the city he was from, Helenus knew a wider range of songs that the rest of us had never heard and proved to have a very nice singing voice. He and Chryseis sang a duet from one of the more popular love ballads. Briseis, not to be outdone, made my throat close up and drew tears to Chryseis' eyes with a slow, sad song about a Muse who fell in love with her poet but could never be with him other than in his dreams. Finally, after much prodding, to leave the evening on a high note,

I picked one of the less rowdy songs I knew, one that our workers sang in the harvest fields to help with the strokes of the scythe and sickle, and I sang that with Bithia's help for the women's chorus.

By the time we were done evening was coming on and the wide sky above us was painted in beautiful colors that streaked slow and brilliant across the darkening blue.

"We should start back." I stood as I said it and the others rose to their feet as well. Chryseis threw her arms wide and tipped her face to the sky.

"What a beautiful day!" she declared and danced a little in place. "I've met an old friend and made new ones!"

I suddenly wanted to hug her fiercely to me, as if to keep her as she was in this perfect moment and I did not know why. Instead, I shook my head at her with a smile.

"Every day with you is a beautiful day," I teased it and yet I meant it sincerely. She must have known for she grinned impishly back at me and I saw love in her eyes.

"Oh, Andromache, with you, some days are perfect!"

VII.

Bithia was resorting to braiding my hair again the next morning when Zoe scratched on the tent flap and then let herself in. My father looked up from the map he was poring over. She approached him but she shot a look my way that was both hesitant and unsure as she did so.

"There's a young man outside," she told him, sounding uncertain as she added: "He says he is one of Princess Andromache's friends from yesterday?"

I blinked at her, while Bithia made a thoughtful noise behind me. My father and the two brothers that had not already gone for the day, looked at me as well.

"Helenus?" I asked which was silly because I didn't know any other men that I'd met yesterday and she didn't know the name of the man I had. When she gave me a helpless look, I smiled. "I'm sorry," I told her as I turned to look at my father. "We met a prince of Troy yesterday. Bithia, Chryseis, Briseis, and I. He took us to see the Monument of Ilus."

"Briseis, Chryseis, and you --" my father's voice was thoughtful. "And it is your tent he comes to today."

I felt suddenly guilty, though I didn't know why. Automatically, from old habit, I offered my hands, palms out and fingers extended.

"I don't know why. Maybe he wants to talk to me about Chryseis. He noticed her first

156

yesterday."

My brothers were watching me silently, faces expressionless, but my father's mouth turned upward in an almost sad, quiet smile.

"My little bird," he murmured. Then he clapped both his huge hands down on the table in a decisive move and turned his attention back on Zoe.

"Send the boy in."

Helenus stepped into the tent a moment later and his eyes scanned its interior, noting me, before they focused on my father. He bowed.

"I am sorry for the short notice, King Eetion. I'm Helenus of Ilium. One of Priam's sons. I was hoping, with your permission, to take the Princess Andromache into Troy today."

My father was watching him thoughtfully.

"You're very fast," he commented and the remark that puzzled me only had Helenus nodding.

"Yes," he agreed comfortably. "I find that when moving over thin or shifting ice my safety lies in speed."

Father chuckled.

"Who were you intending to have accompany you?" he asked and our visitor looked over at me directly for the first time.

"I am hoping for the princess' company. And that of her lady, of course." He looked back at my father, and I saw he was measuring something inside himself. "And whoever else of your household who would like to see Ilium from the inside."

My father nodded.

"Then you will have my daughter. For the morning. And her maid. And her brother." He turned to Callias, sitting next to him, and said: "Go tell Kleitos that Andromache needs an escort today. Tell him that she's going sight-seeing in Troy."

Inwardly, I cringed even if I didn't give any outward sign. My brothers and I had been getting along, if not well, then at least much better since the raiding this season past. Kleitos, however, would not be happy with me if he had to spend all day dragging around behind his little sister. Callias shot me a bemused look as he rose and walked out past me. He was probably glad he wasn't the brother that had gotten the task dropped on him.

I still wasn't sure why the task was being dropped on anyone. If Helenus wanted to sound me out about Chryseis, or even Briseis, he could have done so here, in our camp. My father looked over at me and the look in his eyes was different from any I had ever seen before.

"Go on," he told me. "Enjoy yourself but don't stay away too long. I need your brother back here during the afternoon. You'll return with him."

I stood up and was surprised to find I was nervous.

"Yes, father," I told him and walked over to lean in and press a kiss to his cheek. "I won't stay away too long."

He gave me an odd smile and there were thoughts in his eyes that already took him away inside. I took my veil from Bithia and left with Helenus.

"So that's the mighty King Eetion?" Helenus commented as we waited just outside the tent for my brother to arrive. He shook his head slightly. "The stories they tell of his strength..."

That did make me smile. I was very proud of my father.

"He is a giant," I agreed softly and he looked over at me, face changing to something much more speculative.

"Do you mind this?" he asked. "I thought you might want to see Ilium a bit closer than yesterday. She's a very beautiful city."

"I don't mind," I assured him quickly. I hadn't been interested before but now that the offer was in front of me, my curiosity about the holy city was growing. They said it had great streets that were wider than two chariots racing next to each other in some parts of it and I was curious to see buildings stacked on top of each other. In my own land, houses spread outward, not upward. I looked at him from the sides of my eyes. "But if you wanted to ask me about Chryseis or Briseis, you didn't have to go through the trouble of impressing my father and showing me a city."

He looked at me in surprise and then a little half smile twisted his lips. His eyes were strange, as if he was both caught and yet felt too sly to be caught. It confused me.

"What makes you think I want to talk about

one of the others?" he asked. I shrugged, feeling a bit out of my element but determined to be honest. I couldn't make matches for my friends – but if I could help steer someone toward their fathers who they might enjoy being married to...

"Most men would," I told him. I was no expert in wooing or romance though I was learning a little by watching the servants. If Helenus was talking to me instead of one of my friends' fathers than perhaps he was interested in wooing one of them. It wasn't necessary for a marriage of course, but it would certainly make a man's home life easier for him if his wife enjoyed his company. "It's good to know what makes a woman smile. It helps in winning them over."

"So what makes you smile, Andromache" he asked and I looked at him with a sharp jerk of my head, eyebrows coming down after a minute when he didn't smile or laugh the comment away.

"Why?" I asked instead, suddenly feeling guarded. And then he did smile. It was a secret, quiet smile but I had seen too many of those within my mother's rooms to feel anything but foreboding in seeing one now.

"Perhaps I like your company."

I didn't exactly know how to answer that and so I said nothing.

"I understand why the others need to be around you. You make everything calm and safe. It's nice."

"I think you're overrating me," I protested

and he shook his head. Still with that secret smile. He said nothing in reply.

One of my brothers joined us then but it was Podes and that surprised me. He still grumbled about it though and I wondered how he had gotten tricked into taking Kleitos' place. Helenus led us to the chariot he had nearby. It was a wide chariot and we all fit closely into it behind his driver. I curved my long hands around the railing as the four horses in front started forward and looked at the passing landscape. For once my mind didn't want to ask any of the questions it should.

From the edges of my eyes, I watched Helenus.

He stood, tall and steady against the movement of the chariot, one hand resting casually on the rail while he talked to my brother. From time to time he made economical motions, illustrating a point or gesturing at something as we passed through the field of tents and Troy's walls loomed. He didn't look at me as he talked to my brother but I was sure he knew I was observing him. In my head, I twisted the mental puzzle he'd given me, trying to work its riddle out. If I were a man, I would have loved Chryseis for her personality. If I were a shallow man, I would have lost myself to Briseis and her teasing gray eyes. Yet I was the one in Helenus' chariot, not either of my friends. I didn't understand why.

The chariot passed through the first gate and the guards at it nodded to one of their princes as he returned. I saw their speculative gazes fall on my veiled face as well and wondered what gossip would pass through the servant's quarters about me tonight. I listened to gossip. It was often so wrong that it was like listening to a very well-told story. Sometimes, though -- it held the truth too.

I was glad to be wearing my concealing veil.

Then we were passing under the great wide walls and I forgot to worry about gossip. I almost forgot to think at all.

My home was a palace. But it stood by itself. The various towns of my father's lands were spread out and rural. Ilium felt as if it would try to hold an entire nation within its walls and somehow, being inside made it seem so much bigger than even seeing it from Ilus' tower had. I gaped.

The buildings on the outer edges of the city were simple and solid. Helenus explained that they were the newer parts of the city that had sprung up around the older buildings. Yet even these outer homes were several generations old. There were signs of repair on some of them. I had heard there had been an earthquake during the summer on the Troiad but I hadn't thought beyond that. Due in part to the fair but also to its position in the world of trade, there was very little space between the buildings that was not taken up with more temporary shelters and I saw many of the rooftops had small shelters or tents on them as well, signs of the people from farther away that were staying with friends and relatives that lived in the city. We passed up what seemed the main road, white and paved in long stone, and I held onto the railing and simply stared at the variety in front of me. Here, there was, if possible, an even more rich mixture of people than what I had seen on the Fair grounds, for not only were there wealthy merchants and traders but slaves and refugees and passing travelers and sailors as well as mercenaries and foreign priests. Some of the buildings were shops and some were homes and some were simply gathering places and each one was decorated distinctly, marked by the color of its paint and the things hung from its roof and windows. The deeper we rode into the city the more varied and grandiose the buildings became. There were older buildings built singularly and over a period of time instead of in large groups to accommodate the growing influx of residents and so they were more distinctive in shape and form, their edges rounded with time and wear. The road was wide and well kept and it met others like it from time to time in intersections. Something inside me said a person alone could easily get lost once the main roads were left and I was suddenly glad we were in the chariot. I could run barefoot and unworried through our trackless forests back home but this was a different kind of forest entirely and as foreign to me as the thought of cutting off a breast and joining the Amazons. I looked back at my brother and he too was watching everything, though his eyes were narrowed inside of as wide as mine felt. Helenus still spoke but I doubt either of us heard him and I wondered, when I saw people and architecture, what my brother saw when he looked at the same things.

Our chariot turned down one of the intersecting roads and we passed through a second set of walls. The tops of these were also manned by guards but in much more ceremonial armor. The buildings in this area were much larger and set further apart. There were more gardens here too. The clothing on the passing people became much richer and there were fewer people. Anyone could see we had passed into the area for royals and priests.

"Hector has a house near here," Helenus stated, voice the measured calm of someone practiced in giving nothing away, and I looked over to catch him watching me. "Or he will. They're just starting work on it now."

I looked at him, looking at me, glad again for the slight concealment of my veil. Wondering what in his mind when he watched me that way. Low, he asked:

"Did you want to see it, Andromache?"

Something in me carefully drew shields about my thoughts then, instinctively and automatically. Things suddenly felt the way they did when my mother asked me one of her trick questions and stood waiting for the impossible 'right' answer. Podes saved me from having to answer by snorting.

"What? A vacant lot full of stones? That's

what you brought her here to see?"

Annoyance flickered momentarily in our guide's eyes and he looked over at my brother, breaking eye contact with me. I started to breathe again, feeling, inexplicably, as if I had just escaped something nameless. Helenus gave my brother one of his quiet smiles.

"No. I actually had something else in mind." His eyes moved back to me. "Something I think you might be interested in seeing."

I didn't ask. I understood that this was his surprise and he enjoyed the chance to show me something unexpected. But also because – whatever he'd woken in me that usually lay dormant outside of my mother's lair, it was wary. And it wondered just how long he'd been planning this for me. I knew it was an unfair suspicion but my mind was too used to my mother's games to ignore it or let it go. I found that I suddenly had no more questions left for this prince of Troy. It did not mean that I understood everything.

The horses pulled us around a corner and ahead of us I could see a huge temple rising as we started down the street. We had temples in Thebe. They were well-kept but simple buildings. The reigning philosophy, never spoken of out loud of course, was that it was better when the gods left you alone. When we sacrificed, it was to ensure their apathy toward us, not to try to cajole them into action on our behalf. It seemed to work for us. It had been decades, for instance, since any of the gods had decided to pay a royal woman a visit and leave her either sprouting branches or a child. Ilium, apparently, had no such worries.

This temple was a work of amazement, truly a home to lure the gods down from Olympus to visit. The sun overhead caught and glinted on gold, silver, bronze, and electrum decorations. The stones of the building were polished to shine. And there were so many priests - more than in all of Thebe - though I thought most of them were probably visiting. The street was full of them, priests and priestess, acolytes and slaves, visiting supplicants in every form, each dressed in all the colors of the rainbow, some outfitted so regally they could have been kings and queens. Even as the horses started down the narrower street that led to the temple on its lone hill, the smells washed over me from the dwellings and shops that lined the street to either side. I smelled incense, perfumes and ash, burning meat and grains, precious woods and spices. The lingering smell of old blood. I watched a pure white bull with golden horns and garnet earrings in its ears being led up the stairs of the temple, and I heard the lowing of cows and the bleating of goats where they must be kept nearby for ceremonies. Everything here screamed for the notice of the gods. I was afraid to pray for their continued inattention to my existence because prayer here might actually be heard.

"Where are we going?" I asked and the voice that came out of me was the one I used when I spoke to my mother.

"To the temple of Pallas Athena," Helenus said. "There is a thing there I want you to see."

I nodded and my eyes went back to what we were passing. Maybe proud Ilium had the right idea - calling down the gods' attention so. She was a prosperous city. Yet, I still could not help feeling vulnerable and exposed as we passed down the open street. Granted, the amorous gods, like most men, only chased beautiful people and so I was safe from that. But -- there were other ways the gods hurt women, and, if my mother's blood ran true in me, as I feared, I was a singularity outside of what women had been created to be. Like Medea before me, I would never fit any story as a proper woman should but rather as a strange aberration. My hope lay in being forgotten by gods and grand events. Medea had not, and it was well known what had happened to her when a god's hero had brushed against her life. Podes was glowering too and he placed one of his thickly muscled arms behind me on the railing. Whether he had intended it as comfort or just a bracing against the movement of the chariot, I was still grateful for it.

We stopped in front of that grand temple that the entire part of the city seemed built around and I could not help but stare. Its pillars reached toward the wide blue sky, polished to gleam as white as the clouds and the whole temple seemed to be stretching silently upward as if to find its home above instead of bound to the earth under it. There were none of the smaller, more personalized touches here. No scattered shells and bronze wind chimes like Poseidon's temple, no bright faced youths and flowers like Aphrodite's. Those small temples and shrines, Helenus had told us, were deeper down, in the outer section of the city. Here... this... it was simply too grand and massive for emotions and gifts so small and mortal.

"The temple of Phoebus Apollo," our guide stated, stepping down from the chariot. Apollo. I had seen his bent sun symbols scattered throughout the city. It was not surprising his temple should be so vast. He was supposed to love this city. Helenus took my hand to help me down and his touch was very dry. I very much wished to be elsewhere but I was here already. Too late realizing it now. I would not show weakness and run. Things only got worse if you tried to run. As much as I knew all I had to do was say no, too much of me was trapped in the pattern of visiting my mother now and I had no voice left.

"He has given my sister and I the power of visions." Helenus said factually and I looked up at him. God-given visions. My mother called them a curse and worse, in her mind, useless. She said they were traps laid by laughing gods and only came true because people forced them to. I did not repeat any of this to the prince of Ilium. I did not excitedly ask about what he might have seen.

He did not offer to tell me.

My brother looked up at the tall building in

front of us and grunted thoughtfully. He too offered nothing by way of comment. The gods took offense at unpredictable things at unpredictable times. It was better to remain silent and not give them the chance.

"This way." Helenus started forward but he did not mount the great wide stairs to lead us up between the many pillars and into the courtyard beyond. Instead he started down a side path that lead away to the side of the white temple. The path was surprisingly unpaved, a simple wear in the earth from hundreds of feet that for some reason had also chosen to circumnavigate the stairs of Apollo. Folding my hands together in front of me, I followed and Podes came next. As a slave in a holy place, Bithia stayed with the driver. I envied her.

We followed the dirt trail and it wound away to the side of Apollo's temple and into a grove of old trees I had not seen from the front of the building. I looked back at Apollo's temple before the branches of those woods closed around us and I saw that smoke rose from the center of it. The back of the temple was a great porch where I thought I could hear water running and the low murmur of voices. Apollo was god of the sun, but he was also god of healing and prophecy and music. And, like his father before him, he was also a lecher and fickle with his heroes.

The trees blocked out all sight after that and, with surprising suddenness, I was deep in an ancient wood. It was strange, for I knew the city lay just beyond and yet, here, it was dark and silent. The city of Troy did not exist in this place. Perhaps no world outside of its rooted borders existed. There were no birds and no small creatures of the forest. The trees themselves were forever old and had grown twisted and knotted. Their branches caught sound and swallowed it whole. This place smelled of secret hidden pools in the night and the slow rot of green things. It made me want to shiver, the sudden lack of constant sun running a chill up my skin, but I was too well trained by my mother to give any sign. I thought I could almost hear the trees, eternal and endless in the shadowy twilight under their dark canopy. Our feet were silent in the fallen leaves no one had cleared from the winding path.

Helenus didn't speak but he paused and stepped to the side so that I could draw even with him. I was sure it had only been a short walk – but it had felt impossibly long to me. In front of us, I saw a hole in the earth. The sun broke through in patches here and ahead, in the center of a perfect circle cleared of everything including the oppressive trees a large stone, three times as tall as a man, rose out of the barren earth. It might have risen higher but some long time ago, it had broken and its other half now lay against it. It formed a doorway of sorts and old, well-worn stone steps of some dark gray rock led downward into darkness. I did not move but everything inside me took a step back. I could see the second door in my mother's inner chamber as clearly in front of me as if I were physically there.

"Come" Helenus took my hand and I let him. Unresisting. "This is the oldest part of Ilium," his voice hushed in the heavy silence of this place. "It is why Troy will never fall."

I went forward because I always went forward. I didn't know any other way. So I went down those shallow stairs with their worn middles. The air smelled damp and the darkness was thick with it. There were oil lamps in niches carved in the earthen walls and they gave off a smoky, unsteady light. My eyes adjusted and I did not lift my veil though I would have been able to see better if I had. I smelled old earth and stone and wet clay. I smelled old blood. And I smelled the rot of wood. The stairs stopped and the floor was hard packed earth under my sandals. There was a thin layer of water across the floor and it damped the hem of my dress and seeped up over the edges of my sandals. Its touch was bone cold. I heard Podes swear quietly behind me as he took his first step into it unexpectedly and it pulled the edges of my lips upward and I suddenly loved him fiercely for it. My jaw and teeth ached and so did my back, as stiff and straight as a steel bar. The flickering light hide more than illuminated the room but I felt as if the roof above me must be very low. People in hooded robes moved in the darkness of the room but my eyes were drawn to the center with horrible certainty. There was a spring in the middle of the downward sloping floor and its water bubbled up silently at the base of something my mind would not translate for me for a moment.

It was stone and it was wood and it was not a connection of both but a mating. Tortured wood had wrapped and twisted around a darkly faceted rock that had lodged in the center of the tree's heart once long long ago. The tree was dead now and from its contorted branches small stone lamps of oil had been hung that sent weird shadows capering up the sides of the tree as the air from above breathed down into this hole below. It had not been a tall tree. Its empty, dry branches hardly grasped desperately for the sky at the level of my head. But, in its struggle, and loss, it dominated the room. And I knew, while the tree had died, that what was in its heart had not. That black faceted rock was still alive and because it was, so was the tree. Not alive and yet unable to die entirely either. I could feel the truth of that tree as if it were silently screaming and twisting still, trying to grow past what had burrowed into the very center of its heart. I shuddered and, despite my training not to, I could not help backing up. I backed up into my brother. Both of his thick arms went around me and I had never loved anyone before as I loved him in that moment.

"It's Pallas Athena." Our guide was ahead of us and had not noticed my retreat. Instead, he stepped forward into the deeper water of the spring and spread his arms in worship of that horrid, ugly rock. "Her Palladium. Sent from the sky for us. As long as it remains, so does Ilium." I saw it then. In one of the flickering draughts of meager light. When shadows fell a certain way against the rock, it was a woman's face - and she was laughing. I shuddered again and turned my face into my brother's shoulder. Not wanting to see more. Because now that I could see her face I could see that it moved in the light and shadows. Always there, always changing. Always watching. It reminded me of the distant echoes of Aeris madness on the faces of men in battle. What was in that face was too much for a mortal mind to hold, too raw and wild. The woman in the tree was even more terrifying than my mother to me – and I had never thought I would find anything to match the terror of my mother.

"She's beautiful," I heard Helenus' quiet voice but I was used to beauty and I knew the difference between truly being beautiful and being terribly so. So did Podes and he picked me up without a word and carried me back up the stairs. There was no part of me that considered protesting. He didn't say anything as he walked back up the path through the woods and I did not move from where I was curled, face pressed hard against his shoulder. The walk back seemed so much shorter than the walk in, though I knew, in my head, that they were the same distance. I heard Bithia make a wordless noise as we reached the chariot where she had waited. I knew that were were out of that den, that we were past the trees and so I knew it was only a matter of time before my skin would start to feel the sun that must be shining on it. My stomach felt as tightly sick as it did after one of my mother's sessions though and all I wanted to do was find the safety of my own bed and hide under the covers until my mind let go of the shadows again. This was not supposed to exist here. My mother's darkness was supposed to live in only my childhood home. The rest of the world was supposed to be safe for me. The gods themselves were not supposed to be reflections of what crawled into my mother's eyes during those times of darkness and fire in that buried second room of hers. My brother sat me down on the edge of the chariot and his one word was disgust and explanation to Bithia's wordless worry.

"Cities."

It made me smile weakly, grounding me, however tentatively, in the reality of my brother's much more straight-forward world and I raised my head.

"Thank you," I whispered to him and he shrugged and rolled his eyes. And I knew, suddenly, that he loved me dearly and I wondered how it had happened. Gentle, I touched his hand and then shook my head at Bithia as she fluttered in front of me.

"I'm all right," I told her. And I was. I was not entirely settled inside, not yet, but I was free of the clinging darkness and I could feel my world starting to right itself inside again. I looked over her shoulder as she crouched down to rest her hands on my knees. Helenus had not accompanied us and that his driver was standing to the side and kindly pretending he didn't know what was going on in the back of his chariot. I closed my eyes with an exhale and lifted my veil to tilt my face to the sky and the heat of the still climbing sun. And I wondered, in my heart of hearts, if there was any god, any where in the world, who was not twisted inside.

"Whore!"

The slap managed to rock me backward in my seat. My eyes jerked open, less at the sudden pain, which was slight compared to what I was used to and more in surprise. I had a brief glimpse of a sickly pale face and pale eyes under wild dark hair. Still half lost in the sickly shadows of my own mind, it reminded me of the face of the drowned woman we had pulled from one of our wells when I was a child. Beautiful and dead. The face in front of me was alive though, and I forced myself to wake up inside, narrowing my eyes to try to focus my mind on the present instead. My brother had easily caught the wild woman into a tight hold, though she was straining for me and Bithia was standing protectively between us now, seething with her own rage. I could only stare, waiting for my sluggish mind to make sense of the strange, sudden woman. I was positive I had never seen her before.

"You will be remembered for being faithful but you spread your legs for every man that comes

along! Trojan and Achaean, brothers and sons, your
husband and his murderer! You'll hide your oldest
child and let another women's be killed for yours!
How many of my brothers will you take away from
me?! Harlot! Whore! Murderess!"

I was just as lost as to why she'd struck me
by the end of her tirade as I had been before before
and didn't make a move to rise. None of her words
made sense, too specific for general slurs but too
unrelated to anything in my own life to apply to me.
The wild girl fought uselessly against my brother's
grip and Podes gave me a look over the wild mane.
Looking - more tired and stoic than surprised or
shocked. As if he dealt with this kind of thing every
day and was getting tired of the repetition. Despite
the situation, his reaction was so *normal* and
grounded in the face of everything that had recently
happened that it tugged a weak smile out of me in
answer. Not because things were funny but because
there was still a strange, long patient humor in it
somehow. The wild child saw it and screamed. We
were attracting a crowd now and I found myself
more concerned by that than the accusations the girl
had screamed at me. There was no way she could
know me and she was quite obviously insane but we
were also visitors in this city and some places
treated their mad differently than others. I had no
idea what Troy's laws were when it came to the
god-touched but I did wonder how she'd gotten out
here by herself. There were no restraints on her so
she must have had a guardian of some sort. Where

were they and why was everyone was just standing there watching instead of offering to help or at least identifying her. Despite the hair, she was dressed richly.

"I'm sorry." I looked around the watching crowd. "Does anyone know where her guard is?"

"Me! Speak to me!" she demanded and her voice was raw as if she'd been screaming for too long. I didn't make it a habit of talking to wild people and I slid her a look that probably said as much. It was not as if Thebe did not have its share of the mad. The gods were fairly free with insanity. No one else spoke for the girl. It left me little choice.

"All right. Where is your watcher?"

"You mean my captor," she sneered.

"Yes," I agreed. She blinked at me and I watched her face go owlish. I felt sorry for her. Most of the mad knew, at some level, that they were mad. I could not think of anything I treasured more than my mind.

"Did I hurt you?" she asked, voice younger and only then did I remember that she'd struck me. It had been an inexpert and glancing blow. I thought it would be cruel to tell her that though. So I touched my cheek with the tips of my fingers and answered instead: "It's all right."

The way her face went angry and dark again told me that had been the wrong answer.

"What's going on here?" It was Helenus'

voice as he pushed his way through the crowd. The girl in my brother's grip turned large, pleading eyes on him and her lips trembled.

"Helenus. They're hurting me!" I watched in astonishment as a tear rolled down her white cheek. My brother snorted.

"And the red mark on my sister's cheek is just for fun," he snapped and Helenus' surprised eyes focused on my face. I watched his jaw firm.

"Let her go," he told my brother but Podes only raised a dark eyebrow. My brother was just as much a prince with just as much arrogance and rule as Helenus. Helenus' light eyes snapped in anger and then he drew in a breath and let it out. His eyes went clear and calm again. But I had seen...

"Let her go," he repeated softer. "She is my twin sister. Cassandra."

I looked at the young girl in shock as my brother released her and she immediately threw herself into Helenus' arms, sobbing and trembling. For some reason, I thought of Briseis.

I found myself surprised and not at the fact she was Helenus' twin. I could see that now. It was in their eyes and their angular faces. My surprise was that this was the Cassandra Hector had spoken of so long ago. The one that had wanted to be born a boy. The one I had envied.

I certainly didn't envy her now.

Helenus looked tired as he stroked his sister's wild hair and murmured soothing things to her. She clung to him and, through her sobs, begged him to send me away -- substituting 'harlot' for my name since she didn't know it. I couldn't say I was insulted. I'd been through a bit too much in my life to consider a stranger's name calling a hard thing to endure. Bithia took insult for me however and I watched as her lovely eyes narrowed down even as her hands found their way to her hips. Both Helenus and his mad sister were moments away from a stern tongue-lashing and as much as I loved her for it, I could not let her do something that dangerous to herself. I interrupted before she could start.

"We should go."

"Thank the gods," my brother snorted and reached up to help me down from the edge of the chariot I was still sitting on.

"Wait." Helenus shifted his sister to his side despite her attempts to remain in front of him and he looked at me with his pale eyes. They were apologetic. And - something else. He was waiting for something from me but I had no clue what it was and I was suddenly tired of playing his guessing games. "I'll take you back," he said. "Let me try to save the last bit of your tour at least."

I gave him a smile I didn't feel, just wanting to be home again. Willing to walk forever if it would get me there instead of here.

"It's all right," I reassured him but his eyes were determined and he shook his head.

"No. It's not. But I'll make it right." He looked down at his sister who was shooting me a strange look under her lashes. Her eyes were surprisingly dry and unrimmed with red considering the storm of tears she'd just displayed. All the women I knew looked a mess after weeping that enthusiastically. "Cassandra, you need to go back to the temple now. I'll leave Lycurgus with you." The driver didn't look thrilled by the prospect but he didn't protest either as he turned toward the couple. Cassandra's eyebrows came down over her pale eyes. "I'm taking the Princess Andromache home now."

The girl's eyes flamed then and she pulled back sharply from him, rage and fury on her pale face again and, to me at least, it looked as if she felt betrayed.

"Andromache! Eetion's daughter?! You brought her here so Pallas Athena could see her and would remember her face! You wanted to lay claim to her in front of the goddess!"

Helenus' face was very stiff and still.

"You're staying here," he repeated and she backed away from him, fingers curling into claws at her side. I gently nudged Bithia out of the way and behind me before she realized that was what I was doing. I was familiar with women's claws.

"You just want her because of our brother! He liked that she was clever. You heard him talking to father when the cattle from Thebe arrived. Now you want to be able to tell him you've had her first when he comes back! Don't you ever get tired of tarnishing his toys, Helenus?"

Helenus turned his back on her and gestured for my group to get back on the chariot. His driver stepped forward to take Cassandra's arm but she pulled away from him nimbly and, blinking back tears, snarled at her twin:

"I hate you!" And then she was flying down the road, legs bared to the knees and dark hair spinning behind her. I noticed she was barefoot as she ran. Helenus sighed and climbed up into the chariot next to us, taking the reins with a practiced move. We, so used to family secrets ourselves, said nothing and he turned the horses and started the chariot back the way we had come while his driver pounded down the road after the mad, fleeing princess. I turned and watched her run.

She ran as if she was trying to outrun the entire world.

There were no words spoken on the ride back and I was glad for it. I just wanted to be home, even if home was only temporary tents at the moment. I wanted to be surrounded by my own people and my own things and the familiar habits and patterns of my own family. When the chariot arrived, Podes practically leaped from it before it had even had a chance to stop. He immediately turned to lift me down. He was angry. Very angry. The level of it I saw on his face surprised me. The look he shot Helenus was not friendly at all but he said nothing as he set me down on the opposite side of him from where the Trojan prince was.

"I am sorry," Helenus told me from his spot

on the chariot and I shook my head. I did not know what had been his fault or if I had anything to blame him for and yet I was secretly glad to be out of his company. Podes gave Helenus a sharp nod of dismissal. It was a very final type of nod. And, though it was rude to part without polite talk and thanks, I let Bithia draw me into the tent and only when safe inside did I sink down onto the bed in a slump and exhale a great sigh of relief. I was shaking.

I did not see my father or Podes for the rest of the day.

That night however, as we were getting ready for bed, Zoe brought me a small delicately carved wooden box no bigger than my fist.

"From Prince Helenus. He asked that I give it to you," she told me and then lingered in curiosity. I did not send her away. I had the gut feeling that the fewer secrets there were about that Prince of Troy and I there were, the better.

The box fit together cleverly and when I opened it gold glinted back out at me. When I saw what it was, for the first time, I was forced to wonder in full how random his meeting of my group yesterday had been. It was not a comforting thought at all. Bithia, watching over my shoulder while Zoe tried to look over the other one, made a jerking, quick noise as I, without touching what was in the box, dumped it out onto the cover of my bed. In the oil light, it glowed. Zoe was the one that named it and her voice held all the awe and significance a secretly given gift of that sort merited.

"A signet ring."

VIII.

We left the next day.

I hadn't been expecting it. I knew we had been planning on staying several days more and I had gone to sleep wondering how to avoid Helenus without losing my chance at enjoying the Fair. When I woke in the morning, however, to the sounds of packing outside the tent and my father told me we were leaving as soon as the wagons were loaded. Somehow, Bithia got word to both of my friends, even at that early hour, and Chryseis arrived along with Briseis to bid me goodbye. Chryseis promised to give my ribbons to Nemea and swore that we were friends for as long as the sun rose in the sky. Briseis was less effusive, but did promise that she would cajole her father into letting her come and visit. I felt sorry for my poor brothers if she did but it was nothing but the truth when I told her I would be glad of her company. I got good, full hugs from both of them and then Podes was lifting me up into his chariot and I was watching first my friends and next the fair itself fading in the distance behind us. Ilium itself took much longer to disappear and I watched it as it did. Our departure had happened so quickly that I hardly had time for it to sink in and watching Ilium's great walls dwindle as we traveled, I could not decide whether I felt relieved or disappointed. Something, I didn't know what but I felt it, had just been beginning there, even before Helenus' arrival, and now it was stopped in its tracks and gone forever. I felt strangely as if I should mourn it – and yet I was glad that, whatever it was, it had passed me over and gone on its way alone. I would again be small and safely forgotten in the enclosed world of my father's house. I was content with that.

****

The messenger from King Priam, wanax of Ilium, came little over a month later.

I was in the stables, convincing one of my father's aging horses from Ilium to eat the wine soaked grain I was offering him. He had become finicky, and, I suspected, thanks to me, spoiled. Zoe came dashing into the stables as I was resting my forehead against the horse's much wider one and he was gently lipping grain from the palms of my pale hands.

"Princess! There's a message from Troy!"

"Oh?" I asked mildly, but my stomach tightened. I had been busy in this past month, preparing for the winter that was already tapping its fingers impatiently against our door. I had buried the small wooden box with its dangerous gift in the bottom of a clothing chest with the hopes of forgetting about it. I had tried not to think too much on Ilium either. Each time I had the confusion and strange lonely feeling had risen again and, since I didn't understand it, I thought it better to avoid it all together. I missed my friends but they were not there anymore anyway and I did not miss Helenus and his strange, waiting riddle. There was nothing to miss Ilium over and so I had determinedly turned my thoughts to the practical instead.

Yet now Ilium had found me again.

"He came by chariot! And there's a huge chest in the back of it!"

"Did you give him something to drink and make him a warm place by the fire? Did you send someone to tell father?" I asked, voice still calm. I did not move away from the horse.

"Yes!" Zoe sounded slightly insulted and I was proud of that. Before I had taken over the household the man would have had to fend for himself. "The king is talking to him now!"

"Will he be staying for dinner?"

I heard her foot slap the packed earth behind me and smiled. I knew I was baiting her but it was so much easier to think of that then why Ilium might have come to Thebe. The horse grunted low in his chest.

"Don't you care why he's here?" Zoe asked, exasperated.

"He's here to talk to my father," I surmised and she blew out a breath. I knew what she was thinking. I was thinking it too. I was just not sure how I felt about it and if I was not sure myself, what kind of response was I supposed to give her?

I had been all the talk of the servants when we had come back, or rather my brief tour with Helenus and his gift of his ring had been all the talk. Since Bithia and Podes had offered nothing, a great deal of it was speculation. In one story, he had even taken me to the tallest roof in his father's palace and swore to lay all of Troy at my feet. It felt as if everyone in the servants' quarters had been waiting for this single moment and now that a messenger had come from Ilium, the stories were all being proved true

Helenus. As my husband. I remembered his light eyes and shut my own. No great, sweeping emotions rose to the surface and that worried me. Wouldn't most girls my age either be delirious with joy, or nervous with uncertainty, or even shot through with dislike? Yet I felt a low discomfort in the pit of my stomach and a silence in my chest. I felt as if I were waiting for something still and I was not sure how I would react when it finally came. I inhaled and told myself that my imagination could easily be running away with me. There were many reasons the king of Ilium would want to talk to my father, even bribe my father, and only a single among the many had anything to do with me at all. I latched on to that and managed a smile that must have looked real enough when I turned around, for Zoe gave a little bounce on her sandaled feet and smiled brightly back. .

"I should get ready." I kept up my act. "Father will want me at dinner tonight."

For whatever reason the messenger had come, I still had my duty as the Lady of the House. My mother had mocked me about the role the last time she called me to her rooms after we had returned from the fair. It was the only time she had sent for me since our return and the session had

187

been surprisingly mild, almost as if she was only going through the motions. I would not complain – and, though she had meant to insult me by calling me good only for housekeeping, I had found myself proud of the thought. I was good at organizing. I might not have had the beauty that drove men to great deeds, but I could lay a good table and I could foresee my guests' needs before they realized them. I could see to it that when they reached for a new goblet of wine or a blanket against the sudden cold, it was already waiting. Father liked having me in the room when he entertained guests now. I was proud that I could, silently and unseen, make things flow. Whatever the message was about, it was my job to see that the silent running of our house impressed him.

Zoe danced along next to me as I made my way to my room. I knew she thought I should be there because I was on display. The bride my father and the messenger bargained for...

I hoped she was wrong.

Bithia was waiting for me and so was the bronze bath full of hot water that I had grown so devoted to. It took up too much of the room and crowded everything else but I considered that slight awkwardness more than paid for. It was my one indulgence and I forgave myself for it. Afterward, once Bithia had dressed my hair and I'd put on one of my nicest dresses, I made my rounds, checking on all the preparations and pleased to see the way the servants had everything under control. When the summon came to join my father for dinner, I, and everything else, was ready. The routine had helped to settle my nerves but they came back as I walked into the main hall. I was one of the last arrivals and saw that father had set my place between himself and his guest. It was an odd arrangement but I took my seat anyway, looking curiously at this man from Ilium from the edges of my eyes.

He was close to me in height and slightly shorter when he relaxed. His eyes were straightforward and he was giving me a frankly appraising look as the dinner was served. I saw he had the same dark hair I had come to associate with Ilium, though his was straight. I thought a great deal about him looked loose and casual, even though he was supposed to be the king's personal messenger. His nails even still had traces of dirt under them though his hands were immaculately clean. A scattering of strange short scars ran across his cheek and under his beard, pale against his tan. He caught me studying him and he smiled. It felt, strangely, like meeting an old friend.

"I'm Cebriones," he introduced himself and I was surprised when he offered me his wrist as if we were warriors meeting on a field, instead of a woman and her guest. It did not stop me from clasping wrists with him automatically all the same, though his larger hand engulfed my own wrist easily. He chuckled at that and turned my arm when I released his to look at the palm of my hand.

189

"Long fingers. But slim. It means you're clever. And your nails are short so that must mean you actually work with your hands too." I blinked down at my own hand and he let it go to rub the pad of his thumb over the tips of several of my fingers. "You weave. A great deal. You've got calluses. Almost like an archer except theirs would be here and here instead." I watched as he tapped the spots on my hand, both curious to learn and bemused by his choice of subject material. He didn't talk like someone that was used to relaying royal messages between touchy, proud kings. He released my hand and helped himself to one of the plates of meat that was nearby, serving me himself which surprised me because it was a servant's job to do that. If it was strange to him for a warrior to serve his hostess, he gave no indication, digging into his own meal once it was proper. Halfway through his second mouthful, he looked over at me.

"He said you talked a lot more than you are," he commented. I realized he was waiting for me to be the good hostess and perform my duties, entertaining him with light banter and small talk -- which, honestly, I had never been very good at. It was why I spent most meals *behind* my father's chair instead of next to it.

"What are you here for?" I asked. It was the first thing that sprang to mind and the only thing I could bring myself to care about. It was perhaps too straight-forward, bordering on rude but he tipped back his head and laughed.

"He did warn me about the questions," he grinned back at me. I expected him to make me guess, to play a game of it, but instead he leaned his elbow on the table and, looking directly into my eyes, he told me:

"You. He sent me to ask for you." He nodded and reached for his wine cup. "He said to ask for Eetion's daughter with the clear eyes and the clever questions."

"I'm Eetion's *only* daughter" I pointed out. He chuckled again.

"He was feeling lonely. I caught him at a weak moment. He gets a bit of bard in him when he's moody."

"Does he?" I asked, trying to fit that new piece of Helenus into the puzzle of him. I liked Cebriones. He was frank. I was having a hard time seeing Helenus sending someone like him though. I had imagined someone more... courtly. I also thought Helenus wore his bard's talent proudly, for the entire world to hear. It was in the way he talked and the way he set things up for effect. My seatmate shrugged.

"He pretends he doesn't but, Hades, he gets bad if he's tired enough."

My lips twitched at the oath and the fact he didn't seem to realize it had come out. I truly didn't see Helenus sending someone like this at all. Though perhaps Priam, who I knew nothing of, might have. It was the type of man my father would have foisted sending an important message off on. I didn't doubt the man next to me, enjoying his meal with such relish, was a soldier. I refilled his cup. Since we were being open... I glanced at my father, sitting silent and watching, on my one side and then turned back to our guest to ask:

"Has my father given you an answer yet?" Cebriones shot me a wink.

"No. He wants to draw things out. Make your bride price and the trade concessions and treaty more powerful. I don't blame him. He's got the best of the dice roll."

I doubted that. All my father had to trade was me. Priam had Ilium to offer. Even a second or third son of Priam's line was a treat on the marriage market. He shook his head at whatever he'd seen on my face.

"He's set on you. Which means we all know he'll pay whatever your father wants. It puts me in a bad bargaining position, so don't mention it to your father."

Considering my father was sitting right there, letting us pretend he was not, I thought he couldn't be very serious. I shot him a look and he set his goblet down to grin.

"Maybe not as verbose as he'd told me to expect but your face talks just fine, I see."

I was surprised myself when I laughed.

"When you go back tell him to stop trying to predict me," it came out as easily as it had long ago when I had first realized words could be games too and his face brightened as he sat up a bit straighter.

"Zeus' balls, you're going to be good for him! You wouldn't believe how quick women are to roll over for him."

"Do they?" I arched my eyebrows at him, though I couldn't say I was surprised. Though it was well outside anything I had experience with, I was not entirely blind. There were women that slept with my brothers simply because they were princes. How much more a prince with the wealth and prestige of Ilium behind them? He laughed, even fuller this time and I had the distinct impression he almost clapped me on the back but stopped himself at the last moment.

"Oh, they'd do that for him too if he even looked cross-eyed at them. It's the simpering that drives you mad though," he confided in me as if we were shield mates instead of near strangers. "He could say the sky was green and most women would add what a lovely shade of green it was too." I laughed too, covering my mouth with a hand, shaking my head at him as I did so. It was impossible for me to feel any foreboding around this man.

"You were a good choice. I'm glad King Priam sent you."

"Priam?!" my guest was surprised. "He didn't send me. Hector did. I may be his bastard brother but he got it in his head that I was the only one that could convince you to push your father to say yes."

My brows came down and I looked at him

closely. Confused. And, in that moment, I was less confused that for some reason Hector expected me to have influence over my father and much more over -

"Why would Hector send you to barter with my father for Prince Helenus' sake?" I asked, surprised to find that my heart hurt at the thought - as if my friend had just betrayed me. It was a silly thing to feel. I had known Hector only a day, which made him neither my friend, nor capable of betraying me by simply trying to see that I married his brother. Confusion moved across Cebriones' rough face.

"What does Prince Helenus have to do with anything?" he asked and I shook my head. Aware, even without looking, that my father's attention had sharpened even more on our conversation. I had too tangled a knot in front of me to pay the attention to that fact that I should.

"Prince Helenus sent you. To ask my father for me. That's who warned you about all my questions. Didn't he?"

The understanding dawned in my guest's eyes and I thought I saw a flicker of anger.

"That little toad," he murmured to himself and then looked back at me. His eyes were very sharp and I thought an eyelash would not fall that he would not see it in that moment.

"Princess," his voice was steady and a bit rough at the edges. "I've come because my brother and my friend, Prince Hector Horse-breaker of

Ilium asked me to come on his behalf. He wants you for his bride. And his queen. And he was very specific that he wants only you."

Everything seemed suddenly very far away and distant and the noise of the hall faded away around me. I actually felt it when the color left my face and the tips of my fingers felt numb and tingled strangely. I was aware of my father's huge hand against my back, supporting me. But for a moment, in my mind, and in front of my sight, all I could see were dark, laughing eyes. I inhaled sharply and realized Cebriones was still watching me closely. My father's hand did not move, but he still did not say anything to interrupt.

"My Hector?" I asked, voice soft and, despite myself, a bit shaky. Asking for clarification because it made no sense at all that the Crown Prince of Ilium would want me. It made no sense in my head that the stranger I remembered from that day that seemed so long ago was the Crown Prince of mighty Troy. The tight lines I hadn't realized had moved into Cebriones' face relaxed and his crooked smile grew.

"I think he'd agree to that," he told me.

The emotions in me that had felt dulled and tangled at what I had thought would be an offer from Helenus rose to the surface now without compunction and I felt as if a great weight I hadn't realized had been there was lifted off my chest. I felt – free -- and relieved. And -- happy. I felt happy. I don't know what my guest saw in my face

195

but he relaxed back in his seat with a chuckle and reached for his wine, apparently content with it.

"You didn't think I'd give you to that pup of a prince from the fair, did you?" my father asked and I shifted on my bench to look up at him, still dazed inside but smiling what must have been a stupid smile. He smiled back and gently touched my cheek. "Podes told me what he did to you," his voice was gruff and I felt Cebriones stiffen in surprise on the other side of me. Apparently, what had happened with Helenus at Apollo's temple wasn't well known. "He might be a respected seer and admired for his archery skills in Ilium but you've had enough of your mother for one life." It was the first, and only, time he ever mentioned that he knew what his wife, my mother, did to me in the darkness of her hall. "I won't give you over to that for your marriage as well."

Helenus was certainly not my mother and in all fairness, I should have protested. I didn't. My head and my heart were too full of everything else. My father's eyes met mine.

"It's only if you want him, Andromache. I'll only send you away if you want him."

I blinked at him in wide-eyed surprise. No daughter had a right to make that decision. Yet -- my father was offering it to me. I found I had lost my voice and all I could manage was a weak smile. There were no guarantees. A man I had met for less than a day could truly be anyone or anything in the world and I would not know until I was already his.

Marriage held little escape. Yet those were simple things every woman accepted long before the suitors even came calling. All I knew was that, for my long ago stranger in the olive groves, I felt something. And, at this moment, it was good. What more could any woman steer by?

I raised my hands and rested them against my father's wide chest. That safe chest I had always made me feel so safe and protected. I swallowed. At a loss as to what I should say. All I managed was:

"I liked him, father. I still do."

That seemed to arrange it. Cebriones left the trunk behind and I discovered it was full of gifts for me. Just for me. The chests sent to my father came the next spring and my own dowry would wait, sent to my husband when I was. That winter was for me alone however and Hector's chest was full of beautiful, strangely practical things. Like the softest of warm cloaks, fur rugs to put on the floor to keep my feet warm against the frozen tile and blankets so thick I thought I would sink into them. There was fabric for dresses, beautiful rich colors that did not run and fade when they were washed. There was jewelry, small delicate, foreign pieces I could not help but imagine he had collected on his wandering and not simply sent a slave to the market to pick up in bulk. I thought this because there were seashells and smoothed rocks that I had never seen in these parts of the coast before included the chest too, things someone would pick up while standing on a beach or river shore instead of looking through shops for. There was a polished board game with little river-smoothed stones delicately carved for its pieces. Tiny figures of animals carved in ivory and jade. I lifted out a tiny ivory horse from the pile of the gifts my friends were happily poring over. All the household women that could had squeezed into my weaving room while I went through the chest and several of the male servants were standing, peering over heads, in the doorway. I ran my fingers over the little figurine. It was older and discolored and its carved surfaces were very worn. Bithia, pulling out yet another bolt of rich cloth, clucked her tongue.

"You're sure you only met him once?" she asked and I chuckled at her teasing. Feeling the little ivory horse growing warm in the heat from my palm.

"Only once," I agreed. "And I chattered like a magpie the entire time too."

"Obviously he's mistaken you for someone else," she teased and I threw a skein of brightly colored woolen thread at her. She laughed as she ducked it.

"This is so beautiful," Zoe sighed, raising one of the fur lined blankets to her cheek. She closed her eyes in pleasure at its touch. "He must want you very badly."

"A wise man," Demetria commented. I laughed quietly at her but she fixed me with a firm look.

"It's true," she protested. "You've made this house something guests brag about visiting. You've softened your brothers and your father. Everything runs so much smoother and quicker now because you figure out all the problems before they happen. You are good and kind and you laugh with us and you make us laugh. You're gentle when we're hurt or sick and you're always right there with us to help when something needs to be done. What man wouldn't want all of that in his house and concentrated on him?"

"Not to mention you're really very beautiful and you've got a voice like honey," Zoe added cheerfully and I loved her for lying to me so enthusiastically. Bithia gave me a warm look.

"They're right. He's the one that's blessed by whatever god wasn't paying attention enough to let this happen. You certainly deserve something good and gentle in your life." She must have seen something in my eyes then because she chuckled and handed me the cloak, so soft and warm that where it rested across them, my legs sighed in pleasure. "No man who sends his bride such soft, sweet things is intending to use her as a brood mare and forget about her in the meantime. He wouldn't have sent you anything at all if he'd intended that. You know a future bride isn't entitled to gifts until the day of the wedding. Trust me. I have seen it when I was in Rhodes. A man does not give gifts if he's only thinking of a business transaction."

I wrapped my arms around the cloak and

hugged it tightly, little carved horse folded safely in my hand. Hector of Ilium's betrothed. Hector of Ilium's bride. Hector of Ilium's wife.

It took some getting used to – saying those words in my head. I thought I was starting to learn to like the sound. I smiled over at Bithia.

"I hope I can make him happy. As his wife," I said quietly.

But it would be seven more years before I would see Hector of Troy. And when I did, I would not be his betrothed, much less his bride or his wife.

IX.

I did not know then, of course, that my future was so unsteady before me. Winter came upon us heavily and there was even the rumor of snow in some of our higher fields. I was kept busy with even shorter days than before. It was no small thing to keep men occupied that were trapped inside when they were used to having an entire outdoor to contain their energy. Guests did not come as frequently either but the ones that did come stayed longer and those were nights full of songs and stories in the light from the fire pit. Sometimes I would fall asleep in the corner of the room and dream of the figures on the walls dancing in that light to odd stories that never made sense when I woke later on. During those darkest days, my mother would summon me to her rooms. She had taken an interest in me now that she had not had before. My lessons expanded beyond simple pain and foul darkness to taint other areas of my life as well. Herbs were no longer the herbs I had thought they were and words were no longer the words I had been familiar with when I was in my mother's dark rooms. It frightened me. For there was power in my mother's lessons and they woke something in my blood that was hungry, always, for more. The pain it cost became secondary to the knowledge gained with each drop of lost blood, each swallow of poison. Each time I left her darkness, I was shaky and sick to my stomach as always, but now it was with the knowledge of what I had been taught.

To my shame each time I was summoned back, I went hoping to learn more. My mind was like a dry sponge and I soaked up what my mother was beginning to teach me with a hunger - and understanding - that terrified me.

For, if I craved it, if I loved the new dark knowledge, if I found I had a talent for it, what did it make me but exactly like her?

When I was not in my mother's rooms however, I set my new learnings aside in a dark corner of my mind and pretended they were not there. There was a great deal to take up my time and concentration. With new determination, I dove into the daily routine of running a house, down to the smallest detail, trying new methods and developing the old. I had a purpose now, a future to plan for and I would not fail the trust that had been placed in me.

I was not cold that winter. Hector's gifts kept me warm, in body and in my heart.

It was so strange to me, to reach out my hand and feel something that had been given to me alone. Not a cast off or a secondary thought or a thing of necessity, but something that was unnecessary and yet given to me with thoughts of only me in it.

Stranger still to reach out and touch something from Hector, my dark eyed memory of a day and a night. Strange too, in the night, to draw a blanket over myself in the cold and feel the weight of wool and the softness of fur and to realize, half-asleep, that somewhere, someone had thought of me and sent this. That a man, for surely he was a man by now, had remembered me, had remembered me and had collected things for that memory. Like a small family shrine, hidden in the woods, these were thoughtful gifts of personal choice and intent that had been laid at my feet. Not yet a woman, for my body stubbornly resisting turning from child to adult, there was no fear of what was expected of me in return during those sweet moments of realization, only the comfort of being remembered. Hector, so far from me, kept me warm that winter and it was with so much more than his gifts.

As if to make up for the harsh winter, spring came early that year and the fields were full of newborn animals and busy farmers in the fields. I tried to be everywhere and my mother left me alone for those glorious days of blue and green. Each year I learned more, tried my hand at more and this season was no different. Miltiades would not let me help with the oxen but he sent me out into the fields with the sheep. It soon became a consuming job and the shepherds did not mind the extra help when it came to hunting down where the stubborn ewes had snuck off to give birth. It was not the job of a future princess of Troy but the driving need to understand everything about what went into the life of a household hard hardly abated inside me simply because of a shift in my future. I would come back late in the evening reeking of sheep so that Bithia made terrible faces and ordered me into the bath without willingly touching me first. I loved it. I could run a household of a hundred or more, I could set a table for guests in any number, I could remember without error the contents of any of our storehouses, but it was in seeing those new lives, safe and cared for, that I felt the best pleasure. It was a promise of life and a future and more than ever it meant something to my heart to see it.

My father and brothers stayed home that year. Still, during the springtime and summer, we heard of Achaean raids further along the coast. Every year it seemed they grew bolder, raids coming more and more often to our side of the ocean.

I thought of Hector when I heard of those raids and for the first time it was not the memory of a raid gone past that sprang to mind. It was the worry of raids yet to come - and battles he would fight because of them.

I found a strange dark pleasure in my mother's lessons during those times. I think it might have pleased her, though she never suspected my reasons.

Spring sank quickly into a long, hot summer, full of olive trees and growing heads of barley, dusky green all of it in my mind. We cut new dresses for me out of the fabric from the chest since I was outgrowing my other clothing. My body seemed intent on growing but it was growing wrong - upward, always upward, when I wanted it to grow outward instead. For the first time, as we measured me for the fabric, I was aware of the way my body lacked curves. I was not soft and round like beautiful Bithia, and for the first time, I cared. I wanted to be full and lovely and instead I was tall and thin with my pointed face and my restless hair. For the first time I was aware of the strange scars, awkward to explain, on my body and the calluses on my hands and fingers. Impossibly, I felt shy about my looks for the first time, painfully aware of them and embarrassed by them. Trying not to let it show, I began to imitate Bithia's nightly routine that kept her beautiful. Mortified to even do so, much less at the thought of being caught at it, I felt both hopeless and strangely driven to try to change myself despite it. Bithia caught me - of course she did - but she was kind enough to pretend she wasn't aware. Instead she began teaching me - now, finally, after all this time a willing student - in the arts of being a woman.

There were creams and salves, ointments and perfumes, hideous smelling muds for my face, my body, my hair, my hands. She polished my feet and fingers, my elbows and knees, with rough pumice stone until they were red, soaked me in milk and other things I didn't even dare guess at. I suspected that she was over doing things - drastically - and yet I continued to submit to them, hoping they would make my freckles go away or give me golden skin, that they would tame my hair or somehow - most desperate wish of all - make me look like a woman instead of a girl.

Aside from my smell, I noticed little change. I continued with the routines despite it. My mother discovered it somehow and she mocked me, ugly creature, for wishing to look as I did not. It made me more determined to prove her wrong, and yet more hopeless, because I knew, deep down, that she was right. I would always be tall and thin and speckled. I had always known it, really. It was just that - for the first time - it mattered.

By autumn I had given up most of the beauty routines. There was too much work to be done and where my hands and feet had been softened, they blistered and reddened from tying the sheaves of grain together and helping with the grinding and the harvesting, the storing and preserving and curing. Nothing made my hair decide to either be straight or curling and not both and my freckles refused to be hidden or chased away, remaining like small stains of honey in strange smatterings from place to hidden place on my otherwise pale skin. Like everyone else I wore the sticky salve to keep my skin from burning in the sun and so I came home at the end of each day smelling sharp and strong with dried sweat on my skin. If I were ever going to become a woman it would take far more than Bithia's magic to make me so. I resigned myself to it and yet, looking at the ivory and jade figures with their delicate carvings in the promise chest I kept in my room or the sweet, careful earrings, I would still feel a twinge.

Hector was waiting for me to become a woman. How long would he wait until it became apparent I wasn't going to?

He did not care that year. Just as the last of the harvests were brought in and the fields covered over for the approaching winter, another chariot came from Ilium. I did not recognize the driver but there was a cedar chest in the back of his carriage and again it was full of things meant only for me.

My father and brothers said I was being spoiled and that Hector would regret training a wife to expect gifts. I thought perhaps they might be right. I had already been waiting, hoping, telling myself not to.

More cloth, more trinkets, more toys. I was suddenly rich in my possessions with both this year's and last's. In my newfound wealth, I was generous and the women of the household did not protest long or hard enough against it.

Hector had sent me three lamps of bronze and a carefully wrapped jar of oil that smelled sweet when it burned. There were more skeins of thread than last time, as if he had been told about my loom. Dice of pink coral and spinning tops with exotically painted designs that made pictures when you spun them. More furs, more jewelry, more rare and beautiful things. Enchanted, I curled myself around my hoard that night and slept with his gifts against me, one of the furs over and another under me, needing, in a way I could not explain, to feel the press of them against my body, to feel their foreign weight and solid form in my arms as I slept. It was not for the gifts themselves... but for something deeper I could not explain. Bithia, used to my odd ways, did not comment when I woke up the next more deeply content in my soul and very stiff in my body with their marks against my skin where they had pressed in the night.

I was at my loom later that day, unable to resist the lure of those bright colored threads I had been given. Outside it was one of those clear, cold days that should have given us a sky that went on forever and yet somehow instead seemed to make outside into yet another small room. Bithia sat on a stool in the corner of the room mending clothes, a never-ending chore in our large household. I sat at the bench in front of my loom and the colored thread in front of me spun itself into a golden summer in my head. I knew weaving was considered work but it never ceased to soothe me and steady my thoughts and mind.

It was not until Bithia cleared her throat that I looked up from my weaving and realized that someone had come into the room. I was not usually so oblivious but my weaving took me away. It was Enoch and I gave him a smile of greeting even though his appearance puzzled me. I worked closely with Enoch now. He was still the steward of my father's house but he was aging. I did a great deal in his stead because of that and in return he taught me more than I thought anyone else could have ever known about the running of a household and the world around it. I was used to seeing him in his own settings however, for I always went to him. He rarely came to me unless he was summoning me for my father.

If he had been summoning me for my father though, he would have simply spoken his message and gone. Instead, he stood there expectantly and so I quickly offered him a seat near the brazier and a blanket as well as a cup of water from the pitcher nearby. All of which he took with pleasure and I knew he thought that a great deal of my hospitality was a trait learned from him. Some of it was.

Perhaps in some families, there would have been mild conversation before reaching the true point but in my family one tended to simply say what was on their mind or risk being forgotten before they got the chance. I wasn't surprised that, as soon as I was seated, Enoch explained what he was doing visiting me. Though - being Enoch - it was as much a lesson as an explanation.

"Come spring, I am going to have to buy a boy to train." He watched me as he said it and I simply looked blankly back at him, not understanding until he explained: "To be steward of this house, Princess. So he will be capable before I grow too old."

I think I must have blinked but I otherwise sat still. A part of me felt hurt however. I had thought that I was doing a good job of taking over his more strenuous work. He was telling me that I was going to be replaced though and that meant I was not good enough. I had very little of myself I took pride in. My ability to run things smoothly was one of my greatest prides and, I had thought, a gift I could give him in return for his teaching. He smiled softly, a rare expression for him.

"I will need someone to replace you, Princess, when you leave for Ilium. I think we all pretended you would stay with us in this house forever." He looked pointedly at the multicolored threads at my feet and the smile was quiet and not unpleased. "But we are being forced to realize that it won't always be that way, aren't we?"

I looked down at my hands. Embarrassed, proud, pleased? It was hard to tell. It was true. I would leave one day. I had known it always, long before Hector's promise; it just hadn't seemed to matter to my present life. The future had, and to me sometimes still did, seem very far away. Enoch's quiet face was gentle.

"This house will be less when you leave." A compliment of the highest order coming from him. He so rarely gave praise at all and again I felt that confusing mix of emotions at it. He showed mercy and did not leave me there, instead moving on to his true point.

"Have you thought of what you will bring to your husband's household when you go?" He asked and the sudden shift made me frown but my mind caught it immediately.

"Father has provided me with a dowry." The raided treasure from that storehouse across the sea that felt like a lifetime ago. Enoch nodded but I knew it had only been a leading question because, of course, he knew what was set aside in the locked chests in the room near my father's chambers, perhaps even better than I.

"Gold and silver is good. A man whose bride brings that to him can be proud. You can use it to set up your own house. Your father has provided a great deal for you. Much more generously than most men even for their only daughter. He's never touched so much as a ring of what he's set aside for you to pay his own debts, you know." Enoch's eyes shifted to mine, calm and mild. "But gold and silver run out eventually, even the greatest amount of it. A woman should have her own investments against times of hardship."

Death. He was talking about Hector's death - my widowhood - before I even was married. It was not uncommon enough for a widow to be left destitute that I would not realize what he spoke of. My mouth felt strangely dry but I only nodded and he nodded in return as if pleased with my response. My mind shuddered suddenly at the new thought though. Not yet used to being a bride and already, suddenly, reminded that to be a bride was to chance being a widow, especially married to a man of war. Mercifully, Enoch appeared to change the subject and my mind turned toward it eagerly.

"Come spring, I will be leaving with Miltiades. One of your father's neighbors has had a good three years running with his oxen. Last autumn we picked out some of the new born bulls and paid him to keep them with their mothers for the winter for us. Chances are we will come away with more bulls than we paid for. And he might part with some of his cows as well."

It was all he said and my brows sank over my eyes. I was not a fool. Enoch had mentioned the wealth that waited for me and then an increase to our herds for a reason. The closest I had come to wealth I truly considered my own and personal purchases had been during the Great Fair of Ilium almost two years ago. I had not thought of my dowry as money I could begin spending *before* I married.

Oxen, called horned wealth. They were mobile and self-multiplying and if taken care of, they easily paid for their care and fodder. It was a gamble, of course. There was plague and drought and, especially now, raiders to consider. That mobile wealth could be driven away and it was impossible to lock up in chests. Gold locked in chests however never became anything more than exactly what it already was.

"Do you think father would let me have my dowry early?" I asked him. In another family it would have been unheard of for a woman, a mere girl, to have access to her bride price but... I was coming to learn that most of my restrictions with my father were the ones I had placed there myself trying to be 'proper' and 'good'. He had let me choose Hector -- though I cannot say he would not

have chosen him anyway if I had said no. Perhaps -
- perhaps, he would let me do this too. Not with all
of the gold. Not even with half of it. But perhaps
with a quarter of what was locked in those chests...

"I cannot speak for your father," Enoch
answered calmly, even though his eyes were proud.
He was acting as if this were entirely my idea and
he had only come to relay unrelated information. It
was yet another reason he was a very good steward.
Again, he was watching over my interests and I was
still not sure what I had done to merit his favor. I
was grateful for it though.

"I think you know him well enough to know
how to approach the subject with him though."
Then, as pointedly as he'd come, Enoch thanked me
for the hospitality and took his leave. Leaving
Bithia and I sitting in a strangely stunned silence as
it began to sink in.

I was about to become a businesswoman.

My father gave me permission and gave me
the keys to one of the chests. My hoard was large
enough to spare its loss, I supposed, having no idea
what men gave for their daughters as dowries. So,
that spring, I found myself accompanying Enoch
and Miltiades, Bithia and Podes with us, as we rode
north.

I had never been in this direction before for
more than a half day's journey and kept my eyes
open and curious the entire time, indulged in my
questions by everyone that rode with us.

The man that we were to buy the cattle from

had two sons and he eyed me curiously until Podes casually mentioned who I was betrothed to. It was surprising the change that came over him and I found myself suddenly treated like a visiting dignitary. It was the first time, though hardly the last, that I realized that, though I had belonged to the name of my father before, my betrothed's name was even more powerful. It was not strange that Ilium was more powerful than Thebe but rather that *I* was considered more powerful than Thebe. It was my first lesson in how being attached to a powerful man changed the way the world reacted to me personally but it was hardly the last.

He gladly sold me oxen, going so far as to, to all our surprise, offer the healthy ones immediately instead of hiding them until last to see if I would take the poorer ones off his hands first. Miltiades walked through them with me and pointed out what I should be looking for, good and bad, and soon we had a small herd sectioned off just for me. The price he wanted was high - apparently being Ilium's bride was respected but also expected to be wildly wealthy. I bargained him down to a reasonable price on my own, even though it seemed to amuse him to be bargaining with a female over cattle. I saw Enoch's nod of approval afterward, however, and it reassured me.

I felt as if I were swimming in water too deep - and yet the thrill of it kept me from turning back to safety.

Mine. As we drove the cattle back home

and I lay in the bed of the wagon that night and listened to them, I was filled with a fierce and almost overwhelming sense of... of what it was I didn't know. But it was strong in my chest whenever I realized that the heads I looked at, the shedding winter coats, the large, liquid eyes and the stubborn plodding – they were mine. Only mine and shared with no one else. They were creatures of my own to grow and worry over and care for. They were my responsibility entirely and if I failed or succeeded, it was entirely mine to live with. It was overwhelming and freeing at the same time.

I kept them in a pasture that was deeper inland than the fields my father kept his in. The division helped keep the two herds separate in all our minds. It also kept my strange investment away from my mother, which seemed like a wise decision. Miltiades lent me a few of the younger boys and one of his older men to watch them and they were soon as excited by the idea of my own herd as I was. Since every one of my questions started with the word 'why' we were soon sorting through what was merely tradition and what was sound practice when it came to raising and caring for a small herd. All spring and summer, I spent almost every free day out in the fields with my small company of fellow herdsmen and, by the end of that first summer, we had settled into a system that worked for us and the cattle. I was pleased that, as we drove them down to the lower pastures for the winter that my herd was just as glossy and fat as the ones that Miltiades drove for my father.

A third cedar chest was waiting for me in my room when I came home at the end of one last, long autumn day.

With all the gifts I had been given, I rarely had reason to wear the jewelry that came in those chests of cedar. Something in me balked from arraying myself with those trinkets of delicate metal and gems in front of my family. Unlike the practical gifts or even the games and silly trinkets of pleasure, the jewelry did not remind me of a dusty hot day in an olive grove and a dark haired boy with a soft voice. The jewelry made me think instead of a future day, when I would wear jewelry always and of a city so large that a stranger could become lost in it. There was something vaguely overwhelming about it, as if I heard the thunder of the storm in the distance and, not seeing it, still knew it was coming, so I chose not to think about it at all. And yet - I did love the jewelry too. Each time he sent me new jewelry, I would deck myself in the long jointed earrings, the strand after strand after strand of clever wrought beads and polished jewels that draped around my throat, the tinkling bracelets, the expensive beads for my hair, the clips of polished metal with their imbedded pictures, the light circlets for my head and hair. The bronze mirror in my room reflected me back golden and distorted and yet it still showed me how what I wore caught the lamp light and glinted all around my odd, sharp face. It made me feel foolish and beautiful at the same time, old and yet like a child in her mother's clothes. Myself... and someone I did not recognize at all. The treasures Hector sent me to adorn myself with were never common, always exotic looking pieces that made me long to ask him where he had found them and what their stories were. Some days I thought they had been traded for in foreign courts he visited. Some days I thought they were the spoils of battle from burned cities whose last owner had no more joy in them - or any joy at all now. Yet I could not help but treasure them whatever their history for they told me without words that I was remembered still. It was no small thing to me. Nor was it a small thing that he sent me gifts a woman should receive, and not just a child. Even though my body stubbornly refused to be anything but a child's despite yet another year having passed. Each cycle of the moon came and went with no hint of the bleeding that would signal that I was finally a woman and my body stayed straight and as curveless as a boy's.

After my first indulgence however, I would tuck the jewelry away again and only take it out in weak moments to look at. I had not imagined I would be wearing it before I set out for Ilium one vaguely distant day in the future. I was wrong.

An invitation came by messenger early that next spring. It was from Briseis. She was going to marry and wished me to be in the maiden train that would attend her until the ceremony. My father agreed to let me go.

Briseis... Man-clever, sharp eyed Briseis. I had enjoyed her company years ago but, standing in my room with Bithia, trying to decide what to bring - I suddenly felt awkward at the thought of seeing her again. Suddenly, without entirely understanding it, I was glad of Hector's expensive gifts of cloth and jewelry. I did not know if that made me older - or simply smaller and more petty but Bithia approved, which did nothing to answer the question. With the help of some of the women in my house, we made me new dresses, designed to hid my awkward angles and pretend at graceful curves and a woman's figure. I felt older in them, more calm somehow, though I had not felt restless before. My father provided me with new shoes of soft red leather.

Hector's jewelry came out of its chests and joined the dresses.

I did not travel alone to Lyrnessus, of course. Bithia came with me but she also insisted that we bring more servants with us, for we represented not myself but the family of Thebe. Thanks to my position in Briseis' train, I would bear the brunt of representing my family. I had never had to do that before in a situation I knew I would be scrutinized by the other Houses over. It was intimidating – and yet I was surprised to find that I looked forward to it. All these years, all this training – I was a hunting hound suddenly let slip from its leash for the first time. My father sent several of his older soldiers as well and, to my horror, he sent Podes. In another time, I would have been glad of his company, reassured by it, but by the time we began our journey, it was beginning to stretch into a long, lazy summer and my father and the rest of my brothers were going to march down the coast to try to find Achaean raiders to engage in battle. The Achaeans came in larger numbers every year now and they stayed longer. Our Hittite allies to the east had offered to send troops to help us fight but they only wanted the excuse to have their soldiers on our lands and so Ilium politely refused them. Our men were more than eager to march out to battle and win glory for their names anyway. My father and brothers would march out directly after I departed for Lyrnessus. Podes, who had been left behind once before, was now left behind again. And again, he was guarding a little sister while the rest of the men in his family went to win honor for themselves and plunder and fame in battle. I had not asked my father for Podes but surely he would still be angry with me simple as the object that kept him from deeds of valor and fame in battle.

What could I say to that? No apology or explanation would be accepted and I watched his broad back from the covered wagon I rode in with my women as his chariot led the way along the worn path to Lyrnessus. The movement of the oxen that drew the cart made the earrings set in my ears chime quietly and they tickled faintly as they rubbed against the sides of my long throat.

I had to admit that, despite all the worry and responsibilities, I was looking forward to seeing Lyrnessus. It was several cities away from my own father's lands, lying closer to Ilium and tucked in against the side of Mount Ida instead of along the coast as my city and most of our neighbors were. It was considered safer from the Achaean raiders because of it, both for that distance and the walls it had.

Approaching Lyrnessus in the evening twilight, I saw it was a sturdy city, walled and clean, and little houses crowded up near those walls, many looking newly arrived in the last few years of Achaean aggression. And yet, it seemed - small to me. The buildings inside the walls consisted of the royal house and several houses I thought must belong to important people in the country. There was a small barracks building and, of course, the housing for the servants and the slaves as well as storage rooms and stables, a black smith's forge, the potter's house. It was larger than my own father's house and more crowded together than the people that lived on our lands - still it seemed small to me. It took me a long time to realize, as we entered the gates of the city and passed quickly into the courtyard, why. It was small because it was walled and those walls made me think of the only other walled city I had ever seen. Lyrnessus, as sophisticated as it was compared to my own more rural home, was a small shadow after having seen Ilium.

Servants rushed out to greet us and I was soon separated from the men and brought to a room full of girls my age, each dressed richly, giggling and talking happily among themselves as if they were all friends from childhood. I immediately felt awkward and out of place. Bithia began to set up my things in the area of the room that had been set aside for me according to the servant that had lead us there. Nowhere did I see Briseis. It left me on my own to deal with this new situation and I knew I could either stay where I was with my things and forever remain that way, nothing more than another piece of my luggage, or I could venture into the rest of the room and seek out company. Why was I so self-conscious and aware of the possibility of rejection or mockery though? I had no trouble befriending giant, hulking soldiers or newly arrived slaves. Why would girls my age seem so intimidating to me? Self-conscious I touched one of the earrings I wore and heard it chime like a secret whisper in my ear. I could do this, it whispered, or at least I pretended that Hector's gift would have whispered it to me if it could have. I simply had to watch how they were together and find a place to fit myself into. I had done it with my own servants. I could do so again here.

Watching closely though, I soon realized that not everyone was as bonded as I had first thought and not everyone was equal. Even though most of the girls sat close together, the longer I studied it from outside the circle, the more I could see distinct groups that divided them. I saw who the heads turned toward most to listen or ask questions or seek approval, who the sly looks went to, who sat near one of the groups and yet was not included. It was like a great knotted puzzle and once I began to see the end threads, I found that I enjoyed picking it apart.

I watched too long though because one of the girls from the center of the group looked over at me with her kohl dark eyes and asked with scorn:

"What's the matter, girl? Haven't you ever seen noble women before?"

I heard Bithia hiss behind me and knew she was about to get us both in trouble with her sharp tongue. I did not need a defender though. I had been watching long enough. I understood the dynamics of the room and I knew, if not who, *what* the girl that had addressed me was. Understanding made me feel more steady on my feet and I felt calmer and more myself now. Reaching up I calmly lifted away my veil and gave it to Bithia to keep her out of trouble. The girl in the center of the room was the most influential girl present; I saw it in the way the other girls turned to her. The girls that were in her inner circle and sitting closest had coveted positions, drawing their own power and influence off of hers. It was like a small court, complete with other small groups that, while yielding her power, did not seem quite so disposed to do so cheerfully. My choices were to attempt to join the center circle or to attempt to join one of the outer circles. How I reacted to the girl in the center of the room would show which type of position I intended to try to win for myself.

My pause and lack of immediate response did not do me any favors if I wanted to join the girls in the middle of things. The longer I was silent the more their leader saw it as an insult, or possibly even a challenge, to her. I let my silence last anyway, a part of me that I probably should have resisted, stubbornly rising to the surface. I had been attacked, mocked, before I had even opened my mouth or made the first gesture of greeting. Perhaps I had grown to used to the respect of the people in my own home, but it was a respect I had worked hard for and a part of me angrily rebelled against the thought of being cowed now by a girl no older or more powerful than myself.

"Once or twice," I was far too well trained by my mother to let any emotion but calm show in my voice. My mother had taught me the power of words and how to layer them to say many things and I used her lesson now, perhaps more hurtfully than I should have. "My house is full of warriors so there is little room for women."

There was a chair that sat nearby, unclaimed so far and outside of any of their circles and I sat down there, careful to spread my skirts the way Bithia had trained me so that they fell gracefully without looking as if I had made an effort to have them fall that way. Bithia brought me one of the fur wraps Hector had given me to drape over my legs -

even though it was not really that cold - and I asked her to bring me some of my sewing. She brought me back the blanket I had been embroidering with small gold and amber beads for the baby one of my brother's wives would give birth to shortly. Ignoring the rest of the women, I bent my head over it and picked up where I had left off.

I knew I was flaunting the riches Hector had sent me, and felt the slightest bit like a pretender with my needle of bronze and the gold and colored beads in my lap. A greater part of me felt justified however and so I pushed aside the weakness of uncertainty and acted as if I used extravagant materials like this every day. It was only my mother's training though, which let me hold the needle and sew instead of my hand trembling the way it wanted to. I was still very angry... and very outside of any situation I had ever been in before. A part of me wanted to go home, but the greater part of me was too proud to be driven off the battlefield. So I sewed abstract patterns instead.

It was only a matter of time before the retaliation came, I knew. I had thrown my mocker off balance by not acknowledging her obvious position in the room and, more, I had insulted her family, whoever they were, by insinuating that apparently they were full of women and not warriors. My wealth was a challenge to her position as well, for wealth always meant power. Perhaps worse of all however, I would not play the games that were going on in the room and ally myself with one of the groups there. The last, at least, was not intentionally done on my part to provoke her but rather because I knew it was a game I could not win. I had no skills when it came to dealing with girls of my own class and they obviously were well acquainted with the game that was being played. I could play by their rules – or I could choose not to play. I chose not to play, and apparently I had taken a road untraveled before. Perhaps it made me a coward, but even if I did win my way into one of their circles, what would it earn me? Bithia would guard my side of the room well enough that I would not have to worry about spiders in my bed or oil spilled on my clothing. A place in their shifting positions would last a handful of days and never matter again. For the first time, I realized that I would have to face this battle in truth when I went to Ilium and the thought terrified me. But this was not Ilium and this was a battle I had no need to fight.

My mocker stood up to deal with me. She was dressed in the looser, more modern style of dress while I had opted for the more traditional one. Another contrast between us and I pretended to have not noticed her rise.

"I am Thais of Lesbos." She expected me to recognize her name. I did not. I raised my eyes briefly from my work to look at her before returning to my sewing.

"I have always wondered what it must be like to live on an island," I answered her mildly. I was not about to be drawn into a naming contest with her. People drew glory and power from their city, from their family and from the people they were associated with. It occurred to me now that Briseis would have wanted the most notable names she could manage in her wedding escort. Since all her women must be virgins, it meant that Thais must either be the daughter of the ruler of Lesbos or else one of the daughters of a very prominent citizen there. Her next statement verified my guess.

"My father is Acacius. He is the head of the king's council there."

Lesbos was a prominent island and the city of that same name that was on it was walled and well known, I knew that much. It was certainly better known then my home of Thebe. Yet she was the daughter of a council member and I was the daughter of a warrior king. My father was better known then hers. Thinking these things though -- we would both be measured by our families, not by what we were ourselves at all. It was the way of things and yet, for that brief moment, for the first time, I wondered at the point of it all. It made me even less willing to measure names and reputations against hers. Unmarried we weren't even measuring husbands' deeds against each others, just family, which we had no influence over. We were all children in garments we had borrowed from our parents and I suddenly understood why it was so important to my brothers to make names for themselves. I could be proud of my family – yet, what had I done to earn any name or reputation of my own? So I didn't rise to her challenge and volunteer my own information, even though it would have put her in her place and asserted my own importance. All for the families we had had the luck to be born into. Instead, I nodded, losing my anger of earlier and realizing that we were all the same. They were as powerless on their own as I was, measured by their protectors and established in their positions because of those men in their lives.

"A difficult position. You must be proud of him."

I would not mock her. The game seemed hollow to me now that I saw the core of it. That did not mean that I could simply step aside though. Until I was safely fit into a position in the hierarchy in the room, I was a challenge to every position. Thais folded her arms over her chest, puzzled and glaring. I continued my work.

"I am proud of him. The king listens when my father speaks."

"An important position then."

She shifted on her feet, feeling her position among the girls changing and not sure how or why. Perhaps my jewelry and dress made her hesitate or maybe it was the way I was acting but she finally asked, in a slightly less antagonistic voice:

"Who is your father?"

"This is Andromache of Thebe." I looked over toward my unexpected herald. Briseis entered the room, all aglitter in golden jewelry. Something in the way she swept in made me wonder how long she had been standing outside the doorway and listening. She was beautiful and smiling and she held out her arms in greeting for me. "She is betrothed to Hector, Horse-Breaker of Ilium."

As I rose and went to her arms, I wondered, perhaps unfairly, whether she had wanted me here for myself – or my betrothed.

Apparently the name won was enough though. From that point on I was not only left free of the female jostling for position but I was actually sought out as a means in that constant, silent competition. That night, while they stayed up and talked and I listened, they asked me for the story of my betrothal and, when I proved reluctant, they told their own stories of Hector. To hear it, you would think he was a second Heracles, an idea I found myself both proud of and yet slightly bewildered by. I knew he was a hero. News reached even woody Thebe. But I knew he was also a man who sent shells gathered from foreign shores mixed in with the golden treasures in their cedar chests and a dark eyed boy with wild hair and ears too big for the rest of him who taught his horse to whistle. Some of the stories they told about him, apparently in complete belief, seemed a bit impossible for a mortal man to manage. However, if I believed anyone capable of such things, it would be Hector -- not for his legend but because I remembered the look in his eyes when the raiders had come into my house.

During the day, I could not help but notice that Briseis kept me always close to her. A part of me liked to think it was for friendship's sake and that I was familiar to her in a world that was not. I did my best to be what she needed me to be, distracting or steady or practical or simply present depending on the moment. My name might be greater now than it had been before, but she had been my friend before that and I believed in that still.

Our time was not all gossip and female politics, of course. There was a great deal that was expected of the bridal party surrounding the new bride. There were several days of mixed feasts and several more where Briseis, as queen in training, hosted dinners for the visiting women who had come with their husbands for the upcoming wedding or already lived in the city. There were endless superstitions and gods to be appeased, so many that we had a priest assigned to us who did nothing but tell us what was expected and when. There were last minute details about everything, from the flowers to be given out at the wedding to the decorations sewn on the edges and center of the bedding for the wedding night and, in the organization part at least, I proved so useful that finally everyone gave the position entirely over to me and simply asked what they should do. And, there were, of course, the gifts, the constant gifts that came flooding in from every city and family within a day's travel of Lyrnessus. Briseis paid more attention to those gifts than to anything else. I had brought my own gift for my friend, of course. It was a golden diadem with links that dangled down to flow past her shoulders. Briseis was delighted with it and insisted she would wear it at the actual wedding ceremony. I was pleased and did not tell her it was from my father's plunder of long ago Achaia and not from among the gifts Hector sent me each year.

In fact, I was reluctant to talk to Briseis about my own betrothal or Hector simply because she was so curious about them. It was an awkward situation for me to talk about to begin with, too private and strangely personal for me to want to put into words. The way Briseis asked about it however - something in me shied away from sharing my thoughts and feelings with her. Firstly, because she had never and never did, ask for my thoughts and feelings on anything else and secondly... there was something in her voice, her eyes, when she spoke of Hector. Something greedy. I didn't understand it - Briseis was marrying a king. Mynes seemed like a good enough man on the rare times I saw him during my brief stay there. He was suitably older than my friend and was not rumored to beat the women in his family. He was obviously enthralled with his young bride and she spun out the full power of her personality when she was with him. Already he gave her whatever she asked for and she was not shy in her asking. There was something in the way she tried to make me promise to bring

Hector to visit once we were married though, something in the way she pushed me to promise to invite her to stay in my house once I lived in Ilium with Hector... Something in the way her eyes changed when she said his name...

I managed to avoid promising her anything. Deep inside me, I thought I might just go out of my way to make sure I did not bring Hector to her. I didn't understand why I felt that way entirely but I felt that way anyway. Misplaced on my part or not, I didn't think I would ignore the warning hesitation in me.

X.

The day of the wedding dawned without clouds and the priests declared it a good omen. In fact, they declared almost everything that happened that day, from a pair of flying doves to breeze that ruffled the ivy we passed in the garden to be a fortuitous sign. Even though I had my suspicions about the priest's enthusiasm of all things good, I too did my best to make sure that every last moment need was prepared for in the hopes that if the first day went well, so would every day that followed for the marriage. And, so much more personally, I wanted my friend to have a lovely day. For the first time ever I had seen fear in Briseis' eyes this morning when the girls had joked about the wedding night. I think I was the only one that had been paying enough attention to see it and Briseis had hidden it quickly enough but it had made me all the more determined to give her as wonderful a day as I could. She was my age and becoming a wife already. We had all heard that there was pain, only pain, for a woman her first time with a man. And sometimes... only pain forever after as well.

For myself, I could not feel fear of my own wedding night when I thought of it. It seemed much too far away and - it was Hector. My dark eyed boy from the olive trees. I knew I should but I could not find fear of him. With my head, I knew he was no longer the boy in my memories but my heart thought he was still and it would not let me fear anything he might do to me because of it. I let my heart deceive itself because I did not want to feel fear, not the kind I saw in my friend's eyes.

If the fear stayed with Briseis past those first few moments of gossip while we prepared her for the day though, she did not show it. By the time she was finally dressed and blessed and anointed, she glowed. I had never seen anyone so beautiful in all my life and I was proud of her. She kept me by her side for all the ceremonies the women had to go through to prepare for the wedding itself and I thought, that for this day at least, she kept me nearby my familiarity and friendship instead of my name. We sacrificed carved toys to one goddess, flowers and many seeded fruit to another, spices and incense to yet another. We gave different sacrifices to so many gods and goddesses that I lost track of them. Local gods, city gods, family gods, great gods - not one could be forgotten or slighted or their wrath could cripple the marriage. Fickle gods, I thought in the privacy of my own head as we bowed before yet another alter and offered small cakes of bread, ignoring when someone did right and only too eager to notice and punish when they did wrong.

It reminded me of my mother.

Finally, we were allowed to slip back into the women's rooms and take a little drink and food. Briseis was laughing and light and breathtaking but I noticed that her eyes sparkled like a fever victim. I thought of something my mother had taught me, a mixture that if done with a light enough touch, would help her relax and, almost, I offered to mix it. I would have to explain it though if I did, and how I had come by it, and I did not dare do that. Too many questions I could not - would never - answer.

The wedding ceremony itself was surprisingly short given the amount of preparation that had gone into it. This was the legalizing part of the wedding, the contract agreement between two Houses as much as between two people. The bride and groom stood in the front entrance of the building and we, their wedding party, stood to either side. Briseis promised piety, harmony and faithfulness. Mynes promised protection. The men who stood as witness swore oaths to defend Mynes' marriage claim should it ever be questioned. To finalize everything, a bull was brought to the steps of the house and slaughtered there. As its blood still cooled the priest examined its entrails and proclaimed good fortune and a fruitful marriage for the new couple. And with that, the ceremony was over. My friend was now a wife and a queen. Together she and her husband reentered the building and we followed, the girls singing a song of celebration and blessing even as the bull was left behind to be divided on the stairs and sent in pieces to various temples and houses in the area. I whispered the words of the blessing song so that my less than impressive voice would not ruin the music and I meant every hopeful word of it for my friend. And, perhaps, I selfishly thought a little of myself too.

The feast was already waiting for us when we entered the main hall. It would last all night long and possibly into the morning if anyone was still sober enough for that. I found my seat at the side with the rest of the girls from the wedding train, glad that we were safely outside of the main part of the celebration. Like most feasts this one would start calmly and grown more boisterous as the night went on. Given the strength of the wine being poured, I suspected this one would get more rowdy than most. There were speeches given, beginning with the traditional one by Briseis' father, a lamentation for the loss of a precious daughter and the pleasure of a stronger alliance with Lyrnessus. Mynes answered it with a claim of happiness at gaining such a good father-in-law and reaffirming the bond between their Houses. Tradition satisfied, the rest of the speeches went everywhere from dignified and flowery to raucous and heavy with innuendo. After a while, they became a background noise as the celebration rolled forward. There were platters of basted meat, bowls of steamed fruit, honey cakes of toasted grain and the ever present wine that never let out cups empty. I spotted Podes in his place across the room and he did not seem furious to be there. I took that as a better omen for my future than any bird sign the priests might proclaim.

Briseis was shining and beautiful. Her laughter flowed through the room like delicate bells and she was pure wit and adoration next to Mynes.

Mynes looked as if he was unbelieving of his luck every time he looked at the woman at his side. For some reason -- I felt a little sorry for him and I could not say why. Thais sat next to me throughout the entire meal and together we watched the newly married couple. While the other girls laughed and enjoyed themselves, the two of us did not seem inclined to. Finally, Thais sighed.

"I hope my father finds me a fool that thinks he's in love with me," she murmured before turning to her wine. I watched Briseis charm the entire room and made no answer.

Long before the sun set, Mynes rose to retire to his bedroom and the men near him joked with him about his eagerness for his bride. Brisies pretended to blush and laughed her beautiful bell laugh and would not meet my eyes from across the table. Once Mynes was gone, the rest of the girls from her escort and I rose and surrounded her, spiriting her away from the room to the slightly drunken and cheerful calls of the rest of the guests. I slipped my arm around her smaller shoulders and held her close against my side and, while she still laughed and teased the other girls around her, she leaned into my side tightly and her skin felt cold under mine.

Again we bathed, dressed and anointed my friend and I thought the chatter seemed even more intentionally distracting and foolish than usual. What Briseis was about to do, we would all do soon enough ourselves and that unknown future made us all, I think, more determined to keep her mind from it as long as possible. Briseis pretended not to notice and not to be frightened and I would have believed her if she had not clung to my hand the entire time. Finally, we could stall no longer and so we led the new bride out into the hall where we were joined by hired actors in animal masks and children bearing flowers. Together they sang and danced around her as we lead her down the hallway to her waiting husband's room. To me, at least, the brightly lit hallway seemed very long and shadowed in its corners but I only smiled reassuringly and held my friend's cold hand wrapped safely in my own. The door to Mynes' bed chamber was already open and waiting for us. He sat on the bed and his eyes and smile found Briseis when we brought her in to him. The smile she gave him in return looked beautifully genuine but her nails left red crescents in my palm before she let go of me entirely and let herself be playfully tugged over to where he waited, laughing her beautiful laugh. The last I saw was his arms reaching out for her and then the swirling band of dancers pulled us all out of the room and the door was shut. Without noticing the walk, I found myself outside in a courtyard with them, surrounded by laughter and dance and drink. I put my hand over my heart where it hurt and did not feel like any of that. Instead, I retreated to my bed where Bithia was waiting for me. I was not the only girl in my group that retreated early that night and the room was strangely silent for once. As Bithia carefully stripped my finery from me and helped me prepare for the night, I curled my fingers around the marks Briseis had left on my hand as if they were secrets she had given me. Strangely -- I wanted Hector. I wanted to see his dark eyes again and be reassured. And I wanted to marry him. So the wedding night could be over with instead of somewhere in the darkness ahead of me, waiting...

****

We left the next day. Married, Briseis had no more use for us, or at least, tradition had no more use for us. I wondered if she might not have wanted us to stay a bit longer with her if she had been given the choice. Ceremony said we were unnecessary though and so my things were loaded onto their wagon and my people were gathered and Podes strode out last of all, looking bleary eyed but not half as miserable as men from the other families that were arriving to take their women home. Briseis came to the front steps to thank us and wish us well but she did not come down them to stand with us. Her servants circulated with her gifts to us and our families but those were given from servant to servant, not from Briseis' hands to ours. There was a formality to her speech now, a distance between us. She was a wife and a queen. We were all unmarried daughters. I did not think the distinction was as necessary as she made it but I thought she made it as a protection for herself against our departure. I could not see her eyes from where I stood and so I did not know if her smile was real or not.

I felt guilty for leaving her.

"Andromache, ride with me."

Podes surprised me with the request and I felt a brief spark of hope that he had forgiven me. As soon as we were out of the city, he gave me the reins and let me drive, shutting his eyes and bracing his hands against the railing in the way soldiers did when they had long travel ahead of them. I knew no matter how tired he was or how ill from drink, he would not ride in the wagon. Only the old, infirm, or wounded ever rode in wagons. I was careful to guide the horses along at a sedate pace and kept them to the smoother sections of the road.

"Frightened?"

We had been traveling in silence for quite a way and his voice surprised me almost as much as the question. I glanced at him from the corners of my eyes but his eyes were still closed and his face was showed nothing. I pressed my lips together and was silent for a moment.

"Of?" I finally asked. Not willing to give away anything that was inside me by accident. For all I knew he could be talking about driving such a long distance and not about what was inside my mind at the moment at all. He opened his eyes and they were surprisingly clear as they looked at me.

"Hector."

"…oh." He *had* been thinking as I had and I concentrated on the road ahead of me. I was surprised a man would think about a maiden's fear of marriage. He did not prompt me and I was quiet for a very long time, thinking. Finally, I answered him quietly.

"No." I picked my way over my words slowly, wanting them to be true. "I am not afraid. A little nervous - but I do not think I am afraid."

He grunted in his chest and didn't say anything else.

We did not talk the rest of the way home and we never again spoke of weddings or female fears or the marriage bed - but I never forgot that my brother had asked. He had cared.

We returned home from the wedding long before my father returned from his march along the coast and so Podes and I again fell into the pattern of running things smoothly between us. He seemed content, though I knew he could outfight some of our older brothers. For the first time I realized that, perhaps, he was simply more content to live the life of a farmer instead of the one of a warrior. My guess could have been wrong, but I think I loved him even more for it. My mother did not send for me often during those summer days and when she did her dark lessons were short. I felt as if she was biding her time and it made me wary, worried. She would not follow me to Ilium. I would be free of her there.

Surely?

I assured myself that I would be and, like so many things I had no control over in my life, I pushed that fear into the depths of my mind and did my best to ignore it. My cattle were a good distraction and, whenever I could find the time, I went out to where they grazed and talked with their keepers. Sitting there in the grass, watching their solid, slow forms helped me settle my thoughts and it made me content - and hopeful. Hopeful of a future.

When father returned in the fall, he did not bring much plunder back with him, though all my brothers had been bloodied and had the names of warriors they had bested to brag about. Podes and I had a great deal to show for our less glorious efforts too, for the harvests were good again that year and the cattle had stayed healthy and strong.

My cedar chest came just after the last of the harvest had been tucked away in the storehouse and for the first time I did not open it right away. I knew it would be full of beautiful things, lovely things, gifts from dark eyed Hector. For the first time though, it didn't seem enough -- or rather it seemed the wrong thing. I realized as I looked at it sitting in my weaving room with its newly created clasps of bronze and fragrant red wood -- that I wanted Hector himself, not a box of toys and pleasures. It seemed vaguely greedy and I felt guilty about it and yet, it did not change things. It was a foolish, pointless wish too because I was not yet ready for a man and he could not come for me until I was. My body stubbornly refused to give that single sign that would indicate I was ready to marry, to have babies of my own. I was trapped in the world of children until then, and yet, I did not feel like a child in my mind any longer. I wanted Hector - not a chest of treasure.

It was ungrateful of me and I did open the chest and exclaim in pleasure over the things inside it. The women of the house cooed and congratulated me, again, on having such a rich and attentive betrothed. No one had ever head of a man sending his future bride gifts after the first offering and yet Hector sent them year after year in equal abundance. I was pleased with what he'd sent. As always there were things of beauty and usefulness and he had included things to engage my mind as well as my fingers. I found myself searching through them and wondering what had been on his mind when he had decided to send this or where he had found that, searching for hints of the man he had become while I remained a child.

Late that night, as I lay wrapped in a new blanket of strange weave that felt as soft as fur against my skin, I decided that I would do whatever it took to convince my body it was time to become a woman. I was tired of waiting. Not so tired of the waiting itself but tired of being caught in-between, as if I were falling and yet could neither catch at what I fell from nor find the bottom of what I fell toward. It was horribly frustrating and, deep in the night, I sometimes feared something my mother had done to me in all my years under her cruelty had broken something inside me so that I would never change but always be a little child no matter how tall my body grew or how many years passed.

I could not ask my mother, of course, but I enlisted Bithia's help and all winter long we tried every superstition and remedy and prayer and offering and wives' tale we could think of. I got sick several times but that was all. My body refused to bleed, though it did grow in height again until I was almost as tall as Podes by the time spring came.

I had never been in this kind of situation before. I was used to life falling into two categories, the outside ones I could not control that happened to me and the ones that involved just me that I could control. Suddenly I found myself dealing with something that was me and me alone, and yet I had no control over it. I knew I was not the only one that noticed. Spring came and the animals had their young and I knew that my father looked at me and wondered -- and if my father wondered would not Ilium be wondering too? Waiting for news from my family that I was a woman finally and ready to be married and yet year after year no word came. How long would Hector wait for a bride that would not leave childhood behind? Briseis had now been married a year -- an adult -- and yet I was still in my father's house, nothing more than an overly tall child.

I felt trapped and frustrated. The world was moving on around me but for the first time I felt left behind, trapped in time, like that insect in my amber bracelet. Often, I pretended not to realize it and sometimes I would forget entirely during the business of sowing and animal birthing and housekeeping, but then I would remember and it would be as if it had never been absent, only eating away at me silently. It made me want to scream sometimes, to stamp my foot like a child, this endless waiting when I was ready *now*. I gave up on the superstition that activity in a woman delayed their bleeding. I had sat still all winter and nothing had come of it. I took to running whenever I went from place to place outside. In running down the forest paths or through the fields, I could almost outrun my failing and, if I exhausted myself, that night I would sleep instead of lying in bed and looking at the darkness above me.

There was something wrong with me, a flaw inside me. I was not just overgrown for a female, I was not entirely female. I knew it, fought against it. All these years my mother had mocked me about not being enough and I had never really believed her. I had always been enough for myself and that had been what had mattered to me. Yet now I was no longer enough for myself - and maybe she had been right all along. My mind rebelled at the idea and yet - my mind could not argue with the facts in front of me either. I was not enough anymore, not even for myself.

Spring turned into summer and summer turned into autumn. I pretended nothing was wrong but Bithia worried that I was losing weight on my already sparse frame and -- deep inside -- I worried too. What if no chest came from Ilium this year? What if they gave up on me?

What if Hector realized there was something wrong with me and married someone else?

I had no right to be hurt by the thought - but it still made me sick to my stomach and strangely, vaguely panicked each time it bubbled thickly up in my mind. He had settled too firmly into my picture of my future. When I thought of my someday husband, his dark eyes were what I saw. If I lost them... what future did I have left? I wanted Hector. Not some variation of Mynes.

Not to turn old and grey in my father's house.

Not a single god or local spirit was interested in any of my increasingly frantic offerings or bargains. Winter was coming and yet again, my family had no message to send to Ilium. My father said nothing about it, but there could be no way he was unaware, that he did not wonder, about this daughter of his that would not become a woman and yet had not been born a boy. I knew that most girls my age were already married or else preparing to marry. It felt as if I were the only one left in the world that could not bleed and leave childhood behind.

I found myself beginning to worriedly watch the road that led to far off Ilium.

Hector's cedar chest came without fail yet again that fall and again it was full of sweet gifts for me. I opened it in private and cried.

He had not abandoned me. He had waited another year and his gifts showed no complaint or rebuke toward me, as luxurious and intimate as always. Something in my heart calmed and the ants that had seemed to live under my skin all summer long grew quieter. I was still a child. I was still broken inside. But with Hector, I still had time.

I was determined to show him what that meant to me. That I was not inactive and lax in my time despite what my body might say. I wanted to be more than a faraway face and blurred memory. I called Bithia into my room as well as Zoe and several of the other girls I felt closest to and for the next two days we poured over my colored threads and drew patterns on wax tablets so often that the wax hardly had time to harden between ideas.

It was not traditional for the bride to send the groom gifts. I was determined though. By spring, I would send Hector a tapestry created with his gifts of thread and worked by my own hands. What I could not say with words, I would show him in cloth. I wanted our lives together. If my body never matured, it would not matter. But it seemed important to let him know anyway. I suspected that a man that sent seashells and river rocks might understand that.

It was a good distraction that winter. For the first time I felt as if I could do something for my future but sit and wait, even if, with my mind, I knew that a single tapestry was not enough for a man to wait for a woman over. My heart hoped that the meaning behind it might be though. I was careful and picky with my weaving those long dim days in my room, testing each thread, each shift in the weave of my slowly growing tapestry. It had to be perfect because it carried all the hopes for a future together that I held in my heart. There were evenings Bithia had to slowly pry my fingers from the shuttle and thread and lead me, groggy and stumbling to bed. I was determined to have something to send Hector by spring and all of my free time went toward that work.

Then, during one of the longest nights of the year, while I was deep in my mother's rooms, sick and shivering from what she had done, my body finally caught up with my mind. I would have wept in relief if I had not been so weak as I realized what the dark liquid slipping down my thighs meant. In disgust, she sent me away and I found my way out of the rooms to where Bithia waited for me. She held me in her arms and wept too and I think we were both aware with new strength that Ilium would be my escape as well as my new home. I recovered in the privacy of my room but the news did not wait for that. Despite the time of year and the bad weather we had been having, within days my father sent word to Ilium.

I had finally become an adult. Hector could come for me.

Once I had recovered, I spent the rest of the winter preparing. Despite my previous determination, my tapestry sat on my loom, half finished. I would send more than just cloth to Ilium come spring if all went well. Designs of sunflowers on blue could wait to be finished there. Instead, Bithia and I sewed a dress of richest, Sidonian purple after the dresses of the queens of old with their high waists and their bell skirts. We spent many long evenings embroidering it in gold and purple thread. My cattle far outweighed the amount I had spent on them and Miltiades brought me an exact count of them as well as his predictions about how many more I would have by the time the calves came in the spring. I would go to Ilium wealthy beyond what most women dreamed of. Late in the evenings I would sit in my weaving room as I embroidered and listen to the girls around me talk in the golden light from the fire about what they thought Ilium would be like for me, what kind of house I would live in, how many rooms it would have, who would serve me, how often I would go to the royal palace to see the wanax and his queen. I wondered about all of it myself - but more then anything - I longed simply for Hector.

It was foolish. I knew that. I had no idea what kind of man he had become or what he looked like. I had nothing to tell me about him but the grand stories that always followed his name these days. And the chests he sent me. He had a new name now as well as 'Horse-breaker'. They called him 'Man-killing Hector'. I should have worried. How much of what he sent me in his boxes of treasure was from burned cities and defeated foes, from captured women and ruined kings? Who had worn the earrings that now tinkled in my ears as I wore them in waiting for him before me? Had the necklace I now wore at my throat been an offering of ransom for a defeated husband or taken from a cold neck? I knew I should fear what he might have become. Yet when I filled my hands with foreign sea shells or played a game of Hounds and Boars with its tiny carved pieces or drew the soft furs up over my cold hands - I saw his dark eyes in his young face and remembered his kindness to me in that olive grove all those years ago - and I found I could not fear him.

I longed to know who he had become, but my heart whispered that whoever it was, he would still have his dark eyes and his thoughtful look.

I could however grow nervous and, as the spring came I found that feeling only increased. That strange flutter inside my stomach, the tingle in my palms, the catch in my chest -- they would startle me at unexpected times and I would find my eyes looking in the direction of Mount Ida and Ilium.

Most wedding preparations took long months but my betrothal had been longer than most. I assumed that, as soon as word came in response to my father's news of the winter, I would either be sent directly to Ilium with its return or else follow shortly after. The delay between that winter day and the coming of spring was simply that Ilium would need time to prepare for the marriage of its oldest son before it could send for the bride. Perhaps I should have felt upset that my family and friends seemed so eager to see me go – yet I was so eager to go myself that I did not think I could have born it if anyone had tried to keep me longer.

Despite the expectant wait for Ilium's messenger, life still went on. I was kept busy with the usual activity of spring. I was no longer allowed to go out into the fields or pastures so that I would not show up at Ilium sun burned and wind worn but there was still plenty that needed me. I went through the store rooms with Enoch and his new apprentice, sorting through what was left over from the winter months and what went to planting. I made sure that my family and the rest of the servants working in the fields were well supplied with food and water and that when they came home at the end of the day, the house was ready for their return. During the day, I took the women of the house and, as we did each year, we went through all the rooms and cleaned them completely to get rid of the smells and dirt of winter. Only my mother's rooms were left untouched and I did not see her or her dark slave during those days of bright sunshine and green growing things. It was if the upcoming promise of Ilium was something even she would not threaten with her touch. It gave me even more reason to hope. And all that time, the sudden flutter, the unexpected clench -- and I would look down the road that led to Ilium. Waiting.

No one came that spring. I told myself that

men went off to war during the spring. He would come in the summer. The bees droned lazy and the olive groves were thinned as the sun heated the days into golden dust. I left flowers around the tree he had found me in all those years ago in thanks for her help. And still - no word came from Ilium.

My father questioned the messenger he'd sent and the man swore he had delivered the message to Priam himself, though Hector had not been in the city at the time. My father took to watching the road to Ilium as well when he thought no one was watching him. I carefully folded away the dress of purple now that it was finished and put it in a chest so it would be kept safe and clean, determined that nothing would threaten our hope, even as it began to grow fragile feeling in my chest. Hector would come. I was ready. I had not wasted too much time.

Harvest came upon us and we were all busy. I was grateful for the distraction and threw myself into all of my work in an effort to stave off the whispers of doubt in my head and the feeling of disappointed looks I imagined from my brothers and father. I spent my days up to my elbows in olive oil and honey preserves when I was not busy with harvesting herbs from their secret places or working with Enoch and his boy. There was a small skirmish just down the coast from us with Achaean raiders that had stayed longer than usual and my brothers found two of the men that had escaped the sinking of their boat and killed them as they stumbled onto our lands. We drove the cattle further inland, just in case, and went back to work. The harvest would not wait. Yet, at the end of each day, I found myself standing in one of the small side doorways of our house and pretending to watch the sunset when I was actually watching the road to Ilium. Still waiting. And my chest ached.

Winter came and no word came from Ilium.

For the first time- - no chest came for me either.

I pretended it was not winter for as long as I could and then I pretend I had not noticed the lack of attention from Ilium. From Hector. I didn't know who I pretended harder for, myself or for the rest of the House. I saw the looks I was given though when they did not realize I was aware of them and I knew. My father did not speak of it but I saw the growing storm clouds on his forehead whenever he glanced in the direction of invisible Ilium. The look on my own face kept Bithia from trying to say anything to me in attempted comfort. I was not interested in pity or comfort. The lack of a chest from Hector seemed, somehow, even worse than the lack of word from Ilium. I told myself he had not sent a chest because he was planning to come himself and for a very long time could almost believe it. Except winter stretched on and on that year and no one ever came. No matter how long I stood in that doorway each evening in bare feet, wrapped in fur - no one came. Bithia complained that I was losing weight again but I had no interest in eating. Even my loom lost its pleasure for me. I did find I could stare almost endlessly into the fire though and I passed a great deal of time that way. No one was interested in coming to my rooms those days and gossiping and sewing to pass the time. There was only one thing to talk about - and no one wanted to talk of it. My heart felt as if Medusa had breathed on it and turned it to stone. It would not ache, but it would not feel anything else for me either. Inside, I felt frozen and I was afraid of what might happen to my heart if it were not that way. I did nothing to shake off the winter that had settled inside me as well as over the outside world.

I felt a burst of hope come spring though and shook off the apathy of winter. Surely, this was the year. Any day a messenger would come from Ilium with apologies and a sound reason for the delay. Hector had waited longer than a year for me to mature. If it was a test of my faith in him or my faithfulness, it was one I would pass. It helped that work took a great deal of my time too, even more than usual. My brothers and father had left. Achaeans were swarming up the coast and news had come to us belatedly that last year the city of Teuthrania had fallen. We could not help them now but we could avenge them and so the men in my family, Podes included, left to join other kings and they took most of the men with them so the women and I took over the chores of planting and shearing. I was kept so busy that I should have found no time to look toward Ilium. I still did though. Soon, my heart promised me. He will come soon. Wait until the Achaeans are driven away and then he will come. My selfish heart worried about Hector almost more than it did my father and brothers.

I became a surprise midwife. Ours broke her arm thanks to an angry sheep and everyone turned to me to take over. I had never delivered a human baby before though I'd helped once or twice with the livestock when they had had problems. Now I found myself doing the same for women, the midwife over my shoulder giving her instructions while I carefully did exactly as I was told. I held two newborn lives in my long fingered hands that spring and cleared the mucus from their mouths. It was my breath that entered them first to let them cry. For days after each birth, I walked through my duties with my mind unwilling to concentrate. Even Ilium did not seem so important for those few days.

Our men returned during the summer, unable to find enough Achaeans to fight. It seemed they had burned Teuthrania and fled last fall, going back across the sea to their homes, taking the women of the city and its wealth with them. Hiding across the ocean. My father talked of sailing another raid across the Aegean but there were not many kings that had not suffered from raids in the past few years and less still that were willing to leave their own homes exposed to raid distant shores. Summer stretched, dusty and baked, and my father grew restless. I found that I had grown strangely emotionless and tried, once I realized it, to hide it. I stopped looking toward Ilium but I still could not seem to find the energy to weave or even pick up my embroidery during the evening. I seemed to grow tired faster and I slept a great deal more, blaming it on the drugged heat. I did not dream while I slept.

Visiting guests began to bring whispers of Ilium and its oldest son. At first I did not hear them and was only aware of their existence by the way the servants began to act toward me, of the way conversations stopped or changed when I walked into a room. I thought they were whispers about me until I began to pause in doorways before entering rooms and began hearing whispers of 'Ilium' and 'Hector'. Of 'Sparta'.

It was early fall when my father finally drew me aside early one day to speak to me. By then however, I already knew what he would tell me and I felt barren and hollow inside. I had listened, gathered the pieces of what I heard together, and used my own mind. It had been a puzzle and I had never been able to resist a puzzle.

Sparta, far off Sparta, deep in Achaean lands, had offered an alliance with Ilium. It was a small country, its king only a minor king and not wanax the way Priam was but one of Sparta's daughters was married to Agamemnon, the king of mighty Mycenae. Agamemnon, who had united all the cities of Achaia and its kings under his rule. It was no small thing to have him as a brother-in-law, especially as each year the Achaeans pushed deeper into our own countries and stayed longer. The king of influential Sparta wanted an alliance with Ilium. He had no sons left to offer, both of his twins dead.

But he had a daughter...

Helen. Beautiful swan-born Helen of Sparta. To marry her was to become king of her father's lands - and to have the woman that was claimed to be the most beautiful in all the world in your bed.

Sparta wanted concessions on Ilium's trade goods that came down through the Hellespont. It wanted a king for its throne strong enough to keep Sparta strong. Ilium wanted an end to the Achaean aggression that had been weakening our empire for so long. It wanted influence on the Achaean mainland.

Sparta offered Helen. It wanted, in return, Ilium's first son.

Hector.

My Hector...

I stood by my father's side on top of the hill he'd brought me to with my face to the wind from the water and listened as he told me what I had already figured out. He said they were rumors, only rumors, and that he had sent men to Ilium to hear the truth of things from Priam himself. We stood less than an arm's length from each other, staring out at nothing, and he did not touch me. I think - I think he was afraid to touch me. I did not want him to touch me though so it was all right. Hearing it spoken out loud... I thought if I stood very still and did not move or breathe - perhaps time would stand still for me as well. Nothing would change and nothing would happen.

We stood on that hill a very long time and it was very dark before he finally went down to our house. It was longer still before I finally turned and followed him.

That winter, messengers came from Priam for my father. They brought gold and peace offerings with them - but they did not bring my chest of cedar and they did not bring Hector. When they left, I watched them go from my window, hidden by the curtains. I had listened at the doorway when they spoke to my father. They had come with apologies, not promises.

Ilium did not want me any more.

I went back to my bedroom and no one bothered me that winter. When spring came for the rest of the world, it did not come for me.

I rose in the mornings. I worked in the fields or the house or the barns. I planned meals and cleaned rooms and checked store houses and I never looked in the direction of far off Ilium. There would be no wedding veil for me, no flowers at my feet, or children singing songs. No wedding night to feel nervous about.

No dark eyes waiting for me.

The other kings would see that Ilium had rejected me and they would follow suit. It did not matter that the fault was not mine; I was still a woman that Ilium itself had not seen fit to wed. And I was grateful -- so grateful -- because I could not bear the thought of marriage any more. Of a husband. Children. The very thought felt like ashes in my mouth and all I wanted was to hid away in my family's home for the rest of my life and find contentment there. I could be content with my brother's children, with my duties, with my role as silent hostess to my father's guests. I had, at least in my mind, once belonged to dark forever eyes. I had no desire to belong to anyone else.

My father, however, had other plans for me. I found out about them when the traders he had sent the messages by in the spring returned in the early fall. I found out about them when my father told me there was a husband waiting for me.

Across the Aegean. In Achaean lands.

XI.

I was cold.

I hated that sensation more than almost anything, more than heat, more than wetness, more than pain. I hated the way it settled into my hands and feet, I hated it on my shoulders, hated the way it sank into my bones and lived there. I had always hated being cold.

I had always endured it anyway.

I had been raised to endure. Raised to be patient and silent and ignore what would have damaged me. My father said it was a warrior's trait -- endurance. I thought instead that it was a woman's.

It should not have been hard for me, therefore, to endure the cold that seeped in past the thick woolen drapes over unfamiliar windows and pooled like liquid on all the flat surfaces in the room I lay in that night. It was just cold. It was nothing greater or lesser than I had endured in my own home. In my own room. In my own bed.

I lay in the darkness of the guest room my host had provided, Bithia sleeping soundly next to me, and I told myself I should not mind the cold the way I did tonight. That I should endure.

I had spent so long enduring however over the past seven years and now... now I did not seem to have any endurance left in me. Not even for something as simple as the cold.

Tonight, I slept on Lemnos, island in the Aegean Sea, ruled over by the son of Jason, the so-long-ago hero of the golden fleece. Betrayer of women.

I tried not to think of the fittingness that I should be on this island now. My mother had often warned me I was a Medea. It had always bothered me, to think that blood, that darkness, might run through me as well. It bothered me less because I did not believe her and more because I did. I had never thought I would follow that path all the way to its end, however. Yet here I was, cast aside by one kingdom that had promised to wed me and sent off to another on the other side of the known world.

I was Andromache of Thebe, great Troy's cast off, and I was being sent to Achaean lands to wed King Peleus' second son in far off Phthia. I would be there soon, just a single ocean between myself and my new homeland and yet already I seemed to have run out of my supply of endurance.

How would I survive?

I spent my waking moments torn between panic and despair and I did not dare give in to either one of them, knowing they would consume me if I did. I let the cold soak into my heart and my chest and silently hoped that, if it would not stop my breath, it would at least take my ability to feel from me.

The room I was in was dark, like the inside of a cave and I could only stare blankly at it where I lay. The drapes, drawn over the windows against the cold, blocked out what might have been faint moonlight and I had not let Bithia light the braziers to give the room warmth. I hated the cold. I hated anyone being able to see me when I slept more. Besides, I did not need light to see and there was nothing of worthwhile for me to concentrate on staring at anyway. When the drapes flickered near one of the windows, I watched them without interest. When the man appeared in the reveal of moonlight, for a very long moment my mind did not see him as anything more then any of the other foreign objects in the room. Eyes already used to the darkness, I studied him with a strange detachment as he seemed to wait for his own eyes to adjust.

He was tall, taller than most of the men I was used to. I could tell from where the crest of his boars' tusk helmet reached in comparison to the wall mural the pushed aside curtain cast light on. He was dressed in armor, a beaten leather breastplate without a single bolt of bronze or metal decoration to catch the light. He seemed to take up a great deal of my room, more than a single man should even though he did not seem, physically, to fill any more space than a man might. A god? Hadn't a god come for Ariadne when she had been abandoned by the man that had promised to marry her? This man hardly looked like the moody and fickle god of drunkenness though. He looked like Ares in his dark armor.

Or Hades.

None of the thoughts were reassuring. Yet - none of them terrified me the way they should either. It was as if the cold outside had sunk into me and nothing seemed as important anymore.

Until he moved. I felt a shiver in my chest then and realized I had lied to myself. Apparently, I did care despite myself.

I did not think I had reacted and yet I felt Bithia wake next to me. It was a subtle movement, barely there, and yet the soldier turned in our direction as if he had sensed it. I had a moment to remember that my family had taken all my knives away from me. To remember bitterly that they thought I might try to kill myself in despair at where they were sending me.

As if I needed a blade to kill myself.

His voice came in the darkness. It was a low voice, rough at its edges and deep. It was more than a soldier's voice. It was a commander's voice for all it was so quiet."My lady?"

What was I going to do? Pretend I was not there? Pretend I was sleeping? What kind of person snuck into a room and then politely introduced himself?

"Yes?" I kept my voice level, calm, even though my heart skipped in my chest. My detached mind tried to understand what was happening. We were in the Maiden's Wing of the palace, where the unmarried and widowed women of the royal family stayed. Men were not allowed here. Was he a soldier sneaking into his lover's room late at night? Was 'my lady' the proper greeting for that kind of thing?

Bithia stiffened next to me and her own hand went slipping under the pillow in vain hope of finding our knives. We were unprotected but if he meant harm why was he talking to us?

"You need to come with me." He was confident enough in the dark now to walk to the stand at the foot of the bed and his voice was just as calm and steady as mine had been. It offered no chance for argument though. Unwilling to deal with him lying down, I sat up and felt the cold close around me. I felt like shivering, from so much more than the cold, and did not.

"Why?"

I could not see his eyes in the dark, behind the brow of his helm. Did I imagine that they narrowed? His voice was flat and expressionless.

"Raiders."

Raiders. Something about that voice, that word, brought me back to the night my childhood had ended so many years ago. To the blood and the fear and the unexpected responsibility and necessity. I slipped out of bed and stood up despite the way the chill floor felt against my bare feet. I wasn't even thinking firmly when I immediately went to the inlaid table in the corner of the room and picked up the one thing I had left of value to me beyond Bithia, wrapping my arms around it to hold it to my chest.

Once I had begun my courses, become an adult in the eyes of the world, my mother had stopped torturing me. Physically. The lessons with her however, dark and foul and fascinating, had not stopped. And, somewhere along the way, deep in the depths of her closed off hallways and airless rooms, I had discovered -- I was better than my mother. Not better in any bright or good or noble way, but rather in all the dark ways, all the things she stirred and called into being and did. I could do them better. Instinctively, I had hidden it from her, intentionally making mistakes, diluting what I created, hiding what I knew. It had been instinctive and it had been for survival, for I knew, as much as she needed, compulsively, inexplicably, to teach me, she would never allow anyone to grow stronger than her. Yet I had. And so, when I had left, I had snuck into that hall of shadows and childhood fears and I had taken one thing away with me.

It was a small box the length of my forearm, created of ancient smoked wood and a strange brittle metal like tarnished silver. All my mother's darkest secrets lived in that box. I should have left it behind with her. I should have left all that she had made me become behind and gone into my new life clean. Yet I had found myself sneaking into her rooms that last night and stealing those horrors away. I had needed to bring them with me.

So I had proved her right. I was a Medea. My mother's own creature, no matter how I tried to hide it. Just as I had gone to the box then, I went to it now and gathered it up in my arms like a child. My mother's horrors. And mine. I could not bear the thought of being parted from them.

Even as my hands closed around that familiar wood, I found myself realizing what I had already acted on instinctively. The soldier was lying.

The darkness hid it but I saw. His was no palace armor, no uniform I recognized. The helmet was entirely wrong and he had come in the low window, not the draperies that covered the doorway. Even as I turned back to see his form, barely discernable through the darkness as he leaned over Bithia when she stood, I knew.

There were raiders in Lemnos. He'd spoken true about that. One of them was standing in my room.

I backed up then, my bare feet silent on the floor, lips pressed together against any sound. Raiders… on the one night my ship to Achaean land was beached here. My chest felt tight with the sudden fear. The last time I had faced raiders, my father and brothers had been there. My people. Hect - I had not felt helpless then. I did now. That helmeted head swung in my direction as if he could hear my thoughts - or sense my weakness. He stretched out a hand to me.

"Come," his voice said he knew. He knew that I knew him.

His hand was not directly lifted to me, though. He could not see me in the darkness the way I could see him. The way I could see Bithia raise her face, trusting and curious to him in puzzlement; the way I could watch the understanding flood her features as she realized what I already knew. She jerked suddenly but his other hand was ready and curved around her upper arm. Bithia, at least, was going no where he did not want her to.

And I?

It was all I could do not to press my free hand to my own mouth, not sure what sound I would have made anyway. I could go. There were windows near me and he could not see me in the dark, could not anticipate me. If he was being quiet, it meant he was here alone or with a small party. The palace still belonged to its royal family. Its guards still walked the halls. I could run and he would not catch me before I found myself safely with my hosts. I was free.

Bithia was not…

"Don't," my maid said it softly, as if she could read my mind. Perhaps she could. She was a slave. The chances were good that he would leave her behind if he lost me.

"Now," his voice was firm and his hand did not waver.

He could leave her behind with a slit throat…

What was one slave to my life? To the treaty between my family and Phthia that my marriage sealed? To the gold it would cost to buy me back from raiders -- if they left enough of me to sell me back at all? To what rough men would do to women in their power? What was one slave?

What was my Bithia worth?

I stepped forward to him again, this huge, dark man who had come in the night to steal me away. Used to being equal in height to men, this one towered over me and for the first time in a long time, I felt small.

"I'm not Dora," I hoped beyond hope he had come to the wrong room tonight, that he was here for Lemnos' beautiful daughter. He snorted in the darkness, a whisper of derision and I thought he sounded angry.

"I didn't come for Dora."

He dragged Bithia to the door after that, assuming I would follow. I did. The look she gave me was furious and for a moment, a moment of insanity, I almost smiled. She was angry at me for not deserting her. How I loved her for that. Then the drape covering the doorway were pushed aside and I saw there were other men in the hallway, in mismatched armor that labeled them as mercenaries as well and one of them held a torch that burned dully. It's suddenly light had me squinting and resisting the urge to show weakness by shielding my night sensitive eyes against it.

Our captor handed Bithia over to one of the men and reached for me. I flinched away from his hand. He caught me anyway and drew me up close against him. I felt the inflexibility of his breastplate against my own chest and stomach through the fabric of my nightdress, felt the way his hand wrapped almost entirely around my upper arm. I would not let go of my mother's box and it pressed painfully into me where it was trapped between us. I caught the scent of leather and sweat and ocean. His fingers on my arm did not bruise me. Standing as we were he blocked out the rest of the world and filled it with only his presence. His voice was very low.

"No screaming," he told me. "No running. No tricks."

His eyes were very dark in the depths of his helmet but the fire from the torch caught glints of amber light in them. I looked into those eyes and could not help that the edge of my lips twitched.

We were in the Maiden's Wing. What was I going to do? Scream and draw those innocents out into the hallway to also be kidnapped -- or worse. The girls would be defenseless creatures. In the darkness of his helmet, my captor's eyes narrowed slightly.

"No screaming." He turned his head to growl it at Bithia, who was already being held around the waist by one of the other raiders, obviously putting up more of a fight than I was though she was still by the time I looked at her. She glared at him in return and if looks were spears, his spirit would have already been loosed from his body and on its way to Hades from the venom in her eyes. I knew her though. She would do nothing until I did. I did not make a sound or protest as we were hurried down the silent hallway.

I should have. It was the first right of any

captive to try to escape. Yet - where would I go? A captive needed somewhere to escape to and if I escaped I would not be returning to my home where my small bed in my cramped room and my battered and loved loom were. I would be escaping to continue my journey to Phthia, to marry Peleus' son. A foreign bride in a foreign land with a sea witch for a mother-in-law to rule over me. People spoke well enough of Peleus. Of his sons... the rumors were not so gentle. What exactly was I supposed to be wanting to escape to?

What did it say about me that I actually weighed a short life used by raiders against a long one far from everything I knew?

We did not go out by the main way, which would have led us through the main hall, and any number of household servants and guards. Instead, without hesitation, we were led in the opposite direction, deep into the hallway until a drape that looked just like the other draped doorways was brushed aside. I found myself in a room that appeared to store blankets and fabrics for the women of this wing. I looked back the way we had come as I was dragged into that thicker darkness and wondered, with the first beginning jolt of panic, how they had known this room was here? How had they known they were not walking into someone else's bedroom? The only way they could have known was if someone told them -- someone that lived in this palace. Somehow, that betrayal frightened me more than the armored men or the uncertainty of my future. I balked for the first time.

It must have angered the man that was taking me away because he drew me sharply up against him again and I lowered my chin in response as my brows came down. I had learned how to take a blow. The tail at the top of his helmet swayed as he looked down at me in the dull orange of the torchlight, but no blow came. Instead, impossibly, one of his huge hands cupped itself around my upper arm and rubbed briskly. It was such a simple move, warming my skin with his as if we were companions – I could only look blankly at him, feeling off balance and confused. Someone drew aside the shutter over the window and so I knew it had not always been a storage room. There were men outside already, waiting for us. Bithia went through like a wild cat. She was still silent, waiting for my signal to break that, but she made no attempt to make her abduction easy. It took three of the men to force her through the window and pry her hands and braced feet off of its edges.

I should have been doing the same thing. I should not have been standing patiently against the side of my kidnapper, holding my mother's box and feeling forlorn and lost while he rubbed absent warmth back into my cold skin. A woman abducted is not at fault. But what if she goes willingly? Is it still abduction?

And yet, somehow, stupidly, I was less terrified of my kidnappers than I was of my future in Phthia. At least their threat was one I had lived with all my life. I knew what to expect and it would be terrible but it would end when my family bought me back. Phthia... Phthia was absolutely unknown to me but I had heard enough rumors even over the sea to feel fear. Phthia would hold me for the rest of my life if I went there and there would be no ransom away from it.

The others passed through that window and then it was my turn. For the first time, my body rebelled against me, balking despite my determination to face this with dignity and the soles of my feet skid against the stone of the floor as I resisted being pushed to that opening. I told myself I was brave and that if I had to endure this I would do it with grace but my nerve almost broke. My mother's box left red grooves in my pale skin I was holding it so tightly. My captor came through directly behind me and we both paused at that window. He could have manhandled me through. I might have broken and started screaming. Instead, he rested his hands on my shoulders and didn't push anymore.

"It's only a window."

It shouldn't have mattered what he said and it certainly wasn't a sentence to give someone courage – but for some reason my muscles unlocked and the air flowed in my chest again. Pressing my lips together, I climbed through the window as well and he followed behind me. One of his men sealed the shutter back over the window as silently as he had drawn it away.

Lemnos had grown up around fishing huts and than market places. There was no design to its buildings or the roads that cut between them. The houses that cluttered, haphazard, around the palace had grown up over the generations, built and rebuilt to suit. A city set on an island, there were no walls built for protection. Where the mercenaries had exited the palace, there was very little in the way of houses to hinder their retreat. Now that we were outside the Maiden's Wing, I knew now was the time to draw attention to what was happening, but even as I thought it I felt my abductor's hand close over my mouth as he drew me close again. It was just as well. I could not bear the sound of my own screams.

"Almost there," it was a murmur near my ear, though I could not tell if he said it to me or to himself. It sent a shiver through me and I shut my eyes tightly -- because I knew. It was not the voice so much as the way he said it. In that instant, I knew who my kidnapper was. I thought, deep down, that I had somehow known it all along.

Suddenly, it did not matter what I ran to, only what I was desperate to run from. *Who* I was desperate to run from. In all the world, the man holding me was the one person I could not bear to face. Not now. Not anymore. I sank my teeth into the flesh of his hand as I brought the heel of my foot down on the instep of his. The sound he made was low and I brought my fist up and backward over my shoulder so that it connected with the line of his helmet right where it met his brow. For an instant, his hold on me loosened and I twisted myself free. I was desperate in my need and careless of how I had to twist my limbs. The cold bit my skin and I ran into the night. Like a startled deer, I ran.

I should have screamed. I should have run back along the wall until I came upon a courtyard and people. I could have even tried, at a risk, to lose him in the jumbled city streets. But when I heard his footsteps behind me, all I knew was that I could never let him catch me -- and that my recent history had already been played out in front of an entire continent. I did not want anyone else to see this.

The air was cold as it poured down into my chest as I ran. My bare feet made soft thuds that didn't drown out the sounds of my inhales as I raced over first stone and then packed dirt paths. When I ran, I flew and I had no intention of stopping now. My feet carried me away from the city. Toward the cliffs.

The dark warrior was right behind me.

I stumbled as I reached the rocky area outside of the city and was surprised to hear my breath sob into me in response. Back home I could run forever. Why did my heart feel so tight in my chest and my throat already hurt here?

I saw, with sudden clarity, where the ground ended in the moonlight ahead of me. I saw the forever ocean, beyond that cliff. I thought of the numerous times gods had turned falling women into birds. But I hesitated, still far from the edge, and my pursuer's caught me in that moment. His thick arms closed tight around me and all the fight went out of me when they did. No god appeared to turn me into reeds or a passive tree. I shut my eyes hard, sobbing in cold air and told myself it was only that and not the great heaving twisting of my heart that wrenched those sounds out of me. I tried to curl forward but his arms held me still and through the rigidity of his armor, against my back I could feel the way his chest rose and fell with his own heavy breathing. He bent forward too then, his head next to mine, and for a very long time we seemed to stand that way. Breathing and not moving. I could not control what raged inside of me, too many emotions to name. I felt as if I could not bear them all and my fingers dug hard against the wood of my mother's box.

"Andromache."

I shook my head mutely where I had it bowed, in denial of him, in denial of the name, even I could not say which. It didn't matter. His voice on my name drained everything out of me, left me dry and hollow, utterly adrift. As quickly as my panic had come, it again fled and I had nothing left to me with it gone. I felt as small and scared inside as I had that night so long ago when my life had first been invaded by the outside world.

He picked me up in his arms and carried me down the rocky path we had both raced up earlier. I held my mother's box in my arms and tucked my head. I wanted to wake up. I wanted to wake up from everything and find that seven years had never happened and that my heart was still safely in my chest where it belonged instead of sacrificed for a Trojan prince and a striped future. My captor was silent as he walked, offering nothing more.

There was a boat beached on the shore. It was out of place, a long, sleek hull meant to travel distances, not the rough little fishing boats that were scattered around it. More soldiers in mismatched armor moved on that boat and at the water's edge, preparing, silently, to sail into the moon covered dark ocean.

"Let my maid go," I whispered it and his answer was just as quiet. "No."

I pressed my lips together. "Let me go."

He stood on the beach with the quiet sounds of canvas and water on wood around us and he lowered his head to me. I did not look at him but my fingers tightened on the box I held. My heart felt very fragile in my chest and I held my breath. For a very long moment we remained that way. The ship pushed back from the shore. Finally, quietly, he told me:

"No."

I shut my eyes and felt him move forward. I flinching away automatically from the water I heard under me as he waded into the surf, anticipating the first seep of cold into the fabric of my dress, not sure I had anything left inside me that could bear being cold and wet after everything else. He held me high against his chest though and, when the water grew close, he lifted me. I felt other hands offered down to collect me and I let them pull me unresisting the rest of the way onto the boat's deck. Bithia, fire in her eyes, was already there and she pushed through the men onboard to wrap her arms possessively around me as my captor hauled himself onto the deck as well. I was glad of her warmth but, even more, I was glad of her high burning emotions. Mine felt as if they had faded to ash. My captor was the last aboard and, even as his feet found the deck, the men were already bending silently to the oars.

They were taking me far from the promise of Phthia and my future there. I leaned into Bithia's embrace and watched the dim shapes of the island's city begin to grow faint. I wondered if I should cry, but there were no tears in my chest or my eyes. Only that hollow, waiting feeling.

"She's not going to jump," Bithia hissed in disgust at two of the men that seemed to have been stationed between me and the sides of the ship. "The water's cold."

It broke a silent laugh out of me, a single exhale, and I shut my eyes and laid the side of my cheek against the top of her head. Tonight my world had fallen apart. Again. And yet, somethings would never change and for that I was grateful. I suspected it was my only hope of sanity.

"I thought you were free," she told me and her voice was very quiet and vulnerable. I freed an arm to wrap around her and held her tightly. I couldn't tell her why I hadn't escaped. It all caught in my throat and threatened to stay lodged there forever.

"No."

"Did you really bite him?" She sounded both worried and proud and that flickering smile came over me again. Beautiful Bithia, for distracting me from the hollow circling my thoughts were doing in my head.

"Yes."

She muffled a laugh against me and I hugged her again. I was not alone. It was selfish of me to be glad about that, but I was. With an inhale I lifted my head. Lemnos was growing distant on the horizon. I was not alone, and that meant I needed to wake myself up inside and begin thinking again. I could not have done it for myself, but I would for Bithia's sake. A soldier approached and took off his helmet. I recognized him too.

"My lawagetas says I am to take you below and show you your bed. He told me to give this to you as well." He offered me a heavy woolen chlamys, the short cloak of a warrior. In the moonlight it was as red as drying blood and I drew it around myself and Bithia against the cold. My eyes lingered on my tall captor as he stood at the front of the ship. *Lawagetas.* 'Leader of the people'. Bithia tugged at me to remind me to move and I turned my attention to following our escort to the trap door that led to the narrow hold.

The ceiling was low below deck and I could

hear the rush of the water and the tap of the oars on the hull. In the back was a small section, marked off from the rest of the space by a hung canvas wall. When the soldier drew it aside for us to enter, I saw a raised wooden platform with two narrow beds on it along with a wooden chest. The raised floor would keep my feet out of any water that might leak in or trickle down from the trap door and I was grateful for that. The soldier gave the lamp to Bithia, trusting either the damp wood or our self-preservation. Even if I had not known the soldier's face, I would not have worried to be in this small space with him. Even if we were considered *lawiaia*, 'captive women', warlords divided their spoils, not the men that served them.

"There are clothes in the chest," he stated, looking at me. I nodded. His eyes searched my face but I gave him nothing back. My mother had trained me well and he was not a comrade or companion that had a right to my thoughts. With a quick nod, he left and at my gesture, Bithia moved to the curtain to watch him and make sure he truly did leave. When she gave me a nod, I sank down onto one of the beds and drew the cloak, now warmed with our shared heat, closer around me. Bithia gave me a worried look from her post by the canvas screen and I returned it, feeling old and gray and frail inside.

"I think we are in trouble," I told her.

In another time and place, it would have drawn one of her dry looks that went with the mocking arched eyebrow but it was a sign of her own worry that she didn't think to respond to me that way. With a determined inhale, I stood up, dipping my head to keep it from brushing the ceiling. I could do this... whatever *this* was. I was my place to protect my friend and the only way I could do that was if I was determined and active.

The chest was not locked and inside it I found several dresses. Good thick woolen ones which made me bless whatever woman had packed them. There were clasps for my hair, as well as an ivory comb and some ribbons and I realized, whoever the stranger packer had been, she had wanted me to feel not entirely abandoned and alone. Bithia shifted on her feet and I glanced at her from the corners of my eyes, saw she was trying to watch out past the canvas and me as well and that she was starting to look a bit green at the edges of her lips and eyes. My poor Bithia. Poseidon's ocean made her sick at its mildest. I had seen it first hand on the voyage to Lemnos. I knew it was a sign of her love for me that she had not once complained of the sea voyage that was to take me away from my homeland. To distract her, I lifted up the fabrics and scattered the ornamental hair clips on the bed along with the bracelets and necklaces that had been in a small box at the very bottom. She eyed them and I could tell she was deciding their market value, not to sell, but to see if the people that had supplied them had spent enough money on decorating me that she would be satisfied with them. Her sniff indicated it was enough -- for the moment. Then she peered intently at my face in the subtle light from the lamp.

"You think you know who they are," she stated in surprise. "That's why you're being so calm about this."

I didn't think calm was the right word for what I was feeling but I had no idea what the right word would be. Waiting, I suppose, came closest. Everything inside me felt as if it were waiting and I wasn't sure what it waited for. If she thought I was calm though than that was good too. If I was calm than she wouldn't feel fear either and if my captors thought I was calm they wouldn't be so quick to try to take advantage of me. At least that was my hope. Frowning to myself, I shook out one of the dresses for her and then one for myself, gathering my thoughts as folded away the others. When I finally did speak, I picked my way over my words like a barefoot girl hunting in an oyster patch.

"I recognize the man that brought us down here." The last spare dress went into the trunk and I very slowly, very deliberately shut it. Bithia was starting to give me a narrow look but I was not stalling for dramatic effect or to tease her. It was that I felt as if I said the wrong thing, somehow it would suddenly all become too real and crash over me like a wave. There was a numbness around my heart and a clarity in my head and the balance between the two felt very thin. I met Bithia's eyes.

"That was Cebriones. He is the soldier that

Hec - that was sent from Ilium - to ask for me." I stumbled across the words badly despite my determination and winced at myself. I was better trained than that. Certain words had become sharp to my throat over the years though and I had learned to be careful how I uttered them. I did not enjoy swallowing broken pottery, not even in verbal form.

Bithia's eyes went wide however and she almost dropped the lamp. Her other hand went to her mouth.

"Troy?" the word caught in her throat as the realization that this was no simple kidnapping sunk in. As the implications of what that might mean sunk in. *"Troad Ilium?"*

I shot her my own dry look from the corners of my eyes because we both knew there was no other Ilium and began to change into one of the woolen dresses. It turned out to be too short for me but I had little alternative. My silence and activity gave her time let the new knowledge settle. To wrestle with the same question I was.

Why?

"He's here?" Bithia asked suddenly and looked from me to the hatch we had come down and then back to me. Thunder began to build in her eyes. "He's the tall raider, isn't he? The one that caught you."

I didn't even pretend to misunderstand who she was talking about. I sat back down on the bed and my voice was not as firm or full as would have wanted it to be when I answered:

"Yes."

It was strange that I could not sort through the emotions I felt but, from the looks that flew over Bithia's face, she experienced them all for me. Finally, it was fear and worry that settled strongest.

"What are we going to do?" she asked, letting the canvas fall to come and sit by my side on the bed, hands reaching to take one of mine. That was what it came down to. What was I going to do for both of us about this? How was I going to protect us and try to see a way clear of this horrible marsh we found ourselves in? That was my duty to keep us safe while hers was to follow where I decided to lead. I folded my hands around hers in my lap so they would not go weak and give me away.

"First, you must dress," I told her factually. I saw the way the relief filled her eyes. She had too much faith in me and thought I was already well on the way to taking matters into my own hands. All I could do was wonder what I would do on the day I failed that trust of hers. "Then we will bind our hair back and I will go speak to - " My heart was carefully shut against that name and so I simply nodded. "I will go speak to our captors."

We bound my hair back after Bithia had changed, making it a simple tail that hung down my back. Perhaps, I should have used the gold clasps for my hair and the beads but I would not. True, it would have marked me as a princess and worthy of better treatment but the gold was not mine. My gold, my wedding treasure, was back in the ship that rested in Lemnos' harbor. Perhaps it was the pride in me that resisted the idea of having to rely on borrowed gold, or maybe it was that I was simply not willing to accept any more gifts, of any kind, from Trojan hands. Either way, I let Bithia bind my hair with ribbons.

When she was done, I rose and, lifting the hem of my dress more from habit than need considering it didn't come near my ankles, I let Bithia lead the way to the ladder that led back up to the deck of the ship. I had not been sent for. I was hardly concerned with etiquette.

Bithia stayed below with her lamp.

The ladder gave me no trouble; being raised with brothers, I had learned to do most of what they did with my much longer skirts. No one stopped me as I pushed the hatch aside and stepped up onto the deck. The night was deep and thick now and I saw no land from where I stood, only the forever ocean as black at pitch. I wondered what swam below us in those depths.

The soldiers looked at me from their benches but no one approached me. My kidnapper was still standing at the prow of the ship. My one time promise.

He had taken his helmet off as well as the breastplate and he did not turn around as I came up behind him, even though I knew he was aware of my approach. His stillness gave me a moment to study him, this man I had not seen since he was barely more than a boy. His dark hair was still curly, worse perhaps because he had it cut shorter than our Achaean neighbors wore theirs. His body had grown and filled out since I had last seen him, entirely a man now without a hint of boyish awkwardness to reassure me. He turned his face after a moment, when I didn't say anything, and looked at me. I held my silence and forced myself to focus on his face instead of letting it blur in my mind's eye. He had grown into his nose and ears.

And he still had the dark eyes I had never forgotten...

Not willing to accept what I saw in his dark eyes, I spoke to the emptiness over his right shoulder.

"I formally ask you to put us ashore near Thebe." I had never been so glad for my mother's training in hiding what was inside me and appearing calm as I was at that moment. I would not give him my thoughts and emotions again. I had made that mistake once. I felt his eyes on me and knew that I wouldn't have known what my emotions were even if I had been inclined to share them.

"You think I would do that?" he asked, voice low. "After your father's broken promise to me?"

Of course, I had not thought he would do that but, as in any bargaining, you ask for the moon and settle for the mountain. I let my fingers weave calmly together in front of me. This was only the beginning skirmish in a very long war, I knew and I would not show any weakness during it.

"Is a promise broken by the second man if the first man has already broken it? If you will not set us ashore in Thebe, I ask to be placed in a neutral city under its ruler's protection until this dispute is settled."

"You know who I am. You know why I came for you."

I finally met his eyes then and I raised my chin. I had an emotion quite suddenly for him as it flared to life in me and it was anger.

"I know who you are, Prince of Ilium. But there is nothing between us that merits your actions."

His eyes held mine and they held their own quiet anger. It should have frightened me. I was entirely at his mercy and there were heroes famous for their quick, mindless tempers. For some reason though, his anger did not feel as if it were pointed at me and it was strangely calm. We watched each other for a long moment, and I weighed what I saw in his eyes and on his face. I suspected he did the same to me. At my back, I could feel his men pause in their breathing. He was the one that finally turned away.

"Then you won't understand why I won't let you go again."

I waited but that was all he offered. It was too much already, striking too close to wounds in my heart that had never healed and half dreamed futures I had once had. Anything I would say in that moment, I knew shouldn't be said. Instead, I turned and silently made my way back to the hatch and a little way down the ladder. There I paused and put a finger to my lips for Bithia. I had not closed the hatch and no one else moved to do so. We waited but no one said anything else to him and finally I finished my descent and joined Bithia on the wooden floor.

Bithia stayed quiet until we were back in the alcove. I noticed she was breathing through her mouth and her eyes looked tight at their edges. My lips shifted in sympathy for her. She swallowed and asked stoically, "now what?"

"Now we pray. And tie down anything we can," I told her. "There is a bank of clouds building over the horizon and I think we are in for a storm."

I was not done with my wayward prince, but first we had to survive the night.

XII.

If I had thought the gods noticed women that weren't attractive I would have thought Poseidon was furious over my abduction. And, like most gods in a fury, his response was threatening to drown me as well as my abductors.

I had never seen a storm like the one that overtook us on the ship that night. It was a storm dredged up from the very bottom of the ocean floor, I was sure of it, and the waves seemed to me to be huge mountains of liquid glass. Our ship seemed tiny on them, an ant in the middle of a lake, the wooden sides small and fragile defenses against the ice cold water we rode in. Each time the wood shuddered I did as well deep in my bones and the sides of the ship leaked water like salty tears, groaning as they did. I understood then why sailors swore their ships were alive, for our ship was all that stood between us and becoming nothing more than forgotten spirits drifting the bottom of the ocean with the many legged monsters and nyraids. We were all nothing but small, helpless children protected in its wooden arms as it painfully strove to keep us alive.

Bithia was sick. Sick beyond sick and soon even though I held the small bowl for her there was nothing left in her stomach to give the fish. The bed she lay in rose and dropped and we both were not always touching a surface as it happened, her, laid out and weeping she was so miserable, me frozen down to the bones of my wet bare feet. Even on the platform my feet were underwater up to my ankles and I tried not to think about that as I moved from one end of the ship to the other. I was below deck, of course. Most of the men that were not absolutely necessary were below deck now as well, sent there for fear of losing someone overboard as the green water threw itself across the deck. The hatch was shut as well but water still poured in small waterfalls down the outline of it and, when it opened from time to time I could not help but look up to see those great glass mountains rising against the dark and angry sky.

It was just as well that there was little cargo in the hold of this ship for it let the men bail the water that poured in back out at every chance they got. Though the chances they got were fewer than the water pouring in did. It did little to deter them, however, since the alternative was not bailing at all and letting the water win without a fight. Soldiers, sailors, men - they let nothing best them without at least a fight.

I could hear the crash of Zeus' mighty lightening in the sky above even through the wood of the deck at times. Just as, at times, I could hear the sounds of hoarse shouts torn away by wind and water from the crew still on deck. Once... once I thought I heard something long and slick and alive brush along the outside of the hull near me...

I had asked and so the men below told me that the mast had already been cast off, too much of a danger as it rolled, and that the oars had been lashed down tightly to preserve them. They would be all we would have to move us when the storm ended.

If the storm ever ended.

Bithia was delirious and she kept catching at my hand and begging me to find a coin, any coin, for myself. So, I assumed, when we drowned, I, at least, would be able to pay Charon to ferry my soul across the River to the afterlife. I could not imagine wasting the time to try to find a coin when there was so much happening around me. Besides, if the fish ate pieces of me, wouldn't that be the form I would wear in the afterlife?

Strange, the priests and oracles never thought to address those kinds of questions. Someone should have.

I had stopped passing back and forth with the bowl to give to the man near the top of the ladder. It had been a useless effort anyway, but it had kept us all pretending we could make a difference. Bithia had nothing left to give the bowl though she was still retching. It worried me, that her own body might harm her by not stopping when there was nothing left for it to do. I went to my mother's box.

I had tucked it into the chest, which, like the beds was nailed to the floor. I was not sure I had liked it sitting there, looking so innocent in with all those simple and helpless clothes, but anywhere else I left it, the box might have seen it soaked or swept out into the bilge that sloshed on the floor. Bracing myself on the edges of the chest, I leaned over and opened the box while I held myself steady with my other arm. The all too familiar bottles and small stone jars and boxes with their arcane carvings on them -- the needles of bronze and minuscule golden and stone knives -- the cords of stained black leather and coils of sinew and dried skins, the ink and chalk – they all seemed to look eagerly back out at me, waiting. And all of it as carefully and meticulously organized as if Chaos himself had never existed in the world this box lived in. I felt it steal over me then, that strange competence. It was as if something in me relaxed and calmed, slowly blinking itself awake with thick lidded eyes. It was the way I always felt whenever I looked into the secrets the box held since I had first taken it. I knew them all. There were a hundred uses for each and every thing in front of me and each one was just a few touches away from me bringing it to pass. The rest of the world was impossible and confusing but in that box, I knew exactly what everything was. I knew what *I* was.

What hid in this box belonged to me as surely as my eye color or the freckles on my skin.

What I wanted came to my hand without having to search, fingers so instinctive I could have found it without sight. The world around me seemed perfectly still and silent, frozen in a single moment. I shook a small amount of the sticky brown powder into my palm before I closed the jar, closed the box, closed the trunk and the world went back to wet chaos. Except, with that powder in my hand, it did not seem too wild and impossible to resist. It was just a minor powder compared to what I could create but even that small piece of control over my circumstances was like a bit of warmth in my closed fist.

I was not helpless. I was not incompetent. I was not lost.

Holding my hand close, I dumped the sticky powder into a small wooden cup and managed to get a little of the water from the water skin into it. I sheltered it with my hand and body to keep the sea from leaking its way in and finding access to Bithia's body. I knew what it did. There was not a powder, potion, oil or herb in that box I had not experienced myself. My mother had made sure of that. There was no temptation to share Bithia's drink though. I could not bear the thought of something happening to me that I was not awake and aware of. Even death.

Perhaps, especially, death.

Bithia drank when I propped her up and held the cup to her, not because she wanted to but because, even delirious, she obeyed me when I used the right tone of voice. I held her upright and tipped her head back so that she had to breathe through her mouth, sheltering it with my hand so the water that dripped from the ceiling could not fall into her throat. Twice, she tried to vomit and, twice, I stopped her. The mixture stayed down and soon Bithia was unconscious to the world and far from the raging storm. I rolled her onto her, using the blanket to keep her in place by winding it through the slates of the bed frame on either side of her body as a kind of makeshift strap. On her side, she would not drown if the water came down on her from above or she vomited again. If the water came from all around... then no position I placed her in would save her. I was just finishing when I heard a crash that was not the lightning overhead and the cries of the men that were below with us.

Sensible women did not rush to find the source of noise and shouts of alarm. I did.

There had been jars, great jars of stone, lashed to the fore and aft of the ship's hold, jars that held the water and food supplies, carefully sealed against sea water. One of the stone jars in the front of the ship had broken loose. Now, it rolled like Hera's carelessly tossed giant stone spindle across the planking, threatening both the men and the fragile wood of the hull. The rope that bound it must have frayed, though I knew they must check it regularly against just such an occurrence. In that moment, there was only one of the great stone jars loose but the broken rope was beginning to slide away from the rest and the one that was loose rotated drunkenly in the storm tossed hold. One man had already been crushed, staining the water with his blood as his friends tried to pull him clear, and I realized with a moment of absolute clarifying horror what would happen if the rest of the jars broke free and rolled. The next time the ship lifted they would roll back to the rear of the ship to join their brothers still secure there. And the ship would never settle level. We would sink like an arrow shot into a pond after fish.

"Oh please...!" It was a desperate, automatic prayer, but to whom? What god was the kind that claimed responsibility for stone jars? Even Poseidon, who claimed the sea, did not seem interested in stopping what he was doing.

I saw it all a frozen moment of time, a single, thick heartbeat. Horrible things so often happen in that single moment of time that seemed to stretch on forever. The world balances, I have been told, on single moments of time like that.

"The rope!" I shouted, though I couldn't have been the only one to prioritize the situation. Almost before the words were springing from my mouth, men were leaping forward to catch at the slipping ends of the ropes, to make themselves into human chains to hold the rest of the jars in their places against the ship's plunge.

"Stop the jar!" Men seemed to already be rushing to catch it by its handles, and if not haul it back, at least keep it from rolling further. I spun back to my room and snatched up the blanket over the other bed, almost tripping as I splashed forward into the water of the hull as I raced back to where the men with the jars were.

"I need a knife," I cried and found one thrust into my hands. It was a good sturdy fisherman's knife and I used it to cut the blanket into jagged stripes, trying not to cut myself as well in the chaotic bucking of the boat. Once I had the strips, I knotted the wool, which, soaked, pulled tight as we pulled the ends. Awkward, we bound the makeshift woolen rope through the handles of the upright jars, rewrapping the rope as well. Because of the missing jar, we had enough space to pull them all tightly together though they shifted alarmingly in their makeshift home. That still left the one that was free. If we had been on deck, I would have simply said to roll it over the side and into the water but we didn't have that choice.

Eventually we managed to wedge it awkwardly on the side of the ship and several of the men stayed to keep it there. It was a graceless, temporary solution but the only one we could come up with at the moment. The contents of the jar were utterly spoiled, adding their grain and soaked break to the bilge on the floor. Finally, I could turn my attention to the man that had been caught by the first break of the jars.

Little wonder I believed my mother when she told me I am a twisted thing. What kind of human was I that I looked to the wounded man last?

His name was Melanippus and his leg was badly broken. He was pale and shivering on the bench his friends had lifted him onto and his eyes were glassy, even as they darted to watch me. I gave him a smile that was meant to be reassuring but wondered how effective it was considering the way I probably looked, as dripping wet as if I had just come from the bottom of the ocean floor myself. He stayed calm for me though and he answered me when I asked him about his family. I told him he would see them again and he smiled and I knew he did not believe me. I was not sure I believed myself. The bone poked through the skin and, if infection set in, I was not sure anything I did would be strong enough. He was already feverish. I smoothed my hand over his brow and leaned low to study his face while I assured him that I had something to make the pain go away. His pupils were the same size and he was cognizant so it was only his leg and not his head that had been struck. He even managed a weak smile for me before I left him to again open my dark box and braced against the side of the chest to mix a potion for him. It was not quite what I had given Bithia, who roused a little when I leaned over to check on her, but something stronger with additions to fight poisoning of the blood. Carefully, I sealed everything back together when I was done and hid it away before carrying the cup back to him. Trying to shield the surface of my mixture from an invasion by seawater, I staggered like a drunk with the motion of the ship until one of the men came forward to catch my elbow and help steady me. Melanippus drank the mix down and I wondered why no one ever seemed to ask me what I gave them when I told them to drink something. My household back home had gotten used to drinking down my cures without a thought but here was a stranger who drank it just as easily and with as little compunction. What if I was poisoning him? Didn't it cross his mind to wonder? I watched it relax him and, when it the potion had enough time to soak in, I had his friends hold him down while I reset the bone as best as I could. Setting bones was honest work and I did not think it gave away too much of what I truly was. Even at the best of times I tried to hide my real abilities and I certainly didn't wish to see the men around me drawing away in horror. I had no desire to end up another Ariadne, stranded on an island and abandoned.

The splinting was easy after that and I laid a paste over the leg before I wrapped it in an already soaked cloth. Nothing was dry on the ship, least of all us. The bench was better than the bed for his leg because it was hard and straight and so we decided to leave him there, tied carefully in place while one of his friends stood watch over him.

I realized then that my joints felt suddenly weak and I would have sat down, except there was only water to sit in and it was cold. I was cold. And wet. For the first time I realized that the ship wasn't pitching all of us off of our feet. It still rocked and not at all peacefully but we did not rise in the water alarmingly as we had been. I looked to the hatch and one of the men climbed the ladder quickly to crack it open and peer out. Water pelted in but when it hit my face, there was no salt in its taste. Rain. The waves were beginning to stay on the outside of the boat and the rain could finally touch us. We were coming out of the storm. I drew in the first deep breath I had managed in what seemed a very long time. The man standing next to me smiled, but then he did an odd thing. He reached out and, very carefully, very gently, touched a bedraggled strand of my hair that snaked down the side of my arm. One by one the other men stepped forward to do the same and they did it in a strange reverent silence. I stood there and let them because it seemed the proper response even though I had no idea why they were doing it. Still not explaining, once they had each touched a strand of my hair, they went back to work bailing out the hull.

My mind was too tired even for my usual love of puzzles and so I set aside their strange ritual in my mind and left them to their work. Returning to my room, I checked on Bithia again. She slept on and, my mind was suddenly exhausted, as if it had been storing the feeling away until it was overwhelming before letting it free. Bithia's binding made her bed awkward and so instead of joining her, I lay down on the edge of the other one and closed my eyes, thinking to take just a moment of rest before getting up and seeing if there was anything else I could do to help.

Miserable, wet and cold, the sounds of the men manning the buckets in the background, I still fell asleep almost immediately.

There were no dreams for me in my sleep, too thick and sunken for even that. I did have a strange feeling steal over me as I slept though. It was warm and covering, a solid feeling of safety that, even asleep, I registered as strange – but welcome. Damp and hungry and worried, there was no questioning it, nothing alarming about it that roused me from my rest. I turned into that warmth and it made all things right. My sleep sank peaceful and deep sleep.

Eventually, I woke, slowly slipping up through the layers of sleep, not at all eager to leave the comfort and peace behind. My skin felt stiff over my bones, sticky and crusted where the salt had dried. My clothes were also damp and stiff, uncomfortable as they stuck to me. Strangely though, I was not cold. And - on the tail of that realization - I realized I was not alone either.

I was used to sleeping next to Bithia. It was for warmth and for simple comfort but even still half asleep I knew it was not Bithia next to me. It was not the fact that I remembered I had left her unconscious and tied to the bed -- that only came later. It was the scent and the heat.

The smell was salt. Storm. Ocean. Under that however it was - under that it was warm. A warm smell. It smelled warm the way rocks smelled after they had been basking all day in the sun. IT was the way oxen smelled when they came in from the fields with their coats hot to the touch and their movements lazy and content. Instinctively, I inhaled that smell, pressed my nose against it, wanting to absorb that heat into my own body so that I would never be cold again.

My movement woke me a bit more though. So I was aware that there were details to the warmth I pressed into. It was long. Large. Skin...

For a moment, I stopped breathing, frozen with the realization. I was against a body and there was no mistaking it for Bithia's. Or anyone female for that matter. It was entirely male, and even with a mind clouded with sleep and confusion and salt water, I knew who it was.

Ilium's favorite son.

The boy that had once sent me chests of treasure each year to remember him by.

He was no boy now.

And I had been forgotten in favor of a demigoddess.

So what was I doing on his ship? In his arms?

My eyes opened through the stiff lashes that had salt stuck to them and they felt dry and hot. I did not dare reach up a hand to rub at them, afraid to wake him. He was asleep against me and deeply so from the feel of the slow rise and fall of his chest, the feel of his breath against my throat. My own throat felt closed over and tight and it had nothing to do with the salt water of the storm.

What was he doing? What was he doing to me? My heart hurt as it had not since I given away Nemea and I felt the threat of tears in the edges of my eyes. I refused them, just as I denied the pain in my chest, forcing myself instead to focus on what was now. Forcing myself not to think of what I had once dreamed might be. Instead, I would be practical. I would be safe in my practicality.

I was turned on my side into him, pressed chest to chest, hip to hip, even my feet were tangled against his ankles. He was so tall, so huge that it brought me a moment of panic, a feeling of being overwhelmed. It quieted quickly however. He was asleep, nothing could happen to me while he slept. After I had that reassurance - and the realization that, as wrapped around me as he was, I wasn't going anywhere without waking him - I lay there for a long moment, wondering what I should do. I was still fully dressed. As tired as I was, I still could not have slept through my own rape. His thick arms were around me and his face rested against the side of mine. It distracted me, the feeling of his cheek against mine. The bristles of his short beard were rough against my skin but his exhales were warm, soothing in their slow rhythm. The restless, hurt circles my thoughts were traveling in slowed and relaxed when I concentrated on the brush of his breathing against me. I stared at the dark skin of his throat. I shouldn't be lying with him, letting him make me think how nice it was, how safe I felt, how warm and right-where-I-belong being this way felt. He had promised me this once before – and utterly ruined my whole world when he'd broken that promise. I should be shrieking to wake the storm again at finding myself in his arms now. I should be flailing and biting and clawing, driving him off with my fury. He had no right to touch me sweetly. I was not his betrothed anymore. The only thing left between us now was the violence of a man to a captured woman.

I did not want that kind of violence. The threat to my heart when he lay with me this way though seemed somehow worse, a danger I would not recover from. Whether I still belonged to another man or this kidnapping had ruined me for that, my future was not in this prince's arms. And I should hate him for showing me what I would never have instead of feeling such impossibly deep loss and sorrow to know it.

Once... this had been meant to be mine. I had treasured that dream. Once.

He sighed in his sleep and his arms tightened around me, pulling me closer against him before he settled again. It felt good, to be held like that, knowing there were no hidden secrets in sleep, just honest wants and desires. To feel desired honestly and not feel fear as a result. The bitter mixed with the sweet pain inside me.

For so long, I had stopped myself from thinking about it. It had hurt too much, too many broken dreams, too precious a future snatched away. I had thought I might have been happy in that life. I had truly liked the young man I had met that day in the olive groves. I liked this feeling now. I hadn't been scared of going to Ilium the way I was scared, so quietly, bone deep scared, of Phthia. I kept my eyes open, seeing nothing but bronzed skin where my face was pressed against him. I could have had this…. in a different world. I could not tell if I hated him or loved him for making me feel those lost dreams again.

I shouldn't have, but I must have slept again, surrounded by his scent, his warmth and the solid feel of him around me. I woke again, faster this time, when I felt him move against me. There was another voice in the room. From old habit, I had was lax at waking, and I stayed that way. Being caught awake could be dangerous to me now. Hushed voices came to my ears.

"Thracia, he thinks. Not too far off course."

The body next to mine stirred, and I was surprised by how carefully he moved, easing me softly down to the mattress as he let me go and sat up.

"Cities?" His quiet voice was rough at its edges with sleep and tight with swallowed salt. He had not been below deck during the storm.

"Not yet. Phereclus is looking for a natural harbor or river mouth we can pull into for repairs."

"Good. We don't need any company." The bed moved as his weight left it. A long pause, the sound of fabric. Then silence and I felt eyes on me. I didn't react. Canvas parted and footsteps splashed away from me. For a long time I laid still, thinking about what had just happened. Behind me, I heard Bithia quietly trying to fight her way free of the blanket and then her own soft footsteps went to the canvas, paused, and went out as well. I waited until

I was sure she was gone, then sat up. His heat lingered on my skin and I kept my feet out of the water, shuffling myself sideways on the bed to the chest, where I dug out the comb. I was patiently, slowly, working it through the salt-encrusted tangles of my hair when Bithia came back. With my head bowed and my hair in the way, I did not have to look at her.

I was not sure how I felt. The rage I knew I should though was not there and the sadness was so quiet and deep I did not dare touch it. Bithia was painfully silent and I could hear her feet moving restlessly. In mercy, I asked calmly:

"Are you feeling better?"

"A little," she answered. I realized it probably hadn't been kind of me to remind her. I just hadn't known what else to say.

"I was worried."

"I was too." Her voice was soft, almost silent and young. Oh, my poor Bithia... She'd been awake to see me in a man's arms then. I tipped my head to look at her through the red and brown fall of my hair. She looked guilt-sick and miserable, probably thinking she had slept through my cries for help when Ilium had taken me. Except I didn't ever cry for help. And Ilium's son... Ilium's son had done much worse to me just now than break the seal of my body.

"Nothing happened," I told her, voice low and calm. Very, very sure of it. I gestured to the bed, which, damp, still would have showed signs if it had. I was not so innocent of the way men were with women. I had brothers who enjoyed women. Often.

She sat down in a rush next to me and put her arms around me. I lost track of which sections of hair I had combed and which ones I had not yet, my careful concentration that had kept me from thinking too closely about anything but the safety of combing hair broken.

"I woke up and that -- that brute was all but swallowing you with his body." Her voice was tight and shaking. I traded my distracting concentration on my hair to distract myself with concentrating on her. "I thought -- I thought I'd failed you. That he'd raped you. Damn him for never treating you as you deserve! Troy is nothing but a den of pigs and barbarians!" She railed the last in an insulted way that told me she was starting to feel better.

My lips twisted up wryly at their edges and I stroked her dark hair.

"Nothing happened," I assured her, soothing when I should have been the one in hysterics and in need of reassurance. "He must have just been tired and wanted to sleep somewhere that wasn't hard as a rock."

Bithia sniffed.

"He should have slept above deck. Or on a bench. You were in the bed first."

Given our situation as captives, it was so impossibly irrelevant that it made me laugh and I held her as I did because I had the fear inside that if I did not laugh, I would cry. And at least the laughter was over quickly. She pulled back from me to look at my face, searching carefully and I worried about what she might see.

"Still," her voice was firm as she simply took the comb from me and began to work it through my hair. "It is far too familiar of him. It makes him think things that he shouldn't. You can't let it happen again. He's just a man. They all think the same things." She lectured me like a nursemaid and I patiently let her, glad to think of practical things. Bithia didn't understand the real damage he had done to me.

He had left my body intact, but he had made me feel safe and warm for the first time in a very, very long time. I was not sure how I was supposed to survive that.

XIII.

The pilot found a small river and our ship crept up that flow until a sandy turn in its shallow bend gave us a place to put the ship aground. Bithia and I were lifted ashore and an awning was set up at a comfortable distance from the ship to give us a place to rest. The sand was warm under my toes and I was surprised by how important fresh air untainted by damp was, by how important I suddenly found green, growing things to be. The canvas over our heads stank of damp and wet but the sun was persistent and dried it, just as it also dried Bithia and I as we sat in the grass and sand near the shore. For the first time I saw our ship in daylight and it at once looked larger than I had thought it was and yet somehow more fragile with its red painted hull and its unblinking eyes near the long curling prow of its nose. I thought of how it had saved us and almost joined us in death. Helplessly, I loved that little ship and its thin sides.

The men were divided up into teams and I watched curiously from the rise on the shore I sat on. Some were sent further up the river for clearer water, some inland for food, and the rest divided into work forces. The main one of those was sent to create a mast to replace the one we had lost. There was an extra sail below deck but giant masts were not so easily stored. I watched in fascination as another group of men began to move over the sides of the ship, patching and repairing as they went. The pace was leisurely. No one came to shout at anyone to move faster, to hurry. My kidnapping was apparently not on a schedule. I couldn't tell if that made me feel better or not. In the end, I didn't suppose it mattered. It was already too late. I had been abducted -- gone in the company of men for more than enough time for anything they wanted to do to me to have already happened. I wrapped my arms loosely around my ankles and rested my chin on my upraised knees as I watched the activity in front of me. It did not matter that I had yet to be touched. To anyone in my family, to anyone in the world, I was now compromised. Any child I bore in the next nine months could belong to one of my captors and no man would touch me until well after that time period if he expected any child he had by me to be unquestioned as his.

Abducted women were not uncommon, especially during times of war or raiding. From the lowest hovel to the queen of a nation, no single woman was ever entirely safe. To the strong went the spoils and captive women were nothing more than golden jars or household idols - things of value to be carried off to foreign lands and made to serve there, until you were ransomed or your family won you back -- or you were taken again on yet another raid by yet another stranger. It was not seen as the woman's fault but rather the fault of the men that were supposed to protect her. They had failed her, left her undefended. Often the children born after those kidnappings were adopted into the family of either the kidnappers or the men that came to reclaim the woman that had once been theirs. Helen of Sparta herself had been a kidnap victim until her brothers had rescued her. Rumor said she had born Theseus a daughter. It certainly did not diminish her beauty or value to other men. And yet...

And yet women were not golden pots or gods of stone. We were flesh and blood and hearts and souls, and I could not imagine that being ripped away from the safety and security of your family and used by the men that had done so -- I could not imagine that any woman returned to her people after that – or who lived out the rest of her life in her captor's house – would not be changed inside. Golden pots washed clean no matter what foul mess you poured into them and left no sign of what they had once carried. Women, I thought, did not lose the sign, or the memory, of what had been poured into them so easily.

Strangely, as common as Achaean raids had become, I had never seriously thought that I would be a war prize, one of the lawiaiai. I wound my long fingers around my ankles tighter and watched the work on the shore in front of me and wondered why anyone would want to claim Eetion's over tall, over thin, odd-looking, forgotten daughter.

I wondered how long it would take before I found what it was that my captor wished to pour into the golden jar of me.

"You should drink something." Bithia settled down to sit next to me, practical and solid. I smiled weakly as I took the offered cup, wooden, not golden, and sipped at the water inside. She moved her small feet in the sand and for a long time we said nothing. Perhaps we were both thinking the same thoughts. Bithia squinted upward.

"You should be wearing your veil. The sun will make you freckle."

It was an old argument and I smiled tiredly at it. Apparently, we were going to pretend things were normal. I wasn't going to disagree with that.

"It's probably still wet. I would drown."

She shot me a look and hid a smile. It made me relax little as I looked back at our little red ship. For a very long time, Bithia was silent next to me but by the way her shoulders kept shifting minutely, I could tell that she was thinking of something, trying to decide whether she should say it or not, or perhaps just how to say it. I sat patiently, pretending not to notice and let her wrestle with it.

"Could you – " she stopped and I watched her from the corners of my eyes as her own skipped backward toward our awning refuge. "Could you - stop them?" She would not look at me.

I exhaled silently and did not look back at what she was. My mother's box. Or rather, mine now. I had carried it when I had been brought ashore and it rested, half hidden, in our shelter.

"I could," I answered after a long minute -- for I could. What was in that box could paralyze a man, kill him, drive him insane or send him off into forever dreams until he died of starvation rather

309

than wake. With what was in that box, I could turn the men in front of us into beasts, at least in their minds, or I could make them see gods. And the horrible thing that lived inside me had already thought of that, long before Bithia had. With the right time, and if I could find the right ingredients, I could poison the very river that sparkled in the sunlight in front of us and send a plague seeping downstream that would bloat and boil anyone that drank its waters until they died in agony, laid low by Apollo's arrows. Or rather by my own, just as invisible and effective as the god's.

My mother's legacy. For the first time I wondered who *she* had learned from.

And how my father could have ever borne to father child after child upon her.

Bithia loved me. She was very good at not hurting me. So I pretended I did not see the way her eyes widened with horror when she quickly looked back at the box. Because it was not what was in the box that terrified her -- it was me.

And she did not even know everything I was capable of.

"But what would we do afterward?" I said mildly. I swept a long hand to indicate the ship, the river, the men. I loved Bithia. Little matter if I had to hide parts of myself to make that easier. "I heard the talk. There is no settlement nearby but there might be bandits. Even if we did find a city, who is to say its leaders would do anything to us other than what we can expect now?"

She nodded with a slight frown and I wondered if she had been serious or not, whether she thought she had been serious or not. For myself, I had found, the easier it became, the more reluctant I was to consider murder. Even my captors, who, short of almost seeing me drown - and to be fair they had almost joined me – had been considerate and surprisingly polite.

"What about the lawagetas?" Bithia asked, voice lower, and it was my turn to be surprised. It was a hard hatred I heard in her voice. It made me turn and look at her. She was looking fixedly at the ship, though, avoiding my eyes.

"Ilium's warlord?" It was a ridiculous thing to use his title when I had known his name almost my whole life but still, I could not bring myself to say it. It was as if, in saying it, I would loose something into the world again -- and I did not want it loosed. Not ever again. Bithia said his name instead.

"Hector. Could you kill Hector?" And, despite the fact I knew she feared my skills, she looked me in the eye when she asked it. That, more than my answer, made me pause for a very long time.

"I could," I finally answered slowly, watching her. "But he is my protector now. If he dies, I am fair game to every man in the area."

Strong enough to take me from my own protectors, he would protect me now until someone stronger came along. While he had no obligation to protect me from himself, it was his duty and a measure of his reputation as a warrior how well he guarded me against others. That was the way of the world I lived in. If I killed him, there would be no protector and every other man would be allowed to try to take me. I understood enough to know that I might not wish to survive that myself. If I went on nothing other than common sense, it was better to be the prey of one man over the prey of many. As prey went, so far I had been treated better than most women in my position would have been by now. Bithia frowned and looked away.

Maybe she thought I was making excuses -- that I could not kill him because I did not want to.

Maybe she was right.

But I would rather think about Bithia's emotions than my own, so I lowered my head, bringing my face closer to hers, and scooted a bit closer so that our hips bumped.

"You hate him."

She glared at the trees further inland.

"He hurt you." Her voice was just as low as mine but it was full of emotion. "He said he would take care of you and he forgot you when it was convenient for him. He made a promise." She was emphatic about that. "To you. And he broke it. And you stopped laughing. Your smiles weren't real anymore. No one cared that you'd been hurt. Not your father, not your brothers, not even your mother noticed and she enjoys you in pain. They were all full of the insult to their name, to their house, to themselves. While you were wilting inside like a flower brought in out of the sun. And no one cared. Not even you!" She accused fiercely, even if she still wouldn't look at me. "I had to watch you die while your body kept moving. He deserves to die for doing that. I don't care who he is."

It was a viciousness I had never heard in her before. I knew she had come from a very hard place before she had come to me. She had only spoken of it once but it was in all the things she hadn't said, all the details she'd glossed over. I knew that her love for me was fierce because of it. She defended me like a lion with its last cub, still holding herself guilty for never being able to stop my mother. It never mattered how many times I told her otherwise or pointed out that even my father left me to my mother's devices, she blamed herself. Bithia would protect me against the whole world if she were able. I had just never realized how deeply that fierceness went.

"You should hate him but you don't. So I hate him for both of us."

I didn't hate him? No. She was right. I didn't. I wasn't sure what I felt for Ilium's favored son at this moment but it was not hate. Gentle, I reached out and put my arm around her waist, drew her, resisting slightly, so that her head rested on my shoulder. After a long moment, she relaxed but I could tell she was still angry. I rested the side of my cheek against the top of her head.

"I will not harm him," I finally told her softly. "Nor will you."

"He will break you again. And I will kill him."

"No," I said just as softly. "You will not."

And even though she was silent, I knew she would not disobey me, not for anything, not even my own death. The way she loved me bound her to my word more strongly than her own will. It was something I had known for years and had never taken lightly. I was careful how I used it. I used it now.

We sat in silence for a long time and, on the beach, one of the parties returned. They had a deer carried on a makeshift pole between them and, when they were closer, I saw hares as well. The baskets they'd left with were full now as well. We would certainly not go hungry tonight. The workman on the ship put aside their tools to wander over to see, and there was a flurry of hand motions as they talked, indicating stories being told. Eventually, they divided up into other groups with the food, for cooking and preparing no doubt. I watched with mild curiosity as three of the men approached us, trotted over the dunes to where Bithia and I were. The one in the lead was grinning and he offered me a long wooden bowl.

"They found these. Last of the season. We thought - " he looked back at the other two who were smiling as well and, oddly, reached out and touched a strand of my hair. "We thought you should have them."

Pleased and puzzled and strangely flattered, I took the bowl from him, full of blackberries. Another of the men stepped forward to leave us another full water skin. The last shyly set down a handful of tiny unbroken shells and didn't say anything at all. We all hesitated over this strange gift giving and then I said 'thank you' and it seemed to be what everyone wanted because they nodded happily and trotted back down the beach to rejoin the others.

Bithia looked at my suspiciously as I reached out to pick up some of the tiny shells, thinking what a pretty necklace they would make.

"They're acting like the servants in Thebe," she said. "What exactly did you do to them while I was sick?"

I exhaled an amused sound and scooped up the shells to pour into the lap of my skirt.

"I don't know what you're talking about." I offered her a share of the berries. It didn't pacify her but it did keep her from asking questions for a little while.

They brought us dinner in the same fashion when it was ready, along with some blankets they had rinsed out and dried in the sun. I was getting used to the hair touching. It was always the same, hesitant, strangely reverent gesture, just the slightest finger tip to the edge of a strand of my hair. I thought I was beginning to understand what was going on. Maybe. It was... odd and I wasn't sure how I was supposed to react. Being grateful for their gifts seemed to be enough for them though and I did notice that we were given the choicest pieces of meat and some of the last horse bread that was left over and unspoiled by the salt water. The other parties came back and after a while I grew aware that we were not alone anymore. There were guards appearing silently in the growing dusk, taking up positions around our shelter, while staying far enough off to give us a measure of privacy. When Bithia and I went downstream a bit to wash, some of them followed and stood facing away to again give us privacy.

I wondered if they were here to keep me safe or to keep me from running again. Bithia apparently was thinking the same thing because she muttered:

"Too many to bite them all."

It made me feel like laughing, something I hadn't expected to do for a long time, and I followed her back to the covering of our shelter, glad of the sun-warmed blankets now that the sun had gone down. We folded them over and under us and the sand underneath was not an uncomfortable bed. I should have felt frightened or been kept awake with worry about my situation but almost the moment my lay down, I fell asleep.

When I woke, the moon was bright and high overhead. I never slept a full night unless I was sick or recovering. Bithia slumbered peacefully next to me, and I lay there for a while, looking out the opening of the awning at the night sky. The stars were very bright. I traced their familiar patterns, letting the stories they represented wash over me while I finished waking. Finally, restless, I slipped out of bed, careful not to let the cooler night air under the covers to wake Bithia. I often wandered in the night. It helped clear my mind and usually afterward I could sleep for a little while longer. Tonight, I had more on my mind than usual but I wasn't sure I wanted to think about any of it. If I lived in the moment, I could be calm, but I had a great fear in me that if I looked too closely at my future, I might fall apart at how large and nebulous it seemed. Concentrate on the grain of sand and ignore the shore.

The night was quiet as I stepped out from under the shelter of our awning, and paused to let the night fill my senses. The river was a peaceful sound and small things stirred in the night in the forest behind me. The night air had chilled and, outside of the shared warmth of our shelter, it filled my lungs with its crisp bite as I inhaled. With all the moonlight, my eyes hardly needed to adjust at all to the darkness and I looked around, picking out the almost hidden shapes of the guards that stood watch over us but did not approach our tent. I wrapped my arms around myself, cupping my elbows with my hands and pressed my lips together, toes dug into the cool of the sand.

What did they want? What did *he* want?

I would have to ask him if I wanted the

317

answer and, despite the disadvantage of not knowing, I was reluctant. Asking him felt as if it would give him even more power over me and he already had too much of that. I could admit to myself that I was less afraid of what he would do to my physically than I was of the danger to my still wounded heart. Physically, he had been careful with me so far but I knew from experience my heart did not merit the same treatment from him. He already held my fate in his hands, the thought of asking him for it made me feel even more vulnerable.

An owl called in the woods behind me and I almost shivered before my training took over and held me still. Athena. Not since I had seen her mad laughing face in Ilium's sacred grove had I felt she was what was claimed of her. Wisdom? Then why was she a goddess of war? Practicality? Then why were all the stories of her about her jealousy? She had lied when she had told man what she was. Whatever she had been when that stone had seen her face and reflected it forever back was what she truly was. Perhaps more than any other god, because of that she frightened me.

I turned my feet toward the river instead of into the woods when I began to walk. This far from home, I thought to stay in open ground anyway. Who knew what lived and roamed in the darkness of the enclosing trees? The worse I would run into down by the water was a river god and they had never bothered pay attention to me before. I could not see one starting now.

I was aware of being followed. I had expected no less. One of the guards that had been standing near the trees, no doubt, and I could hear his footfalls, almost silent at a distance from me. I was not afraid of his company. Perhaps we could both use the walk and he certainly had nothing else to do. As long as their lawagetas claimed me as his own, I was safe from everyone else on the group. Strange, to think being a war prize actually made you safer...

The river wound slowly back away from the sea and I followed it, in no hurry, stopping when something caught my eye to examine or explore it. I began to gather things in my hands. Little rocks that had shone in the moonlight, small, white flowers that had not been open during the day, an herb or two I recognized and had to pick up from sheer compulsion of never letting a potential pass me by. Eventually, I found a patch of mint and settled down in it, far enough from the river to be alerted if anything came out of it. The fragrant herb released its wild smell into the cool night and I rubbed some between my fingers as I looked up at the stars that moved through the night sky. I had been taught to read the messages written in those stars but tonight, I was not sure I wanted to know what they said. How long could I get away with thinking on of the moment before I was forced to confront the nebulous future? Tonight, at least, I was determined to try.

My guard approached and it was warning enough that he did not remain at a polite distance. I knew who he was then and my stomach clenched. I went very still, confronted with what I had been trying very hard not to think about all this time. He was very huge and dark as he approached, blotting out the stars in the sky.

He settled down in front of me, sitting as I was. I had remembered that he had dark eyes but in the moonlight they were black. As I watched, wary of what came next, he leaned forward and opened his hand to me in obvious offering. I saw the tiny black pebbles I had seen along the shore as I had walked here. My eyes went to his face and he looked steadily back at me. I thought... strangely, I thought he looked tired, even though there was nothing in his face to make me think that. Gingerly, I reached out and touched the sleek, black stones in his hand and he simply held them steady for me. I took one, because it seemed the right thing to do, and as I drew my hand away he moved his, just a little, but enough so that the tips of his fingers brushed my retreating wrist and heel of my hand. It sent a surprising heat skittering up my arm and, strangely, I again had to resist the urge to shiver. Instead, I looked at him then, truly looked at him for the first time since this had all started.

He had grown, this half-boy, half-man I had once met. He had been tall for a boy. He was huge for a man. All height and strength. His forearm alone, now relaxed across one thigh would have easily fit both of mine inside it and his shoulders were the shoulders of a warrior who carried armor and shield and sword and spear and could use them all. He had grown into his nose, though, perhaps, not his ears. The breeze from the river blew at his dark curling hair. The hand that held the pebbles was huge and long fingered and I could see the scars from weapons handling on the inside of it where the rocks did not cover his skin. He would swallow a woman if he drew her against him, I thought, and then remembered that Bithia had used the same words when she'd spoken of finding us on the bed together.

What was I supposed to do, confronted by him for the first time since my kidnapping? Should I scream? Curse at him? Should I turn my face from him and ignore him? My heart was in none of those responses even if he deserved them all.

Reaching out, I laid the tip of my finger against one of the scars on his palm. When he did not move, I very carefully traced its white path down to where the pebbles buried it. I felt him relax. It was just a quiet, soft thing, a barely there lowering of his shoulders in the dark, but I felt it all the same. When I raised my eyes he still looked tired but not so tired. What was I doing?

What were *we* doing?

"Why?" I asked softly, almost afraid to let the word out into the air. I was not even sure which of my 'whys' I asked, or if I even wanted an answer. He looked down at the pebbles in his hand, the way my finger still rested on them. Then he looked back up at me and his voice was just as low. Just as soft and unsure about letting the words out into the night.

"Because... I think I need you, Andromache."

I drew my hand back and he let me, dark eyes on me as I frowned at him. It was only later that I realized how strange it was that, instead of accusing him of lying, I corrected him instead.

"You're wrong."

It hung in the air between us for a forever inhale. Then, reaching out, he gently added his pebbles to the collection of my own things that I had put into the lap of my skirt. He was careful not to crush the flowers.

"No." He shook his head and his voice was easier, deep and warm with currents. Where his beard didn't cover his lips, I thought I almost saw the small whisper of a smile, there and gone so quickly I wasn't sure. "I think I'm more sure of it now than I was before."

I shot him the look before I realized I should probably be playing a bit more diplomatically. Of course, that probably meant I shouldn't have corrected him either.

"That's ridiculous. You can't need someone you don't know. And I am not the only woman in the entire world either." My hand moved, pale in the moonlight. "Go find someone else."

He grinned then and I saw white teeth in his

dark face and the way, under the dark hair, one of his cheeks indented.

"You can't just tell me to go away," he argued calmly with me, as if we were disagreeing over the price of dye in the market. "And I can't find someone else. I don't want to find anyone else."

"Hector," I said his name before I realized it and was shocked when it did not wound me. It did make me pause though and regroup my thoughts. Talking to my captor was not supposed to be so easy. So natural feeling. More calmly, firmly, I told him: "Don't be foolish. You already found someone else. That is why I'm marrying Peleus' son. That is why you're supposed to be sailing to Sparta. That is why we are *not*," -- I emphasized the word -- "supposed to be sitting here, together, tonight."

The laughter had faded from his eyes but he did not look away from me.

"Is that what you'd prefer? Would you rather be sailing to Phthia than sitting here with me tonight, Andromache?" He reached out and took one of the flowers from my skirt before looking back at me and there was so much in his eyes that I was sure he did not want to be there. I saw pain and I saw vulnerability in that darkness and he had a right to neither. And yet, it made me want to answer him honestly.

"It's not my choice."

His eyes narrowed as he looked at me.

"That's not what I asked."

"No," I agreed, quietly, and I could all but feel the jostle of who we really were inside our bodies. "But it is my answer."

He looked down at the flower, so impossibly small in his fingers, and his brows came down. It was a long moment and then his head moved, as if nodding to himself.

"All right," he raised his dark eyes back to meet mine. "Would you like to keep sitting here, with me, for a little while longer, Andromache?"

I knew what I should say. I knew what he deserved to hear from me. It warred inside me with what I wanted. He sat silently and waited. In the end, being sincerely asked for the first time, I gave the only answer my heart would let me.

"...yes."

XIV.

I sat in front of our shelter the next day and rolled over in my head what had happened the night before. We had not talked after Hector had asked if I wanted to stay with him. Instead, we had sat in silence, watching the moon reflecting off the river. It had felt strangely comfortable. When I had finally risen to return, he had helped me carry my treasures back to my tent and this morning, when I had woken and stepped out from under the awning, I had found a small woven basket, empty and waiting for me. For my collection.

It had reminded me of the chests I used to receive every year from Ilium. No -- not from Ilium. From Hector.

He was gone when I stepped outside into the morning light. The men that brought me breakfast told me that the right kind of tree to use as a mast had been found yesterday and cut. Today, it was being trimmed and prepared. Hector was overseeing the work. If all went well and the gods ignored us, we would sail tomorrow. It would be an unweathered, unseasoned mast but one that should be enough to get us where we wanted to go. To Troy.

And then what?

What would happen to me after I reached Ilium?

Last night I had not asked and it had not been offered. In my mind, I was still turning over from what had been said last night – and from what had not been said. I looked at it from every angle I could think of and it reflected back a dozen different possibilities, all of which worried me. All of which came back to the fact that Hector had used the word 'need'.

Strangely, now, I wasn't afraid that he would use my body for pleasure or children. I did not think he would hurt me physically. But he sounded -- need sounded like the kind of word you used when you were determined, when you were not going to let go of something. Someone. Need sounded very powerful and very stubborn and deep down it scared me so much more than if he had used the word 'love'.

Need did not sound like the kind of thing that would ransom me back to my father or Phthia.

That frightened me. Not that I would not still go to Phthia or my father's house, though that should have been what I worried over. Instead I felt a smaller fear and it was closer to my heart. Too close. For, deep down inside of me, I wanted someone to hold on to me, to be determined not to let go. I yearned for the security of that feeling. Hector could not be the one to do that for me though. I had believed in him once already and my trust had been wrong. It had cost me more than I was willing to admit to, or even look at too closely. I would not make the same mistake again. Helen had not vanished from the world and the reason I had been abandoned the first time was still valid now. There was no future for me down the road to

Ilium, not anymore.

I would have to tell him so. Surely my abduction had been the decision of a moment. Now, with more time to think, I was sure he would see reason.

Decision made, I stood up, dusting sand from my skirt. It was simple. I would explain things, he would see the sense of it, things would be set right. Last night had been dangerous. To me, to my heart that wanted to believe in him, that had once dreamed of him. I couldn't let that continue. I knew myself too well and the longing in me to believe in Hector was too great despite knowing better and having lived the proof of my folly for years. He had listened to me last night though and it gave me hope that he would listen to me again now.

It felt good to be listened to.

One of my guards was Cebriones and he sat in the shade with his back against a tree, carving forearm length pegs for the ship. Though it had been years since I had seen him before just last night, he did not frighten me, perhaps more because of than despite the scars on his face. He was the one I approached with my plan. He looked up when I stopped in front of him.

"Where is your lawagetas?"

He smiled at me.

"Your little maid will be furious," he warned. I pressed my lips together and told myself that I should not to feel like a child about to get away with something their parent would never approve of.

"Bithia is down at the river," I pointed out and he set down his carving in the pile next to him and stood up. We were almost at eye level. There was a glint of mischief in his eyes before he bowed his head.

"Then we'd better make our escape while we can."

He led me into the trees and I picked up the hem of my skirt and followed him, bare feet silent. Even in the daylight, the wood were shadowed and swallowing. I felt the shiver down my back as those branches closed off the sun. My mind didn't need much opportunity to show me how much my future had suddenly become like these woods, trackless and tangled. I hoped that Athena's owls did not nest there as they did here.

Sooner than I had expected, we came out of the trees and I could see where we had only actually cut through a small curve in them, for the river was still visible to the side of me a little way away. I followed my guide down a slight slope to see where a long tree had been felled and dragged into the open ground, men busy stripping it of branches and bark. The smell of sap and crushed grass filled my nose. Most of the repair work on the boat had already been done and I wished I had asked to come here earlier so I could watch the progress here too. Bithia and I were too important a trophy to let do any actual work and as much as I didn't mind the stillness, I felt much better with something to keep my mind occupied.

I spotted Hector before Cebriones did.

He was standing to one side of the tree, working the other end of a long saw to take a thick branch off at its base. His upper body was bare and there were chips of wood and bark on his skin and in his darkly curling hair. There were bruises, several days old and ugly, over his ribs on one side too. The man he was working with said something and he laughed and even from this distance I saw his teeth flash white. The branch fell away with a thud and, as if he had been waiting for that, Hector lifted his head and turned it to find me where I stood with my escort. As if he'd known I was there all along.

He said something to the man he had been working with, setting down his end of the saw and his long legs swallowed the distance between us.

"Cebriones." He nodded at the other man, who simply smiled and ducked away, going back the way we had just come. I felt a moment of sympathy for him if it was to face Bithia's wrath. Then Hector stepped closer to me and I forgot about Cebriones or Bithia as I tilted my head to look up at him. He blocked out the sun and it lit the edges of his darkness but I could see his face.

"You're standing very close to me," I observed, which was not at all how I had intended to start the conversation. He grinned and lowered his head. Even in sunlight, his eyes were dark.

"I like standing close to you." I was surprised by how soft his voice was. If I had reached out my hand, even just a little, I could have laid it against his chest. I could smell the sap and sweat on him and, below that, the sun warmed smell that I was coming to recognize as his and his alone. It warmed the air between us.

"Why?" Again, not what I had meant to say and his smile softened.

"I like the way you smell," he told me, with a bit of rumble in the back of his voice. "I like watching you tip your head to me. I like the way the light catches in your eyes like honey. I like the way you don't step back when I step close." Again, the smile. "I like the way it makes me feel."

"You don't stand close to Bithia," I pointed out, though in truth I'd never seen them close enough to count as even being in the same area. He chuckled.

"She doesn't smell like saffron."

I tried to send him a chiding look but it was hard not to smile. I had forgotten our long-ago banter and had not realized how I had missed it until just this moment. Then I realized what we were doing and shook my head and raised a hand in front of me. The tips of my fingers brushed his bare skin with the move and I drew them back, aware of the way his heat lingered there despite the loss of contact.

"You need to stop this."

He didn't pretend to misunderstand. There

was no insult to my intelligence in him. He just shook his head.

"No."

I felt my brows coming down again.

"You're not making any sense," I told him, as if he was a small child refusing to understand. "Whatever you are thinking about me, you need to stop. There is no reason for what you're doing and you need to send me home."

His eyes squinted and he looked away from me for a moment, gazing off into the forest with his brows low over his eyes. In no way did it take away his surrounding presence from me.

"The sailors think you're their good luck charm," he said after a long moment of silence, looking back down at me. "They think the ship would have sunk but that you stopped it somehow. They say you saved Melanippus' life and possibly his leg too. I've seen them touching your hair to rub that luck onto themselves."

It was a little embarrassing and a little bit warming to hear it. I had suspected something like that but I hadn't been sure. Not that I had actually done anything, but truthfully, it hardly mattered what I thought. It was what the sailors thought that mattered to them. Feeling a bit awkward and knowing he had a point to what he was telling me, I nodded. His eyes changed color, black to brown and I thought I saw that tiredness in his eyes even though I could not say why I thought it was there.

"What if you were everyone's good luck?

What if everyone that saw you, everyone you talked to or came in contact with, even your own parents and brothers and sisters, thought of you that way? Everywhere you went, every time you spoke, everything you did was considered a part of the fact that you were good luck. Every day of your life from the time you were a child until today. How would you feel?"

He asked it softly and as I looked up at him I understood what he was telling me. Who had not heard of Hector, hero of Ilium? Gods loved and undefeated? Man-slaughtering Hector. Hector, Breaker of Horses. Hector of the Flashing Helm. Hector, Defender of Sacred Ilium. Everywhere it was prophesied that Troy would never fall as long as Hector stood to protect it. What did it do to a man? To be the good luck of an entire country? Day after day, year after year...

I could not help it. I reached up and gently touched his cheek and his eyes lidded for a moment as I did so. His breath whispered soft against my palm. No wonder I thought he was tired. I was surprised he had not run away from the responsibility as Athens' vaunted Theseus had. Or broken under it the way Heracles' mind had.

"I'm sorry," I murmured and he smiled a little and shook his head. I noticed he was careful not to dislodge my hand. I also noticed I had not pulled away the way I knew I should have. The touch of his exhales sent their warmth all the way down my arm and curled inside my chest.

"I was born for it," his answer was neither bitter nor resigned nor proud. It was simply fact to him.

"What does that have to do with me?" It was an honest question. I understood, perhaps only a little, what he had wanted me to understand, but I did not see how it was an answer to my first statement. Which was that this, taking me, keeping me, was pointless. He reached up to curve the fingers of his hand around mine as it rested against his cheek.

"Do you remember the day we met?" His question was serious, as was his face, but I could not help narrowing my own eyes at him and giving him a reproving look. He laughed then and it was soft and warm and, on seeming impulse, he turned his head and pressed a kiss to my palm. The strange way it tingled distracted me enough so that I almost missed the way his voice sounded when he murmured low: "And you wonder why I need you."

Before I could begin to protest again, or even deal with the odd way his touch had sent something shivery and hot and cold down from my palm to my elbow, he continued.

"You had no idea who I was. In fact, I think you hoped I was a mercenary or raider. You even promised I could be your beekeeper. You didn't know I was a prince or even my name, much less my reputation, but you climbed down from that olive tree and treated me as if I was important to you. Just as any other human being in the world and nothing special except that you had decided I was simply because."

"You did have horses," I murmured. "That whistled."

He laughed again and leaned closer so that the curling hair at his forehead almost touched mine. Somehow our fingers had become entangled. I wanted... I wanted my face to touch his. But I stood very still so that it wouldn't.

"Andromache. My tree nymph. You didn't care who I was, you just wanted my story. And I have never felt so important, just for being me, before or since. That is why I wanted you then for myself. And that is why I want you now. When you look at me, all you see is who I am. I'm not letting you go."

He was so sure, so determined and unbreakable. I think if anyone else had said something like that I would not have believed them capable. I believed him though. His determination didn't scare me, what did was that I wanted, needed, him to be that sure, that determined. Yet the second I trusted that – him – I would open myself all over again for the pain when he forgot about me again. I couldn't face that pain. Not a second time. If there had been a god I could have prayed to for help, I would have but there was no one. For, oh, how I wanted...

"My lady."

It was Bithia's call and close by too. I shut my eyes because I could not seem to pull away from the darkness of his eyes. I could not bring myself to draw away from him. I wanted...

"There you are!" Bithia sounded as if she had lost me somehow and was now proudly reclaiming me. I turned my head and opened my eyes finally and I felt the way the tip of his nose grazed my cheek as I turned my face away from his. When had we gotten so close? His hand continued to hold mine. Bithia's face was pleased and smiling but the look in her eyes would have killed the man so close to me if she'd had any say in the matter. I wished she had not found me, and yet I was so relieved that she had I could have hugged her. Cebriones stood back near the woods and looked apologetic. I drew away from Hector and he let me, though his fingers slid against my palm as he released me and his eyes followed me, not Bithia, as I drew away and she approached.

"I was so worried." She was acting the effusive, bubbly maid she so often played in others company. "I came back and you were gone! I thought a wild animal had dragged you away until Cebriones was kind enough to tell me otherwise."

She was overplaying the act a bit and I shot her a look that said as much. She was deeply in the 'innocent, concerned' servant role however and pretended she didn't notice.

"Of course if I had known you were with the lawagetas, I wouldn't have worried." It was certainly safer for Bithia to hide the way she really felt about Hector but it was still hard for me to keep from giving anything away with a reaction she was overplaying it so completely.

"You are right," I told her, voice nothing but conciliatory and it was her turn to give me an odd look. I slipped my arm through hers. "I am tired. I think I will go back and lie down for a while." I did not look at Hector. I was not sure what I would see in his eyes if I did and I needed time to think without their darkness crowding my thoughts.

I could have found my way back on my own but Cebriones accompanied Bithia and I, seeing us safely back to our shelter before reclaiming his spot at a distance and going back to his carving. In my mind I twisted over what had been said. What Hector sought was not a small thing. Acceptance, being loved just as you were? Maybe most people were loved unconditionally by their family and friends. Maybe they had nothing dark or threatening inside themselves. I did though. And Hector did too. To be accepted - cared for - just as you were without hiding the things that were ugly or broken, without needing to? It was no small thing. How could I pretend that I did not understand exactly what it was Troy's blooded many times over warlord craved from me?

Deep down, I craved it too.

I did lie down after I returned to our shelter. The men had offered to move it onto the deck of the boat once the repairs were done, but I had declined. Poor Bithia did not need her stomach rebelling against being inside her any earlier than necessary.

I rolled onto my stomach and pressed my face into my folded arms and thought about being accepted just as I was. I thought about being desired to the exclusion of any other. I thought about being held with a determination that didn't let go or grow tired. I exhaled and thought I might as well dream about climbing rainbows or growing wings. Things like that were easy to claim but personal experience said they were not so easy to see through. Eventually, I dozed.

I woke when Bithia quietly entered the shelter and sat down next to me. Slitting a single eye open, I watched her very deliberately folding a blanket. *Very* deliberately. Her beautiful face was very set and very still and her motions were very careful. I sat up.

"What happened?" I asked. Wondering what could have happened surrounded by all those men and no more than a stone's throw or two from where I was sleeping. The stillness of her features alarmed me. Had something happened to her, someone hurt her? Had I misjudged the safety of our situation so badly?

Bithia looked down at her hands and took a deep breath.

"I tested him."

My eyes narrowed down into slits, a sudden suspicion making my stomach tighten painfully.

"What?"

"I went back to the clearing and I tested him. We both know he is fickle." So recently thinking it myself, I nodded automatically but my mind was busy sorting rapidly through what she was telling me. Her eyes met mine and there was a guarded confusion in hers. "If he is fickle, it is not with me."

"Hector?" I clarified and she nodded.

Bithia had snuck away while I had slept and tried to seduce Hector?

It hurt. But for some reason it hurt to think that he would have accepted her advances, not that she had offered them in the first place. She was everything I was not, small and delicate and curved and soft looking. She was beautiful and he had forgotten me for another beautiful woman already once before. I frowned at the fact it still caused my chest pain and Bithia scooted closer to me, reaching out and touching my knee as if to reassure herself. "I told him you would not mind. That I could reassure you he was a good lover. I said that you had sent me to him."

It made my stomach hurt to hear that. I would never have offered my Bithia that way. It had not even crossed my mind to keep an eye on her as I probably should have. I was too used to her taking care of herself. The guilt hit me hard – and made me realize that I already trusted these men, that one single man, far too much for our good.

"You could have been hurt."

She scowled.

"He is a man. I wanted to distract him from you so you would be safe. I saw the way he looked at you when you walked away."

"What if he had accepted your offer?" Both the anger and the fear began to catch up to me and the anger was what showed in my voice. "You are not my whore, Bithia. Have I ever given you the thought that I wished you to be?"

"He's a man," she repeated stubbornly. "I would do more if it would keep you safe."

It made me angry with her and yet, I understood it was her love, her devotion to me that had made her risk herself that way. A sound escaped my throat but I hugged her against me.

"He did not hurt you?"

"He didn't touch me," she almost spat it. Then she shivered and the anger faded. "He smiled at me like some great cat. All dark and hunting and confident. And he told me that, while you might not mind sharing, he did."

XV.

I waited until Bithia had gone to sleep that night, waited while the stars slipped out and the night settled low. I listened to the barks of the foxes and the murmur of the owls in the woods. I waited until the world had settled in comfortably and gone to sleep. Then I rose and shook out my hair and stepped from our shelter. I drew the night into my lungs and let my eyes adjust to the light of the moon before I began to walk. I walked toward the sea this time and I did not stop and gather things as I went. I was not walking for the sake of curiosity or boredom tonight.

He fell into step next to me as I left the camp behind and I knew that he, like me, had been waiting. He was silent and tall in the moonlight, as dark as the moon was bright. He did not say anything and neither did I. Instead, we both simply walked with our long, loose steps, a warlord and his prize. A captive princess and her abductor. Andromache and Hector.

I cupped my elbows with my hands and listened as the river gave way to the ocean beyond. The forest turned to simple shore in a slow, easy slide and I felt the way the grass changed to sand under my bare feet. Pressing my lips together, I raised my face to look at the moon's reflection on the ocean. Salt lived in the breeze that came off of it. We would leave -- tomorrow? I thought so. Most of the work was done. And after that Troy.

"I do not want you touching Bithia," I said

quietly but firmly. I knew what she had offered but, it was not her right to offer it. She was not my sacrifice. His voice was a dark rumble.

"Good."

I turned my head slightly, just enough to slant him a look from the corners of my eyes and he was watching the sea as well.

"That is not a promise," I told him and watched his eyes tighten at their edges.

"I don't want your maid." His voice was graveled and low. Steady and controlled and yet, I felt in him...

"You are angry," it surprised me and I turned my face to look up at him. "You are angry that she offered herself to you."

His eyes, very dark under his low brows, shifted to look at me. I could see the denial of it on his face but the anger was in his eyes and it had leapt for a moment when I had confronted him. It made me stop walking and I turned to face him entirely, looking up at him in curiosity. Angry? That a beautiful woman had offered herself to him? Or angry because he realized she was a test and that I did not trust him?

"Most men would not be angry that a woman had offered to join them in their bed," I told him factually, strangely feeling as if I was lecturing him. He shot me a dark look and did not answer. I folded my arms in front of me.

"She can't possibly be the first woman to make the offer." I didn't believe women left him alone any more than I believed the gods were loyal. He was a man of power, of rank and position and I was not blind. I could see he was a handsome man. Women would come after him for every reason from ambition to being Eros-struck. "You are our captor," I pointed out, wondering where my head was that I would point out our vulnerability to him as if he needed reminding.

"You're mistaking me for my father." The look he gave me with wasn't friendly. Instead of driving me away however, it made me step closer so that I could peer up into his eyes.

Priam, a powerful man of a powerful people. A man who had already had three wives and, if Cebriones with his half-blood legacy was any indication, had even more children outside of those wives. Oh, we liked to joke about Priam, the merchant of women, in Thebe but that was not what I was judging Hector on.

"I am not. I am seeing a man that has two marriages arranged for him."

He exhaled and there was a frustrated sound buried in it.

"Ilium gave its oath twice. I only gave my oath once." He reached out then and I felt his fingertips brush mine. Waiting. My brows came down over my eyes but I gave him my fingers. He wrapped them in his own and drew me over to sit down on the beach with him. He sat in front of me so we were facing each other and, even sitting, he managed to be too close to me. I should have moved away, especially now that we were touching on the heart of what had lodged like a spear in my chest for so long -- but he blocked the cold of the ocean breeze and he was warm. He rubbed at his forehead with his free hand for a long moment and I sat in silence, waiting. Finally, he lowered his head to me so that we were on eye level.

"I'm not used to explaining myself. But I am going to try. For you, Andromache." Somehow, he managed to shift closer and block out the rest of the world. I thought I felt his hair brush against mine.

"You're clever. I don't have to tell you the Achaeans are growing more aggressive in their raids or that our neighbors are testing our borders. Each year in the spring I ride out to war. I stop being Hector the man and I become Hector the soldier. I'm rarely in Ilium during those days. When autumn comes, I ride back to my city with the ashes of the men that cannot ride back with me in pots." He raised his eyes and looked up at me and I saw in his look what he would not, or could not, say with his words about what that cost him. His fingers curled around mine.

"I knew when you were ready for me. But it was hard for me to think of you as an adult. I thought I would wait another year, two at the most. It's not unusual and I made sure you received your gift each year in the fall so you would know I had not forgotten. The year I meant to ride to claim you, the Achaeans burned Teuthrania. They tried to settle there. I spent that year driving them out and was brought back to Ilium in a wagon myself, though I wasn't in a jar thanks to the thickness of my helmet." He raised our clasped hands and touched a spot on his head, under the thick curling hair, rubbing my fingers over it. I could feel a twisted scar there. He let me draw my fingers away when I reacted to the horror of it, not at the scar, but rather what that scar had almost meant. Under the skin of my fingertips, I could still feel the memory of its raised, rough surface. As well as the soft touch of his dark hair.

"Things got worse after that. Each spring before as I had ridden out, I swore that it was my last time as Hector the soldier. That, come fall, I would return and once I had remembered what the world smelled like when it wasn't covered in blood, I would try to be Hector the husband instead. I would promise myself that once I could sleep without the screams in my head, I would go and fetch you and that I would stay in Ilium as your husband and let someone else go to fight Ilium's battles. But each year, I found myself riding out in the spring to war again. The winter after Teuthrania, I spent a long time walking through shadows in my head. The only reason I could give myself to find my way out of them was you. The promise of being a husband." He exhaled and his gaze moved off to watch the tall grass where it moved in the sea breeze. For a very long time he was silent. Hesitant, I reached out and touched his hair again, over that hidden scar. His eyes came back to me and his smile was tired but there. He reached out and brushed the hair from my cheek where the wind had blown it.

"I was recovered by the time this past spring arrived and so I rode out again. And as I did, I swore to the gods that it would be my last season of war until after I had married. I fought all year with that in my head, in my chest. And then I rode back to Ilium in the fall to find that in my absence, I'd been sold off to a higher bidder. My father has over fifty sons, but I was the one that Sparta had heard of, fought against, and remembered. I was the one they wanted for their – daughter," the last word surprised me because it sounded angry again. Almost as if he had meant to say something else. He snorted out through his nose, a sound of anger. "The negotiations had been going on a very long time, much longer than I should have been unaware of, but my attention hadn't been on politics while I recovered. And the councilors that were pushing for the treaty made sure to keep it from me." Something in his voice darkened and I had the distinct impression, he had made it a point to find out their names. "My father agreed. I had already given my body and blood for Ilium. This was just the same but with less metal involved. Why would I refuse the *honor*," his voice tinged the word, "of marrying a renowned beauty? When had I ever refused to do anything for the good of Ilium? It was settled. Your father had already heard of it. You were being given to some long-haired Achaean on the other side of the world. What was left to discuss?"

His eyes met mine and there was no mistaking the exhaustion I saw in them now.

"All I ever wanted for myself was what you gave me without even knowing it. I had learned to rely on that promise during my years of war. Learned to dream of the day I could be husband instead of warlord. And then you were gone. It was all gone. The one thing I had claimed for myself. The one hope I had let myself come to count on."

He looked so tired, sounded so tired. I could not help but touch him, want to comfort him. Gentle, I laid my hand against his cheek and he closed his own hand over it and turned his face into my palm, closing his eyes.

"So you came for me," I whispered the words and my voice was weak. My life would have been easier if I could have disbelieved him. I didn't. Against my palm his lips moved as he nodded.

"I came for you," he answered and his voice was just as soft.

I reached up with my other hand then and stroked his hair, watching his face while his eyes were still closed.

"I am nothing compared to Sparta."

I felt his lips curve against my palm and his eyes stayed shut. He lifted his head though, for a moment, from my palm so I could hear him clearly when he stated:

"I don't want Sparta, Andromache."

"You don't know me," I protested.

"I know you walked out here tonight expecting me to follow, wanting to talk to me. I know you are loyal and protective to the ones that you love, like your little maid. I know you are clever enough to know how to approach a situation and wise enough to be aware of more than what is on the surface. You've already proved you're brave, both when I was in your room and when you were on the ship during the storm and I know you're kind because you let the men fawn over you," his eyes opened and found mine, "and because you will sit on the beach with a soldier and stroke his hair when he's tired." His fingers found mine again as he watched me. "You treat me like a man, not a lawagetas. And you're not frightened of me. Even when you should be." He reached up with his other hand and I felt his touch, very gently on my chin. "I know that your eyes are always sad and I know that I want to be the one to change that." His lips shifted upward at their very edges. "And I know that it isn't a makeup box you carry with you everywhere you go."

My eyes must have widened in horror because he chuckled quietly, just a rumble in his wide chest.

"I haven't looked in it. It's yours. But considering you haven't worn makeup once on this

347

journey, I doubt you find it as important as you find whatever is in that box."

I shut my eyes. He had been honest with me tonight, laid his soul bare. I could not do the same. I could still warn him though, that what he wanted when he wanted me was not as clean and straight as he must think.

"I am other things too," I told him quietly. "And they are not - " I could not find the right word. Strangely, he provided it.

"They're ugly," his voice was low and calm. "I know. I see it in the way you draw your shoulders inward sometimes. What lives inside of me isn't wholesome or beautiful either. Sometimes it frightens me -- what I know is hiding in the darkness inside me. Sometimes it pleases me even though I know it shouldn't." His fingers touched my chin again and tipped my face to his. I opened my eyes to watch him, searching for the lie in his eyes but there was none. Tonight Hector, warlord of Ilium was laying himself bare for me and there was a need in his eyes to do so. "But I don't frighten you. You know, you must know, that there's darkness inside me but you never back away. Your eyes never hesitate or flicker. Andromache," his steady eyes held mine. "I'm not afraid of you either. If there is a god's severed hand in that box -- I am still not afraid of you."

It would have been easy to dismiss his word as being unaware of the fact a woman could torture and maim and kill just as well as any man, but --

looking into his eyes -- I did not think he underestimated me as a woman. If he did not know exactly, what was in his eyes said he knew enough. I wasn't sure I believed him. And yet -- I was not sure I could *not* believe him.

I lowered my head. It was a lot to believe, that someone would accept me completely as I was and not need me to hide parts of myself away in order to be acceptable. I didn't trust that assurance. He had yet to see how very dark and ugly I could be. And yet, hearing him talk, he knew his own dark ugliness. It frightened me how strongly I did not want to be alone with my darkness anymore. Raising my eyes, I looked at him from the tops of them.

"What now?" I asked, phrasing my question vaguely to see what he would answer. He said he wanted me. I was willing to accept that, even believe it as unexpected and strange as it was. Tonight, I would lie in my blankets and think over what he had told me under the moon here. For the moment, however, I accepted it. It still left me with the question though, what of me? What would happen to me now?

He gave me a sad smile.

"Now I take you home with me. We should be able to sail tomorrow with the tide. I will bring you to Ilium and not as my war prize, Andromache."

I watched him, pressing my lips together for a long moment before I quietly asked:

"And is Helen already waiting for you in Ilium?"

His eyes did not leave mine and I saw the dark anger flare in his eyes, yet I knew it was not directed at me. He shook his head.

"Helen is still in Sparta, as far as I know. She will stay there. Ilium will no doubt send one of my brothers to formally apologize and explain things. If we pay Sparta enough," he stated wryly. "They'll forget to be offended. Andromache," his voice softened. "I am tired of fighting. I will not invite it into my house as well. My mind hasn't changed in seven years. It will not change now."

My brows came down. He made it sound like such a light thing, thwarting the desires of three nations. I knew it was not.

"It is not as easy as you are pretending. It will cause problems," I looked at him. "No one will take this lightly."

He surprised me with a smile that flashed across his face, making him look young – and I thought, I saw a dangerous light there as well. It reminded me that I was talking to Hector of the Flashing Helm, the man whose reputation for his deeds in battle and against the odds reached all the way across the sea.

"I know. But for just this once in my life I'm going to think about myself first. If Ilium is not happy with me, they can find another lawagetas." Again, the flash of his smile and it was fuller and more relaxed this time. "It will give me an excuse to spend more time at home with my bride."

My lips twitched upward in response to that and I could not seem to stop it. He sounded like a young boy, that light was in his eyes for a moment as he answered me. Hector's bride.... I had once had to adjust to thinking of myself that way, then it had become as natural as breathing to me. I found that I had to adjust to that thought in my head again now. I was not sure I trusted it, but the feel of it was not as uncomfortable and sharp edged as I had expected it to be.

"You have thought a great deal about this."

His smile softened and he lowered his head so that his curling hair fell across his forehead.

"I was on that island waiting for you, praying your ship wouldn't go past, for three days." He looked up at me and his eyes were strangely apologetic. "I didn't have time or I would have done this differently. Diplomatically. Something easier for you, more the way you deserve. But I couldn't let you go. Not after so long. And I wasn't willing to risk losing you over the ocean while everyone took too long talking."

I nodded then, looking down thoughtfully. I had been given a great deal tonight. So much new to think over that I wanted to go and lie quietly and turn over in my mind. I should not trust what he told me so completely. And yet -- I did. I always had. It had started a long, dark night ago and it had lodged too deep to remove now.

"You didn't trust my father."

351

"Or mine," he said, voice low. "I thought if I waited and went through the proper procedures and sent messengers and waited for my father and his council's permission, that you would slip through my fingers while I was busy being polite. I've gotten hard because of the fighting. I take the openings when I see them and apologize later." He made a sound and shook his head. "No. That's a lie. I don't apologize."

The admission made me smile softly and I rested my hand over his.

"It's all right." Though he hadn't said it bothered him. "I was --" I pressed my lips together. I was confessing too much. But... he had shared himself with me tonight when he had not needed to. It drew out the parts of myself that I had grown used to hiding. "I was never frightened of you," I raised my eyes to see him watching me. "But I was always, from the day I heard its name, frightened of what waited for me in Phthia."

"The sons of Peleus," his voice was a low rumble and his eyes darkened. I don't know what he saw on my face when he said it but his own softened and he reached out to gently brush my hair with his fingertips. Apparently, the rumors of them had reached Troy as easily as they had reached Thebe. Something dark and hard, like a shark in the deep waters, moved in his eyes. "Your father never should have agreed to that proposal."

It was my turn to smile weakly and I moved a shoulder.

"They are strong. The Achaeans grow more aggressive each year. Having Peleus' sons tied to him by marriage would have earned him both the protection and prestige of their house. He did nothing more than follow your own city's example."

"There are some things more important than safety."

For the first time in my life, looking into those dark eyes, I thought I understood the core-deep difference between my father and this man in front of me. My father would sacrifice me for a promise of his House's safety. Surprisingly, suddenly, a thought sparked in my mind as well. Had my father traded me for safety for himself long before Peleus? For... as long as my mother fed on my pain, she had never caused it in anyone else in the family...

XVI.

Our boat put out to sea with the tide that next morning. I stood on the bow and watched the shore disappear. It was almost frightening how much my life had changed on that tiny strip of forgotten land in such a short amount of time.

"I hope Poseidon likes the offerings better this time." Bithia, standing next to me, was sour, and trying her hardest not to get sick. "If he sends another storm like that, I may just jump overboard to spare myself the suffering."

I turned and gave her a sympathetic smile, which she took as an opportunity.

"What now?" she asked and, since we were alone at the bow of the boat, I knew she was asking what my next cunning move would be, as if I were a master game player and my life was the gameboard. Honestly though, I had no idea what I would do next. Something in me was waiting. I turned back to look at the retreating shore as it disappeared into the water.

"Now, we wait," I answered and knew it did not satisfy her. I also knew she thought it was a part of my plan, when in fact, it was the only plan I had at the moment. If only she knew how often I came up with solutions only in the instant they were needed instead of always having them already plotted out in advance and waiting. In a minor way, I understood what Hector meant when he talked of everyone else's expectations and their faith in him.

I looked back to see him walking to the back

of the ship, watched him stop to talk to the man at the rudder. He was so tall and relaxed in his movements, so unconsciously sure. I thought it was very hard not to have faith in him. He did not seem the type of man to fail and, I suspected, when he did, it did not last long.

"He hasn't spoken to you since the morning they were building the mast," Bithia murmured it and I knew she watched me watching Hector. "I don't like it. He should have talked to you by now. Why haven't you confronted him yet and demanded to be put ashore in your homeland again?"

Because they will only send me to Phthia, I wanted to say. Because... I drew in a deep breath as I admitted it to myself... because I would rather be with Hector than on my way to Phthia. I would rather be here than anywhere else in this world, and what did that say about me?

"We are going to Ilium," I told Bithia instead as I turned back to watch the water, voice intentionally calm. "My father can come for me there. If he wants to."

Bithia was quiet for a very long time after that and I could hear the soft breaths she was taking through her mouth to still her stomach. Finally, cautiously, she spoke.

"Helenus is in Troy," her voice was so soft I could barely hear it. I refused to answer or respond to her or what she suggested and she went quiet again.

Helenus... I had not thought of him.

355

Hector's younger brother by the same birth mother. Looking back now, I realized that I had been unaware that he had been wooing me when I had visited Troy with my family all those years ago. He had been hunting me. Finding me and my friends that day had not been unintentional at all, Cassandra's words had proved that he had been aware of me long before I was aware of him. I shut my eyes and let the wind wash over my face as if it could clear the confusing tangle of it all from my mind. Helenus... I had found him worrisome, puzzling then. Later, with time to think of it and remember, I had found something vaguely frightening about him, as if I were not myself to him but a small, bright jewel -- a thing instead of a human. Now I was older, and I knew I could use that, use him. I thought, if I asked properly and put the right things in my eyes, he might remember that he had once taken me to his goddess for approval. He would remember and help me against Hector. Perhaps, because of Hector. I had brothers -- I understood.

Turning, I looked back down the length of the ship, reaching up to pull my loose hair back from my face. I saw Hector next to the rudder, watching me in return.

Did I want to be saved?

For a very long time we stood that way, watching each other and the rest of the ship seemed to vanish away for me. Then, slowly, he began to smile. He ducked his head. And he came to me, eyes never leaving mine until he stood in front of me. My hair blew against his throat and shoulders, chest and face, and I realized - he had come because of me. Would not have come if I had not turned to him and waited.

Without a word or a movement I had summoned a man.

And it was not just any man. It was Hector of Ilium.

He reached up and his face was relaxed and mildly amused, as if he did not understand what had just happened but did not mind. With a large hand, he smoothed the hair back from my face and it seemed natural to accept his touch.

"Flashing-eyed Andromache," he said with a soft smile. "What are you thinking of standing up here, watching?"

"The future," I was surprised that I smiled as I answered him. "The past. You."

His teeth showed then in a grin and a chuckle sounded back in his throat.

"Tangled thoughts. Am I the minotaur in the maze of them?"

He said it lightly – jokingly even -- but I realized, he was serious. I saw worry hidden in his brown eyes. Was he the monster in my thoughts? Wasn't that what I was asking myself? Now I saw that it was his question too. Was Hector my monster? I should have drawn that out, made him wonder, had my small revenge against him for taking me in the night but I could not. Not with what was in his eyes, not when he worried it in the first place instead of not caring what I thought or felt. I reached up and smoothed my palms over his forehead.

"No horns," I told him. "I think you may be as stubborn as a bull but I am not afraid of you. Not here and not in my mind. I would never give Theseus the thread to find you in your lair."

His face softened and he lowered his head to me. It made my hands slide and I found the curls of his dark hair against my fingers and palms. They were soft to the touch and my fingers curled in response.

"You were playing Athenian to your brother's minotaur the day I found you in your olive tree. Do you remember that?"

I laughed. I had forgotten the details of why I had been up that tree. I was surprised he had remembered.

"I said I was not Theseus and you told me you were not Ariadne." His eyes were watching me, to see if I remembered.

In truth, when I thought of that day, I remembered the warmth and the scent of the olive trees. I remembered his eyes and his horses. I had to think for a moment to recall what we had said and I did not remember it all. It was more the idea of it rather than the actual words. But I remembered the reference to Ariadne because what he had told me afterward had seemed so strange...

"You said you would never abandon me

alone on an island," I remembered outloud and the unspoken 'not even for a god' hung in the air between us as it had not all those years ago. His lips smiled.

"I wondered if you would remember."

"Did you know then?" I could not help but ask. Had he realized, all those years ago, that he wanted to wed me? I had not thought of him that way, being only a child myself. But had he? He smiled and shook his head, which moved my fingers in his hair and reminded me I was still tangled that way. I lowered my hands.

"No," he said. "You were as young as my sisters. I just knew that you seemed so alone and so used to it that you didn't even know it anymore. And that you had already welcomed me into your private world. It was something precious to me. I just knew that you were someone precious."

"When did you decide you wanted me?" I asked and drew away from him to stand near the railing. He followed and put one hand on the rail as the boat moved under us. Salt water and salt wind. It put me in a half enclosure of his arms when he rested his hand there and I did not step out of it. I found comfort in that space in fact. He was once again blocking out the rest of the world but I was growing accustomed to that.

I was starting to enjoy it.

"I'm not sure. Maybe when I came out of the stables and you were covered in blood and soot and were worried about me. Maybe it was in the hall when you shut the windows to stop the raiders. Maybe it wasn't until later when I realized how often my mind came back to you. I just woke up one day knowing that I wanted you next to me." He exhaled and looked out at the water beyond me. "And I realized you were the only one I wanted next to me."

It was quiet for a very long time between us after that. I was still testing out what he had told me last night, wanting to know if he really meant it. If I had really understood it. If I was really that important to him. Finally, very deliberately I turned to him and asked: "Only me?"

His dark eyes slid to mine. He lowered his other arm so that I was encircled by him, the sea at my back. It trapped me but I did not feel enclosed or thwarted. Instead, after a moment of hesitation, I put my hands on his forearms, very carefully and very lightly, still not sure about touching him, only knowing that I wanted to. He bowed his head to be closer to me.

"Only you, Andromache," he said. "Only you in my house, only you in my bed, only you, my only wife. Only ever you."

My face was already raised to his so that I could watch him but now I raised it more. Deliberately, I brought us closer together. I could feel the air between us as if it were a physical thing and my skin was suddenly sensitive to it.

"Women share their men all the time," I carefully tested what he offered me. IT was unfamiliar ground and I was not sure of its reality. His head dipped so that his face was closer still and I could not see all of him anymore, just the darkness of his eye and the plane of his bronze cheek.

"I don't. I don't share at all." I could feel his breath against my lips and it made me feel strange. I had to lid my eyes against it. I heard what he was telling me and I believed him. My head said not to because it was ridiculous to expect that of a man. Yet I believed him anyway. My hands slipped upward to rest against his upper arms.

"I don't want to share either," I admitted. What woman did? We only shared because we had no choice. I could feel his quiet laugh against my lips when it came.

"Then don't," he told me simply. "And I will never ask you to."

I stood very still and thought that he might kiss me. I had not been kissed before. I had been Ilium's promised bride for so long and barring that, I had seven older brothers. He did not close the distance between our mouths though and I was left breathing in the air he exhaled just as he took my breaths into himself. Surrounded by him, breathing him, feeling his sun-warmed skin under my fingertips, I forgot there was anything else. I forgot there was a world outside of where I stood, lulled and swallowed by the rhythm that existed between the two of us. We stood that way for what felt like a very long time until he finally raised his head to press his face into the hair near my temple. I found

I was weak and had to move my hands to his chest to stay steady. I felt him smile against my skin.

What was he doing? What was I doing?

"I didn't expect this when I came for you." His voice was very quiet and a bit thick in his throat. He did not draw away from me.

"Me?" I asked hesitantly, eyes opening to see his dark hair and the blue sky at the edge of my vision. "You didn't expect me to be the way I am?"

After all, who would? Who ever thought little girls grew up to be Furies in fragile form? What had I done that had given myself away? What had I said? What had he seen?

He chuckled against my hair and shook his head but it was more as if he were rubbing the side of his chin against my temple.

"No," his voice was low. Soft. "You are more than I expected. It's -- " he paused and I waited in that frozen heartbeat. "I didn't expect the way you make me feel, Andromache."

"Oh..." I wasn't sure how to respond or what to say. Was that good? Bad? How did I make him feel? For that matter, how did he make me feel? He chuckled quietly against me again.

"Stop worrying," he whispered it. "That's not a bad thing. I'm just used to thinking of you as a child. I'm having to adjust to the way I find myself reacting to you."

I caught the edges of what he was trying to tell me but the completeness of it eluded me. Very slowly, I turned my face so that I could see him.

Found that my lips could brush the edge of his jaw because he didn't move his face when I moved my own. I understood. I did. A little. I had studied Briseis. I had brothers that tended to forget their little sister was in the room. I had watched the servants. There was a physical realm between a man and a woman that I was aware of but that I had never crossed into. Given what I had seen, I had never wanted to. I was not sure I wanted to now, but I was not sure I did not want to anymore either. I picked my words very carefully.

"I haven't been a child for several years now."

He made a low sound in his throat and I watched the edge of his mouth curve.

"Are you trying to seduce me, Andromache?"

Was I? I thought -- I thought I just might be. Except seduction was all about teasing and pulling away. It was about not being there when he wanted me. It wasn't about standing in his arms and sharing exhales. Did I even know what I would do if I did manage to seduce him? And - more to the point – what if this was my version of seduction and it wasn't working?

His arms shifted suddenly and I found myself much more firmly trapped than I had been before.

"Don't," his voice was gruff at its edges. "Don't pull away from me, Andromache." His face shifted just enough to look at me from the corners of his eyes and then they shifted at their edges, wrinkling slightly into laugh lines. "I like what you were doing. I've never had someone try to seduce my soul out of me before."

"I was not," I protested, not sure if I had been intending that or not but knowing it was the kind of thing to deny. I was rewarded with his smile as he lifted his head to look back out to sea.

"Ah," his response was noncommittal. "Well, it's what you were doing whether you were trying or not."

I sent him a narrow look, which he ignored. Very intentionally, I turned in his arms so that I was watching the sea as well. He kept his arms on either side of me and after a long moment, I rested my hands on top of his on the railing of the ship. Together we watched the blue sky and the wine dark sea.

Eventually, he moved away. There was a discussion about supplies, which we had little of thanks to the ruin of the salt water from the storm, and Hector finally stepped away from me without a word and strode over to involve himself in the decision. For a very long time before that though, he had been content to do nothing more than stand behind me in silence as the water had padded past. I found that I had found a quiet peace being that way as well. After he had gone, Bithia came slowly over to join me, putting her own hands on the railing next to mine, even though she closed her eyes and lifted her tight face to the wind to avoid looking at the motion of the water.

"If I didn't know what you were doing, I would be worried," she told me in a soft voice so it wouldn't be overheard. I gave her a mildly curious look from the corners of my eyes, wondering what she thought I was doing considering I wasn't sure myself. With her eyes closed, she missed my glance but after a moment she continued quietly:

"You're making him care about you. So that he'll be less likely to do anything that will hurt you. The more he likes you as a person the less likely it is that he'll treat you the way men treat female prisoners. You're making him sympathetic to you by being sympathetic to him. You lure people into loving you so that they won't hurt you."

I drew back, just a little, at her assessment. Was that what I was doing? Was that what I did? Was I unconsciously manipulating Hector, and others before him, into thinking tenderly of me just so that they wouldn't hurt me? My revulsion at the idea of manipulating anyone hit first but there was a small, sound part of my mind that asked: and what if I did? I was a captive. Wasn't it my right to do whatever it took to make sure my captors didn't abuse me?

Bithia must have felt me move because she turned her head and looked at me suddenly, surprise in her eyes. She reached out and caught my arm as worry moved into her eyes.

"It's wise," she protested, voice still quiet, face sincere. "There's nothing wrong with it." And then her eyes changed and she looked stricken. "It's not as if that's why people love you. Not people that really know you. I don't think you do that to me. I love you no matter what you do."

The theory hadn't worked its way through my mind enough for me to begin worrying that she would think that I manipulated her for her friendship. I still hadn't worked my way past the thought that I might be manipulating people without even meaning to.

"It's all right," she assured me. "I don't think he knows it."

"How do you?" I asked, surprised by how calm and unworried my voice sounded. She responded with a smile.

"Why else would you let him act the way around you that he does?" She turned back into the wind and shut her eyes determinedly as she battled her stomach. "I was worried until I realized why you were being so accepting."

I pressed my lips together and it was all I could do to not look back to where I knew Hector was. Accepting? I thought that was a... kind word choice. I did not think 'accepting' was the proper word for what I felt when he stood close to me and lowered his head. It sounded far too mild. I was not about to try to correct Bithia on what was truly happening inside me when he came near though. I could not even explain it to myself. Better she think I was in control and knew what I was doing. Seducing - manipulating - accepting? What *was* I doing? I didn't know.

****

Our ship moved forward. The wind was
wrong at first and so, for a little while, the oars were
at work, propelling our ship through the water in
steady continuous moves that beat like a human
pattern on the vastness of the sea. When the ship
was in position to catch the wind right however, the
men unfurled the sail and it came down with a great
rushing noise, like a giant wing on a down sweep.
The wind caught it even as they secured it at its
bottom and it filled with a brisk snap. It reminded
me of the way a man will clap his hands together
just before he gets down to real work and it made
me smile to think our ship did the same thing. With
the sail full our ship scudded forward and the men,
finished with lashing the oars back in place, found
themselves with free time.

They did not approach me but I felt their
glances from time to time as I stood at the bow of
the ship and wondered if I wasn't, unintentionally,
feeding their superstition about me being 'good
luck' by standing at the front of the ship like some
wooden guardian. The alternative was going below
deck and I had no desire to do that so I stayed where
I was and let them think what they would. They
would think it anyway whether I was there or not.
But I did watch them. I had always wondered,
when my father had set out to sea, what men

367

trapped on a small ship did to fill their empty time. On the way to Lemnos, I had not found the energy to care but now I found my curiosity again. It was reassuring to feel more like myself again.

In some ways they passed their time much as they did on dry land. There were the usual games of luck and chance, made with small chips of wood or stone or bone that they tossed and aimed for certain symbols on. I recognized several of the dice games. One man played a tune on a long lonely pipe, stopping often to rethink and replay notes almost as if he were making it up as he went along and then memorizing it. Several of the men were stretched out and napping, while others worked on carvings. It made me remember the little carved horse I had found in the very first chest Hector had sent me and how rough and determined it had looked. It was easy to imagine him as a youth, still learning, as he carved it. The thought that he had shared it with me warmed me deep inside. I still had it. Or rather, I had. It was safely tucked away in my personal chests, which were in Lemnos now. Or perhaps they were on their way back to my father. I was not sure I would ever see any of them again.

I suspected that, in other times there might have been old sails to patch, nets to weave, mild repair work to do below the hull. We had lost so much in the storm though that I doubted we had any old sails or nets left and the repair work had just been done less than a day ago. Several of the men were trailing lines over the side of the ship, hoping for fish fast enough and determined enough to keep up with the ship long enough to get caught. It was a peaceful, quiet stretch of time and it soothed me. I wanted to stay on this ship forever. Life was very simple and I did not have to face any of the things that would be waiting for me once we reached the shore. Eventually, I went into the small shelter they had set up at the bow for Bithia and me and went to sleep. Relaxed enough, feeling safe enough, and tired enough thanks to the salt air and the sun, to actually sleep deeply. Bithia, lying on the deck on her back next to the makeshift bed, kept a determined watch over me - and her stomach.

I opened my eyes much later, judging by the angle of the sun. I realized why I had woken when I heard a scratching at the entrance of our small tent. Bithia started at the sound and so I knew it was the first time. I just had a very hard time sleeping when people moved within a certain distance from me.

"What?" Bithia's voice, logy with sleep.

"My lawagetas wishes to speak with your lady," Cebriones answered.

Formality? It made me wrinkle my brows.

"My lady is sleeping." I sat up on my elbow.

"No. Not anymore. I will join him shortly."

"You should have made him come to you," Bithia hissed at me after we had heard Cebriones' steps depart and I gave her a soft smile and leaned down to touch her cheek.

"Stop fighting for me," I told her gently. "I have my own battle plan and I would not see you caught in it."

It settled her. What was one small lie to take the fear out of her? I felt no guilt over pretending I knew what I was doing to give her comfort. With a long inhale, I stood as much as I could in the shelter of our tent and then ducked lower still to be able to step outside of it and into the daylight. I had not slept so too long. It was late afternoon. I wondered if we would reach Troy tonight but when I turned out of habit and looked at the horizon I was shocked to see land. It shook me in a way I could not explain and I froze for a moment.

What lay ahead of me was not large enough to be more than an island or perhaps a peninsula. Not Troy then. We were close enough though that I could see the vague impression of houses on it... and the smoke rising from it in a thick dark plume like a visual scream of horror, black against the blue and empty sky. Raiders?

I turned to walk back to Hector and he was already there behind me. How had I not felt him approach? It didn't seem as important as that black column of smoke somehow.

"That's the island of Chryse, Andromache." His voice was calm and its usual low tone but I thought I heard thunder at its edges. "Apollo's high priest lives there."

But Apollo's high priest wasn't the only

one. I knew someone else that lived there. And my heart tightened in my chest.

Chryseis.

XVII.

The island of Chryse was burning. Apollo's sacred temple, the people that served him and the pilgrims that came to the holy site, the market places and the shrines... all burning.

"Raiders?" The word was dry in my throat as I thought of my laughing, light friend. It had been so many years since I had seen her but she was as immediate to me as anyone here. Chryseis had been my first friend and she had never asked about the darkness that curled around the edges of my life when I was with her. Hector's eyes were narrow as he watched the smoke.

"Not necessarily," the answer was slow and thoughtful. "That's the watch beacon. I convinced the priest Chryses to install it a few years ago. The Achaeans are sacrilegious dogs and they've been looting smaller temples along our coast in the past few years. Yet they still claim the gods take their side." He paused and I wondered if what I heard in that silence, so close to a mirror of my own thoughts, was really there or if I only imagined that I might not be the only one to question the nature of the fickle gods. Hector looked down at me, brows low over his eyes. "I told him that if I or any of my ships saw his beacon burning, we would come to help."

Suddenly, I understood what he was telling me. *I* was on his ship, the woman he said he was taking back to Ilium to marry. His bride because he was done being Hector the warrior. And now one of his allies called for him while I stood right in front of him, representing both his promise to himself and his duty to protect.

"My friend Chryseis is the daughter of Chryses," I told him quietly, meeting his eyes. "She holds my laughter inside her."

His face tightened and he lifted his head to watch the smoke. Already, we were drifting closer.

"If it is a raiding party of one or two ships I can stop this. If it is more - " he looked down at me. "Andromache, I took you from the safety of Lemnos. I will not let you be taken as lawiaiai by some Achaean animal while I still draw breath."

He was hesitating for my safety. It felt strange to be the first thought on a man's mind instead of the last. I pressed my lips together in thought and looked at the rising smoke with him. We were standing very close, almost shoulder to shoulder.

"Is there an approach to the island that is away from the port?" I asked finally. "Can we land without the city knowing?"

He smiled at me and I saw something strange in his eyes. He did not seem upset with my suggestion though, even if I had not had time to phrase it so that it sounded as if it were his own idea.

"We are already coming in from an angle." He gestured. "The port is that way, just around the lip of the island where it is protected from the sea. The city rises above it. There," he lowered his head to be on level with mine and pointed. "Is a small cove. I warned the priest to sink stakes in it or run a chain across the last time I was there to dissuade raiders but he refused. Too many locals from the mainland use it, he claimed." His look was dry. "Smugglers in other words. I'm going to land there and send a small party to see what is happening before I committed all my men." He paused and looked down at me with something soft at the edges of his eyes. "I don't remember Eetion's sons being good at strategy," he added mildly.

I thought he might be teasing me, that he was not upset with me for offering a strategic suggestion that had not been asked for. I glanced up at him from the corners of my eyes.

"They are not so fond of suggestions," I said and he chuckled, reaching out to touch my cheek.

"War is men's work, Andromache. I would never want to see you with a sword or breastplate on. But clever thinking -- I would never want to see you without it. I will do the fighting. But always give me your thoughts before it."

Given that most men I knew paid attention to a woman's looks or her abilities at homemaking, I thought it was an odd thing to hear him say. Yet, I was being reminded, Hector focused on things that others didn't. So I nodded. His smile was real but I saw the distraction in it too as he focused on that plume of smoke again.

"You are more precious to me than a burning city." His voice was rough. "If something goes wrong I will expect you safely away and in Ilium no matter what is happening on Chryse."

I understood. He would do what he could. A man driven by the gods or by glory would have sacrificed everything. It made me think that Hector was more driven by his duty to people that looked to him for protection. He would do what he could and when he could do no more he would save what he could. He was a practical fighter and I admired that so much more than what I could only see as hollow glory. And I, apparently, was not to be risked in this situation.

It would take some getting used to, being held so highly in someone else's priorities. I thought I could learn to enjoy it – and yet I also thought it could be a blade that bit both ways.

The ship came aground in the small cove and men jumped out to drag it on to shore enough to stall it against the tide. I did notice however that it was not as far ashore as usual and it would take very little to push it loose back into the water. Everyone was lacing themselves into their mercenary armor again, quick and efficient from obvious years of repetition. I watched Hector emerge from below deck in the familiar dark leather but this time he carried a spear and a shield was slung across his back, smaller than the large battle ones I was used to polishing for my brothers and father. This was a scouting party and they meant to travel fast and light. Cebriones approached and handed him a cloth wrapped bundle, which Hector casually stripped away to reveal a helmet of shining bronze, the tall horsehair crest proud and defiant at its top.

Hector of the Flashing Helm.

He put it on his head with both hands and suddenly, he was someone, something, else entirely. Even without the bronze armor to match it he looked taller and more terrible than I had ever imagined a man could. That helmet turned toward me and I could not see his eyes in the depths of its cheekpieces and nose guard. I still nodded. He was terrifying, but in the depths of my own dark mind, it was comforting to know. I did not fear him, there was no need, but our enemies would. The crest swayed as he nodded in return and then he was over the side of the ship with a handful of his men and they moved quickly up the beach in the gathering dusk. I stood on the bow with Bithia at my side as if I were standing upon a city's wall and watched them until they were long out of sight.

And I found myself silently praying. For the safety of my laughing friend. And that Hector of the Flashing Helm would come back to me.

Apollo disappeared from the sky in his sun chariot.

I wished I knew what the city looked like. I thought, if I could picture it in my mind, it would be easier for me to imagine what was happening or what might be happening. I was good at waiting. I had been doing so all of my life in one aspect or another. But that did not mean I enjoyed it.

Was it raiders? A monster from the sea? Had one of Poseidon's growingly common earthquakes sunk everything into the port? Plague? I kept my watch from the bow and I was careful not to look as uncertain as I felt. The men around me did not need that. Bithia did not need that. And I - I did not need that. I still hated not knowing. More than anything in my life I hated when I did not know something.   The last light of the sun disappeared, leaving only stars in a moonless night in its wake.

Finally, there was a flash from the sentry stationed at the cove's entrance, a flare of his fire that he had kept hidden until then. Cebriones was at my side in an instant. The fire flashed again. I looked at Cebriones. Was that good?   Was that bad?   The fire flared a third time, then burned steady and Cebriones relaxed next to me.

"He's coming back," he stated and did not have to tell me who 'he' was. I finally let my fingers grip the railing as tightly as they had previously wanted to, eyes searching the gloom. I needed to see for myself before the strange knot in my chest would relax.

Only three men came down the beach but even without the helmet, I would have recognized Hector among them. One of the men with him was his, in the familiar mismatched armor, but the other man was dressed in a priest's robes. Apollo's broken sun symbols decorated its hems, I saw them as he drew closer. Hector stopped on the beach and gestured and Cebriones leaped down to join him as if he were an arrow shot from a bow. Together, they bent their heads near the priest. I could hear little more than the murmur of their voices, counterpoint to the waves on the shore but I strained my ears anyway. Whatever they decided, no one would tell me what it was. Men didn't tell women things like battle plans. It didn't mean the women didn't know. We were just very good at listening well and putting different overheard sentences together into a larger picture. I was very good at finding things out before all of my own brothers were aware of them. If it had not been so obvious, I would have leaned down over the railing to try to hear better but part of hearing what was going on was not letting the men realize that was what you were doing. They didn't guard themselves against what they didn't realize.

"He still has his spear," Bithia's voice was a whisper next to me. Both Hector and his soldier still carried their spears. If they had been fighting, those would have been the first things to be lost. They were thrown and once they were thrown, there was no point in retrieving them until after everything was over. Whether they'd struck home or not, they would still be useless after the first throw, until their bronze tips could be reheated, straightened, and sharpened. Yet Hector still wore his helmet. In a friendly city, the helmets were the first things to come off to both show good intention and to reveal who was under them. My fingers moved against the railing silently and yet Hector's helmeted head rose as if he had heard me. I could feel his eyes on me, even though I could not see them. For a very long time, he watched me. We watched each other for so long in fact, that the men with him paused in their talk and lifted their own heads to look from him to where he was looking. The beach was very still and the priest whispered something. Hector's helmet turned from me, crest swaying and I heard him chuckle, though what he said was too low for me to hear. He turned and strode over to the ship, stopping when he reached the hull to stretch up his arms for me. There was no doubt in my mind that I would want to join him and I turned to look for someone to help lower me down. One of the men was already there with a smile and I gave him one of thanks in return as he lifted me and then lowered me down into Hector's waiting arms.

Hector took much longer to lower me to my feet than most men did when they helped me off a ship.

"Your friend is all right." It was the first thing he said to me as he finally set me on my feet and the breath shuddered out of me in relief. I had not dared think too long about her before because I had known that the fears would try to eat me inside if I did. Now though, I shut my eyes for just a second and let myself feel the relief. There were so few people in this world that loved me. I could not have guarded any of them carefully or closely enough. Hector's face softened and his hands moved against my upper arms where he held me, the same steadying, gentle chaffing for warmth he had done when he had first taken me. His voice was low and just for me.

"The priest thought you were Athena on the prow of my ship, come to defend her shrine here."

I hardly thought I fit Athena's description, even in her most terrible disguise. I don't know what Hector saw move over my face but he chuckled.

"Softer than Athena," he murmured and I looked up into the darkness of his eyes under the rim of his helmet. Lightly, he touched my cheek. Then he exhaled and looked back the way they had all come.

"You were right. Achaeans. One of their minor warlords. He's blockaded the port with his ships but he can't get into the city itself thanks to its walls. So he's stayed and issued a challenge rather than go home in disgrace."

Challenging the priest of Apollo. The Achaeans truly were without fear of the gods. Or else they feared their countrymen more. Then I realized what he was doing and looked up at him in surprise.

"Why are you telling me this?" I asked.

He gave me a mild questioning look. "Don't you want to know?"

"Of course."

"Then that's why I'm telling you." It meant

so much to me that he would so causally share the news that my heart hurt. And yet it sparked my mind too and I laid both of my hands on his chest, to look solemnly up at him.

"Tell me more."

He chuckled and his large hands curved warm on my upper arms.

"The challenge is for your friend. He wants to marry her but her father isn't willing to give her up to an Achaean. Or the dowry the same Achaean is demanding as her marriage price. So he's stated that he will stay where he is and blockade the harbor and keep them shut up in their walls until someone comes down and accepts his challenge to single combat. The winner decides the high priest's daughter's fate and the loser goes home in a jar."

I stood very still.

"He must be very intimidating, if none of Apollo's men will go out to meet him."

Hector's eyes slid to mine.

"I've heard of him," he admitted. "I could go to Ilium and come back with enough ships to fire his in the harbor and leave their bodies on the bottom of the ocean floor. But he's issued a formal challenge. Not even the gods are allowed to ignore that kind of thing." He sounded, surprisingly, less enamored with honor than the men I knew and more intent on the practical side of things. I pressed my lips together and watched him. He gifted me with a look. I exhaled silently.

"When do you fight him?" I asked softly.

"Dawn," his answer was simple and there was no apology in it. Though there was rue there. The edges of my lips curved weakly. I could not help but lift a hand to touch his cheek under the metal of his helmet.

"And what will I do if you are the one sailing home in a jar?" I whispered.

"Thank the gods that you were delivered from me, demand my father handsomely pay to restore your honor and have a full Trojan guard to escort you home to your father. Or claim I married you here and live in Ilium as my widow as long as you like." He said it lightly, as if it were an easy thing, yet he'd obviously given it serious thought. It made me want to slap him. And throw myself in his arms and hold him very tightly. I stepped closer instead.

"How bad is the Achaean lawagetas?"

"He's older than me, younger than your father," Hector answered me. "They call him 'The Bear' in his homeland. I've never fought him before. I don't think he'll be expecting me though. And I think he's probably tired of waiting. He'll try to end things quickly. Because it's a personal challenge in front of his men, he may try to show off as well. It's a good way to get killed on the battlefield."

"Do I have to wait behind?" I laid my hand against his cheek as I asked it and watched his eyes lid at my touch, in response to me. As I had hoped he would. I was not used to being an influence of this kind on men but I thought I was beginning to learn it.

"Yes."

"You do not want me to see?"

His dark eyes opened then, catching light from the torch one of the nearby men held, but he did not raise his face from my palm or draw away from me.

"I do not want you to find sanctuary, Andromache." His voice was rough at its edges. "The largest shrine to Apollo on this side of the sea is in that city. If you reach it, if you throw your arms around his statue's legs, even I can't drag you away. Even my own men would never allow it, much less the priests and my father." His eyes were very steady on mine. I noticed he had not mentioned Apollo's reaction. "You ran from me once when you realized who I was. I am not going to give you the opportunity to escape me this time."

"My captor."

He did not flinch.

"If I have to be."

I was silent for a very long time and he watched me. All that we were, he and I, balanced on this one thing. How willing was I to be with him if I had other choices? How much was I his captive woman and how much was I his bride? They could be the same thing, but they weren't. We both knew it. How long until I ran from him again? As much as I was coming to enjoy my present, even I didn't know the answer to that. I could not promise to never run. Not yet.

Finally, I lifted my eyes and focused on him.

"What if I promise to come when you call for me? Wherever I am?"

He went very still at that. I stepped in closer to him so that we were almost touching and his eyes glinted briefly at my move. We both knew I was standing so close because it softened him to me.

"Any time I call. Ever."

It was a hard bargain. Much, much more than I had offered. It would bind me in ways I couldn't control or plan for. I narrowed my eyes at him with a frown. I should say no. Say no and stay on the ship. I had waited in uncertainty before and it was not as if I would never know how the combat turned out. I would most certainly find out shortly after it was finished, one way or the other. He was asking too much.

"While I am on the island of Chryse," I bargained but he shook his head.

"Anywhere. Ever."

"You will abuse it."

"No. I won't."

"I am not a dog to be called."

"No. You're not. And that's not what this is."

Mentally, I twisted at the restraint like a snake in a snare. I should say no. What he wanted would cost me more than what he offered. Finally, I raised my chin.

"All right," I agreed. "I will come to you

when you call for me. Anywhere. Ever. Which god do you want me to swear to it by?"

"Swear it on whatever is in that box you carry. That's oath enough for me."

I gave him a narrowed-eyed look but he didn't flinch from it. So I sent Bithia to fetch my box. And shortly after that, I found myself among the group of men that Hector was bringing back into the city of Chryse with him. He even let me bring Bithia along.

I watched his back as we traveled and I wondered. Why had he not simply asked me not to run from him in the first place, instead of having me promise to return when I inevitably did?

XVIII.

I was sure that if we had approached the city from the harbor and the front gates I would have been very impressed with it. Even in the dim light of the night, I could tell it must be a large city and its silhouette against the night sky was towering and layers. We approached it from the back though and so I was left to imagine what a new arrival would usually see. Chryseis has mentioned stairs and climbing and even approaching from the back of the city, I soon learned it was so. There was not a great deal of island to build on and so the city had climbed upward upon itself to find room for its growth. Apollo's great temple stood in this place. And, thanks to Chryseis' stories, I knew there was a goddess that cared for and was known on only this island as well, some secret, sacred mystery. I wondered what those two immortals thought of what we did so far below them. I wondered if they noticed at all or cared when they did. Strange that I should want a god to care about what happened, and yet be so relieved when the gods that ruled my world ignored me.

The priest went before us and led us through a small back gate in the city walls. I looked up as we passed through it and saw that the walls were not very thick at all. From the outside they looked that way but passing through I saw that it was a trick, using large stone blocks that weren't half as wide across as they were tall, affording the city just a little bit more room for buildings. It was a clever trick because it keep the Achaeans on their ships. I thought I might have been tempted to build thicker walls when the next opportunity presented itself though, if I were the one living in this city.

Bithia took my hand in hers while we walked and I wondered what she thought as she walked into a besieged city. I also wondered how many ships the Achaean raider had, how many men he had, how long he had been here, how he was supporting himself and his troops and whether the city had attempted any raids in the night or not on the ships in their harbor. I did not ask though. I understood when I should pretend to be silent and simple.

The city was crowded. The entire island had hidden inside these small walls. I wondered where their water source was. It was late in the night but people still peered out of doorways and the shelter of their tents as we moved past and in the torch light I saw their faces and their large dark eyes. The air was thick with the scent of too many people and animals packed in too small a space. I wondered where their water source was and how long their supplies would last. The only raids I knew had always been fast and quickly over but this was another thing entirely and I wondered how long so many people could last fit so tightly together.

We were brought to the Apollo's temple and even in the darkness, lit only with torches, it was a magnificent sight, putting, I thought, even Ilium's temple to shame, for it stretched upward forever, reaching for the sky. From between its painted pillars, a priest appeared, dressed so simply that it was not until he'd come all the way down the stairs to meet up that I recognized him as Chryses, Chryseis' father. He moved with as much ease as I remembered but his face looked so much older and I wondered how much of it was the years and how much the Achaeans. Some of the age faded though as he approached Hector. I lifted my head while they exchanged greetings and searched the temple's pillars and openings, wondering if my friend spent tonight in the god's shelter or at home in her own bed.

As if in answer to my searching, a form moved into one of the arches, looking small and delicate. Even after all these years, my heart recognized her even before my mind did and I gave

Bithia's hand a light squeeze before I let go. I should have waited with the rest of the group but seeing her, nothing seemed able to stop me from starting up the stairs. I felt Hector's eyes on me suddenly but he made no sound and my movement attracted the attention of the girl at the entrance. I watched her hesitate and then I saw the way she all but jumped in surprise before she was calling my name and flying down the steps to me like a bird loosed from a cage. I had never had the simple sound of my name make me so happy before.

I met her halfway up the stairs and had to brace myself for the force that she flung herself into my arms with. I returned the hug and held her so tightly I thought I might hurt her but she was holding me just as tightly. My friend. My first friend. I lowered my head to press my face into her hair and heard her weeping against me in between exclamations of surprise and happiness. I shut my eyes and let there be nothing in the world but her and the way she welcomed me even after all this time. Finally, she pulled back enough to look up at me and her face in the moonlight was just as I had remembered, beautiful and young and true, with tears in her large eyes.

"You came!" Her voice was the same too, exuberant and full of life. She cupped my face in her tiny hands to study me, hope in her shining eyes. "Oh, you came. I should have known. You always knew what to do when something bad happened. I should have known you'd be the one to come and save me."

Impulsively, I hugged her again.

"No. I came with Hector. He is the one that's going to save you."

She looked past me at the knot of men standing as the foot of the stairs and her hands, which had fallen to clasp my upper arms, gave a squeeze.

"Hector? Of Ilium? Oh!" She looked up at me in sudden understanding. "Your husband! How did you convince him to bring you too?"

Chryse was not Lemnos. News, apparently, did not travel here the way it did to larger cities. I pressed my lips together to try to decide how to even begin to explain but then Chryseis smiled past me and waved.

"And you brought Bithia! It's almost like old times." Her smile was as bright as the god she served as she looked back at me. And then I watched the shadows move into her beautiful eyes and knew we could both wish I had come for a different reason. I wrapped my arm around her shoulders. She clung to.

"I am so glad you're here, Andromache." The relief in her voice was real and sincere. It made me want to protect her from the world. It drove home to me how terrified she had been with some Achaean raider outside her walls and her future no longer her own. Not long ago I had known the feeling too well myself. I turned my own head then, looking over the top of her own, and I looked back the way I had come. Hector stood among the group of men and though he spoke to them, his head was lifted and it was me that he watched - but he did not call me back to him.

He had given Chryseis back to me.

I stood there with my arm around her, watching him watching me for what seemed like a very long time. Finally, I turned with her and we both went up and into the temple together.

Once we were inside, Chryseis drew me to the side and into one of the small rooms set aside to hide the practicality of the worship of the gods from their petitioners. A temple had to be self-sustaining and yet seem to be untouched by mortal needs and so all of the storage rooms and cleaning areas and small resting places for the priests that must always be on duty were all hidden behind hanging drapes of fantastic scenes of the god's work or through cleverly disguised doors in corners of the different chambers of the temple. Chryseis held aside a curtain depicting Apollo being given the first lyre so that Bithia could catch up and join us and then she stood there for a long time with both of my hands in hers looking at me once the heavy cloth had fallen into place to conceal us again.

"You've gotten so beautiful," she told me wistfully. "Like one of the statues of the gods." The safe way to speak of someone being as 'beautiful as the gods' without risking offending those same selfish gods. I gave her a sideways look and a sideways smile at her exaggeration and her eyes widened.

"But you do," she protested. "You've always been elegant but you've grown beautiful since I saw you last. You were beautiful before," she quickly stumbled over it and I laughed to ease the awkward conversation away, finding a seat on one of the couches so that she would sit too. She settled herself on my couch as well instead of putting the distance between us by finding her own. There was a great comfort in being able to be close, for both of us I suspected.

"I want to talk about you," I told her, taking her hand in mine, forestalling her questions about my own life in the past few years. "You must have been so worried."

"I was scared," she confessed it in a low voice, shooting a look at Bithia before focusing on me again. "That - that Achaean," she spat the term as the curse word it was becoming on this side of the Aegean, "he's huge! He caught some of our fishermen when he first came here and he killed them. Right in front of our walls so that we could all hear them scream. He laughed! And then he said he wouldn't go away until I married him. But I won't!" Her hand tightened on mine as she looked back at me. "He just wants the temple's gold as my dowry. It's sacred to Apollo. He thinks he's so clever. If we give him the treasure instead of him taking it by force, than the curse falls on us and not him." Her eyes narrowed in fury. "As if Apollo wouldn't know the difference."

Yet I noted that they hadn't given him Apollo's gold either and I had to wonder if they were right to hesitate, weighting the hope of a god's understanding. I did not remember any stories of the gods being understanding. I gave her hand an encouraging squeeze.

"But your father lit the beacon. That was better. And now we are here and you are safe."

"You're here," she agreed as if somehow my presence made a difference. "I know everything will be all right now." Then her smile went brighter and lit her eyes. "And your Hector came too."

Something must have showed on my face because she sat forward, scenting gossip. I might as well have been a deer trailing blood to a lion.

"What's happening?" She scooted closer. "Something's happening. You've got to tell me! Please," she wheedled. "It will take my mind off of my own problem."

I gave her a narrow look and she only smiled at me. Bithia sniffed. I inhaled and gave a long exhale and I suddenly found that I wanted to tell her.

Slow but with her coaxing, I did. We spent the rest of that night in that little room, crouched together on the couch, voices low like little girls whispering after their parents had sent them to bed. I had never had sister. I did not know about sharing secrets and dreams and stories beyond my single night so long ago when I had first met Chryseis. That night Chryseis might as well have been my sister from the womb, just as she was tonight, for she was the sister of my heart.

At some point in the long night, Bithia left to fetch us food and so we ate as we talked. Nemea also found his way in at some point and let me hold him, though I could not tell if he remembered me or not. I had missed him and I buried my face in his soft fur.

I was glad of Chryseis. She was much less judgmental of the entire situation than Bithia. She already thought of Hector as a hero and I had a sneaking suspicion that my story only increased his stature in her eyes, even though she was very careful not to be too obvious. To her everything seemed much more romantic and adventurous than I thought of it as being and I had to stop and laugh more than once at her questions or comments.

The talking solved nothing, of course. Yet it settled something inside me, gave me a strange comfort and peace I had not found before. Things seemed not really so horrible at all when Chryseis repeated them back to me and by the morning we were both more relaxed, I suspected, than either of us had been for several days. With the morning, however, came a throat cleared outside our small room and Chryses let himself in. Giving me a formal bow and greeting, he then turned to his daughter.

"It is almost time for the morning prayers, daughter. Today we ask Apollo to favor the warrior that fights on his behalf."

I had my doubts about a god's favor. It was not that I didn't believe the gods did favor some men over others but -- what happened when two different gods favored opposing warriors? How did the gods decide who to let win and who to let die? And – even when a god did favor their warrior -- how of our stories were about the gods failing that same warrior at random? I would pray though, I would pray to any god that would listen that Hector triumph today.

The morning ritual was simple. Spices were offered on the coals of the fire at the statue of the god's feet. The priests sang his praise while we stood silently by and the smell of the spice rose in the early morning air. The temple was open to both the east and the west and had been built in such a way that the light from the creeping sun cast directly onto its alter, burnishing the gold so that it shown like a second sun. I raised my eyes to the sky where the stars were still visible and as much as I feared a god's attention, I could not help but silently pray that, if any god was listening, they would step down from their lofty realm and guard what I loved today.

Hector entered the sanctuary afterward, a man of war stepping into the sacred, and he stood in front of Chryses to be anointed with the holy ash from the fire. He was dressed in burnished bronze armor now and the sun hit it as he stepped forward to take the blessing. He glowed, warm and gold, everything a god would be proud to call his own, and it added to my already more earth bound fears for him. It made my heart feel tight and my breath would not loose in my chest. I did not know what exactly we were to each other yet. I just knew that I did not want to lose him on this island, in this place. I was not ready. Hector's dark eyes found mine over the priest's head and the look in them was restless. Once the ask was pressed to his skin, he reached up and pulled on his helmet of the night before and the tall horsetail crest of it swayed as it settled into place. He was something else now, something that belonged to Ares on a level that I would never be able to understand or share. I had my own dark shadows though and he did not scare me, even now. Turning, Hector gathered up a longer shield than the one he had carried last night and the same spear and turned and walked out of the temple. A roar of approval greeted him then and I guessed that the people of the island had gathered to see Apollo's chosen defender.

Bithia had refreshed my and Chryseis' hair, winding gold into the strands and braids of it and we had been given mantles to drape over our dresses to suit the occasion. For the first time in many days, I wore bracelets again and they chimed quietly each time I moved. I was dressed for a noble occasion as we followed Apollo's anointed warrior out of the temple and down the stairs to what waited beyond.

Why was men killing each other considered noble?

And yet, what was there instead? Some men only responded to violence and sometimes the only way to move a problem was to destroy it.

There was a place for us to watch from the open gate. The walls were too thin to support large numbers of watchers and so someone had set up a raised platform in front of the city gate. It hardly mattered if that left us exposed. If Hector won, it would not matter. If Hector lost... well, it would not matter then either.

There were seats on the platform and I was given one of them, Bithia standing behind me to one side. Cebriones surprised me by taking a position behind me on the other side. He looked dark but I did not see fear in his eyes and I turned my whole attention back to the marked off place in front of us.

Across that open space, the Achaean raiders had amassed but they were not in battle formation. Some of them were not even in armor and none of them had drawn swords. They, like the island people behind me, were not here as participants. We were all here as witnesses, nothing more. I saw the way the Achaeans looked at Hector when he stepped into the emptied space and it was obvious they knew who he was. There was a rippling motion through their ranks and, even from where I sat I could hear as his name rose like a wave among them. There was fear and awe there, in those voices – and anticipation.

Their own warlord stepped out into the space next and he was huge. Built like a great bear in his own bronze armor, he moved like one too, lumbering and round legged but with a looseness that whispered of surprising speed. The heralds called the terms of the battle, the prizes to be won or lost and then gave the names of who fought today. Men. I shut my eyes for a moment as my stomach rolled sickly. It was all about the glory for them. Not half so important if a battle was won or lost as long as their own personal glory increased. My father had told me stories of men that broke rank and ruined battle plans just to fight the most renowned name on the other side of the battlefield. He was bragging about it too when he did so. Men lived and died by their glory, not by their nation or leader's name.

Yet... I would rather two men fight and decide than have armies die and in this case, what choice did we have anyway? I opened my eyes as the chips were tossed. Hector lost the first spear throw.

After that, everything flew forward with a speed I wasn't ready for. The Achaean threw first and my heart twisted in my chest as that great, bronze bound length whistled through the air. Hector dropped his shoulder and twisted to the side in a sudden move and I heard a great ringing sound as some part of the spear must have touched his armor. It still passed over his shoulder and into safety. Hector's response was immediate, his own great spear flying free even as he stood, the entire motion like a snake's strike through the early morning air. The bronze point bit and tangled in the Achaeans' shield, doing no damage to the man but he was forced to drop his shield, made unwieldy by the impaled spear. Without a pause, both men drew their swords and closed on each other like rushing storm clouds.

I found my hand, fingers clenched hard, against my lips. I had seen men fight before. Of course, I had. Who were my brothers and father, after all? Men enjoyed fighting and they enjoyed even more, I had discovered, fighting in front of a woman. My brothers always fought harsher and more violently against each other when I was there to witness it. Training aside, it was lucky that their weapons were blunted for the practice. It was not just my brothers either. We had visitors in our home and sometimes there were bouts of practice and skills at arms. My father liked me to be present for them and from what I saw, when the men knew I was there, they were much more aggressive. I suspected it was a male reaction the entire gender shared. So, though I had not seen actual battle since that confused night of the Achaean raid on my home as a child, I had seen men fighting most of my life. I had never managed to pretend I was interested or enjoying it, but I had grown accustomed to the loud crash of metal against metal and the painful sounding smack of weapons against flesh.

So I had no excuse for the way I found myself wincing now.

They were both big men, though Hector was much taller. I could not look away as they fought, as the bronze caught the rising sun, tinting it as red as the blood that was beginning to flow from both of them. I pressed my lips together and concentrated on staying very still, as if any movement I made would somehow, impossibly, weigh the balance wrong in the fight. I also found that I had stopped blinking, as if by simply bearing witness and watching I could somehow insure protection. I knew they were small, useless things but I felt useless and they gave me some measure of pretend control. The Achaean was strong. I could watch the bronze on the shield visibly shudder each time Hector caught a blow with it and already the metal was dented. To me, it seemed that Hector was faster though. As I watched, I realized, slowly, that he was not aiming as many blows as the Achaean was. Not even half as many. Considering his opponent didn't have his shield any more, I knew it was not from lack of opportunities. My brows came down as I watched, trying to understand. I saw the Achaean overswing as Hector moved suddenly to the side and in that instant, open and exposed, Hector brought his great shield around in a wide motion. It slammed into the other man while he was unbalanced and, even at that distance, we all could hear as much as see the way knocked the Achaean's head backward. Hector's bronze sword flashed and suddenly there was a wide line of red, raw and angry up the entire length of the

Achaean's sword arm. The foreign sword fell to the dust. My eyes shot back up just in time to watch the flat of Hector's blade connect with the side of the man's head.

Those final moves had taken what felt like only the space of a single heartbeat. Chryseis' would-be-husband collapsed like a felled bull into the dirt and Hector stood over him. The world was entirely silent.

And then it started, like a great roaring wave finding the shore. I could not tell what started first, the heralds announcing the winner or the crowd behind me going mad with noise as the enemy that had tormented them was brought low before them. The people might even have rushed forward to savage the fallen man had Hector not held up his arm. Just that. Yet the entire crowd obeyed him. With a gesture, he summoned one of the Achaeans to him and he spoke to him quietly. I could not hear what was said but the heralds snuck in close to eavesdrop. This would be a tale around the fires this winter and every detail was precious. The Achaean returned to his own shifting, silent line of men and Cebriones came forward to join Hector, vaulting down from the platform to stride across the field. There was a nod in passing, but not a word spoken before Cebriones knelt and began to strip the fallen man of his armor. Hector remained in his place, a guardian statue between the city and the restless Achaeans. From nowhere, it seemed to me, his own band of men, heavily armed, suddenly appeared, stepping out of the crowd to stand in a solid line behind their leader. It was enough. The Achaeans came forward to collect their naked fallen leader and carried him away. Hector gestured and his men followed their silent retreat, to be sure they kept their terms of the agreement. Hector turned to us.

I was on my feet, not aware of when I had stood, and I felt his eyes find me past all the others. My heart beat hard in my chest and yet I felt tears I did not understand in my throat as well. His eyes left me and he tilted down his great helmeted head to speak to Chryses as the man hurried forward to receive him. His voice carried easily for the waiting crowd.

"They will go and not return. In your harbor they will leave everything they have taken on this raid and each of their helmets. Put the helmets on your wall or in Apollo's temple before his feet, to do with as you please." His voice was hard and steady. It was the voice that belonged to the flashing helmet. "My men will be sure of it. It would be wise to keep watch on the horizon for several days. Just in case."

"Apollo won a great victory today," Chryses intoned solemnly as his people broke into cheers and I watched Hector's lips moved tightly under the cover of his helmet. The priest looked up at him. "He does favor you."

"The gods favor whoever is strongest," Hector's voice was flat and while it made the priest smile, I thought I had heard a different meaning behind his words.

"You must stay," Chryses was telling him. "We will celebrate in your honor. A feast tonight blessed by the gods. You have saved my daughter and our city." He drew Chryseis over to his side, and perhaps I imagined things, but I was reminded suddenly that she was now free to marry and that it was common for heroes to marry the women they rescued.

"Thank you. Oh, thank you." She was as effusive as ever and she took his large, bloody hand in both of her own. "I knew you would win." Her smile was beautiful. "I knew that anyone Andromache brought to defend me would win."

His lips did soften and smile under his helmet then and he leaned down to kiss her forehead.

"Andromache makes men need to win," his voice was a rumble. "So that they can come back to her without shame." Then he turned to Chryses. "I must decline. We sail with the tide. I am bound for Ilium. If you would thank me, give Andromache a wedding gift."

It drew the attention I had been hoping to avoid back to me and Chryseis immediately left her father to rush over and throw her arms around me.

"I would ask you stay," she whispered. "But I think you would go anyway."

My eyes lifted to Hector's where he watched me and I wrapped my arms around my friend.

"Yes," I agreed in the same whisper. "I would go anyway."

XIX.

Our ship left the island almost as soon as we returned to it. We paused only long enough for Hector to strip his armor and wash off in the sea next to the boat. I watched the way he replaced blood and sweat with salt and noticed the methodical way he went about it, as if it were an old habit. I supposed it was for him and it made my heart twist strangely in my chest to watch the way he was so painstakingly thorough about it. Chryseis, along with a great many of her people, came to see us off and she carried Nemea in her arms. She had offered to return him but our worlds were not the same anymore. He had found his home too long in her temple on her island for me to try to reclaim him now and so I only told him my good bye. I left him in my friend's arms, a part of my past that, like so much else, I would never find again. There were tears in Chryseis' eyes but she promised that now that I was so much closer, she would see me again soon. I hoped so. She made the world a better place whenever she was near and I had missed her in a way that the years between us had not changed.

There were gifts too. Gifts of gold and bronze, shell and coral, cheese and oils. Chryses insisted on giving Hector one of the great shields that had been crafted for Apollo's temple, saying that the god had favored him and would favor him again. The shield would be Hector's proof on the battlefield. Hector accepted it graciously, but left me to accept all the other gifts on his behalf and his farewells were polite but short. I had the distinct impression that he was not fond of thanks, or long speeches and so our leave taking was short. Hector went to the back of the ship while it pulled away from the beach with its long thin oars and I stood on the bow with Bithia and raised my hand to Chryseis until we were out of the cove and making again for the open sea.

"Did she have to make the cat wave?" Bithia wondered dryly, but I knew from her smile that she was just as fond of the other woman as I was.

"I am glad I was able to see her again," I murmured, and Bithia nodded next to me. We fell silent after that and I watched the fading island as she concentrated on controlling her breathing and her stomach. I thought she might be getting better at it out of necessity but decided not to mention it until we were on dry land again. The silence between us gave me time to focus on what was ahead for both of us now.

Troy. I could not see it yet but I knew, the island of Chryse was not that far from Lemnos, where my strange journey had begun. Lemnos itself, was very near Troy. I wondered if we would reach that final city before nightfall and thought so. I did not want to. If I had had my way, we would have sailed forever. Everything changed when we came to mighty Troy. Everything.

The wind came up again and the men pulled in their oars. Off the Dardanelles the wind was fickle but we were not going far. We were only going as far as its mouth, to windy Ilium. I put my arms around myself and wondered what would happen then. I was not a fool. I knew that Hector had taken me without permission and that was not something anyone would take lightly. I did not know how Ilium would react to finding that their oldest son was not going to be a part of the bargain they had brokered with a foreign land. He was going against, his father, his king, over something as simple as a woman. No, I corrected myself, he was going against his king over something as important as his right to choose. I was beginning to understand that.

I was beginning to crave it myself.

I should have wondered if Hector would even stand against what would be brought to bear on him at his return or if he might not simply bow under it and abandon me, returning to what his father had planned for him. It could become very ugly for him if his father desired it and while parents, even kings, could be indulgent of their children, I had also heard of their ability to be cruel to them, sometimes with just cause if it was the fate of their kingdom at stake. When I looked at the man at the back of the ship though, I did not see him bowing to anyone once he had made up his mind. Perhaps not even to the gods themselves. I found that more reassuring than I should have.

So I kept my watch at the bow while Bithia went to go lay down and I let the wind tug at my hair and wished that land would never be sighted. My fate depended on so many men right now, men I did not even know. I found that I did not want to be that helpless. Not anymore. Phthia had not been my doing, but I had gone because it was my duty, because there was nothing else for me.

What if it wasn't that way now though? What if... what if I had a choice this time? What if, somehow, *I* could decide my future instead of leaving it all in the hands of men? What if I could choose?

I would not choose Phthia with its angry sea witch and its terrifying brothers and its foreign language. Nor would I choose to return home, I realized. That place was not mine anymore, grown too small like children's clothing outgrown. I had grown into something else over my years of waiting and I was not content to live in a forgotten room, watching my brothers raise their families around me, living in fear of my mother's shadow. I wanted... Against my will I turned my head and looked to the back of the ship. I wanted...

I wanted what had been promised to me, I thought, and was surprised by how fierce it felt in my chest when I dared admit to it. I wanted Ilium and my own house. I wanted to hear my native language around me when I went outside and to know that the rain that fell on me would soon touch my family. I wanted -- I wanted to not be afraid of the man that would come for me in my bed at night. I wanted --

I wanted Hector.

I wanted Hector. The second time I dared think it, it was stronger, more sure and steady in my chest. It was not a question. It was such a deep desire that I was afraid that, because it was so strong, it would never be allowed. Admitting it to myself seemed to be risking everything. I would not stay the same if I married him. Already I was changing inside from what I had been when I had laid in that cold bed on Lemnos. I wanted that. I wanted who I was now over who I had been then. And I wanted the man lying on the bench at the back of the ship. I wanted to be able to call him my husband. I wanted to hear his voice in my house, and see that smile on his face and I wanted... I wanted him to stand too close to me and lower his head. I wanted to have him be the one that turned to me in the night in our bed.

The wants were a pain in my chest and I pressed my fist against it and tried to breathe. I wanted -- but I had always wanted. Wanting was not enough. I had to do more than simply *want* this time. My life had changed and in changing, it had handed me a chance. If all I did was idly want though, it would not be enough. The realization came hard to me that, this time, I had to act. *I* had to be a factor in my future instead of simply sitting by and watching my future be decided for me. All my life I had been the good daughter, I had let my father, and the other men in my life, decide my fate for me. This time though, for the first time, I had something I wanted for myself and if I was going to keep it for myself, I could not rely on others for that. *I* need to take action. I needed to take the risk. The alternative was unthinkable. I drew in a breath and turned back to the sea, feeling the surety and the determination settle deep in my spine. This was my future now. I had been broken loose from the natural progression of things. I had a chance.

In the immediate, there was little I could do to make a difference but I was intelligent. I would watch and I would see. Just as surely as there had been little places in my life that had been openings for me before, there would be more to come. This time I would use them for more than finding ways to be comfortable with what others decided for me though. I would never again trust men alone to decide my future for me. I would find my own way through their plans. It was both lofty and frightening but my heart told me that if I did not make this decision now, I never would.

Determined to put action to my new decision even if it was only a small thing, I stepped first into the tent Bithia slept in and then slowly made my way to the back of the ship. The men watched me as I passed. To them, I was already something other than just a kidnapped woman. It had made me uncomfortable before, thinking more was expected of me, but now I saw it was what I wanted for myself. I would be more, and I would find a way to rise to what was expected of me because of it. The alternative was to forever be a rag doll, passed from hand to hand with no choice or choosing on my part. I would not be that again. I smiled at the man that was handling the rudder and he smiled back and then I moved over to where Hector rested, flat on his back on an empty bench. Quiet, I sank down on the deck next to his place. The walk to the back of the ship had seemed to take forever and I felt as if there were storm clouds that surely must be rolling in my wake. A part of me was frightened that I was taking on too much, that I was lifting my expectations too high and that tomorrow when it all crashed down around me I would prove what a fool I was for even thinking I was anything but a simple woman, made for trade and children. Another part of me remembered Ariadne. My mother claimed the same blood. Why should I not find my own, hopefully less tragic, way as well? Hector lay quiet and still next to me, breathing deep and slow so that I thought he might be sleeping but after a moment he opened a single dark eye and turned his head to look at me. His lips shifting into the whisper of a smile and I thought... I thought perhaps I would not be all alone in finding my newer, better future after all. It helped calm the beating in my chest. I smiled back at him.

"Your friend made you happy," his voice was throaty with the edges of drowsiness.

"Chryseis makes everyone happy." He offered nothing in response to that and we rested in that silence comfortably for a very long moment while the sail whispered above us and the sea wind kept the heat of the sun at bay. It was strange to find so much peace in someone else's presence, doubly so after what I thought was a rather earth shaking decision on my part, even if no one else in the world realized it. Being with Hector though, it calmed the panicked, wild beating in my chest that the fear and freedom of that decision had given me. It let me calm and center myself again. I would do this thing, I would brave my own future, but the first rush of that slipped away and was replaced by a calmer certainty. Hector's silent presence soothed the jostling edges of my thoughts. Not for the first time, as my mind settled and my chest relaxed over the enormity of what I was going to somehow find a way to do, I understood why the horses loved him so. Why his men did too. Finally, relaxed enough, I tucked my arm up on the bench and rested my head against it. Strands of my hair lifted in the breeze to move across his chest.

"You didn't call me."

His dark eyes both opened and he turned his head to look at me.

"You didn't run away."

I thought I understood then, in the way he said it, why he had not asked me not to run from him before. It was still there, inside him, the thought that one day I would find him frightening and I would run. I reached up with my other hand and laid it over a bruise that stood out, new and red on his bicep.

"You weren't frightening," I told him and

411

watched his eyes change, watched them go soft and dark and his face relaxed as well. He even smiled. He moved the hand that was farthest from me and touched my hair almost reverently with his fingertips.

"Gentle Andromache," he murmured my name. I accepted it as he had meant it and so instead of making me cringe at the falsehood of it, it warmed me. Very gently, I moved my fingertips over the bruise.

"I have something that will ease the aches," I offered after a moment. "It will make the bruises less tender too."

His eyes moved from me to the black box I had taken from my tent and carried back here with me. He might not know what was in that box but I suspected he knew enough to know it was dark. He looked back at me and there was no fear or mistrust in his eyes.

"I would not be a very impressive warrior if I admitted to feeling beaten after a battle," he commented dryly but I saw it was not serious.

"You will have to take your tunic off. I cannot apply the ointment through the fabric."

His smile started to spread then and his dark eyes held light. It striped weariness from him and years as well, so that he looked younger.

"Are you trying to seduce me, Andromache?"

"Never," I told him, innocence in my voice. Though, for the first time in my life, I thought, perhaps I was.

With a low noise he sat up, careful not to bump me while I moved aside for him. I noticed the ginger way he moved as he shifted, how each motion was done with the least amount of action possible and it welled up a strangely protective feeling inside me. He had been hurt, and for the first time I realized fully that he was mine to take care of. Terrifying warlord of Ilium. Given to my hands for care. When he was finally sitting up completely, I stood as well and set the box down on the bench next to him. He looked at it curiously but there was no terror or disgust in his eyes. He did not know what it was capable of but I also knew he was too aware to not wonder what lived inside it all the same. For the first time, someone that was not my mother's blood saw its interior. That was my choice too, to share this part of myself, albeit obliquely, with him. I opened the box's first level and took out one the opaque jars. He watched but he didn't ask and he didn't hesitate to tug off his tunic for me either as I moved to stand behind him.

He had a well-muscled back, smooth and layered without being painful looking or knotty. His skin there was almost as bronze as the skin on his face and arms. I could see bruises and raw spots from where armor that hadn't been his had sat on him wrong or absorbed a blow. Very gentle, I touched his hair as it curled against the back of his neck and I watched the way his shoulders lowered and relaxed in response. He bowed his head and I could see the way the lashes touched his cheeks as he shut his eyes for me. For the first time, belatedly, I realized that he was a beautiful man.

It was trust that had him baring himself to me and trust as well that he did not question what was in the bottle in my hands. He gave himself to my care because he chose too and I was finally beginning to understand just how powerful that was. We were both stepping outside of what was given to us to reach for more. It helped shore me up inside to realize that I was not alone in that. Pooling the oil from the bottle into my hand, I returned the bottle to its spot and then leaned my face close to breathe the words of power over the liquid I let shift to fill the cup of my palms. Then, as I had been taught, I began to slowly work it into his stiff muscles and bruised flesh. This was not the first time I had cared for a man like this. It was the first time I had touched Hector though and it felt... different... The skin under my hands was mine, if I wanted it; the muscle that moved under my touch would move again to protect me if I asked. I remembered the warmth of sleeping with him after the storm and realized that I would feel that again, soon, and that there would be less clothing between us the next time. What I felt under my hands, I would soon feel against the rest of me and it was a frightening though and yet it was something I found I was curious to discover. I had heard stories and heard and seen things in the night in a house full of brother and servant and soldiers but Hector was different to me and I found I wanted to know more. I did not fear him as I had my future husband in a foreign land across the great sea. I let my hands linger on him, let them feel the sun soaked warmth of him and I let myself grow used to the idea of touching him. It was not so frightening at all.

There was no great magic to what I did. I had done the same for my brothers and my father before, on some of the soldiers in our house. I had even used this potion without whispering the words and still seen the ointment, a collection of oils and herbs and minerals, do its work just as well. If the words did not hurt though, they could only help. It felt important that I do things to my best when I did them for this man, not because he asked or would even know otherwise but because I wanted to. This man was mine alone to care for and it was a good feeling to have.

My hands were strong from years of work and the sharp smell of the oil brought me back to a hundred times before. I knew what I was doing and I could feel it working as his muscles loosed under my strong fingers and the breath escaped him in silent long exhales. It filled me in a strange way to think that he was not used to this, that I was the one that could give him this. He would not have even known to ask me for it and yet I could give him the gift of it all the same. It was no small thing to take care of someone strong. It was no small thing at all to take care of someone you cared about.

"You came back to me." His voice was

deep with sleep and I saw the way his breathing had deepened but he fought it. It made me smile, reminding me of a small child and giving me yet another facet of the man I had decided I wanted for myself to see. I knew he meant that I had come back to the back of the ship to see him when always before he had had to come to me.

"It seemed cruel to make you walk," I told him and was surprised at how easy it was to be lightly teasing with him. I saw his lips smile and he opened one eye to slant it back at me over his shoulder. The wind played with his salt dried curls.

"Gentle Andromache," he called me again and again I could accept it from him instead of feeling guilt for not being what he said.

I took took my time with him, careful to work my craft completely. It was also my secret excuse to acquaint myself with his body, storing away my new knowledge of his scars, his skin, the way it felt to touch him. By the end, his head was nodding and I could not stop the soft smile that created on my lips. I did not know if he had slept last night and then he had faced a giant in a battle that had not been short. I slipped my hands one last time over the full expanse of his back, murmuring for him to lie down, and he did, relaxing on the bench again. I gathered up my box and would have walked away, leaving him to sleep in peace, but his hand caught the fabric of my skirt. It was a new skirt, one that Chryseis had made part of my 'wedding gift' and it was actually long enough on me. I paused and turned my head to look back down at him, not startled so much as willing.

"What would make you happy?" He muttered, eyes still closed.

I had not been expecting anything in particular from him and his question caught me off guard, so that I had to pause, brows coming down. The new bracelets on my wrists chimed gently as the wind caught at them.

Happy?

"A kitten." It was the first word that came out of my mouth and I immediately realized how stupid I sounded, asking for something so silly and simple. His lips only curved up into a sleepy smile though and he nodded against the arm he had folded up under his head.

"A kitten," he repeated and let go of my skirt. I shook my head at his strange question, which he couldn't see, and then made my way back up to the front of the ship. Cebriones looked at me as he sat there.

"Thank you," was all he said but I thought it was more than enough. I gave him a shy smile and ducked back into the tent set aside for Bithia and I. Bithia was already asleep and I slid the box quietly under my own mat and then lay down as well. There had been no sleep for me last night either and as much as my mind wanted to circle around all that had happened to me and all that was ahead, I took the escape into sleep instead. It had long been my friend when I needed to forget for a time and my mind ran away into the darkness of it again as I closed my eyes.

I woke when the sailors began to move with a purpose and, looking outside I saw that we were indeed nearing land. That stretch of shore, I knew, could only be one place. My future would be decided there and it was time for me to start laying my own hand to it. I woke Bithia and, groggy, she did not wonder at my change of attitude when I had her brush and fashion my hair with the gold and amber beads I had been given or help me fasten the waist of my dress with the gold and silver pins. I had no sandals but I still had her clean and anoint my feet. I touched the saffron oil to my skin. By then Bithia was awake enough to be aware and she looked as if she torn between suspicion and approval at my actions. She was right to be suspicious. What I did, I did with a purpose this time. I even let her set the veil over my head though I drew it back so that I could see clearly and, more importantly, so that my face could clearly be seen. She fastened the necklaces of gold and amber that matched the beads in my hair around my throat and in my ears she set earrings that chimed softly each time I moved my head. I let her darken my lids with charcoal and my lips with color and waited until she gave her soft grunt of approval. She thought I was as adorned as a woman of my stature should be. That was the point. When I stepped out of the tent and straightened it was not as the casual Andromache I had been. I felt the impact and the pause in the men and knew that, for this ship at least, I had succeeded.

I was not lawiaiai. I was no war prize. I would come to the city as a bride. I had made my decision. I did not, however, have the nerve to look for Hector as I assumed my usual position at the bow of the boat. He did not join me.

Our little ship pushed into its harbor. It was coming home again and content to do so. It had carried us safely through the storms and across the trackless seas and all it asked now was a safe harbor to lie in until it was called upon again. I caressed its rail with my hand and murmured my thanks to it. For so many reasons.

The nose of the ship brushed up against the sand of the shore and immediately there were men there to catch its ropes and pull it farther up. They saw me. The crews of the two other ships that were lying next to ours saw me as well and I was aware of their eyes. I stood straight and tall and unflinching before them and I knew the sun caught on the gold I wore. I came here, if not of my own freedom, as my own choice at least. I would not cower as if I were ashamed. Presentation meant more than words. Let my first impression be of what I wanted for my future and not what someone else would decide of it for me. The men handed me down reverently onto the sand of the beach and it was hot under my feet despite the cool of the weather. Ilium... I had finally come to Ilium, so far from my wedding day. I could see the Monument of Ilus from here and Troy's great white walls beyond that... My heart beat hard in my chest despite the way I kept my face serene. I had been here before, stood on this shore before, seen the city rising before me once before, but everything was different. I was not safe in anonymity this time and there was no father or friends or brothers to stand by me. The plain and the city beyond it did not seem larger so much as... brighter. For that second, my heart caught in my throat and I was sure that I could not do this monumental thing I had set in front of myself.

A chariot came next to me then, no doubt from where it had been waiting nearby for important visitors and when I lifted my eyes there was only Hector in it, reins held competently in one hand as it stopped next to me. His eyes were very dark – and very soft. He held out his hand for me.

"I would like to show my bride her new city." His voice was very gentle and yet I knew pitched to carry to everyone that was nearby and no doubt listening intently.

Gathering my skirt's hem, I took his hand and joined him.

XX.

I wrapped my cold fingers around the railing of the chariot. It had been sitting in the sun before this and I could feel its warmth of its wood against my palms. I pretended I could soak that warmth into my lungs and drew in a breath to steady myself as the horses started forward at Hector's low command. He waited until we were well past the men who had stopped their work to watch and then he chuckled.

"Someone taught you to drive." His voice was very low. I turned my head to look at him and I could not help the small smile as I saw he was looking at me from the corners of his dark eyes.

"How can you tell?" I asked, both proud and embarrassed, and I watched his lips twitch as he turned his eyes back to watch as he guided the chariot at a steady walk.

"You're not standing like a passenger. You stand like a charioteer." I kept myself from looking down at my feet in automatic response. "You've learned how to balance the basket."

I pressed my lips together, then remembered they were painted and I should not smear them. I had forgotten that Hector paid attention where other men did not.

"My brother Podes taught me. The year after you first came to Thebe."

"Good," his eyes were ahead as the horses found the more hard packed road that would curve and take us into the city itself. I gave him another sideways glance because it was not traditional for women to drive chariots but there was nothing on his face or in his voice that said he was not being honest with me or that there was mockery hidden underneath. Somehow, I had not thought it would bother him.

"Have you ever traveled behind the golden walls of Ilium?" His voice was soft but mine was softer.

"Once," I whispered and did not tell him more. Instead, I raised my face as the vast white expanse of massive walls and the growing sound of a city full of life drew closer. And I felt the awe of it that I had not felt when I was younger. Now, older, I could understand much better what I saw when I looked upon the city that had once promised to take me in as one of its own. I could appreciate the grandeur and also the brutal force that keep it alive and thriving. I could feel the cold metal behind its beautiful front and I could appreciate its determination to exist despite threats both foreign and closer.

Vast Ilium's walls rose tall, taller than two men on each other's shoulders. Its wide white stones were perfectly fit so that there was no mortar between them and thin coat of pale paint over them smoothed their surface as it arched upward toward the forever blue sky. They were walls built to endure forever, a steady, strong promise that this city would last. I knew men had built them but it was easy to see why people believed it had been the gods themselves. Towers, even taller than the walls, rose at the various gates with their crowned heads and the men that moved on top of those seemed small. I wondered what they saw from such a height.

I wondered if I might join them to look outward and see the world spread before me as well someday...

Before we even reached the city proper, I saw that smaller houses, shops and animal pens had grown up around Ilium's base. I did not remembered them from my last visit here and I saw that a deep ditch with a wooden and mud brick wall had also been added to surround the impromptu town, small shield and fortress outside of the greater one. It was silent proof of Achaean interest and Ilium's response to those greedy eyes. How many of these people, I wondered, had once lived somewhere else and been driven to the protection of Ilium's shelter? How many small settlements and towns had fallen to foreign forces in the past years and escaped to huddle here?

It was late in the day and the streets were busy with people but everyone moved aside for Hector's chariot and they stood silent and watching as we went past. I kept my eyes ahead so I would not have to meet their curious gaze, feeling awkward in my chosen pretend role of confidence but determined to see it through to the very end. I knew. People reacted to what they perceived, not to what was necessarily really there. I would not be the spoils of a raid to be treated carelessly and argued over by men of power. I would be a bride and treated with the respect due me as Eetion's daughter. I could not change the circumstances, but I could change the way other people saw them. At least a little. Hopefully, it would be enough. As we drew closer to the city proper, children began to run to keep up with the chariot and I heard the growing murmur among the watching people. Gossip would forever travel even faster than the wind and it was obvious that something more was going on than a simple return of Ilium's favored son. Hector's eyes slid to me and I watched the edges of his mouth shift upward from the corners of my eyes. He stood as straight backed and calm as I did, though he had done something to the horses with his touch and they arched their necks and all but pranced as they clamped along. I realized we were going the long way around the city.

"You're doing this on purpose," I murmured, barely moving my lips, and he grinned suddenly, teeth white and beautiful in his tanned face. Then he laughed. It was a wonderful laugh, real and unhindered and it filled the air. And -- suddenly -- everything changed. Someone in the crowd raised their hands, shaking them, bracelets of shell rattling. And then another set of hands rose. And another. Soon the air was full of those pale palms and the cheering began. It started small but it grew. The children were joined by young men who ran next to the chariot, smiling wide grins that matched Hector's. The deeper into the little town we came the more people there were on the streets, lining up along our path to wait for us to come by. The first shower of flower petals surprised me and I turned my face to blink into it by reaction, finding their pale colors falling around me like large, lazy snowflakes. Then there were more. And more. We had hardly given them warning or time to prepare, yet young girls and small boys still darting forward to intercept Hector's slow paced chariot. They pressed flowers and the traditional sheaves of grain into my arms but, unprepared, they also made do with what was available to them. I found carved horses of various quality in my hands, small trinkets of shell and stone, flax and wool and hemp in various stages of preparation. They gave me small jars of decorated clay and double handed cups, even a bracelet of tiny brass bells. I had never been welcomed before and certainly not by an entire city. By the time we reached the great, thick walls of the city proper, I had already had to put three armfuls down awkwardly in the basket of the chariot. My careful, protective calm had shattered and I felt overwhelmed and yet lighter in my chest, confused and yet happy and entirely unprepared myself.

"But they don't even know who I am," I protested as I turned where I stood to look back at them as the chariot finally passed through one of the giant gates of bronze and wood, moving into Ilium proper.

"They know enough," Hector told me as he

nodded to the guards that looked curiously at me as we drove slowly past. "And tomorrow or the day after when they learn the rest, they will say that they always knew. That they looked and they could just tell."

It made me laugh, though I tried not to, worried about losing dignity. He had explained human nature anywhere though and he was right. Everyone liked to say that they had already known when something strange or wonderful was happening. Hector turned his head slightly to me, still grinning, and gave a flick of his reins so the horses picked up just a little bit more speed. If he could smile and be the warlord of a city this grand and dignified, perhaps it would not be so bad if I smiled as well.

The lower city was much as I remembered it, though not so crowded without the fair. It was just as colorful and busy and confusing as before. Already, the great wide streets that ran through it were crowded with people in brightly colored clothing and they too had flowers and grain in abundance for they'd had more time to prepare. The flower petals fell like rain around me as women and children climbed up onto their rooftops where their grapes and figs were laid out to dry in order to both shower the fragrant petals down on me and to see better. The horses trotted on a carpet of green and colorful flowers and my arms were full to overflowing, but that did not stop the children from coming to give me more. My nose was full of the scents of dusty, sun warm grain and heady flowers; my ears full of the sound of singing, laughter and cheers. Everywhere I looked there were smiling, curious faces. One of the squares had filled with dancers treading the maze and they sang as we passed them.

"Do they always do this when you return?" I asked. For surely -- *surely* -- this could not all be for me. Surely no woman had ever been greeted in such a way. Hector smiled and raised his hand to the people and they cheering him.

"Oh no," he told me calmly without looking away from what he was doing so that the horses, in this close packed, moving crowd would feel his steady hand and stay safe for the people that crowded close. "But you look like a queen out of legend, my Andromache, and you feel like goodness. Your arrival, as unexplained as it is, must be a reason to celebrate." For just a moment, his voice softened. "And it is."

"This is why you took the long way." I was apparently not the only one thinking of setting a precedence. I was glad, and yet, if I had known all this attention would be showered on me, I might have been tempted to try a more secluded way.

Hector's way was the right one though. We would not sneak into his city like thieves. He brought us in like victors.

"This is your city, Andromache. One day, you will be its queen. And queen of all the lands of Troy. How could your country, your people, your home, ever forgive itself it if did not welcome you in when you came to claim it?"

I was glad I was already smiling automatically at everyone and accepting the gifts without having to think about it because if I had not, I would have frozen at the realization.

Queen?

My city? My people?

I had known -- of course I had known, at least in a vague, dreamlike way. Hector would rule Ilium after his father. It was uncontested, even with as many brothers as he had. If he had not been lawagetas, perhaps his birth order would not have been enough, but he had proven himself a leader and the country had already taken him into its heart. Whoever he married would be his queen, to sit next to him at his table and steward the country as a woman stewarded her husband's household. I had known it. I had vaguely worried about it when I was younger, prepared for it as best as anyone could given the limited opportunities I had, but it had never been real to me, not the way being Hector's bride had been real. After I had thought that promise of marriage lost, I had not thought of Ilium since then as anything other than the city that had not wanted me. Except, even not knowing who I was they seemed to want me now. In this moment at least, they were happy to see me, whoever I was, thinking I could only bring them good if I rode with their beloved lawagetas.

If I took my place as Hector's bride -- in the

same step, I took my place as the future queen of these people.

Suddenly, my choice was so much larger than it had been before, even more overwhelming and far reaching. If I took Hector, I took all of Troy. And, if I hid now, if I refused this challenge, I lost it all.

The determination in me hardened. I would not to lose what I had chosen to keep.

So, trapped in my play, I continued to smile and accept the gifts and wave in response to their cheers. I was glad that I had learned to balance like a charioteer or, with my arms too full to hold the rails, I might have lost my balance or worse unbalanced the entire cart. It was not the impression I wished to give being seen by the city for the first time.

We entered the inner walls, past the great gates with their gods set in front of their towers, finally reaching the citadel that housed the royal family, the chosen warriors and the temples of both Apollo -- and Athena. I remembered what lived here. I had seen...

Hector did not turn in that direction though. Instead, he turned his horses as his brother had offered to so many years ago. We did not go to the gods of Ilium. Instead he took me in the direction I had once been told he had started building a home.

It seemed it must have been another life.

The crowds thinned once we were inside the inner walls but it was more that there were not as many people than that they were any less curious or enthusiastic. Here my gifts, along with the flowers and grain, were gifts of gold and amber and pearl, silver and colored stones, electrum and bronze. They were expensive gifts given to a stranger simply because she rode like a queen and stood next to their prince. My mind, not used to the opulence that lead to easily given gifts of value as well as the concept of being unknown and still celebrated, continued to balk but it was growing easier to smile and accept what was offered. It was impossible for me not to feel treasured, even if my mind still hesitated over it, when I was treated so warmly. Ahead of us, they anointed the road with oil and I smelled the way it rose, soaking everything in its expensive fragrances as we passed. The houses were huge here and set well apart, with walls and glimpsed gardens between them. We rode through the very heart of Troy's vast wealth. I could not imagine any city that was grander. Finally, when my arms were growing tired, we came upon one house, set a bit away from the others and, unlike the others, walled completely around. That gate was open and Hector turned his chariot, passing through and we left the crowd behind.

I am sure that it did not truly happen that way but the moment we passed through the gate, it was as if all the noise of the world behind us vanished. Everything went still with a hush so that only the horses' hooves made noise as they slowed and then stopped in the yard. In front of me, a large house rose. It was not as large as my father's house, which held the entire royal family of Thebe but it was larger than any house I had seen in Ilium. It was larger than any house that was not a palace I had ever seen. And it was tall. Three stories high and I suspected that, from its roof, I would be able to see entirely over the walls of Troy. A youth ran out of a small building off to its side I had not noticed and caught the horses' harness, and for a minute I know that our eyes must have matched as we looked at each other and wondered how the other fit into this world inside the walls of this house. Hector tied the reins and, carefully stepped over the acquired gifts I had been given and off of the chariot. I could feel his eyes on me, expecting something I couldn't guess at, and I turned to look at him.

"This is yours?" I asked, suddenly reminded, foolishly, how much more affluent and large Ilium was than Thebe. His hands closed around my waist as he lifted me down and set me on my feet. I was very close in front of him and he did not step back or take his hands from my waist. I was surprised by how powerfully reassuring I found his closeness and I finally exhaled the breath that had been frozen in my chest since I had seen Troy's shore on the horizon. Hector lowered his head and his voice was gentle.

"No, Andromache," there was a note I had not heard before in his voice. "This is yours."

I lifted my face to him and whatever he saw

on it made him smile sadly. His fingertips touched my chin lightly.

"I built it for you." It came out of him in a tired sigh. "All those years ago. Before I even sent Cebriones to your father to ask for you, I bought this land and cleared it so that I could build you a home here. At first it felt like a promise. But as the years went by it just felt empty."

I reached up to touch his cheek, cupping it in my palm. It was like the chests he'd sent to me. At first, they had been promises but as the time had gone by they had begun to feel empty even though they'd been full. I understood.

"Will you show me?" I watched the softness and light touch his dark eyes. "Will you show me everything?"

I watched his smile as he took my hand and I thought that he did not look old at all but young, like a little boy. Somehow that same feeling filled me too and I felt young as I had not felt in many years.

He led me through the house and the grounds. He pointed out the stables, where the young boy was already leading the horses and I knew at once, with a little burst of inward laughter, where he spent most of his time. Then he led me inside and showed me where we would live together from now on. There was the megaron, large enough to be proud of but small enough that it felt friendly and warm. The guest rooms were warmly painted, the kitchen was large and open, the bath was small and cheerfully tiled. The building itself was the same white limestone as the walls of the city and cut like it, so that the stone fit together end to end and perfectly without mortar but everywhere it was overlaid with clay and painted so it was smooth. He'd hired someone to paint the inside of some of the rooms as well and dolphins swam across the walls or dogs hunted boar or warm abstract designs whirled away in bright colors and rich hues. The floors were painted or inlaid with tile as well and where there was wood it was rich and polished. He led me up stairs, through arches and doorways, into and out of rooms and even up onto the roof - where I could, indeed, see over the walls of Ilium. I could from the windows on the top floor as well. I could see the water, stretching on forever in blue and where the Simois flowed into the sea. I could also see the garden that was between the back of the house and the great wall and I saw -

"Olive trees?" Each new turn inside the house had filled me with a happy, hopeful excitement, made me feel like laughing and, strangely, a little like crying. The thought that this was mine, ours, it was almost too much. It made me too happy, made me believe in something too huge and wonderful. Seeing the olive trees though - - I wrapped both of my hands around his upper arm as we stood there, looking out over windy Ilium and this small section of it. He turned his head to look down at me and the wind tossed his dark curls.

"I thought - " For the first time I heard him

hesitate over his words. "I thought you might like them. And remember."

I looked up at him, this tall, dark powerful man next to me. Lawagetas of his people, terror of his enemies, the next wanax of Troy and all its lands and I thought, he had hesitated for me. Wispy, once forgotten me.

"I remember." Of course, I remembered that day all those years ago in a dusty olive grove, and man-slaughtering Hector had planted olive trees because he had remembered too.

Eventually, he led me back down into the house and back to the first floor. On the way back, I could not help but notice how strange the inside of the house was. First of all, it had doors. They were in almost every opening. Not the usual drapes or curtains or simple emptiness but doors. They were thick and solid doors and almost every one of them had an equally sturdy wooden bar to drop across its inside. I thought of the shutters in my father's megaron and how, meant for storms, they had still managed to keep out intruders. Second, I noticed the state of the house itself. It was empty. So empty. There were bits and pieces of oddities and furniture gathered here and there but there was no purpose to them. It was as if the house had been waiting for someone to come and make it real, to turn it from a building into a home. Only the storage rooms themselves were full. There was cloth and household linens in a small room on the top floor off of what I had already started to think of as my 'weaving room' even though it was empty of everything at the moment. On the bottom floor the storage rooms, larger and more ordered, were full of foods and household goods, mostly untouched and still glossy and new. There was one storage room on the middle level and Hector had showed it to me briefly.

That room had been full of the armor and ransoms of kings and heroes.

My hand found its way back to his as we walked and I trailed my other hand across random surfaces that came within reach, needing to touch, to make this real. Looking up once as I did so I caught Hector's eyes on my fingers and would have pulled my hand away, realizing I was acting like a little girl, having to touch everything, but Hector caught my wrist in his other hand and shook his head.

"It makes me happy that I can give you something that pleases you, Andromache. Don't hide that from me."

His words made me self-conscious. I don't know what he saw on my face but he chuckled as he moved around to stand in front of me, raising the hand he had trapped so that it would rest on his chest before releasing it to curve that hand around my waist. He lowered his head to me and I raised my face to his. It felt natural to stand this way with him. It made all of today, so strange and new, seem a little more familiar and easy to accept. It made me want to step closer to him still but I stopped myself before I did, still not sure about where that would lead.

"If it helps, I was also thinking how much I envied everything you were trailing your fingertips over."

Something in my chest tripped over itself then at the way he said that, at the look in his eyes and the tone in his voice. I pressed my lips together and watched the way he focused on my mouth and that made my stomach shiver pleasantly as well. I tried to fight it but despite myself the edges of my lips quivered upward and his eyes rose to mine again. The look he shot me was dark and warning and yet it only made me have to fight harder not to smile. His own smile suddenly split through his dark beard and he laughed, gentle and rumbling in his chest.

"Andromache, my Andromache," he teased and I did not fight my smile then. I did however step closer into him and raised my fingertips to rest them against his cheekbones. His eyes darkened and his shoulders relaxed. Gentle, light, I let my fingers move slowly down his face, curving inward until I could rest the tips of them over his lips. I had never touched a man before, not like this, and I watched as Hector's dark eyes lidded in response. It made something in my chest thrill and he did not see when I smiled this time.

Was this what it was then? To stand in your own house and touch the man that belonged to you?

Through the open window, I heard the

clatter of an arriving chariot, followed by Bithia's voice, though I could not catch her words. My fingers dropped from Hector's lips but I did not step away from him.

His black eyes opened and his voice had gravel at its edges.

"I'll take you to the guest room where you and your maid can sleep. Don't get too comfortable there. You belong upstairs. In my bed -- with me."

XXI.

I woke with the sun the next day and left the guest room, wondering what to do with myself, since I was not, in fact, married to Hector and therefore a guest, not this house's mistress. It did not take long to figure out that Hector was already gone, the house feeling even more empty than its sparse furnishing and empty rooms. Drawn instinctively to what I considered the heart of any house, I found my way to the kitchen. The young boy from the day before and an old man were both there, busy grinding grain in a large dish, adding handfuls more as they worked and they looked up when I stepped into the room, surprised, I suppose, to see me. Cebriones sat on a low stool near a door that opened into the garden in the back of the house, letting in the early morning breeze that smelled like salt air and the faintest tinge of early morning cooking. I smiled carefully at the man and boy, as unsure as how we should greet each other as they probably were, and moved to join Hector's half-brother, shaking my head at the stool he stood up to offer me and instead sweeping my hand across the stone paving of the doorway and sitting there. No one had found me sandals that would fit my feet yet and I hoped secretly that they had forgotten. Now I put my bare feet on the still night cool packed earth outside the door near what I thought might be someone's attempt at an herb garden and looked outward at the thin olive trees, still wet with dew and the half wild bushes of flowers and tall grass that grew near the wall. Cebriones offered me a clay cup that held juice and I took it, sipping thoughtfully as I sat half in and half out of the house, feeling it was very appropriate to be that way.

"He's gone to talk to his father. Priam favors Hector most but he is still wanax and Hector is still his lawagetas," Cebriones said though I hadn't asked and I nodded, sipping the drink again. The boy brought me a small loaf of bread fresh from the oven and I thanked him, careful not to burn my fingers. He gave me a shy smile under the shaggy thatch of his hair and quickly retreated on silent, bare feet to join the old man again. Realizing what I had been given was the flat, tough soldier's bread, I wondered if they knew how to cook anything other than travel rations in this house that had not been a home. After a long moment of pressing my lips together and watching the ever present wind, just a light breeze at the moment, move the leaves of the young olive trees, I asked:

"How likely do you think the wanax is to listen to Hector?"

Cebriones tipped his head back and frowned thoughtfully. The pause and the thought, told me he would not lie to me, even if he knew I would not like the truth. I appreciated that. After a long moment of silence, he exhaled.

"Priam loves Hector more than any of his other children. He'd give him anything he wanted but Hector never asks. Priam is used to that and I think he forgets that Hector is not just an extension of himself sometimes." I nodded when he paused. He looked at me and continued.

"There are many merchants and councilors that are afraid of the Achaeans and the way they've only been getting more aggressive lately. They worked very hard to push the treaty with Sparta on the wanax while Hector was away. Priam is convinced Ilium is invincible but he listened to them anyway because Ilium is built on the trade that the Achaeans are trying to disrupt. Hector has publicly gone against his father's, and his wanax's wishes, by taking you and refusing the Spartan agreement. Priam has enough sons, he can offer another to Sparta. If the counselors had been thinking they would have realized that Hector couldn't go to Sparta. He could never leave Troy and become lawagetas of another land. It's not in him and it's not logical to give our greatest deterrent that keeps the Achaeans at bay to another country. Perhaps they did think of that but decided they'd still rather have Hector gone considering he sometimes disagrees with their suggestions on what's best for Ilium. Troy can buy off any insult Sparta feels over this. They will claim insult though." He turned his head to look at me. "Your family may as well."

I gave him a sad smile at that. I knew enough of the world now to understand that claiming insult was not as straightforward as it at first seemed.

"If my family claimed insult, they would have done so over the fact Ilium cast me aside. We are not strong enough. And none of my father's men would dare challenge Hector."

"Wise," he commented dryly and then exhaled again. "Not everyone will be happy with what Hector's done. Even the people that usually support him. He's gone directly against the wanax's decision."

I pressed my lips together and nodded vaguely, looking out into the garden beyond again and not truly seeing it. I had no power in Ilium, no authority or allies. The cup in my hands grew warm where it sat in my lap as the sun began to rise.

"Hector knew this before he came to me." It should have been a question but it came out of me a statement.

Cebriones grunted.

"He knew."

I drew in a deep breath, then let it out again. I would have to trust him. I had no choice in the matter, but more, it was Hector. Hector, who had come for me even when his father and lord told him not to. Hector who had chosen to take me first -- and ask if he could afterward. I looked at the herbs struggling to find their place near my feet, misplanted as they were. All it would take was a gentle hand and a repositioning and the herbs would learn to thrive. I looked back at Cebriones.

"What did Hector say about me before he left this morning?" I asked and he gave me a companion's smile.

"That you were to be given anything you asked for. Or looked like you might ask for. Or even blinked accidentally in the general direction of. And that you and your maid were to stay here today. No one in, no one out and no confirmation of who you are if anyone asked us." His smile went crooked and he added: "And that if anyone comes for you saying he sent them, it's a lie and we can beat them senseless before we toss them back out the gate."

I slid him a look and did not know whether I should let myself smile or not.

"Is it like that here?" I asked. So many brothers, such a powerful city built on competition and being sly... I remembered Helenus and the way he had gone about things without revealing what he was really after. Cebriones shrugged and frowned.

"He's feeling very possessive and protective."

He'd misunderstood my question and thought I questioned if Hector was always so violent in his reactions. Perhaps it was strange that I had not thought to wonder at it. I shook my head with a soft smile for him as I stood up, still holding my makeshift breakfast in my hands.

"I don't mind."

In truth, I didn't. Violence and force could rob a woman of everything. Hector was prepared to be more violent and forceful to keep it from happening to me. The strongest men made the rules. Hector was making sure he was the strongest so that the rules were his choice. If you were not strong enough - you needed to be clever enough to find someone strong enough and let them make your rules for you. I had chosen Hector. I trusted the rules he would impose on the world. I trusted him not to harm me. I straightened my back as I looked around at the kitchen and the garden beyond. It was time for me to act on that faith and show, in my own way, that I was prepared to be just as strong.

"I am going to go get Bithia," I told Cebriones as he watched me. "And then, after we eat, I am going to start setting this house in order. It is time it became a home." I looked at the boy and older man and saw the way they watched me. If I became mistress here, their futures shifted to my hands. I smiled softly for them. "For all of us."

Bithia, who was already grumbling about how little furniture we had in the room, was more than happy to involve herself in my mission. The first recruits to our mission were the old man and the boy, whose names I learned were Oeneus and Alexandros in turn. We also soon won over Cebriones, and several of Hector's soldiers who were in the house to help move the furniture for us. It was unusual for a man to have his own personal soldiers if he was not king, but, when I asked, I found that it had happened gradually. A fellowship of sorts had formed with Hector at its center, a group of the best and brightest of Ilium's warriors that gathered together and, many of them being single – or escaping wives – Hector's house was where they tended to congregate. Apparently, it had been happening since he was young and his appointment to lawagetas had only solidified the tradition. Ever informative Cebriones told me that there were people in the court and among Hector's brothers that called it a small private army but his father let it happen. Hector called them only his friends but I thought that, if the moment came, they would obey him without question and it seemed most, if not all, of them were soldiers of renown. Their devotion to Hector was in the way their faces changed when I asked for stories and gave them the opportunity to speak of him; it was in their eyes when I mentioned his name. To me it seemed they were like Jason's Argonauts of old, companions and yet shield brothers as well. I found it reassuring and was determined that I would win them over.

It was not very hard at all.

Several of them had been on the ship with Hector when he had taken me and they knew me already. The others had obviously heard of me from the first group. They were curious and, I thought, perhaps as eager that I like them as I was that they like me. We shared a man and it seemed more important that we share him than compete over his attention. I asked their opinions, listened to their advice, showed interest in their stories and begged for more tales. Soon the house seemed full of giant, laughing men, eager to move what little furniture there was for me, each with a story about 'our' Hector on his lips. The charm seemed to work both ways for I found I enjoyed their loud company too.

Having grown up in a house full of men, I had missed the sounds of it in the silence of the past few days. That, and these men went out of their way to remember I was there, to include me in what they did. I was not the sometimes forgotten little sister here. I was the woman their lord had chosen for himself and that meant something to them. It meant something to me too.

Bithia watched it all suspiciously but was not above accepting help from Cebriones when he offered to help her sweep out each room before we moved into it and began to make it livable.

There was so little furniture that I decided to concentrate it just where it was most necessary, either where guests would be or where we were already living. It left several of the rooms completely empty but I made mental notes in my mind of pieces of furniture we needed or that I wanted to ask for. It felt odd arranging a house in a way that was my choosing. I was used to adjusting to what others liked and only my own small bedroom and weaving room back in Thebes had been arranged in a way that I found comfortable. I did not know what Hector found comfortable and -- and he had said that this was my house. I started out carefully at first but soon I forgot to be conservative and the house came together the way I saw it in my mind. It was heady, both the pleasure of making something completely mine and the quieter warmth of knowing that all of this, the house and everything in it, were a gift from a man that treasured me.

We stopped at midday, there was no hurry. I was pleased with what we'd done and had several more ideas for the future but I could take my time. Either I would be here for the rest of my life and so had all the time in the world -- or I would soon be gone from here and it would not matter what I had finished and what I had not. Cebriones had sent Alexandros to market and now we all sat outside in the garden, eating what he had brought back. Olives and bread, oil and herbs, baked fish and goat cheese. Alexandros brought back news as well. Apparently rumors about who I was and what was going on in Hector's secretive house were running wild in the streets below. It made me smile inwardly. Human nature would never change and, from what Alexandros, the mood was more cheerful and optimistic than angry or foreboding. To me that seemed like a good sign and so I relaxed as we sat in the sun and were lazy after we finished eating. I think I fell asleep for a little while in fact, safe under the shade of the young olive trees. Surrounded by men I had just met, I slept deeper and more at ease than I had in my own room back in Thebe.

Eventually, we did rouse from our stories and idle talk to finish the details of the projects we had started. The only area I did not touch was the third floor. It was where Hector's room was. He had showed his bedroom to me briefly, the only room other than the kitchen that seemed to have been lived in. Cebriones came across me hesitating at the bottom of the steps that led up to that level.

"Are we going there next?" he asked and I turned my head to look at him, pressing my lips together with a frown.

"No. It feels like Hector up there. I like that." I could admit it to him. Hiding from Cebriones the way I felt about Hector seemed not only unlikely but also unnecessary. I thought Cebriones might be one of my allies, if only because I suspected he loved Hector and would do whatever he thought would give him the greatest help.

"He wouldn't mind you being up there," he said me with a slight smile. "And I think I can keep things moving down here easily enough for a while."

I gave him a grateful smile and, picking up the hem of my skirt, went up the stairs.

I had not lied. The upper floor felt like the dark man that had taken me from my room on Lemnos. In other ways, it felt like the much younger man that had stood in an olive grove long ago and noticed a shadow in the trees.

The man that had told me a woman could hold a man's heart in her hands and turn it whichever way she chose.

There were only three rooms plus the storage on the third floor. The empty room I had already unofficially claimed as my weaving room. The room that Hector slept in. And a smaller room that might have been too large for storage... but was the perfect size for a nursery.

Had Hector been thinking that when he'd had it made?

Light, hesitant, I touched my fingertips to my stomach as I stood in that small doorway. A baby...

I had thought of it when I had been betrothed to Hector. Whenever one of my brothers' women or wives had started to grow round, I had thought of it and touched my own stomach. I had wondered what it would feel like to carry a small life in me. I had wondered how it would feel -- to my body and my heart.

I had not thought of children after I had been given to Phthia.

Now I thought of them again and wondered. Would they have his dark curls? My eyes? Would they running laughing on stout little legs, unafraid of anything this house held or would they -- the breath choked off in my throat suddenly and I found myself sitting in the doorway of that small room, one hand over my chest and the other still over my stomach.

Would they love me? Hold out their arms to me in trust? Would I – I swallowed -- would I do to them what my own mother had done to me? The hand over my heart moved to my mouth and I felt the physical pain through my body. It was nothing but a memory but that didn't make it any less real. The scar on the back of my shoulder blade throbbed dully.

An old ache.

The room in front of me smelled of faint sunlight, untouched dust, Ilium's breeze - but I remembered my mother's room, that little door to the left of her own bedroom. The smell of the blood that had never seemed to wash away. My blood. My mother's blood. Sometimes in her offerings to the dark beings she called she would mix it, hers and mine. I shook my head to shake away the encroaching shadows of memory, focusing on where I was. The floor in front of me now, full of sunshine and sea breeze, was painted. Tiny crabs in orange and red ran across the blue floor and dolphins and many armed octopus smiled from the walls but my mother's room had been all black. Black with carvings that felt sick under the soles of my bare feet and on its walls, strange animal headed creatures with too many arms or legs and badly twisted bodies that ate themselves. My mother would feed those carvings; paint them with my spit, my blood, my tears. She said they enjoyed blood like mine. Like hers. That it was special.

It was the only time I was ever special to her -- when she spoke of our shared blood.

"The blood passes down through daughters." Her voice had been low and slurred at its edges when she had spoken of it. She had bled us both the day after Cebriones had ridden back to Troy with news that my father had agreed to give me to its oldest son. She had not been vengeful that day. Instead, she had been more interested in going about her dark work than in hurting me for the enjoyment of seeing how long it took me to begin screaming. My muscles had burned from the awkward position she had tied me down in. She had fed my blood and long strands of my hair into the fire that burned in the fat belly of the bloated stone woman without a face that always watched from the corner of the room. The very air had reeked and I had already been sick from what she had poured into the wounds she had made on me. She had been slumped against the wall near me, holding the wound on the inside of her upper arm so it would stop bleeding. While my father grew drunk in celebration elsewhere in response to Ilium wanting his daughter, my mother had celebrated in her own dark way.

"Our blood is stronger than the males that ride us. Our children are ours, not theirs." She had rolled her head against the wall to look at me in the darkness and inexplicably, she had reached out with her wounded arm and brushed the hair that was stuck to the side of my cheek out of my mouth. It made her lose her balance. Her hair had spread out like rare spilled liquid ink where she lay after she had fallen.

"Shhhh," she held one blood-stained finger

to her lips, drowsy with the fumes of what she had burned over the fire earlier to inhale and let her speak to the spirits in a tongue they would understand. "Shhhh. They don't know. The men. But our blood will rule the world one day. I've been promised. It's why they wouldn't let me smother you when I realized you had been born a girl. They said they will use your blood to rule the world."

I had shivered and she had slapped me but it had been an automatic blow. Her mind had been far away from our usual lessons.

"You're useless." It was said so gently, so matter of fact, almost as if for once, she did not mean to hurt me with her words. "But I need your blood. Your daughter will learn quicker than you do. I will have her here one day too."

She had slept after that, hand still firmly over the wound on her arm and I had knelt in that hot, reeking, foul room, waiting for her to wake up and either free me and have Threnody drag me from the room to leave outside in the hallway… or to start again. Around me on the walls the creatures had seemed to dance and I had wondered if Athena's true face was there among all the multi-limbed monsters. My thoughts had been for myself at that time, not for any future children.

I thought of them now though, coming back to myself in a room clean of evil that held no more promise than laughing fish and the smell of the ocean.

I was my mother's daughter. I had the box

that held our evil downstairs where it slept in the same bed I did. What if I went mad when I felt a child beginning inside me? What if I saw their face when they were born and something in me went a little mad? Something must have happened to my mother at my birth. She had born seven sons without taint before I had come. Whatever I had done to her with my birth, it had made her go mad. All because I had been born a girl and not a boy.

Was it only the Fates that had made me the last child she bore? Or was it that she had born a girl...?

Sitting there, I frowned, brows low over my eyes as I stared unseeing into the small empty room. My mother had hated me for being born a girl, even though, as a girl I was the only one with useful blood. Would I bear a daughter some day? Would she drive me mad with her birth? Would I do to her what had been done to me?

Would Hector forget about me if I gave him a girl?

As a child, I had accepted a great deal about my family as simply the way of things. I was not blind though. I knew my father never visited my mother, not even her bed. I had known it since I was a little girl. He always had a woman that sat beside him at feasts, that slept in his bed. Ever since I was young enough to notice, there had always been a woman of one hair color or another, melted together in my mind as they had come and gone. Gone -- I narrowed my eyes in thought.

Gone once they had given him a child. Except - now, looking back I, for the first time, wondered. I had never grown up with half-brothers or sisters. Cebriones was one of Hector's half-brothers and from what he said there were more. What had happened to those siblings of mine by different mothers? What had happened to their mothers? As a child I had just known that they no longer were there at dinner and then, in time, a new, pretty face replaced them but as an adult now -- where had they gone?

I looked around the little room and realized there was so much I had never asked. Never even noticed. Lost children -- vanished women – my mother like a serpent at the foot of the tree --

and my father, who had known what she did to me and never stopped it...

Where had his women vanished to?

Was I the only female he had sacrificed to her?

The only child?

Or had my mother had nothing to do with that at all?

For a very long time I sat there in that silence, watching the sunlight from the open window slowly making its way across the polished floor. I let the silence fill my head so that the thoughts that whirled like leaves in the wind would settle. I inhaled the salt air slowly, filled myself with it and cleansed out the darkness of memories and thoughts. I turned my mind to Hector and to who I wanted to be when I was with him. I thought of the house he had given me and the home I was making. I thought of a child with his forever beautiful dark eyes.

I don't know how much time went by before I finally stood and walked to the center of the room to stand in the pool of light. Out the window in front of me was the ocean but I turned to face the direction I knew the sacred Skamander River lay in. Even though Poseidon was the father of Hector's beloved horses, for this I preferred the steady, constant Skamander to be my witness. My hand was still over my stomach and, very quietly, I whispered to whatever life waited there inside me.

"I will love you. And I will protect you. Whatever it costs me. I will keep you safe."

It was a promise, between whatever little souls waited inside me and I. Just between us in the privacy of this little room. I was not sure what it would require of me in the end but I would not let myself become my mother. My children would not grow up fearing to wake in the night to find me bent over them. I accepted where I had come from but I would never let myself return to that darkness. As surely as I was determined to set my fate with Hector, I also determined this.

I would not sacrifice my children's future to my past.

I came back down the stairs after that and Cebriones and the men that were bringing in wood for the central heating pit in the main room looked up at me. I thought I saw puzzlement pass through Cebriones eyes but they all smiled at me and I smiled back before I went to the kitchen to see about preparing dinner for everyone that had helped me today. I might have just imagined it but I felt as if my footsteps held a solid firmness now that they had not before.

The wood gathering marked the end of our work day. I was more than pleased with how far we had gotten in what I had pictured in my mind and how much of a difference I could already see in the house. It was good to my heart to not only have had the help from the men but to see that, once dinner was finished, they seemed to be in no hurry to leave nor did they seem awkward or impatient with Bithia and I as we sat in the megaron with them. Perhaps Troy's traditions were different when it came to mingling or perhaps it was that I was a strange part of them now for we all, in a strange way, belonged to Hector but whatever the reason, I was included in their camaraderie and no one seemed to be waiting for me to leave the room before they would settle down or relax. It began to grow dark outside and, as the stories finally began to die down and the talk began to grow drowsy, I stood and walked to the door, opening it to look out.

Hector had been gone a very long time.

I turned to Cebriones.

"I would ask one last thing tonight," I said.

XXII.

I stood in front of the wide window and watched the moon over the water. Behind me the lamps were lit, casting a warm, gold glow over everything and the sea breeze was mild tonight, whispering in past me to tug at drapes and the tips of the blankets covering the bed. Bithia did not approve of what I was doing but Bithia was not the one responsible for my future. I was -- and I had decided to wait for Hector until he returned.

I was not expected to wait for him and I understood that. I did not have to stay awake and be watchful. I chose to. To me, that made all the difference.

It was quiet in the sleeping house and so I heard the footsteps outside in the hallway and I turned from where I was to watch as he stepped into his bedroom. Hector's eyebrows were already raised in curiosity but it was not a guarded look and I got to watch the way his eyes changed and went softer and more relaxed as he spotted me near his window. It made something in my chest go odd and weak and I was smiling before I realized it. He crossed the room with his long strides to stand in front of me. Again, he was too close but by now I was beginning to not only expect that but hope for it each time he was near. I raised my face as he lowered his head to me.

"I thought you might want a bath," I said and he turned his head to look for the first time at the bronze tub that I had asked the men to bring up into his bedroom and fill with water for me. The bathroom was downstairs but it was not as private and intimate. I did not think he would have lingered in it. Here, he could.

"Why can I always smell when you have been somewhere? In the hallway, I smelled the sandalwood you must have put on the fire in here. I can smell the herbs or oil that you've put in the bath water." He bowed his head and I could hear his soft inhale near my ear. It sent a skitter of heat up my back and so did his low voice. "And you always smell like saffron."

Why, when he said things that would have made me embarrassed or shy on anyone else's tongue, did I instead feel warm and pleased inside? I lowered my head but it did not move us apart. Instead, it seemed more intimate.

"You smell warm," I told him quietly. "Like sun soaked rocks or the grass when it fills the lazy summer fields."

His chuckle was low.

"Right now I smell like dusty chambers and bickering old men." He stepped away from me but his smile was still there and his eyes were still for me. "And I was in a foul mood until I smelled the sandalwood and realized who it must be." As he pulled off his tunic, he looked at me. "You waited for me."

"I waited for you," I agreed softly and took the tunic from him when he would have absently tossed it over the chair. He gave me a little boy's grin and then moved over to the bath, careless with his nudity the way the warriors I had grown up with had always been. I watched. Growing up in a house of brothers and soldiers, I was almost as used to the male form as the female form. Always before, to me, there had been no real difference. I was aware, of course, of the physical differences but, inside, neither one had ever meant more to me than the other. They had just been bodies and usually bodies that were bleeding or bruised and needed to be set right. Deep down... I had feared that perhaps my mother had managed to strip anything truly feminine from me over the years. I wanted to see Hector though, this man I had decided to bind my life to. Inexperienced but hardly unaware, I knew how a man could touch a woman, what they could do. I had wanted to see how my heart and stomach felt in response to this particular man's body, before I had to worry about my own body under his eyes.

Hector was large, long muscled and bronze skinned. And he was scarred. It was a hard reminder that he was a warrior and his lifestyle had given him marks to remind everyone of that. Perhaps I should have feared those marks for the violence they not only said he had endured but that he was at the forefront of dealing out, but he had given me only gentleness from the very start and no pale marks could change that. I felt the strangest tingle over my palms though, wondering what it would feel like to touch that skin that looked so warm, what it would feel like to be touched by it. I remembered waking on the ship in his arms and it sent a little pleasant shiver through my stomach now at the memory. At the thought of it happening again. I had been worried I would feel revulsion or worse, nothing at all, looking at Hector this way but instead I was surprised to feel curiosity. I was surprised to feel strangely possessive. He lowered himself into the warm water with a low sound in his throat of satisfaction and it sent another warm flush through me. I found myself drawn to where he was without realizing it.

Medea had tricked a king's daughters into boiling their own father with a tub of hot water and herbs. It was a familiar story. Yet, Hector had not hesitated as he'd sunk into the tub of water and oil. Beyond the strange shivers under my skin at the thought of him physically, the thought that he trusted me that much made something in my chest catch and tighten painfully. I took the stones I'd left in the water to keep it hot as he lifted them out of the tub, setting them gently next to the bath. Then he settled down into the water completely and tipped his head back against the lip of the tub. He shut his eyes, his long, muscled throat exposed and vulnerable to me. The need to touch was so strong that I could not resist reaching down to stroke pale fingers through his curling dark hair. I watched his smile come again to his dark face. Everything in the room became small and intimate around me, whispering into the core of my bones and making my stomach feel strange and warm.

"Father is going to leave this decision to me." His voice was drowsy and I could see the way he was slowly relaxing. It was obvious he hadn't been expecting anyone to be waiting when he came home, much less to take care of him. It brought me a deep pleasure to know that I could. That I had. And that, from what he said, I would be able to from now on.

"I can stay?" I asked it softly. This night, this room right now, called for softness. It also served to hide the nervousness inside me. Yes, this was what I had decided I wanted, but it was still a huge change in my life and a great step into the unknown. His dark eyes opened and he looked up at me. What I saw in his eyes was endless. Bottomless. Very quietly, he said:

"I want you stay, Andromache." He was silent for a long moment but his eyes did not change. Finally, he said: "But I can't force you to stay. Not anymore." He straightened and rested his elbows on the sides of the tub. He shook his head and his hair that had gotten wet at the back of his throat curled darkly against his neck. His eyes held me in their darkness. "I was going to make the decision and keep you here. With me. Because I can't imagine coming here without you waiting." He watched me and there was a strange stillness in him. "But I don't want you to stay because I told you you had to. My heart won't leave that alone. It feels hollow and heavy in me." He went quiet then and I did not interrupt it, instead watching, knowing that this was important to both of us. His brows drew down and his face started to darken. After a very long time, almost as if he were talking to himself, he began again.

"What I do is dangerous. I can't promise that I will come back each time I ride to battle. I can't promise to be here to defend a wife. Our children. Sometimes at night, I imagine I can hear my death calling me and it does not promise a quiet end in my bed of old age." His eyes lifted to me, waiting, but I had no withdraw or surprise to offer him. My acceptance of this was even older than my marriage promise to him. I had been born to warriors, raised as a warrior's daughter, promised as a future warrior's wife. I knew that as much as my heart might want otherwise, that that there was no promise of a long future or uninterrupted days of peace. I had known it so long that, even though it still hurt, it was a familiar pain and one that I accepted the same way I accepted breathing. In answer to his unspoken question, I settled down on my heels next to the bath and simply rested a hand on his wet shoulder, watching and waiting for the rest of whatever he would say. I would not run from his future. I had already chosen to fight for my place in it. He exhaled and his eyes narrowed for a brief moment though not at me.

"I met Helenus on the way back here." He took my hand in his, fingers playing with mine and his eyes were inward. The scowl on his face was too. I wondered if Cebriones had ever mentioned that I had, at first, thought he had come to ask for me in marriage to Helenus and then knew he must have. I thought that the quiet rivalry must have been very old between Hector and Helenus and very subtle, like a snake hidden in a bush. Having had enough of the quiet evil in my life already, I was not happy to be any part of it. Hector's callused fingers brushed the tips of mine, sending another of those strange little shivers down through me, and his dark eyes were suddenly for me alone again.

"How can I put you through being married to a man that can't promise to live for you, Andromache? I can't even promise to come home at the end of a battle. How can I marry you knowing I could leave you a widow, caring for children with nothing of a father but a name and a memory?" He shifted in the tub and brought his face close to mine; his eyes were dark with emotion. "I see the light in your eyes and I ask myself why I think I have the right to risk that on a life I have already gambled too many times already. If I marry you, I will put you through long seasons without me, and no promise of my return. Every year. For the rest of my likely very short life. I want you. I want the way my life feels when you are in it. But how can I say I care for you and not protect you from that?"

He was serious. I could see the battle in his eyes and it broke something in my heart so that I could not help but smile weakly and reach up to touch his cheek. Did he think I did not know? Had not always, somehow, known? I knew it with more than just my mind. The knowledge of what was ahead of me was in my very bones, as if it had always been. I would be a widow before I was old. Oh, I knew and I did not take it lightly. In the end, however, it didn't matter. What mattered was what I wanted now and that was worth the cost. For the future I wanted now, I would pay the price at its end. Because it was worth it. My new life, my place here, *Hector* – was worth the price. I would have been insulted and shamed to think that he had turned away from me because I had not been strong enough to carry the debt of that cost in my heart while he yet lived.

There were no promises. There were no gods who cared or would give them. It was far too late for me to begin living safely. I was growing to realize that I had not been born to live a sheltered, quiet life, but, perhaps, I *had* been born for this. Tender, I stroked his cheek and I met his eyes.

"You can't protect me from that," I whispered. "That is the price I will pay and it is my decision to make. Even if you try to take that decision from me, it will still be mine at the end." Leaning in, I rested my cheek against his, feeling the rough scratch of his beard. Some of my hair fell forward to rest on the surface of the water in his bath. This was right. *We* were right together. "I am a merchant who has found the precious purchase and counts the cost a small price to pay to have it in

463

my life."

I drew back enough for him to see my face and know that I was teasing him as I added gently:

"Just make it worth it to me while you are here and I will count it well spent."

He laughed quietly but I saw the shadows leave the edges of his eyes where they had been gathered and it made my heart exhale safely in my chest. Being protected could cut both ways and, in this situation, he could not protect me at all. In trying, we would have both been hurt and perhaps cheated out of a real future. His large hand, dripping wet, reached up to brush the hair at the side of my head; his eyes were tender.

"My little merchant," he teased and I did not mind. Was Ilium not a city of merchants?

I stayed with him a bit longer after that. There was a strange, complete comfort in the silence between us and it soaked into me, soothing the nerves that I knew would linger for a long time as I adjusted to my new life. It was my life to have now though. His wanax had said so. And so it was with a stronger feeling of safety and belonging that I finally left him, slipping through the house and out into the back garden so that I could be alone as my thoughts settled, with only the silent moon to witness.

A place. I had a place here now. This home truly would be mine for all of my days. What the wanax had given, no one could take away and, for as long as I had him, Hector would hold me close here and guard my freedom. I was not a daughter anymore, to be traded away, my future home uncertain, my future husband unknown. I was a woman now, soon to be a wife, and I had finally come to the end of my journey, to the place I would spend my days and build my future. I was home. It was not quite home yet of course but I could feel it growing, becoming more real. More *mine*. This place was mine and Hector… Hector was mine as well. It was a heady though and for just a moment, I let myself spin like a little girl, a short twist in the night of pure happiness. Of all the men I could have been given to, I was chosen by a hero. *I* had chosen a hero. And so much more than that I had chosen a gentle man whose hands made me shiver and whose body made mine feeling tight and weak all at the same time. I could feel that, because I could trust him. I could look forward to joining him in his bedroom because I trusted him. I was nervous, and yet, I was excited too. I had never felt so safe to let my emotions run their course before and they were a jumble as they bubbled inside me. That was all right though. I was home. Here, I was safe to be who I was.

I would never again have to come in obedience and without question when fate came for me in the night to lead me away...

"Andromache!"

The hissed sound of my name had my head coming up in surprise and I looked around in the night, seeing young olive trees and grass and walls but I was alone. The thought of gods come to play tricks on my shivered down through me. I was surprised by how steady and calm my voice sounded as I answered.

"Yes?"

"Andromache," the male voice came from the garden wall and I felt a little foolish for how strongly the relief at such a mundane answer left me. Cautious, I moved closer.

"I've been waiting in the shadows all night hoping you would come out. Quick, the guards will patrol overhead soon."

It had me glancing up automatically at the section of the great wall I could see from this place in the garden, a larger darkness against the still over my head darkness of my own wall.

"Who are you?" I did not even try to keep the sharp edge from my voice as I moved to lay a hand against the stones in front of me. I had no friends in Ilium. Who would come for me in the night like a thief, worrying about guards, whispering from the shadows? When he answered, it was as if I had already known.

"It's Helenus. Now come quickly. Find something to let you over the wall and I will take you away from here. You'll be safe."

Helenus... safe...

I shut my eyes and pressed my lips together for a moment. What had he said to Hector when he had seen him on his way home this night? And now he came to offer me freedom. If I had truly been trapped, I would have thanked the gods for the unfamiliar sound of his now adult voice. I was not trapped, however, and I had not asked for his defense. My palm flattened against the stone of the wall and I was surprised at the strange burst of anger that flared quickly through me. No. No, I had made my decision already and no one else was allowed to try to change that. It was unfair because I knew he was only here to help me.

To help me and to spite his brother...

"No," I kept my voice was low but I was very sure of my decision and it seemed, to me, to fill the night air. "I thank you, Helenus, but I am where I wish to be."

"You can't stay. He'll force you to marry him. He's powerful enough to make it happen. I can help you. Tonight. While there's still time. But you have to be quick and you have to come now."

For just a moment, the feeling came over me. The flicker of the memory of that time in his long ago temple to a buried goddess when he had offered me up without my knowledge or choosing. When he had tried to claim me in front of a god, in secret, to thwart his brother. Of that moment, he had not asked my consent or my opinion and he had tried to make the choice for both of us. I stepped back from the wall with a shake of my head that was so strong it made my hair sway against the backs of my legs.

"I am staying. This is where I want to be.

Go home, Helenus. I don't need rescuing."

He hissed my name at me again but I picked up the hem of my dress and strode across the moonlight yard, careful not to run yet feeling as if arms might reach out to snatch me away at any moment. I did not pause or break my stride until I was safely back in the darkness and weight of the house, the door to the garden shut and barred. He would not dare follow me here, and yet my skin felt cold. Even though I knew it was unfair, a part of me was furious at Helenus for daring to think he knew better than I did. If I truly had been unhappy here I would have rejoiced at the sound of his offered safety – but I was not unhappy and he had not thought to ask. I told myself he was no different from so many other men in my life but I was growing spoiled with Hector and it did not help me feel much more sympathetic. The thought that I still might lose what I'd now been promised thanks to unlistening men chilled me – and made me more determined.

I would not lose the life I'd been promised a second time.

Bithia was drowsing in the bed that we shared but she roused when I slipped into the room, giving me a bleary look of question which quickly faded to a more awake look of alarm as she sat up. I suppose whatever was on my face worried her and her first question was:

"Did he touch you?"

Inexplicably, it made me laugh. He.

Hector. My soon to be husband. Technically, I was his war prize. Hector could have done much more than simply touch me and no man in judgment would disagree with him. She had a right to worry – except he had been nothing but gentle and never overreached what I was comfortable with in our time together. I trusted him. In time, Bithia would have to learn to as well.

"No," I assured her as I sat on the edge of the bed next to her, stroking a hand over her hair in reassurance. I gave her a small smile and, feeling a little shy and a little pleased, admitted: "Though I am coming to wish he would."

She gave me a rolling eyed look but the edges of her lips curved.

"So we are going to live here."

I nodded at her assumption but the thought brought up threats to that promise and so I looked at her more closely as I asked:

"Have you sent a message to Helenus?"

The startled look she gave me was answer enough.

"No. Do you want me to?"

"No." I don't think anyone could have mistaken the finality of my answer and she nodded before tipping her head to look at me curiously.

"You look different," her voice was puzzled and when I arched my eyebrows at her she shook her head. "I don't know. You just look -- older. Except not really."

I laughed and gently pushed her shoulder.

"Go back to sleep," I told her as I stood up and began preparing for bed. "You're obviously tired."

She settled back down in the blankets but her eyes watched me and there was mischief in them. After a moment, she asked:

"You saw Hector in the bath?"

I slanted her a look from the corners of my eyes as I slipped the gold from my hair, trying to keep my face disapproving of her questioning.

"Yes."

She made a humming noise and it was quiet for a little bit. Until she asked:

"Where you pleased?"

I felt the heat on my cheeks but also the way my lips would not stop their curve upward until I was grinning. It only instigated her own smile and soon we both were. There was no help for it.

"Very."

XXIII.

The next morning, I had my first visitor.

It was very early and I was in the kitchen with Bithia and Alexandrois. He was shy and awkward on his suddenly growing arms and legs but he was sweet and eager to help as well and I thought that we would get along well together. Together the three of us were inspecting the cookware to see what needed to be replaced, what could be repaired and what was already in good working order. I felt indulged to have my own, albeit small, bread oven and was running my fingers along the cooled inside of it to check for cracks while Bithia and Alexandrois debated the stability of the cutting table near the door to the garden. The house was quiet, a lazy, early morning, with everyone busy on their own. I cannot say I heard as much as felt it when someone else joined us in the kitchen.

It was the feeling you got when a sick dog crept into the room and I lifted my head and from where I had been crouched down next to the oven, I shifted on my heels to look toward the door that lead to the house. Blank, flickering eyes stared back at me in the faint, early morning shadows there and I slowly rose to my feet. I recognized the woman in front of me. It had been many years but I was not likely to forget.

"Cassandra." I wiped the soot from my hands on the cloth I had across my shoulder, watching her carefully. The last time I had met her, she had attacked me. She did not look far from repeating the action now. We must have been of a close age but she did not seem to have grown or changed the way I knew I had since we had last met. She was still small and pale with her wild, dark hair in knots around her shoulders. Her eyes were still huge, almost disturbingly large for her thin face. She would have been breathtakingly beautiful - if you did not pay attention to those eyes. Eyes that held no recognition of me and for that I was grateful.

"Where is Hector?" Her voice was a child's too when she asked it, somewhere between a tremble and a whisper and somewhere in the back of it, unvoiced, I could almost hear a lost wail. Bithia and Alexandrois had gone very still and quiet where they were by the other door, as if by doing so they could avoid her attention. Perhaps they could that way. Someone so broken seeming should not have drawn instinctive caution out of all of us – and yet, she did.

"He is talking to some merchants." I remembered how he had spoken of her all those many years ago when we had first met. It had been with love, and understanding that she felt so trapped in her role as a daughter and not a son. I had never desired to be a son but I did understand feeling trapped in a role. Perhaps it should have drawn me to her in the hopes of bonding, willing to forget her attack outside the temple years ago. I felt no venom toward her for that attack or her confusing words –

but neither did I find any desire to extend our time together. My gut felt clammy in her presence. She hugged herself and rubbed her tiny hands up and down her arms, a child's hands except they were so veined.

"Is he upstairs? I'm not allowed to go upstairs." Her eyes found me suddenly and they were not so empty or vacant now. Her voice lost its tremble though it stayed wispy. "I'm not supposed to go into his bedroom."

"Try checking the alcoves off the megaron." If she was implying something, trying to shock me and win a reaction, I was not going to be baited - especially not by such an amateur attempt. The best lies were the ones you did not have to tell. If she felt the need to speak about taboo, then I doubted its merit. I gestured with a finger back the way she'd come to emphasize my point. Hector and Helenus' sister or not, I had no wish to spend any more time with her than I needed to. Her eyes were too sane in her frail face.

She didn't leave to find him and somehow I had doubted she would. She was not here for Hector despite what she said and we both knew it. I saw the way she took in the rich dress Chryseis had provided for me, my jewelry, the way I stood. I had intentionally dressed the way I had despite the impracticality of doing kitchen inspection in fine garments. I had not dressed with her specifically in mind but I had known that they would come, the ones that would want to inspect me, judge me, try to fit me into their plans. Appearance could be a type of power as much as anything and I refused to be mistaken for anything but what I was, a royal princess and the future bride of Hector, powerful warlord of Troy. Her eyes took it all in and then narrowed as they went back to my face. I watched the rivalry kindle in her.

"He says I'm too old to sleep next to him. *I* think I'm finally old enough." Her eyes were a snake's eyes, trying to stare me down. I heard Bithia hiss behind me where she was still standing and in front of me, Cassandra looked triumphant, smug in the fact she could get away with talking such blasphemy. "What do you think, strange woman in my brother's house?"

I had been young the last time I had met her and I had held no reason to defend my position, a visitor and a stranger who did not belong. Things were different now. This was my home and my future husband she spoke vileness about. She had come to my territory, my place in the world, to try to beard me and this time I did not have to give way to her. I did not *want* to give way to her. She was Hector's sister but the position of wife was mine and if I would not give it up for kings, I would certainly not give it up for a child that played at manipulation. I knew what true evil was, the power to twist another to your whims and inflict your pain on them and Cassandra only played at it. She was a child at war, coming at me with a sword of wood when I had spent my life facing steel and poison. It was that she would try such a thing on me at all and not the attempt itself that sent the fire flaring through my blood. Who was she to try to wield power over me? She was not my mother, not Ariadne, not Medea. She was not me. All she deserved for playing at power was pity. I should have been kind. I should have been merciful. I *should* have showed her the pity she deserved. Instead, my mother's daughter, I let her see in my eyes exactly how pathetic I found her.

"I think there is no room in his bed for you now that I am here."

She shrieked as she lunged for me and it was the sound of a harpy, high pitched and furious. As she came, she snatching up a bowl that had been on the table nearby, swinging it wild and wide. Indulged and trained by Podes, I shifted my weight to sidestep her rush, prepared to knock the bowl from her hands but Bithia moved faster and put herself in the way. The bowl hit my maid on the side of the head, clay shattering into splintered shards of glossed red and blue. Bithia staggered and went pale. And I -- I felt a fury rise up in me that I had never felt before. With one hand I caught my friend's arm to keep her from dropping and my other hand lashed out. It was only at the last moment, a hair's breath away, that I remembered to lower it so that the heel of my hand struck Cassandra's chin, snapping her head backward instead of shattering her nose and driving the brittle bone upward. The force of it had her teeth cracking together and I felt a moment of regret that her tongue had not been in the way of them to put a more permanent end to her petty lies. She thudded hard into the far wall and I quickly wrapped both arms around Bithia's waist to hold her, too concentrated on immediate needs to feel the panic the situation merited. There was a small trickle of blood along my friend's hairline but it was above her softer temple and when I checked her eyes the dark center of them was equal. I prodded carefully with my fingers but all she gave me was a wince, not nausea or vertigo. She was stunned, but not badly hurt considering the damage the blow could have done if it had been aimed with a bit more calculation. Cassandra was slumped into a ball at the base of the wall and was keening. Loudly. Alexandrois was gone and I hardly blamed him.

A heartbeat later though, I realized where he had gone when Hector came at a run, Alexandrois on his heels.

I watched his dark eyes take in the scene and I met them with my own narrowed ones, still holding Bithia upright, still ready for a fight. In her corner, Cassandra became aware of him as well and her keening shifted to broken sobs. Again, they were louder than I thought realistic.

"She hurt me! Hector, she *hurt* me!" The sound of her voice reminded me of the way men sounded when their wound had gone bad and the fever and pus and sickness was taking them at the end. It made my stomach roll. My eyes didn't leave Hector's though. If he truly wanted me, what must have been in my eyes in those moments was as real as any other part of me he had seen. I would not pretend otherwise.

"Stop her - Ilium will burn because of her! Hector - make her go away!"

He had once told me that he understood what it was to have a darkness inside, and that he did not fear mine. That he carried his own. Nothing in his eyes shied away from whatever he saw in mine now. Instead, I saw a promise in the darkness of his and, perhaps I imagined that I saw a small measure of relief there as well. Whether I truly did or not, he gave me a quick nod before he turned and strode over to where his sister huddled. Leaning down, he scooped her up in his arms. She pressed her face into his chest and sobbed. His eyes met mine again, an expectation that I would be there when he came back, and then he was gone, out through the door and into the garden beyond. I watched him go, still not sure if I had truly seen a measured acceptance of my violence in his eyes or not, and then helped Bithia settled down on one of the stools. What I had just done could easily see me rejected and tossed back to my father's house. I could have just lost everything – but for the dark understanding I was sure I had seen in Hector's eyes. My mind still mistrusted that hope. Bithia pressed her hand against the side of her head and squinted. She still managed to glare with her fierce eyes in the direction of the doorway, recovered enough to growl:

"Bitch," after the retreating sounds of sobbing. I was surprised to feel myself having to fight an inappropriate smile and I walked over to the water jar to distract from it.

"Alexandrois," I said his name gently, the way you would soothe a pup during a thunderstorm. The heel of my hand hurt. I suspected it would bruise. "Please find a broom to clean up the broken bowl. I don't want anyone stepping on the pieces."

He looked shocked but moved to do as I asked, responding automatically to the tone of my voice as much as the words. It was why I had given him something to do in the first place, distracting him and giving him something routine. As he moved past though, I lightly touched his chin with a finger and gave him a wry smile.

"You did right to fetch Hector. Thank you."

It made him go red all the way to the tips of his ears and his mumbled reply wasn't meant to be heard. It chased the shock out of him though and soon he was carefully sweeping up the shards as I brought a cup of water back and attended to Bithia.

It was only a little cut and the area around it was bruising already. Bithia gave in to her years of living with my family and cursed softly under her breath in words she always pretended to be shocked over me using as I rubbed some of the aloe we kept in the kitchen for burns on it and tied a light bandage in place. All of us worked quietly, straining to hear the conversation going on outside in the garden.

Hector's voice was low, too quiet to hear other than the rumbling hum of it. His voice was almost always low, I realized. He didn't have to raise it to be heard or obeyed. Cassandra however seemed to thrive on noise and her own voice rose and fell, shifting from tears to hysteria to wheedling depending on what she apparently thought the situation called for.

She had a very calculated touch with emotional manipulation to be doing it from nothing but insanity, I thought. Especially when she called me a 'double-faced whore' and whatever Hector's suddenly flat voiced response had been had her in contrite tears and childlike pleading. Cebriones came into the room and his eyes flickered to the garden beyond as Cassandra's voice began to rise in a wail. Ilium would apparently burn because of me according to her and she seemed to take an almost unnatural pleasure in describing each collapsing building, each burning child. Hector's voice cut her off before she could work her way into real hysteria. Then she was crying and Hector was walking into the kitchen alone. His eyes met mine and then shifted to Cebriones. It was fairly easy for him to realize we had all been listening, considering Cassandra's growing sobs were easy to hear from where he stood.

"Ilium is apparently going to burn because I won't wed the whore of Sparta," he stated without emotion and I heard the anger in his voice was well as the guilt. Though I did not think it was guilt over Ilium's apparent imminent burning. Cebriones snorted.

"It seems to be going to do that a great deal," his own voice was dry. "Last year wasn't it going to burn if we didn't give Hera that snow white cow? And the year before that I think it was supposed to burn because we were building new ships to patrol the Hellespont. In fact, she's said that if she is ever promised in marriage to anyone, Ilium will burn." Mild, Cebriones stated: "We're going to run out of city to burn eventually."

It was apparent that Cebriones had more practice with this than most because I watched the way it made Hector's face relax. He even chuckled quietly. I was glad to hear it but I also wondered how it felt to a man who was the lawagetas of a city to hear of its destruction over and over again.

"Send someone to carry her home," he just sounded tired now. "She's worked herself up into hysteria and it's going to make her sick the way it always does. Make sure her maids search her and her rooms again to collect anything sharp she's managed to get her hands on."

Cebriones nodded.

"Not you," Hector told him firmly. "I don't need to hear about how you're due to have your head bashed in with a rock."

"At least she's colorful when she describes it," Cebriones shrugged it off almost cheerfully. Hector moved to stand in front of Bithia, looking down at her.

"How badly did she hurt you?" He asked
and Bithia sniffed haughtily.

"She was trying to hurt my mistress," she
pointed out what she considered the truly important
fact. Not failing to imply, I noticed, how he had not
been here to defend me. I laid my hand on his
shoulder.

"She isn't hurt badly," I told him, tone dry
as I shot her a look. "But she should probably go sit
down in bed and have someone to keep her
company for a little while so that she doesn't fall
asleep."

She gave me a narrow eyed glare in
response but Cebriones moved over to scoop her up
in his arms.

"I'll bring her. And I'll send someone for
Cassandra on my way past the megaron."

Hector nodded and then looked back down
at Bithia. His eyes were very dark.

"You are a guest in my house and I let you
be harmed. It was my fault and I will not let it
happen again."

Bithia's face changed at his words, going
strangely young and then Cebriones was carrying
her out of the room. She pouted but let him take her
away. Only Hector and I remained. Alexandrois
had disappeared again. In the garden Cassandra's
sobs were growing louder and more insistent.
Hector made a sour face at it and then took my hand
to lead me into the storage room where we couldn't

hear anything but ourselves. Once the door was shut firmly, he let go of my hands but he did not step away from me.

"Cassandra is used to having her own way. They say Apollo reached down to touch her and her mind could not stand the heat of him." He said it as if it was something he was used to saying. Then he sighed and ran a hand through his curly hair. Slower, softer, he confessed: "I'm not a very good older brother to her. Sometimes -- I forget that that she was once the little sister that used to laugh and chase after me. I forget that I once adored that little child. It's hard to remember now why I loved her then. Why I should love her still. Some days, I forget to love at all." His voice was tired and so were his eyes. He was trying to explain emotions that he probably didn't fully understand himself. I wondered how many years she had been working at him with her twin wedges of guilt and needed protection.

"She was very upset when I told her I was taking what she said was her place in your bed."

His face darkened at my words and his brows fell low over his eyes. It also entirely distracted him from either guilt or anger, just as I'd intended it to.

"She enjoys pretending that kind of thing to shock people. She's not that foul inside."

I had seen the look in her eyes though and I thought he was wrong. For his own comfort, I was not about to correct him on it. She was his family and those bonds were strong. Instead, I reached up and gently touched his cheek. His face relaxed a bit and he gave me a soft, rueful look.

"She needs a husband. And children. To get her mind away from a dream she once had and make her focus outside of herself."

I thought Cassandra would disagree with him on that and threaten another burning of Troy. It didn't mean he was wrong however. I did pity whatever man she would go to – and I pitied her too because not many husbands would be gentle with someone like that after the gloss wore off. I thought she was too set in her ways to try to change now. Tender, I rubbed my hand gently along his cheek.

"You're tired again."

One edge of his mouth shifted ruefully and he shut his eyes and bowed his head into my hand with a silent exhale.

"You were not this tired on the ship," I said.

He smiled quietly without opening his eyes.

"I was."

I made a quiet sound of disagreement.

"You were not tired like this."

His lips shifted and his dark eyes opened to find mine.

"If you don't stop, Andromache, I am going to pull you into my arms and it will be a very long time before I let you go."

He was teasing and yet I could see, in the darkness of his eyes, that he was completely serious. I had a choice, another one. One he did not have to give me but had anyway. I could not stop the edges of my lips from twitching upward even though I pressed my lips together and, because he had given it to me - and because I wanted to - I stepped forward into him and raised my arms to wrap them around his shoulders and neck. His arms came around me completely and he pulled me close, lowering his face to press it into my hair, my throat, my shoulder. It made me shut my eyes and I relaxed into that. Into him. I had been embraced before but those embraces had been nothing at all like this. This was... good. Right. Solid and warm. *Real*. It made my heart melt in my chest when he drew me even more tightly into him and I found that I wanted to be in his arms, that I wanted to stay there. I wanted to be able to have this feeling always. I tangled my fingers in his thick, curling hair and gave myself entirely to this moment, this feeling and only this. Everything else could wait.

Mighty Hector, Tamer of Horses... Why did I feel as if I were the one doing the taming?

"Did you really tell her you were going to join me in my bed?" His voice was low and muffled against me and I thought I heard the trace of a smile in it. Leave it to a man to remember one detail like that in an entire conversation.

"I might have," I whispered back.

"You don't fight me enough." His voice was quiet and I tightened my arms around his shoulders, exhaled a silent laugh as I turned my face into his hair, captured in a man's arms and yet feeling freer than I ever had.

"Hector of Ilium. When I fight you, you hold me tight to keep me from running. When I don't fight you, you hold me close because I am not telling you 'no'. There is no fighting you."

"You're not complaining."

"No…" my answer was an exhale and I did not fight him, or complain, when his arms tightened around me. This new place that was now mine as well was wonderful and I wanted nothing else.

"You can't hide from me from me forever." His voice was almost as soft as mine and I smiled against him as I agreed, content.

"No."

Eventually he let me go. There were still merchants waiting in the middle of talks presumably and at some point Alexandrois and I were going to have to finish our inventory of the kitchen. He was reluctant however and I could not stop the smug feeling of feminine pleasure to realize that he found it difficult to let go of me and that I had made it that way for him. Not used to being anything more than a piece of the furniture or the asexual sister, it was surprisingly wonderful to be a woman and to realize the influence and power that went with that. Watching Bithia all these years I had never really understood the power of a woman's body but I was learning now. So, reluctant, he let go and reluctant, he eventually left. I stood in the doorway to the storage room and wrapped my arms around myself and smiled, feeling young and foolish and happy. I could not remember having felt that happy before.

Alexandrois did come back into the room after a bit. The garden was empty and silent again and the house returned to what it had been before. Except, I thought, perhaps the core of it was just a little different.

I spent the rest of the morning working on my inventory, first the kitchen and then the storage rooms, carefully checking everything and comparing it in my mind to what I thought I needed. My lessons of efficiently running my father's house made it easy for me to adjust and I was eager to put some of my ideas into practice. This was my house, after all. My house in a way that I never could have claimed with my father's house but what I had done to my father's house, I would do here as well. This would be a house of welcome and comfort for the people that lived in it and for the people that visited it. I made notes on a wet clay tablet, using the easy form of writing that the traders and merchants used to keep track of their inventory. My mother's education had extended to my learning several languages, both spoken and written. I rarely used them, preferring to keep that talent hidden, but I did not mind giving this small part of it away. I left the tablet in the sun to dry. It would hardly be permanent but it wasn't meant to be. It was just meant to last long enough to remind me of what I needed and wanted for later.

The afternoon grew long and I helped

prepare food to send to where Hector was meeting with yet another group of men. I did not think I was far off the mark to imagine he was gathering allies for our wedding. I had no desire to be a part of that, trusting him to know so much better than I, as a stranger, ever could who and how he needed. I brought my own meal to Bithia's room and was surprised to find Cebriones still there. Luckily, I had brought enough so we all shared easily. She was fine and I would have thanked a god for it if I'd thought any had cared. It reminded me that I needed to make the proper sacrifices to the gods for my presence here and my occupation of a new house and so after my meal I set that in motion, sending someone else to make the proper offerings at the temples since I could not leave the house and offering the spilled wine and honey cakes at the corners of the house and walls as well as the small family shrine. I gave some to the olive trees as well, remembering their part in my meeting Hector oh so long ago. In truth, I preferred the small gods of hearth and home to the grandiose ones in their temples. The gods didn't care who gave the offerings as long as they were given and I didn't enjoy visiting temples. My mother said my tainted blood allowed me to walk between the gods, so that they did not notice and could not see me, but I had absolutely no desire to test that.

Instead, I worked that lazy afternoon away in the sun outside in my garden. Cassandra may have shed her showy tears here but this place was mine and I claimed it as such each time I pressed my long fingers into its soil or spoke to the plants I was rearranging and coaxing back to health here. Already, in my mind, I was making yet another list -- this one of the herbs and flowers I wanted to try to find so that I could grow them here. My house. My garden. I could finally grow my own choices and no one would ask why or whether I should or not.

I would not have to worry about my mother harvesting some of them by the dark of the moon with her small silver knife or feeding them blood, mine or hers.

As always the gardening helped me relax and I was content and comfortable as the sun began to shift itself lower in the sky. I would have to see to dinner soon and so I stood up and walked back into the kitchen to rinse my hands in a bowl of water. Movement from the front of the house caught my attention and I walked curiously to the window to look out.

I saw men. Armed men who were standing in front of the house. It gave me the strangest sense of double vision, as if I were remembering something that hadn't happened yet and it made my stomach clench. My fingertips felt suddenly cold -- and then I saw Hector striding out of the house to meet them. Cebriones and several of the men that had helped me move furniture and clean the house the other day were with him and I did not have to hear their voices to know the way angry men moved.

It was then that I saw that Helenus was at the head of the armed men.

I left the cloth I had been drying my hands on and ran to the front door.

"I will not give her over to anyone. But I will especially not give her over to you." Hector's voice was all but an animal's snarl, low and rough and throaty with power and anger. I heard it as I stepped through the open door and I saw the way it made the blood leave Helenus' face. Helenus was armed. Hector was not. Yet I did not fear for Hector's safety the way I did for Helenus'.

"Our father will grant her asylum," Helenus' eyes narrowed and his voice was sharp, cut edges and controlled fury. The look on his face was ugly and I was reminded that the gods had made it a special sin to kill your family. I had seen brothers in competition before, having seven of my own. This was far beyond that.

"You know how he feels about abducted women. I'll ask him on her behalf and he'll grant it. No one can stand against a direct order from the wanax. Not even you can do that, lawagetas." Helenus all but spat the last word and I felt the fury, like barely leashed hunting dogs that went through the men that stood at Hector's back.

"I have not asked for asylum." I raised my voice and it carried, strong and calm. I had been raised a princess, even if some of my training had been untraditional. Voices could be power if they were used right. Now I used it to flood the yard in front of me, pitched to carry clearly so that no man could claim to have no heard or doubt what I said. Deep inside me, I was also surprised to feeling the beginning of a rising fury for the second time that day. A fury that was directed at Helenus. I had turned him down in the night outside my house. How dare he come now, ignoring my wishes, to try to take my choices away from me? I had been clear in my refusal and yet he would think to know by desires better than me?

He was not here for me. He was yet another man in my life that thought he knew what was best for me without regards to my own thoughts.

Determined, I walked forward to join Hector and his men moved aside for me. I did not often play at king's daughter but when it was necessary I could be the bronze just as completely as my own father could. I had watched him too many years to have not learned how to look in control and strong. Definitive, I laid my hand on Hector's wrist and then raised my head to look at Helenus.

Who was he to try to take my chosen place away from me?

I did not let the fury slip into my voice though. Calm, control would press my point home more than any emotion.

"Prince Hector has treated both my maid and myself with nothing but the utmost respect and kindness. Until it is decided if my father's promise to the prince of Phthia would have broken the sacred vow I made before the gods to wed Prince

Hector, he has offered to stand as protection over me and guard me against manipulation by outside forces. I have not requested asylum and until my father arrives, the prince, as my betrothed, former and present, is my closest male representative."

This was not an emotional argument. I would not let my wishes be dismissed as a silly woman swayed by a handsome man. I intentionally used my claim to the law in my words. Men ruled and women ruled through them. Who I chose to protect me was my representative in the world of men. I had chosen Hector. I chose him for what he made me feel inside but I was not fool enough to not realize, and, in the moment, use, the fact that he was also the most powerful man in Ilium outside of his father. I was claiming my female right to a representative. Even a wanax, a high king, could not challenge my decision or disregard it once Hector had agreed. I wanted to be very clear so that the men in front of me would understand, and pass on, the fact that I was standing on my legal right. The law was the law and it bent for no one in Priam's courts.

"Word play," Helenus named it fiercely. "He kidnapped you by force. He's only your closest representative because he took you away from everyone else!"

I saw what was in his eyes. I saw anger and hurt at my response – but I also saw a dark hunger and a strange longing there as well. I felt again the way I had felt to realize he had brought me before his goddess to be branded as his. He would not take my freedom to choose from me. I met his eyes without blinking.

"Hector is my protector. I have chosen."

Helenus' eyes changed even as I felt Hector's body tense next to me and for a moment I thought Helenus would actually try to reach out and catch me with his hands. I refused to back away from him or the sudden sweep of lust in his eyes that had nothing to do with a desire for anything as simple as just my body. I would be seen as weak if I retreated even a footstep now, no matter how much my gut told me to put Hector's form between the both of us.

"I can protect you, Andromache," his voice was strained and his hands were clenched at his sides. "I can protect you from Hector. I can protect you from anyone. Come with me and I will keep you safe. You don't have to be afraid of him."

"I'm not." I did not have to watch my voice for that declaration. I was not afraid of Hector. He was a terrifying man, I knew it, but he was not terrifying to me. I shook my head, softening my voice for him in the hopes of taking the blow out of it. Perhaps he truly did think he was doing this for my own good, not realizing what I saw in his eyes. He was not my enemy, but he was not my ally either.

"Let it be, Helenus. I am where I am meant to be and that will not change. I do not need protection from my destiny. I will be Hector's wife.

I will be his wife until the day I die."

He turned in a fury from me then and I saw the pain in his eyes as well. Had he cared for me as anything other than a chance to outdo his older brother? I had not thought so before. Now...? Perhaps. It didn't matter in the end. My decision would not change and as I watched his men turn and follow him out of the gates, I felt strangely washed clean and empty inside. It was not a bad feeling though. It felt as if I had carried something clinging to me from that visit to Athena's grave all these years and now it burned off and was gone. When Hector drew me around in his arms and enfolded me in an embrace I came willingly and stretched to wrap my arms around his shoulders as I settled in close, feeling, perhaps foolishly, inexplicably proud of myself.

Then Hector chuckled and I was surprised to realize that he was proud of me too. It shouldn't have mattered but, as he lifted me briefly off my feet before setting me down again, still in his arms, it made me feel even better.

"My queen," he teased me before his voice softened and he lowered his head enough to look at me with dark eyes.

"Did you mean what you said about being my wife?"

I was no fool. I heard the deep currents in his voice and I freed a hand from his dark hair to lay it against his cheek where the bristles of his beard rubbed against my palm. Something told me to answer truthfully.

"Yes," my brows bent over my eyes slightly and I could not help but tease, just a little. "I thought that was the point of all of this."

"It was," his lips smiled faintly but his eyes did not leave mine and they were still dark and searching. "But I haven't been sure it's what you wanted and not what you were making the best of." Somehow, his eyes darkened even more. "I've been afraid to ask."

It made something in my heart sigh out and break sweetly, all the fire and fight of only moments ago slipping out of me so that I was soft in his arms. I slide my fingertips along his face, watching his eyes watching me.

"Ask me," I whispered it and as I did I realized that our lives hinged on this one moment, on whether he would ask – and what I would answer if he did. "Please, ask me..."

He hesitated. Even with me already in his arms and what he must have seen in my eyes, I saw the foreign fear in him and I realized – if I told him no, he would let me go. As much as it was obvious he did not want to, he would if my answer was for freedom. It made it even more important to me that he ask. His voice was very low.

"Andromache of Thebe, do you want to marry me?"

I had never heard a man's heart in his voice before but this one was here now and it almost brought tears to my eyes. He had once told me, so long ago, how a woman could hold a man's heart in her hands and turn it whichever way she would...

"Oh yes..." I said it and as I did I realized that I meant it with my whole heart and that it was a relief to be able to say it, outloud to him. I had made my decision already but to say it, instead of the weight it had been inside me until now, my heart felt lighter. Hector's lips shifted upward.

"Then will you marry me?"

"Oh yes!" I nodded and the tears were in my eyes now as I cupped his face with my hands and smiled up at him, my heart winging free.

"Good."

His response had my lips twitching in laughter and then he lowered his face and he kissed me. It was warm and it was soft but even inexperienced, I could feel the thread of need and desire in the way his lips moved over mine. His arms came around me and pulled me close into him and I pressed up on my toes and wound close. My world felt endless and suddenly, perfectly intimately small at the same time. It was both the answer and the beginning of everything. For the rest of my life, I would remember that moment, when the entire world was mine.

XXIV.

Cebriones was gone the next day. Bithia noticed it before I did and complained that he knew it was going to be the day for washing linens and that he had obviously found somewhere else to be to avoid helping carry the large caldron outside for the water. Usually we would have sent the house servants with it down to the river to wash with the other servants of neighboring houses but I had not yet bought servants for that kind of work and so Bithia, Alexandrios and myself were going to mix the ash, oil and salt and wash the lines ourselves in the privacy of our back yard. I did not mind the restrictions of not being allowed to leave the walls of our house on my own just yet. Soon enough, I knew, I would be on display, Hector's declared betrothed and I would play the part. Before that time though, I could enjoy having my privacy and no worries about the outside world.

Before we began the long chore, while the others began to gather the blankets and curtains from the rooms, I went in search of Hector. I had hoped to ask for advice from Cebriones but it seemed I would have to trust my own judgment. Last night, lying in bed, still thinking about all that had happened during the day, I had come up with a plan. One that I hoped would make things clearer. It was time to step forward into the future I wanted yet another step and reach out my hand to catch at it.

Hector was not hard to find. He was not

required anywhere and so he was naturally in the small stables that were kept in the courtyard of our house. Most houses did not have their own stables, the horses kept in carefully guarded pastures outside the city walls but this was Hector, tamer of horses. I would have been more surprised to find that he did not have stables.

Hector was unattended when I found him and I paused in the doorway of the stable and watched him. The interior was shaded and cool, smelling of hay and horse and wood and grain. The sunlight filtered slowly through the motes of stirred dust that glinted in the air, gold and warm. It was a quiet place, a slow place, a place that felt at peace and removed from the rest of the world. I knew why Hector loved to spend his time here.

There were only four stalls in the small building, each fenced in rough wood. One of them was empty but the other three held horses. One of those stalls also held Hector.

Chariot horses were not tame creatures. Even the great bulls and cows of my father's fields, though close in size, were slow and uncomplicated creatures. Horses were Poseidon's children however, as wild and restless as their father and I did not find it strange at all that the centaurs that were said to live deep in the forests were wild and vicious creatures given their mixed nature of man and horse. Chariot horses were trained to trample men in combat, as much a weapon as the chariot they drew or the man that rode it. I did not fear them as I probably should have, but I did respect that strength and danger.

Just as I did not fear Hector, though I did respect his strength and danger to others.

He was bare chested and there was a coating of hay dust across his wide shoulders. His dark hair held glints of golden hay as well and I knew he had been taking care of the horses and stalls himself, not because he had to -- he could have given the task to someone else -- but because he wanted to. It was obvious that it brought him pleasure. It was in the relaxed way he moved, in the way his voice was as he murmured to the horse he was busy brushing down with long, competent strokes. It felt good in my heart to see him this way, and to know that he knew I was there and did not mind my intrusion into his world. He was also, I was beginning to appreciate more and more, a very handsome man and I felt a great, possessive pleasure in watching the way his body moved as he worked. It was not that hard to imagine that body against mine in ways that went further than the embraces we had shared and I found I was not afraid so much as curious and even a bit eager.

"I see that you still speak to the horses and me the same way." I kept my voice soft to not disturb the moment and he turned his head to shoot me a laughing look over his shoulder.

"You're never going to let me forget that, are you?" He asked and he didn't sound upset by the idea.

"No." I could not help but smile back as I walked over to the first horse in the line. I had brought a bag with me from the kitchen for just this purpose and now I reached into it and drew out a handful of grain that I had soaked in wine yesterday. Hand flat to keep my fingers out of the way, I offered it to the beast. Who lowered his head curiously to nose at my palms before beginning to lip up the mixture. I had fed my father's ancient horses the same when I was in Thebe and I knew the mixture would be met with approval by Hector's horses as well. He chuckled as his horse gave itself up to the meal and it made me smile again, softer this time, as I watched the great wide set eyes of the horse in front of me as it ate, its lashes as long as the first joint on my finger.

"You're going to spoil him. A trough will be too low for him now that he's eaten from a princess' hands."

I exhaled my amusement at him as the horse in the next stall, seeing his companion eating, tried to stretch his neck enough to both see what was being eaten and get a chance at it himself.

"I am wooing him." I gave the horse another handful and then shifted to the next stall to feed this one too. "So that he will look forward to seeing me and shun the attention of all other princesses."

Hector, and the horse he'd been grooming, last in line, moved to the side of the stall next to mine. Horse-taming Hector leaned his arms on it

499

and watching me with laughing dark eyes as the horse looked over him at his companion's treat and nickered.

"So is that the trick? Woo a male with food and he will never stray?"

I raised my eyes to him as I came to stand in front of the stall he was in and smiled.

"As much as talking to a woman like a horse."

He laughed and caught my face in his hands, drawing me in for a kiss that went longer than, I thought, he'd intended at the start of it. He drew my lower lip into his mouth this time and it did strange things to the tips of my fingers and my toes the way he stroked it with liquid heat. My breath caught when he finally withdrew, one last brush of his tongue. It was worth making his last horse wait over and I realized I felt a little unsteady in my footing afterward.

I was enjoying, a great deal, learning the different ways of being kissed and kissing. Almost, it distracted me entirely but the grain still in my hand reminded me that I had come here with a purpose and so I tried to focus past the pleasant fog in my head to continue with my plan.

"Tell me their names?" It was a little weaker than I'd meant to sound but it was enough to help me concentrate again. Hector's lips flashed a secret, small smile but he did not deny me my retreat.

I did not ask after Epimenides and Marsyas,

Hector's horses that I had met when I was young. Hector had not mentioned them and I thought he would have if they had been alive still. Chariot horses did not often find themselves dying of old age any more than their drivers or the warriors they carried into battle did. Hector let himself out of the stall and latched the gate while I fed the last horse his measure of grain.

"The one you're feeding right now is Lampus," he said me as he came up behind me to put his arms around my waist. Having embraced me once, he seemed to think it was his right to whenever he wished now. I was glad of it, finding myself smiling as I pretended to concentrate on the horse in front of me and instead secretly reveling in the warmth and solid strength of his body against mine. "The middle one is Aethon and the first one you swayed to your side is Podargus. Xanthus is out in the fields right now pretending he's a colt and scaring all the new recruits that are practicing nearby."

Lampus finished his grain and I wiped my hands on the rough fabric of the now empty sack before turning in Hector's arms to face him, letting it dangle, forgotten from one hand. He looked young, the weight and the responsibilities of being lawagetas lifted from him when he was here with his horses. His dark eyes were watching me, his arms still around me. and the straight brows above them began to slowly lift.

"What is it?" He asked and I gave him a

look I tried to make innocent but from the one he returned, he did not believe it. Instead, he gently tugged at the ends of my hair where it rested near his fingers.

"I am beginning to learn you, Andromache. And you have a look on your face that says you have something in mind." His chin lifted slightly at me, like one of his horses testing the reins. "What are you thinking?"

Was I so easy to know? I had never thought so before. Most people seemed to find everything I did a mystery. Was I suddenly so transparent for Hector? Or was he simply paying more attention than anyone had before. I pressed my lips together and rested my empty hand on his upper arm, his skin warm under my touch. Distracted by the feeling of his bare skin against mine, even in such an innocent place, I rubbed my thumb absently against a raised scar that stood out against the bronze and when I looked up, it was to find him still watching me. Waiting patiently. It made the edges of my lips smile and then firm.

"I wish an audience with your father," I told him, meeting his eyes. Then, before the worry could begin to move into his mind, I added: "I wish to speak to him myself. I don't want him to hear that I have said words that I have not. I want to tell him my thoughts, and why I wish to stay with you, so that there are no rumors to whisper in his ears."

I watched the skin tightened around Hector's eyes and I knew. He would have to trust me. He would have to let me decide for the both of us what our future would be. We both knew that if he brought me before his father, and I had lied to him about wishing to stay, that I could throw myself on the wanax's mercy and beg protection. Not only would he be bound by honor and duty to give it to me -- he would do so anyway. Everyone knew the story of Priam's sister, given in ransom for his own life, all those many long years ago before he ever came to power in Ilium. She was an Achaean's bride, bearing foreign children, far across the sea now, sacrificed for her younger brother's freedom. Priam, wanax of Troy, honored her sacrifice by granting any woman that reached him asylum in his holy city. Women ran to this place from far points to risk that promise.

I could risk it too - and free myself from Phthia - and Hector - if I chose - if I could but reach Priam's feet.

We both knew it, Hector and I, and it was in his eyes as he looked down at me. Very gentle, he reached up and he brushed his callused hand against my cheek. I raised a hand to catch it and hold it there against me. I felt the sadness in him. He could have told me no. Instead he nodded, lowering his face so that his forehead touched mine. The scent of him, clean and horsey, surrounded me.

"I will bring you to him, Andromache." His voice was quiet. "You can tell him how you truly feel."

I knew what it cost him to give me that.

Gentle, I cupped his face in both of my hands and exhaled against his lips.

"And then you will know how I truly feel as well. As many times as I have to tell you, I will."

He gathered me close then and kissed me and there was a great deal he said without words as his tongue slipped between my lips. For the first time in my life I realized, that if I were gone, someone would truly miss me. I was not used to being missed.

When I finally slipped away from Hector, I fetched Bithia out of the back yard and brought her to my room. I had meant to ask for a future day to meet Priam but my gut told me to go now, before anything else happened, before any doubts could set in inside Hector and torment him. The wash would have to wait and I was glad I had not begun the messy process already. Instead, Bithia and I searched through my acquired gifts to find the proper adornment for my meeting with the wanax of mighty Ilium. Appearance, despite what some would say, meant a great deal, especially at first. I knew it and I knew how to use it. Today, I would be royal. So we cinched the ancient dress of queens closed at my ribs and waist with gold pins, arraying me with gold and electrum bracelets that chimed at my ankles where the bell like skirt swayed and on my bare arms under the capped sleeves of the dress. Bithia touched my face with makeup, colored my lips and lined my eyes. I wore gold in my ears and in my hair, which Bithia anointed and wound skillfully so it hung like snakes down my shoulders and back. I wore nothing around my throat though or on my feet, leaving those places pale and exposed, a reminder of my vulnerability and that I came as a supplicant as well as king's daughter. Sitting straight backed and motionless in front of my mirror once the work was finished I took comfort in the fact that I did not recognize the regal creature that looked back at me. And I waited.

When Hector came for me, he was dressed to suit the situation as well, warlord and future king. There was gold in his dark, anointed hair and at his wrists in two thick bands. The fabric of his tunic and chlamys was finely woven and delicately embroidered. I turned on my seat to face him and saw the way his dark eyes reacted to me. For the first time since I had entered the room today, I smiled. It was impossible not to. I had never had a man proud of the way I looked before. I stood and then could not help but turn for him to show it all off and he walked across the room to me in three long stride and took my face in his hands. I watched his eyes soften as he looked down at me and he stepped closer, head lowering to me. My eyes fell closed of their own volition and I tipped my chin upward for him.

"Don't mess her up!" Bithia's voice came, stern and unbending from behind me and we both jumped a little, caught like guilty children. "We put too much work into the way she looks for your careless hands to ruin it before it serves its purpose."

A moment of laughter moved into Hector's black eyes and without raising his head, he looked at my maid from the tops of his eyes. He didn't say anything though, offering me his arm instead. He was careful to match his pace to my slightly slower one thanks to the dress as we walked. His men were waiting as we passed through the megaron, surprising and delighting me as they formed an honor guard around us that only a country's lawagetas had a right to. I was not the only one that was intent on reminding others who they were dealing with. Their added presence made me feel more sure that I was doing the right thing. I did not think Hector had meant to remind me what he was but I thought he meant to remind others who I would be if I married him.

We walked to the wanax's palace. It was not so far away but it also let others see us as we passed. I did not mind. It had been several days since I had been able to go walking and my legs had missed it. The faces that peered from windows and doorways, marked our passing and I knew that the rumors would run free before we even reached our destination. That too, served a purpose.

The ruler of Troy lived in a vast palace made of the same white limestone that created the walls of the city and, inside and outside, it was gaily painted in rich colors, marked with the rare royal purple and deeper red. There was no wall in front of it as there was for Hector's home, instead the courtyard was covered in wide, flat stones that were too colorful to come from this part of the world, rosy pink and sunset orange. Guards were stationed here too, in doorways and arches, dressed in rich colors, their polished bronze breastplates a great deal more decorated than what Hector's men wore. They were also, I thought, much less used. The guards dipped their heads in acknowledgment as we strode past and I ignored them. Friendly was for another time and place. Now I was a king's daughter visiting a foreign ruler and I fed that into my very bones as we walked, mentally recrafting the way I moved into what I wanted others to see. The polished stones of the walls, inlaid with rich tile, hung with shields of gold and bronze as well as the rich garments of the people we passed all spoke of wealth and power and it helped me become that myself. We had nothing close to this elegant in Thebe, but I could still act as if we did.

Priam was waiting for us in the megaron on his great stone chair and I did not doubt that Hector had sent someone to tell him to expect us. Not only was it protocol and manners, but his eyes, even across the room, said they had been waiting for our arrival. Around his throne I saw men dressed far too richly and elegantly to not be men of power and authority and I was reminded of the few rough soldiers my own father kept on hand in his own megaron. Some of these men, no matter how richly dressed, had faces that spoke of the same warlike nature. Quite a few did not though and the looks on some of their carefully oiled faces were not welcoming. These then were the merchants and councilors that had sold me away to the Achaeans because they had wanted Sparta to side with them. Oh, I knew who they were and I fed my rage at them for what they had tried to take away from me, gaining strength and courage from it. I was not so foolish as to let it show on my face though, concentrating instead on the single man that sat on that throne at the head of the room.

He was old. He would have to be with a son of Hector's age but even old, I still saw whispers of Hector in him. It was there in his nose, the set of his eyes, the way he sat completely competent and confident on his throne. He was not a frail man and the spear near his chair was not ceremonial. He watched me as I approached and I thought his eyes did not miss much. What was he expecting to see, I wondered, when he had heard I was coming? Someone shy and lost? Someone pushed into this by an overpowering man? Someone set in her determination? His face gave nothing away but patient watchfulness. As much as he had surrounded himself with other voices, I knew that his, in the end, was the only one that mattered to my future. He was wanax. He was higher than a mere king. He was a king of kings and there was nowhere on this side of the Aegean I could go that his voice would not reach. My stomach clenched with that thought - for what I wanted from him I wanted so badly I could hardly bear to put it into words. Like all children I had learned that silence, even unaware silence, was permission unless you attracted enough attention to merit denial. As an adult, things were not that different. I needed his permission though. Things would not rest for me until I had a declaration from him that the world would hear. It was the only way I could protect what I longed for from being stolen in the night by sly men.

Priam stood as we approached and Hector stepped away from me, moving forward to greet him as was custom. I watched the way they clasped forearms and knew that the words they gave in greeting were real, not just words. Then Hector took my hand and drew me forward to stand in front of the one man in all the world I had to convince to see my side of things.

"Wanax." I folded my hands over my heart and lowered my head in front of him in respect. Inside I was trembling but I was determined to show nothing but respect and bravery. He stepped forward and very lightly touched my shoulders. His voice, like Hector's, was low and warm when he spoke.

"Andromache, princess of Thebe. Finally we meet."

I raised my eyes then to look into his and I saw the waiting in them. Like his son, he too wondered what was truly in my heart to ask of him.

"My journey to meet you has been longer and of a greater distance than I had first thought." I had thought long and hard about exactly *how* I wanted to say everything, exactly how I would say everything and now I went to my knees in front of him. I bent forward until my forehead touched the top of his sandals. I could have asked him while still on my own feet but I needed this moment to never be forgotten. I needed it to be dramatic and reach not only him but those watching on an instinctive level. So I called up the old traditions and memories, grounding my request in ancient customs and rights, making my words and actions into a mold that bronze of my future would be poured into.

"Great King of sacred Ilium, I beg for your protection and sanctuary." I raised my face to him then, straightening my back but I remained on my knees. His hands were loose at his sides and I would not rise until he raised me himself. "You would have once been a father to me but I was sold across the ocean to foreign men for the safety of my family. If your son had not rescued me, I would be there now, far from my home and my people. He has brought me before you so that I could beg that you let me remain here, under your protection. Wanax Priam, please let me stay with your son and be a daughter to you once again."

It was, perhaps too short and blunt, a country king's way of talking. Perhaps I should have phrased it in hidden meanings and clever twists. I didn't have that skill though and I would not risk my future, my heart's desire, to a misunderstanding. Let my words be plain and blunt then. They were true and from my heart.

Priam made a soft sound in his throat as I looked up at him and I thought I saw something in his eyes. Recognition? Familiarity? Wanax of many people, he understood the power of custom -- and show -- perhaps even better than I. In that look was that knowledge and his awareness of what I was doing. I did not think he looked displeased.

Were we both actors then? Putting on a show for the rest of the court when both of us already knew our parts and the end scene? It was a surprisingly reassuring thought.

"Daughter," he drew me to my feet then by both hands and pressed a kiss to each of my cheeks. Lower, for my ears, he murmured: "Wise child." It was in his smiling eyes when he drew back from me as well and I pressed my lips together to keep them from smiling the way the edges of my mouth already were trying to. Inside my heart warred with overwhelming hope and the fear that I might have misunderstood it all. Priam looked at his son and then, still holding my hands, he raised his voice to carry, smooth and calm, throughout the room.

"I grant Andromache, daughter of Thebe, my protection. As long as I live, she will come to no harm under my roof nor be forced into anything against her will while in my lands." His eyes found mine. "She will now be Andromache of Ilium, daughter of Priam of Ilium. She has favor in my eyes." The look in his eyes was kind as well as pleased and I both felt as if I had found a strange kindred soul in mask and also as if I were a child again, safe in my own father's arms. Priam could have terrified me if he had chosen and instead he had shown me kindness and seen me for what I was. It found its way into my heart and I treasured it there.

"Now, daughter of Ilium," his voice was gentle. "Have you no other request of me?"

I looked at him, at what was in his eyes, and, suddenly brave without having to pretend, I dared it.

"I would like your oldest son, my wanax. I whould like him very, very much."

His chuckle loosened my heart and I felt Hector move up to stand behind me even though I didn't look away from Priam. His words of answer would be my future and nothing , not even my own father's orders, would matter.

"It seems you are both too determined to have it any other way." Priam was smiling as he said it and there was something, some quiet triumph there that made me wonder which of his councilors he'd defeated. "Hector?"

"Yes, father?" Hector's hands moved to rest under my elbows and I felt the warmth of his body against my back.

"Marry this woman and treat her well. Remember I claimed her as my daughter before you took her as your wife so any harm to her is harm to my name."

"Yes, father." Hector's arms went around

me and I half turned in his arms to curl my fingers against his chest and in the fabric of his tunic, unable to stop the radiant smile on my face for him or when I turned it to his father.

"All the rumors of Priam of Ilium's generosity are too small," I said. "You have given me my life today."

"Then live it well," Priam's smile was warm and indulgent for us but -- I thought – for just a moment, I saw sadness in it as well. With a gesture of his hand he let us go our own way and returned to his chair and the men gathering around him with new plans in their eyes. For the rest of my life, I would remember that smile and his kindness to me, a stranger in his house. And later, much alter, I would remember that final look in his ancient eyes. What had he, so much older and closer to the other world than us, seen when he had looked at me and thought of my future? Or had he only seen the fate of women everywhere and known that one day I too would follow their path – and remake it to be my own?

XXV.

It seemed I had spent so much of my life waiting that now that things were finally moving for me, the pace was so swift it was almost overwhelming.

After so much speculation, conformation of who I was, and what I would soon be, spread through Ilium like wildfire during a drought. Alexandrios, coming back from market on errands, couldn't wait to excitedly tell me, but even if I had not heard it from him, and suspected as much anyway, I would have found out. In going to Priam, it seemed I had opened a wide gate of permission without realizing it and my house was suddenly overflowing with visitors. I hadn't anticipated this aspect of what I had done but as introductions went, it was certainly much easier on me to meet strangers in the comfort of my own house than going to theirs. If Hector would not loose me on Troy - Troy apparently would loose itself upon me. My place with him secured by the wanax himself, Hector did not bar his gates against inquisition anymore.

I had not often received visitors for myself and not for someone else and it was a new experience for me to have people interested in me alone when they visited. Some came for curiosity, some came hoping for favors, some came hoping for influence, and a few, I hoped at least, came for friendship. I treated them all the same, polite and friendly, asking more than I talked, listening more than I spoke. I was still new here and to this position and it seemed safer to do little than too much. I trusted that time would whittle away the ones that were frivolous and bring back to me the ones that were serious.

After the first day of constant visitors, Hector sent me out into the city with an escort. I teased him. I knew it was to win himself reprieve from a once quiet house suddenly full of guests, but I welcomed the chance. There was so much I wanted for our house to make it into the home I saw in my mind and more, it gave me a chance to explore. In my own homeland, I had known every rock and tree within a day's journey of my home. It was not my nature to have something new presented to me, lying in front of me, and not want to see everything that it held.

Cebriones was away on a mission for Hector and one of Hector's cousins played escort and guide to me, making sure I didn't get lost or overwhelmed by curious strangers on the streets. His name was Aeneas and I had never before met a man with such a honeyed tongue for every female he met. Bithia distrusted him immediately because of it but I liked him once I realized he was not serious. When he realized that I knew, we settled into the beginning of a comfortable friendship and he shared enough of himself with me to talk about his wife, one of Hector's sisters. For all his sweet words for everything female, it was obvious that she was something rare and precious to him.

Under his guidance, I was soon sending

merchandise back to our house at the top of Ilium's rise. Aeneas knew the best merchants, both the ones with the fairest prices and the ones with the rarest or most sensible items. All three were not always the same but the discovery was a great deal of the fun for me and I did not mind the extra walking. We could have ridden but I was used to walking and my mind created internal maps better for me if the ground I passed over was measured by footsteps. Bithia, used to my walking was used to walking everywhere herself even if she did remind me that it was below my new rank. Aeneas had just laughed and sent off the litter that had been hired for the day for me. Appearance was important but so was making the life I intended to have a future of her my own.

That meant making a home for Hector and myself as well in the house he had built for us and that meant filling the rooms enough to at least stop them from echoing whenever someone stepped inside them. I had never seen the amazing quality or quantity of goods that I found in Ilium's expansive market place. There was furniture, sturdy or frail, gilded or carved or staunch and polished of woods both common and exotic. There was fabric from across the world, pale and thin from Egypt, rich and exotically colored from beyond the Propontis, strong and intricately embroiled from Achaean lands as well as pelts from as far away as the islands far to the north where copper was mined. There were trinkets from a hundred cities, dealers from across the known world, things I had never even heard of and could only guess at their purpose. Great Troy on the Dardanelles was truly the center of the trading world and all goods came here first. I suspected, if I had imagined something I could not find, someone here would have known how to get it for me. I was very conscious of what it would cost Hector and at first I tried to be very careful about what I bought and what I ordered from the craftsmen but soon Aeneas was teasing me out of my serious nature and, under his encouraging coaxing, I let my heart tell me what to buy instead of my head. My head however did still remind me of the practical lists I had been making of what the house truly did need and I was careful to heed that as well. It was strange having no limit to what I felt I could ask for and receive. Aeneas assured me that Hector, long time warlord of Ilium, had more than enough in ransom alone to give me half the city if I desired it but I had never been free to be careless before and it took a great deal of getting used to. When I did, it was with an odd mix of pure, childlike pleasure, a strange female contentment in being spoiled so badly and not a small amount of guilt that he gave me so much and I had come to him with nothing at all but myself. All that I had had as a bride price had been left in Lemnos and, I assumed, gone back to my father. As a captive bride, it was questionable how much of it would ever make its way back to me. Aeneas, catching one of my guilty and pleased glances as a carpenter happily went off with the wet clay sketch of what I wanted for a set of chairs, was gallant enough to assure me that - to a man like Hector - myself was exactly and all he wanted. It was not a hard thought to believe, not now, but it didn't mean I couldn't wish I had brought more with me than a single box of darkness.

While we shopped, Aeneas introduced me to the people and places he knew and he seemed to know everyone and everywhere. He did not live in Ilium itself but further inland, in the land of the Dardans. He was a prince himself, from a different vein of the same line that Hector claimed his royal blood from, one of those slips of fate not that far back that had given Hector's line the throne of Ilium instead of Aeneas'. Instead of resenting Hector though, or that their positions were not reversed, he seemed to adore his older cousin if his words and the look on his face when he spoke of him was any indication. It did my heart good to see that at least one of Hector's family did not drag at him as so many of them seemed to. Hector had not come with us on our tour of the city, Aeneas confided in me, because he had wanted the city and I to have a chance to meet each other without distraction and, having seen the way Hector had been greeted by his people on his return with me, I suspected he was a distraction indeed. There was no doubt the city loved him and because of that, I found them eager to love me as well.

I was eager to love them too. My entire

future would be within these walls and the surrounding land. At least, I believed so at the time.

We took small, light meals throughout the day, sitting under open air awnings in the squares and watching the waves of people that moved through Ilium's markets like the tides. I saw Egyptians, Hittites, Achaeans, and people even more foreign still. Aeneas even pointed out a small contingent of Amazons from the far east as they strode through the crowds. Every skin color and hair color I could imagine passed in front of me at one point or another and the difference in their dress was as musical as the mix of their voices in their languages. Somehow, this -- *all of this* -- was mine now. One day these people would be my people and I would belong to them, to protect and provide for them under Hector's shadow. It was -- truly, it was too much for me to completely believe, too much to feel real, but I thought in time I would come to understand it and what it meant. I looked forward to the process.

All day, we wandered inside and outside the city walls of Ilium and the town beyond. Even then Aeneas assured me that I had not seen anything but the very tip of what Ilium was and what it held. I had the rest of my life to learn this place. I could not imagine ever growing tired or bored in a city like this. When Aeneas offered to take me to the temple district however, I declined. I was too close to realizing what I wanted to risk a fickle god looking down and noticing. Let the other women go to Athena's temple, I would rather stand atop the Scaean Gate and see the world laid out before me. If I must go to a god at all, the ancient stone gods on their pedestals in front of that tower, so old their names were forgotten, seemed much more welcoming to me than a terrible stone alive inside a tree ever would. Like the Skamander River beyond, I thought the small, ancient gods of this land were much warmer and more concerned with what happened here than the indulgent, younger gods that now ruled the world and were so careless with the mortals that lived in it. I spoke none of that to Aeneas, of course, or even out loud to the wind. What was in my heart was best kept there.

Before the sun began to set however I turned our feet back toward my home at the top of the hill. I was learning that Hector was easy with me and I did not think he would mind if I were late coming home this first time I was freed to roam my new city. It mattered to *me* though. I did not want him coming home to an empty, unlit house. I thought he had done that enough in the years past and I did not want him to ever have to return to that now. It was important to me that I be there when he returned and that his house would be waiting for him.

Aeneas agreed to stay for dinner with us, putting up only a small, token protest since, in truth, his wife was back in Dardania and he had nowhere else to be tonight while he remained in Ilium. I also suspected he was eager to tease Hector about our adventures this day and the woman Ilium's lawagetas had brought home with him. There were already some of my purchases that had come up from the lower city during the day while I still shopped and I had them brought into one of the empty rooms, categorizing in my mind what had arrived and what was still to come, setting aside for another day the rearrangement of our house.

Our house. Such a small word to mean so much.

I knew that teased that Aeneas could not wait to tell Hector about our day but I admit that I watched from the kitchen window for his arrival too and when I saw him come through the gates, I ran to the doorway to greet him first. He had indulged me today, spoiled me, treated me so sweetly and provided so well for me, all without even being present. I wanted to thank to him first. I wanted -- I wanted to be able to put my arms around him and feel his around me and simply be, knowing that action would seal away today forever in my heart as special and precious to me.

Hector smiled when he saw me and it was such a youthful grin that it made my heart rise in my chest. He had something that he was carrying against his back but when I reached for him, he loosed it enough for one of his arms to envelop me and pulled me close into his warmth and solid safety. I had missed him. How had I missed a man I had lived so long without? It made no sense. I had missed him all the same though. I wound my arms around his shoulders and when I lifted my face to thank him, he kissed me instead. That was even better. He had taken to stealing kisses from me whenever the opportunity arose and I pretended that it was necessary for him to steal them in the first place. I found that, given the freedom, I could act young and playful without feeling foolish or worrying that he would think I was silly. I had never before been free to be young and carefree. I could not seem to resist the lure of it with him and so I teased him into stealing kisses and just 'happened' to cross his path so that he would pull me into his arms. I would have expected anyone else to look down upon me as ridiculous but for Hector, and Hector alone, I could be as unguarded as I wished and not worry at how it looked to him.

"I enjoyed myself today," I told him when our lips finally parted and I had found my breath again. I felt him smile as he pressed his face into my hair.

"Good."

"I bought too much."

"Good."

With a smile of my own, I turned my face into his throat and shut my eyes for a long moment, content to simply enjoy the warmth, the solid feel, the smell of him. How strange. I had not, in all my years of waiting, thought of this part of being married to a man.

"One more gift. For today." Hector lifted his head long enough to offer me the wicker basket he'd been holding and I shifted so that I could turn against him enough to take it in my hands without moving away from where his arm held me close. It was a simple basket, woven like a jar and its loose lid seemed to be a mere afterthought. I looked up at Hector and saw his dark eyes were watching me and I saw that there was more in them than a simple gift warranted.

"What is it?" I asked. I was not used to pleasant surprises being given to me and yet Hector's gifts were becoming the well-worn path of pleasure to me as well.

"Open it," he told me softly and so, leaning into him, I did.

The basket was full of hay. And fur. Before my mind even realized what I was seeing my heart knew and the pleased sound broke out of me. I found I was close to tears as I lifted out the kitten that had been sleeping in its nest of hay and the basket, stripped of its treasure, fell to the ground.

"The cats like to have their litters in the stables," Hector's voice was a bit gruff as I pressed my face into the soft fur as the kitten woke. I was shocked to find tears slipping from the edges of my eyes. "I knew you'd spoil this one worse than his mother ever could."

"Hector -" I cradled the kitten against my chest and turned my blurred vision on him. A kitten. He'd remembered. He'd not only paid attention to me but - he'd remembered... and, unknown to him - it meant I was safe. I was finally, truly safe. I could love small, helpless things again and never fear what would happen to them in the dark when I was not there to watch over them.

"Oh... Hector..." He broke my heart and I had never felt anything so sweet before in my entire life. With my free hand I reached to draw him down and press my lips to his. He had not had to - I would have never even known - but he had... I poured my heart into that kiss and the kitten grew restless against me long before we were done.

I named the kitten Chimera and adored him. Bithia, as usual, pretended disgust but seemed to always have a treat for him. Barely weaned, Chimera stayed close to me in the days that followed but each day that went by saw him growing braver and claiming possession over more of his domain. Hector watched it all with faint amusement and indulgence. It took me only a very short time to again grow used to having something small and furred always at my heel or in my hand and at night, Chimera slept across my chest. I felt young, like a child given the best treasure in the world and, more than ever, I found myself just 'happening' to cross Hector's path as we went about our day to day routines. Which just 'happened' to lead to being kissed -- thoroughly and with a quickly growing heat between us. I was growing to crave the sliding heat of his hands and the tight pressure of his body against mine. I still slept with Bithia in the guest room though and I thought I understood why. The longer Hector put off taking me to his bed, the more secure any child born of that union would be. We both knew how I had come to him and that I had been safe the entire time but ten years from now, twenty, it would be important that there was no question as to whose son or daughter I had given birth to if it was soon after my wedding night. In holding off, even for a few weeks, the future for that possible child was that much more secure. There was no guarantee that I would grow pregnant right away and it was a secret fear that I would not indulge that perhaps I never would after all my mother had done to me while my body had been growing. But, if I did, it would be important to have the count of the child's pregnancy clear for everyone. I could wait until marriage, but some nights it was harder than others.

While I waited though, our house began to feel like a home. Over the next few days, the stream of my arriving purchases was steady and I began to settle each room into what I had envisioned it to be in my mind. The rooms were no longer so empty they echoed and, slowly, the house began to feel comfortable and warm instead of hollow and waiting. I saw the way it affected Hector, saw the way he lingered now instead of simply moving pointedly from one duty to another and it brought me pleasure that I had been able to give that to him. For me, the house was a wonder and I was content in it but that I could give such a thing to him, who I was beginning to suspect had never had a home in the truest sense, meant something even more to me.

As I worked on bringing the house to life, Hector labored to set our wedding in place.

It was not that a wedding itself was so difficult. A proper sacrifice, the right offerings to the gods, the necessary people present -- it was easy enough that people married all the time without much notice. Hector was lawagetas however, of mighty Ilium and more, one day he would be its king and I its queen. Our wedding would necessarily have to be a bit more complicated than either of us would have liked. There were feasts to host, oracles to visit, people to invite, gifts to be given, and priests to be bribed to give good readings of omens. I was glad that the only part of that I needed to be involved in was some of the feasts. As the bride I was not supposed to be involved in more anyway but, seeing what was involved, I was doubly glad. Hector, used to handling diplomatics, took it all in stride and seemed devastatingly effective. I felt guilty letting him bear it all and yet there was no hiding my relief and gratitude either.

Through all of this, I began to learn to understand not only the city I found myself in but its lawagetas as well.

For all that I had been betrothed to Hector, I had seen him only the once before he had come for me in the dark on Lemnos, and that had been when I was still a child. I had thought, through first his gifts, and then his silence, that I had learned a bit about the man he had become but that had only been guesses. I was hardly the first woman to come to an unknown husband but a part of me was grateful for this time before the wedding. Living with him, and yet not truly living with him as his wife, I had time to watch the man I would marry and learn how he was. Sometimes, catching his dark eyes watching me, I thought, perhaps, he was doing the same.

That short time before the wedding was not all work of course. The evenings were lazy and relaxed and there was rarely a hurry to bed after the evening meal was finished and cleared away. There were often guests, but after the guests left, there was only Hector and I. I treasured those times most of all. Sometimes we would sit outside in the gardens I had begun to coax into order behind the house. For a couple that had known each other such a short time, we did surprisingly little talking and the silence never seemed to be wrong or awkward. Instead, I found it comfortable and relaxed. Sometimes, I would tell him of the things I had discovered that day and after making him laugh at an observation the first time I did so, I began to search during my day for things to tell him stories about, things to make him laugh again. He was handsome in an impossible way when he laughed and the sound of it never failed to do something strong and wonderful to my chest. I found I enjoyed playing the art of storyteller. Sometimes we would play games of strategy on tiled boards, hound and boar figurines moving across the squares or the small round stone markers being slid back and forth along the lines as we each tried to outthink the other. Hector had a sharp mind but I learned he could be reckless when he thought he saw an advantage.

"I was sure I killed more of your hounds." Hector was sitting across the low table from me in one of the backless chairs that night and his dark brows were low over his even darker eyes as he glared at the gray and white polished stone of the board in front of him. I sat on the other side of the small table, wrapped in a bearskin that Hector had found for me. Spring was arriving in windy Ilium but the nights were still chilled. I hated the cold but I was not sure how Hector had realized it since I was too well trained to ever show such a silly discomfort. He had noticed it somehow though and now whenever the sun began to set and take its warmth with it, I would find myself wrapped in something warm. It touched me but even deeper was the fact that he seemed to not even think consciously about doing so, he simply provided as if it were the natural thing to do. I, at least, realized it was not. We were in his bedroom and Chimera was exploring his bed. I hoped he approved for he would soon be moving up here. With me. Hector had promised I belonged in that bed my first day here and I was not sure how much longer I could wait. The thought brought the usual nerves for my utter inexperience in that area but my eagerness was quickly outpacing it.

"You did," I pointed out calmly, gesturing

with one finger as I held the fur around me contentedly. "Your boar was most vicious."

He shot me a narrow look from the tops of his eyes and then I watched his eyes flicker down again to surreptitiously count the game pieces he had collected from me. I was fairly sure he thought I was cheating and had to hide the smile. If I was inclined to do that sort of thing, I would certainly make sure I couldn't be caught at it. His dark onyx boars clearly outnumbered my ivory hounds on the board and he eyed them suspiciously.

"You should simply concede, warlord of Ilium." Bithia, sitting on a couch to the side of the room and doing mending, didn't look up from her work. "You are no closer to winning this round than you were the last three."

Hector grunted noncommittally at her. They had reached a truce of some sort while I had not been looking apparently. I was no longer worried Bithia might try to murder Hector in his sleep and he no longer baited her temper. After a bit of thought, Hector moved one of his pieces onto a square.

It was a very good move, a very smart move. I smiled as I reached forward and began to click my game pieces into place all over the tiles. Mercifully for Hector, there was a knock at the door before he had to watch me begin to collect his Boars off of the board.

Instead of calling out a welcome, Hector stood up and walked over to open the door himself, firmly between whoever was beyond and Bithia and I. Whoever it was would have had to come through the downstairs rooms and past Hector's people to reach us here but still, when he opened the door, he was standing to the side of it. There was nothing tight or strained about him however and I suspected he didn't even realize he what he moved so defensively automatically. It was another part of him I was learning. That Hector would always be a warrior even when he did not realize it. I did not mind.

I watched Bithia's face light a second before Cebriones stepped through the door with a wide grin. Hector's smile went large and he caught his brother in an embrace of welcome. I felt it too. It was if a part of our strange family had returned at last and I left off decimating Hector's game pieces to smile as I watched.

"It took you long enough." Hector's voice only held pleasure and Cebriones laughed.

"I didn't get to sit around all day with beautiful women," he answered back as Hector drew him into the room. I was just rising to pour him something to drink, leaving the heavy bear skin neatly at my chair, when I saw who stood behind Cebriones in the doorway. My fingers went numb and the world around me went silent and hollow in my ears as I froze. I could not have made a sound or motion to indicate anything but still, Hector's head turned to look at me and I saw the dark fire flash to life in his eyes as his face went hard. He was already between me and the man in the doorway but he put himself more pointedly there now.

"Is this a guest of yours?" His voice was low as he asked Cebriones and Cebriones exhaled, eyebrows coming down.

"Yours, Hector. This is Prince Podes of Thebe. One of the Princess Andromache's older brothers."

Podes looked no more friendly toward Hector than Hector looked toward him but he saluted, fist over his heart.

"My father has come. As a wedding guest." The clarification was necessary, I knew, and I continued to stand, feeling as if I were waiting for something I didn't know. "He has brought Andromache's dowry as well." For the first time my brother looked directly at me but both of us were too close in upbringing to have anything that would speak showing on our faces. The dowry had not been expected. I remembered when my father had laid it out before me. A queen's ransom. Thrice over in my case. Podes looked back to Hector.

"Father is camped outside the city. He has decided that your offer is fair. Better to be bound by marriage than by violence." My father was a strong man. Yet Hector was stronger and his position of power much greater. Of course my father could see that and the advantage of claiming Ilium's lawagetas as his son in law. Now I knew where, and why, Hector had sent Cebriones.

"And I have a message for Andromache." My brother did not look at me and that alone made my breath pause in my chest. It was warning but there was no real preparing for his next words.

"Mother has come as well."

XXVI.

Mother was here...

I could literally feel the blood drain from my face, something I had always thought was only an expression before and I simply sat down where I was. I felt suddenly feverish, clammy and sick to my stomach. Mother... She had followed me even here.

I did not have to look to know that Podes' face would still be expressionless or that Bithia's would be terrified. My own face felt felt numb at the edges of it, as if it were a mask of plaster ready to peel away and leave nothing underneath it. I heard Hector's voice at a distance, low and controlled.

"Get out."

To me, they were just sounds, not directed at me. Tentative, I reached up with my fingers. I touched the edges of my face at the jaw and cheeks lightly. I had been wearing a mask all along and not even known it. It had been a mask of freedom, of joy. Of myself as I had always wished to be. I had thought it was me -- but now I realized that I had been wrong. It was only what I had wanted to be. What I truly was, was the lifeless, stone I felt under the edges of that softness.

Hector's hands closed over mine and I looked up at him, feeling confused without even knowing why. His eyes were very dark, watching my face and he was gentle as he drew my hands away from it. My fingers always grew icy when I was cold and I protested a wordless sound as he drew them to rest against his chest. Even plunged into myself, I was self-conscious about how they must feel through the thin fabric of the robe against his warmer skin but he shook his head and kept them there, over the beat of his heart with one hand while he reached out to draw me close against him with the other. A part of me resisted and for a moment, I did too. I could not be the hollow, stone creature I needed to be to survive my mother when I was wrapped in the warmth and safety of Hector's arms. He did not force me but the pressure of his hand urging me toward him stayed and the part of me that felt suddenly so hopeless and devastated at being so close to all I had wanted and having it taken away, gave in. I closed my eyes and burrowed close. He gathered me into his arms and slowly knelt on the floor, drawing me into his lap as he held me. I knew that I was only stealing these moments before I had to become dead and lifeless inside again. My throat closed over suddenly and I felt tears sting behind my eyelids.

He would ask.

He would ask why the very mention of my mother did this to me. What would I tell him? Not the truth, never that. I would have to tell him something though -- and he would realize I was filthy inside and much worse -- a Medea. I did not think I could bear to see him look at me with revulsion - better I were dead and ash than I ever live to see that look on his face or in his eyes. What would I tell him?

"I'm sorry." His voice was low, rough and soft in his throat as he spoke. His arms around me tightened. "I'm sorry, Andromache."

It was so far beyond what I had been expecting to hear from him that it took a long moment for me to make sense of the words and the puzzled feeling stayed as I lifted my face to look at him. Why was *he* apologizing? I was the one that had brought this darkness with me into his world.

"I should never have left you there. I knew there was something wrong. I shouldn't have left you to grow up in that place and I did."

"Hector..." I curled my fingers against him, remembering belatedly that they were cold, too needy to draw away, trying to understand what he was saying without letting my own thoughts interfere. His eyes met mine and there was no revulsion in them. Anger was hidden in the softness but even then I knew that anger was not directed at me.

"They dressed you up like a doll and sent you out as a lure for me at dinner that first night. Do you think I didn't realize it? That I had never had any other family do the same with a daughter of theirs before? The look in your eyes wasn't what I was used to in sacrificial daughters offered for their family's power though. You looked -- I've never seen anyone look so silently terrified and alone. Not even in conquered cities." He drew me somehow closer into him still and I did not protest, feeling small and still and frozen inside. I was waiting, though I could not tell what I was waiting for.

"It hurt, seeing you like that after the way you'd been in the olive grove for me. It bothered me the way everyone ignored you at dinner. The way, when the raiders came, no one looked to protect you. The way they let you wander alone and unescorted afterward despite the possibility of desperate men still being in the area. That -- closet they kept you in and called a room." The anger and disgust in his voice had been building even though he'd kept his tone low as he spoke and I watched him in surprise. Wondering... was that how my life had seemed to everyone? Everyone but me. "Especially when you had been so open to me. You were so brave and sensible in the face of fear." His lips brushed my forehead and then he rested his chin against the top of my head.

"I could have brought you back to the city, my city, once we were betrothed and let you grow up in the women's quarters. Instead, I left you in your father's house. I thought I knew the limit of how you were treated there. I thought the petty jealousy and bickering here would be harder on you. I was wrong, wasn't I, Andromache? I missed something important and I left you there for seven more years to face it alone. I'm sorry. I was supposed to be your protector."

Of course he had the entire situation wrong. He was taking responsibility for something that wasn't his fault. In fact, I had never placed real blame on anyone for my situation. It had just been the way things were. That my life might have been any different than didn't matter now because it *hadn't* been different and there was no going back and changing things. What I was, what I faced, was what was real. I turned my face into Hector's throat and shut my eyes. He was so warm, so strong. In his arms I felt warm and safe too. It let some of the cold numbness around my mind loosen. Protected by his strength, I could remember, I could think of it safely. He was brave and strong enough for both of us and it let me spend less of myself on being brave and strong and let me think instead.

"Nothing would have changed." I was talking into his throat but he didn't draw away and so I assumed that meant he heard my words. I struggled to keep my voice steady because it was the one thing I had never been able to safely control. "Those years after -- they were no different from the years before. If you had taken me -- it would not have changed that." Though, it might have changed me. To grow into a woman in Ilium instead of my own home? Surrounded by competition for attention and women of power that knew how to manipulate? I would have been before Hector's eyes and not left seven years without him but I would not have been his, or living in his house, or perhaps even in his arms for many of those years of growth. I would have – the possibility made me stop and think about what I had

had while I was growing up. It had not all been bad. Not even most of it. I had grown up surrounded by servants that listened to the sound of my voice and looked to me for guidance. I had learned the cattle trade and farming and household accounts from them. Podes and his strange lessons of competence and ability. Long, hot, golden summers that never ended and crowded megarons of warriors' tales in the short winters. My father's arms. I would have been different inside if I had grown up in Ilium those years instead. Would I have been better, stronger, wiser? Happier? I couldn't guess and there was no reason to in the end. In the end, what the Fates had meant for me was what had happened and it was all that mattered now. It was what I had become and who I was.

Hector did not interrupt me as I silently measured things over in my mind, giving me time to settle inside myself with only one of his hands, stroking my hair. It let me begin to relax, to start to warm and soften again. It was impossible not to the longer I was reassured by the steadiness of his arms. Safe... I had never been completely safe before in my life. Yet here I was and I trusted in his safety when I was like this with him.

"I do not have to see her-"

It was a question and yet – it was a statement as well. I did not. I was only just realizing that. The doors and windows of Hector's house barred shut from the inside, more than proof against a nighttime visit from her. If she came as a visitor during the day -- a visitor was not yet a guest. I only had to have her turned away. Could I -- could I truly be safe from her so simply? I had told her 'no' once before. The memory of my punishment for that made me shudder still. She could not punish me now though. I did not have to go to her summon or follow her if she came for me. I could, quite possibly if I was careful, never see her again on this side of life. I could hide from her forever here. For all my previous revelation and determination about making my own path in the face of what other's did to me, for some reason this was the first time I had realized that I had the power to do the same when it came to my mother. The shock of it was almost choking it swept through me so strongly.

"Your mother," Hector clarified, for he'd never met her, or possibly even been aware of her existence as more than a vague means to an ends of giving life to me. I nodded against him and, finally, I feel myself enough again to begin to move, tentatively slipping my arms around his shoulders. The hand in my hair shifted to soothe gently along my back and he did not let me go.

"No," his voice was steady and he kept it low for me but I heard the steel of a lawagetas' command behind it. "I can make sure she can't even come inside the walls of the city. You never have to see her again, Andromache."

I believed him. It was impossible to doubt Hector. He was the walls of Ilium themselves, just as permanent and steady and solid and dependable. I had chosen him as my protector. He would protect me. If he said I was safe, I would be safe. And, being safe, I could finally have time to realize -

"I must look like a fool to you, scared like this. I can face your father but I hid like a small child from my own mother." Easier to pretend that I had overreacted than that I had good reason for my terror, but Hector would have none of it. I felt his head shake against me and he wrapped both arms around me then to draw me into him.

"No, Andromache. I think you are as brave as any man that I fight next to on the battlefield. Every thread of courage snaps at some point though. For every one of us. There is no shame in running. Only in not stopping and turning to face your fear when you know it's time."

"Your courage hasn't failed." It was a guess but not a hard one to make and when he exhaled I knew it was true. His hands tightened and then relaxed on me.

"No, not on the battlefield. But I will one day. Even the gods break and run eventually and I am mortal and will know death one day as they never will."

I heard the change in his voice and lifted my head to look up into his face. His Fate rode heavy on him and it drew me away from my own self. I lifted one of my hands to stroke his cheek.

"Not today," I reminded him and watched

his lips soften as he looked down at me.

"No," he agreed. "Not today." Leaning down to kiss me and there was no mistaking the gentle possession as his tongue slipped between my lips to brush the inside of my mouth.

"I am safe with you." I sighed it when his mouth left mine finally and it was not because I needed to hear it but because he did. It was finally starting to sink in just how free I was, just how safe my new life had made me. His lips touched mine again.

"You are safe," he answered and I smiled with my eyes still closed as he cradled me in his arms. I was safe and the longer the knowledge moved through me the stronger I felt. He kissed me again, slowly letting it sink deeper, exploring the inside of my mouth and coaxing my tongue to brush against his. His hands warmed me where they moved against me over cloth and against skin. It gave me courage and I caught at it quickly before I changed my mind, needing to confess:

"The box I always carry - "

"I know," his answer was soft and I opened my eyes to look up at him. Gentle, he touched my cheek. "I know there is darkness inside it and I know you are tied to whatever that darkness is. I don't have to know what is inside to know that. But I have seen you draw healing out of that box as well. Whatever is inside that box - whatever is inside you - I trust." His eyes met mine as I searched his. "I trust you, Andromache. Nothing of yours would ever bring me harm."

He trusted me so much more than I trusted myself. I could never see myself wanting to bring him harm, at least not in any way other than that of a normal woman married to a strong willed man might in their years of marriage. It was what I had promised my unborn children when I had stood in their room here and realized that one day, I could become a mother. I would not become what my own mother had. As I had sworn it to the unknown lives inside of me I now silently promised it to Hector as well. He would never know what I might have become, he would only know what I chose to. I was not my mother – and for the first time, I truly believed that I would never be. The small but now rooted belief in that was reassuring. I was tired of being afraid of who I was inside. I was so very tired of it.

Hector lowered his head to me again and when we kissed his was a long promise of determination and warmth. My arms wound around him like the roots in my heart and I kissed him back, long and earnest. Promises spoke without words. Slow, our kisses devolved into simple, pure pleasure as they tended to do these days and for the first time I was brave enough that my fingers slipped down to wander shyly over him as well. I think I might have spent the night in his room if he had not drawn his face back from mine after a long time. His eyes were as black as the stars and foggy as he looked at me. My skin seemed to hum where his hands had moved over it.

"I need to go speak with your father," his voice was rough at its edges and, even warm and liquid inside, I felt the sheer, smug, feminine pride to realize that I had done that to him. Me. I nodded against him but did nothing to leave him and so he lowered his head again and kissed me. I tangled fingers in his thick hair.

"Andromache - " His mouth finally left mine again, a parting that left both of us gasping. His voice was laughing and low when he finally caught his breath. It made me smile but I did not leave him and so he pressed his face into my shoulder and held me close in his arms while I let my fingers move through his hair and against the back of his thick neck. I felt a rub against my skin and realized he was kissing my throat, my shoulder, slow, and the friction of his beard was wonderful.

"I can't ignore your father," his voice was against my skin and I nodded but didn't open my eyes. He laughed softly in my arms and he finally drew back enough to look down at me as I opened my eyes for him.

The look in his eyes was wonderful and it was for me. Me! My smile grew and I stroked the side of his face. This man... What Fate had I pleased or what god had forgotten to pay attention to me that I would be given this man? That, as terrified as I should be in this moment with my mother outside the gates and my new, untested determination about my future, instead I was happy and glowing and humming inside. His lips pressed to where my hairline touched my forehead and I heard him chuckle again, deep in his chest. His voice was a soft rumble.

"My Andromache... I risk offending your father and people all over again just for the chance to keep you in my arms longer." Again his kiss, this time against my temple and he rose, drawing me easily up with him even though I knew I was larger than most women. In his arms, I fit perfectly.

"Go assure Bithia everything is all right," his voice was gentle as my weight settled back on my own feet but I still heard the honey gravel at its edges that I had come to know meant his thoughts were on me instead of practicality. It made me smile again as I rested against his chest and his hands moved slow over my back and shoulders. "I will leave Cebriones here until I come back. You should sleep. Now that your father is here I intend to marry you if not tomorrow then the next day." He drew back just enough to look down at me. "Unless you have changed your mind about me."

I did not even tease him.

"Better tomorrow then the next day," I said instead and contented myself with kissing his throat instead of his lips. He did need to go to my father. As my father but also as Hector's invited guest, it would have been shameful to keep him waiting too long. It still took us still longer to part. Eventually, he left me but it was only when I was in front of my own room and even then it was a long good-bye. I did not make it easier on him but I did try not to make it harder. When he was entirely gone, taking Podes with him I was sure, I turned to my own room and quietly opened the door.

Bithia's pale, frightened face met mine. She was holding Chimera in her lap and her eyes were determined as she stood with the kitten in her hands.

"You are not going," she told me and her voice was firm and sharp with fear. "I will not let you go. Not this time. We can ask Cebriones to stay and watch over you. You don't have to go to her anymore."

It made my heart break just a little and I walked over to her to take Chimera from her. I held him against my chest and noting that all the windows in the room were already shut against the night and barred.

"I am not going," I answered her and watched the emotions chase across her face. It was hard for her to let go of her defiance and harder still to let go of her fear. I understood but it also made me realize that it was not just myself who could have freedom from fear here.

"Good." It was firm but I saw the confusion in her eyes. It made me smile softly, understanding, and I settled down on the bed, drawing my legs up.

"I do not intend to ever see my mother again," I informed her quietly and, like me, I saw the doubt in her eyes that such a thing could be done. Yet Hector said it could. And, I thought, even if it could not, I would never again willingly submit to her. Perhaps she would find a way to reach me but I would never again willingly allow her to. If I could not stop what might come entirely, I could chose not to to submit when it came.

I could choose not to lose what I had become.

Bithia looked at me, hands cupping her own elbows as she still stood in the room.

"You're not going?" She asked again and I shook my head, rubbing gently against my kitten's forehead.

"No."

She sat down on the edge of the bed and looked at me.

"Is that possible?" She was not asking anything that I had not already asked myself. The fingers that were not lulling Chimera into sleep moved upward as if I offered my palms.

"I don't know." It was nothing but the truth. "But I am not going to her."

Bithia nodded and then exhaled. Finally, I reached for her and she scooted close to lean against my side, head on my shoulder as I wrapped my arm around her. She had been my first friend. She had followed me into my future. I realized that we were both still testing out what that meant.

"I asked Podes. Your father brought your dowry. All of it. Even the cattle."

Contemplative, I frowned in thought. I had not been sure what would happen to my dowry. Hector had taken me, not had a contract with his father and while stolen brides were not so rare, it was rare for the family of the kidnapped woman to support it. Most dowries either went to pay to ransom the woman back or else were set aside, sometimes, in generous families, for any children she might have out of the kidnapping but more often, simply to pay for other family goods, the woman considered lost to them as surely as if the sea had taken her. Instead, again, my father did more than most would for their daughter and brought mine to me.

"I suppose the hard goods can join Hector's things in his ransom room." It was my name for it. I did not think he had a name for the room that held all he'd acquired in his years as an active warlord. "I'll have to hire people to watch the cattle and find a pasture for them we can use."

Bithia shot me a look.

"You're rich. Possibly as rich as any woman in Ilium. Maybe more than any woman. And most of the men, I'd guess. Do you realize that?"

It surprised me and I gave her a small smile.

"No," I admitted. "I didn't realize that. I've never had my own assets before - I've only worked with what belonged to my family. I know that what my father brought is mine to use any way I chose – but in my mind, I still feel as if it belongs to someone else and I am only using it because it is good for the household I run." I paused on the thought. "I don't mind. It's my household now."

Bithia chuckled and stood up, moving over to begin taking down my hair and combing it out for the night.

"It is your household," she agreed. "I'm just surprised your father brought everything. Podes was very sure about it."

I nodded absently and pressed my lips together for a long thought. Chimera dozed in my lap.

"I have always wondered why he set aside so much for me. I always knew he loved me but I never thought he valued me so much."

"It's guilt," Bithia's voice was flat and I shifted enough to look at her from the corners of my eyes without moving so much that the comb would pull my hair. Was it? Guilt? Guilt for the years of forgetting me or guilt for leaving me to my mother's hands all those years?

If he had felt guilty -- why had he never done anything to change it? He could have. He could have changed everything for me.

Instead, I, his daughter, was finally strong enough to do now for myself.

XXVII.

As it was, as hard as it was to believe for me, I had little time to worry about my mother. With my father present to allay any of the council's fears that Thebe would withdraw its support from Ilium for my abduction - and, perhaps, to the slight of having been rejected in favor of Sparta at the first - Hector had solidified his marriage claim. He took advantage of that, which I did not doubt was why he had sent Cebriones to my father in the first place. I was coming to understand him a bit more each day and I knew now that he was a man that would do what he felt was right despite other advice, yet, when he did move, he tended to back his choice in as many ways and with as much support as he could. It also showed in the way Ilium's allies came to my wedding and they came in number. My father was apparently not the only one that Hector had sent men to woo to his side.

The wedding itself was a long affair and as I stood next to Hector for a great deal of it and listened to the priests intone prayers and interpret omens over our marriage, I silently prayed to whatever god had let me be ignored all these years to continue with that blessing. The omens, of course, were all good with the usual vague warnings about offending the gods and everyone played their part well and pretended to be surprised and delighted that the well paid priests projected good for our marriage and its future for holy Ilium. Hector sacrificed the first bull with its gold painted horns and its garnet earrings and then the priests took over. The sacrifices to the gods would go on well into the night to be sure that each was done properly and not one of the gods, distant or local, was forgotten. Earlier in the day, as the sun had risen, I had already offered my own sacrifices to the distant deities before going to the two noble rivers that bounded Ilium and laying the wreathes of flowers and gentler offerings that pleased their ancient guardian gods on the surface of their waters.

No one had risen from those waters just as no more fearsome god touched down their holy feet in the temples as the priests pacified them. The closest I came to divinity was when the priestess of Aphrodite adorned my head with a diadem set in the shape of doves and sea foam as they prepared me for the day. Sacrifices were not about wooing the gods. They were about keeping them from growing offended and having their revenge. On my wedding day every temple and small shrine was alight with offerings for my marriage. It was someone else that brought the gold jewelry that Athena coveted and hung it on the branches of her unnatural tree though. I did not set foot in her enclosed domain. Even for the thought of her continuing to ignore me I did not think I would have but it was not my duty anyway on my wedding day and so I was spared having to explain why one of Ilium's holiest places made my skin crawl as if small spiders with long legs ran just under its surface between the flesh and the muscle.

After the gods were pacified, it was time to

pacify the mortals. Wedding days were about being the joining of two being witnessed so that no one else could ever challenge the validity of the union and there were a great many witnesses present. First, Hector and I went before his father for a blessing. Priam stood tall and proud looking and again, he welcomed me into his family and Ilium's world. His eyes were just as sincere and encouraging the second time too and I could not help my smile for him. Parents by marriage could be terrifying creatures but Priam, and Hecuba, Hector's mother, went out of their way to be kind to me instead. My father gave his blessing next and yet, when he hugged me, it was not the same as before. I was no longer a child in need of his attention and, though his eyes were sad, he seemed content to give me up as his daughter. I found myself strangely content to go.

There were guests to greet after our fathers, visitors from afar, the powerful people of the city to acknowledge, Hector's family, my family - of which my mother was not present. Hector had kept his word to me. We went down to the lower city as well and greeted the people there. Aeneas and his wife, Creusa, came with us and she was light and laughing and as adoring of her husband as she was adored by him. I liked her immediately. Everywhere we went, noble space or common, sparse or crowded, the tables overflowed with food, the wine flowed, the music filled the air and there was laughter and smiles and dancing. I was even able to convince Hector to let me lead him through the maze in one of the dancing circles and his face was young as he followed me through the intricate patterns.

He was young. He was young and laughing and, for this one day, untroubled. To me, it was a better wedding gift than anything else that was brought and laid at my feet that day. That this man, my husband, was happy.

I was happy too, happy in a way that was not bounded for once by a knowledge of things to come or memories of things past. There was only this -- *today* -- my wedding to the man I wanted, and, for today, the future ahead of me looked bright and warm and I let myself believe it for the day. For that one day, my life was perfect.

Finally, the day began to fade and, tired and content, we escaped the crowds. Through back ways I had not known about, Hector, smiling, led me back to his house, my hand twinned with his. Smiling still, he drew me up the stairs after him to his room. And then he took me in his arms behind the closed door that sealed away the rest of the world and I learned a new kind of joy.

His touch was sure and it soothed away my nerves. It said that I could trust him, that he would not hurt me, that there was nothing to fear about this unknown part of our lives. He was slow, exploring as if I were some wondrous foreign treasure with hidden secrets he wanted to know and it surprised me. It... made me feel beautiful. I was so used to being over-tall and too thin and too sharp angled but next to Hector's body I was delicate and soft and just the right size for his arms. He held me close and he coaxed away my shy awkwardness, made it a soft game, lured me into finally being brave enough to explore him as well. It was the soft tangle of fingers and mouths, the waking of skin and the strange growing need for more of what he did. As I had led him through the dancing earlier, he was sure-footed and steady as he led me through this older, more intimate dance. Brushes turned into caresses, caresses into tugs, tugs into the clench of strong fingers and the light scrape of nails. His mouth and fingers touched me and I learned new things about my own body I had never suspected. And even in the fire, when the flames between us flared hot and demanding, he was patient and coaxed me into discovering his body as well. His pleasure at what my innocent attempts uncovered only made me bolder for the next time. When he finally claimed me, I did not feel like a vessel being filled with someone else's desires. I felt like myself, perhaps for the first time, and full of both my own surprising need and the impossible satisfaction of being with the one that I had come to not only cherish but adore as we were sated.

My old life ended that night. My new life started.

I spent the next day in his arms. Learned touches I had never known, words I had never understood, feelings I had not imagined. My new husband was kind and caring, he was dark and consuming, he was easy and teasing, lazy and slow. He encouraged, delighted in, my innocence and my curiosity and I delighted in learning what made him groan. I was safe in his arms, safe to explore, safe to ask, safe to want. I had never been safe that way before -- until Hector. It melted away my hesitation. I did not have to hide who I was and he, somehow, thought I was wonderful. Such a simple thing and yet, to me, it was everything. I had not been wrong to have wanted to wait all those years for this single man.

That night I slept in his arms, woke in his arms, slept again. There was nothing in me that wished to leave him to wander in the moonlight or restlessly ghost through the house. I was content, at peace, just where I was and no evil memories rose to trouble me or drive me from our bed. I was warm and I was safe and I did not think I would ever grow to take that for granted or forget what it could have been instead. I silently blessed the Fate that had woven this into my life's thread. For all the times it had been cruel, this one kindness made up for everything.

We woke late the next morning and, thanks to wandering hands that had led to more, it was later still by the time we rose to bathe. Most of the house servants had been sent away as well as all our permanent guests. For the next few days, I would belong to no one, and have to give my attention to no one, but Hector, just as he had temporarily set aside his duties as lawagetas for me and this time. It would not always be that way. It would probably never be that way again. For this short time though, we had only each other and I stored it away in my heart to always shelter and remember.

I made us both something to eat down in the kitchen while he sat on the familiar stool in the doorway to the garden beyond and watched me. He was barefoot, dark eyed and tousle haired, and I thought he looked young and happily content. I had not thought so much would change in the simple act of marriage, in sharing our bodies, but, in strange subtle ways it had and each new awareness of that was a surprise and a pleasure to me as I discovered them.

"I can't think of what I'm doing when you watch me like that," I told him, slanting him a glance from the corners of my eyes and trying not to smile. His gaze was like a touch now when it rested on me -- and I had learned that I very much enjoyed his touch.

"Liar," he grinned back at me and his dark eyes were full of light and laughter. I could not resist him when he was like that and I left the basil I had been chopping to drift over to him, reaching down to curl my fingers in his dark hair. All of me softened at the way his eyes changed at my touch. How could I be loved so very much?

"I am not," I answered back, playing like a child at the game and his hands came up to close around my waist and draw me closer. I could feel their heat through the thin fabric of my dress and all of me seemed to sigh in contentment as he drew me down and gathered me into his lap, where I curled in pleasure.

"I was just watching. Not touching," he mumbled it against my shoulder where he pressed his face. "You're not supposed to get distracted until I'm touching you."

I laughed quietly against him, pressing my own face into his hair as I tangled fingers in those dark waves against the back of his neck and the fabric of his tunic. I reveled silently in the way it felt as his arms tightened around me in response.

"Your eyes were touching me. They are always touching me now," I told him softly, shutting my own eyes as I relaxed into the now familiar feel of him. My husband...

My Hector.

"I can't spend all day wandering around with my eyes closed, Andromache." He pointed it out logically but his long fingers tangled in my hair where it lay against my back. I knew he was smiling. "I'll walk into things."

This playful teasing was new to me. I wasn't used to playing like this. It was fun, strangely intimate and personal.

"You don't have to keep your eyes open if you stay in bed."

It was his turn to laugh and I felt that throaty rumble through my own body as it moved through his. I had never known a better sound. He made a humming noise.

"But I do keep my eyes open in bed," he told me. "Now. The view is suddenly worth it."

It made me delightedly embarrassed, an emotion I wasn't used to and I could not stop my helpless smile as I ducked my head, pressing my face against his. After these past days and nights I could not doubt him when he spoke that way, not after the way he'd been with me. Not after the way he reacted to me. His lips were near my ear now and so he whispered the rest.

"In fact, I may never sleep again."

It flushed that wonderful emotion through me again, made me feel shy and wonderful and pleased. He moved his head, began rubbing slow, lazy kisses along my throat, taking his time and I tipped my head to the side so he would continue, giving him more. He murmured his approval and his hands shifted on me, drawing me closer and more intimately against him. I left my eyes closed and realized I was smiling as I wound my arms around him. Worth any price... These moments were worth any future price I would have to pay.

"My prince." The voice came from the doorway that led back into the house and I very much did not want to hear it. Hector paused in what he was doing but did not lift his head and I felt the way his hands tightened on me where they were curved. I wound the fingers of one of my hands in his thick hair. I was not embarrassed to be found with my husband this way and I was no more happy with the interruption than he was.

"What?" Hector's voice was sharp and low and a bit muffled against my skin. I almost felt bad for the messenger that had invaded our house. Almost. We had left the front door unbarred but it had not been an invitation.

"It's your sister. Cassandra." The man sounded no happier to be here than we were to see him. Hector lifted his face from my skin and looked at the man in the doorway behind me. His face was lined in stone.

"And - " he prompted.

"She's having one of her fits. She's screaming for you. They're afraid she will hurt herself."

"Tie her to her bed," Hector's response was flat and there was a flicker of anger in his dark eyes. "I'm not going to encourage her by coming whenever she throws a tantrum. The palace should know that by now."

"Yes," the agreement was slow. Hesitating. "But your mother said this is not one of her usual fits. Her mouth is discolored and her pupils are too large. She has a fever already. I am to tell you that she is not ranting as she usually does."

Cassandra had not come to our wedding. I had found out during the celebrations afterward that she had been intentionally kept away. I had overheard that before the ceremonies, she had shrieked to anyone that would listen about the doom of Ilium and so it had been decided to lock her in her room with her maids instead of risk her doing the same during the wedding ceremonies themselves. I had thought it was sensible. I had also wondered however if she might not attempt revenge of some sort. Apparently, she had and in the only way she knew how. Yet the discolored mouth bothered me... Hector exhaled, a noise of annoyance and anger.

"Go. Tell them I'm coming."

Hector's eyes met mine as the man exited and I reached up to gently stroke the side of his face, giving him a soft smile. He returned it and I saw that the edges of his eyes were tired again. Leaning in, I kissed him.

"Go," I told him softly. "And then come back."

He stood up and kissed me again as he set me on my own feet. The kiss lingered, started to heat. I found myself laughing as I drew back.

"Go." I reached up to pull him back to me for another kiss that only ended when I added: "And come back."

He moved to the door with me following and then drew me up against him again for another kiss. There was laughter in his eyes.

"Come back," I murmured against his lips and he kissed me again. His voice was a lion's purr and it sent a delighted shiver down through me as he agreed.

"I will come back."

I let him go and didn't follow him to the

front door even though I wanted to. I knew if I did it would be a very long time before he left the house and I wanted him to go so that he could have it over with and be coming back to me. My throat still felt the rub from his beard and I touched my lips and found them smiling a woman's pleased and content smile. Then I wrapped my arms around myself and danced on bare feet back to where I had been preparing the food. I felt young and silly and since I was in the house alone but for a servant or two, Bithia was politely hiding in her room, I let myself be young and silly. Who was there to see?

Chimera was on the table next to the food, tail curled around his feet as he sat and waited for me. It only meant that there was nothing in front of him he'd wanted to eat. I picked him up and held him against my chest and he tolerated my female mood and let me. Covering the food with a wide clay bowl, I picked up another as I moved to the herb garden. I would wait for Hector to eat, so instead I went to my knees in front of my carefully chosen plants. Chimera hopped from my arms to stalk off along the side of the house and I used my nails to pinch off the herbs I wanted. Hector's shoulder grew stiff during the night, an old war wound. I had noticed it and thought I knew something that would ease the tightened muscles. The sharp smell of the herbs on my fingers woke my mind.

A discolored mouth...

I wondered what color Cassandra's

screaming tongue and teeth had been. Something swallowed? Something swallowed to bring her before the gods? I went very still and my lips thinned as I pressed them together. Strange, wasn't it...? That Cassandra should find something to drink that would pull the gods down from their thrones to live in her head... That she should find it now of all times... Now, when my mother resided in her darkened tent outside the city...

It made the edges of my face, the tips of my fingers, feel cold. It was possible my mother had nothing to do with this at all but it was much more likely that if Cassandra had known of such a drink before now she would have taken it already. If she'd intended to take it at all...

What did my mother gain by poisoning a mad, helpless princess? Was it a warning that her hand could stretch even into the very inner courts of Ilium no matter where I tried to bar her body from? The rosemary in my fingers broke and its sharp smell filled the air.

My head came up as I heard something inside the house. It was too early for Hector to have come back but perhaps Bithia had seen him leave and decided to come out of her self-imposed exile. I left Chimera and the bowl outside with the herbs and stepped back into the house. Beginning to cross the kitchen to the door that opened into the megaron beyond, I caught a glimpse out the window to the courtyard beyond. My brows came down. A wagon? And loaded with long bolts of cloth? I stepped closer to look, thinking that I had accounted for all the cloth I had ordered. Even more, all of Ilium knew better than to bother their lawagetas and his new wife during the days that followed immediately after our wedding. Puzzled, in the process of turning to stride into the next room, I heard another sound -- and it was the sound of breaking furniture and a cut off cry. It reached my mind just as two men, too large to be cloth merchants, burst into the kitchen from the megaron. My heart reacted before my head, going cold and small in my chest and I was turning and bolting from the kitchen for the garden even before my thoughts caught up to my racing heart to tell me why.

Strong fingers tangled in my hair, caught at me, and I reacted on instinct, suddenly furious. The bowl that I had covered the food with was at hand and I caught its edge and swung it like a discus, putting my shoulder behind the swing. I caught my temporary captor by surprise. Brightly painted clay, the bowl caught and then shattered against the side of the man's face. His grip loosened as he fell back. I saw blood. I also saw two more men piling into the room. I turned and ran. My mind, bent on escape, offered me no answers as to who they might be. The *why* of why they were here seemed to involve pain and no choice of my own and, for the moment, that was more than answer enough.

They caught me in the doorway and I threw my weight forward so that the man holding me was entangled by the stool at his knees. I twisted my way free as he lost his balance. My nails caught the next man that reached for me and only his quick jerk back saved his eye though I left furrows in his skin near it. There were too many of them and even if I did reach outside, there was nowhere to go. It was a walled garden too high for me to climb easily. Those facts didn't seem to matter. I just knew I could not let myself be taken.

A hand lashed out and I saw it coming, pulling my head back desperately. The move softened the impact but the blow still made my eyes go dark. Arms closed around me then, hard enough that I felt my ribs creak as I was lifted bodily off my feet. I brought my head back hard. The impact made me see stars but it was the back of my head against the front of his face and his grip loosened. I drove my elbow backward and felt it strike solid flesh. Twisting my way free as he faltered, I darted forward, toward the other side of the kitchen now and its open windows to the courtyard. A body struck mine and sent me flying. I hit the table, felt the fire of the impact flare and then spread across my ribs. Hard hands closed on me again and it was only then -- so late, too late -- that I realized I should scream. I was in a city of soldiers but who would know to come to my aid if they didn't know I needed it? This time, for the first time, help would actually come if I screamed as it had never come for me as a child. It was exactly why my attackers were trying not to make sounds as we struggled. A blow to the side of my head had me sagging before I could reach the window. I didn't know if I knew how to scream. Someone covered my nose and mouth with a hand the consistency of horn, blocking off my air. Furious, pinned, I let all of my weight suddenly go, knees giving way and the sudden shift let me sink my teeth into the hand. I locked my jaw as he tried to jerk it away.

The next blow stole consciousness from me and the darkness swallowed the light.

XXVIII.

It was hot. Hard to breath. Dark.

I slit my eyes open and saw -- nothing. My head was beating in time with my heart and it hurt terribly. My mouth felt dry and I realized that there was cloth packed into it and bound there with a gag. It cut into the edges of my mouth and my jaw hurt. I blinked and still saw nothing. Trying to move them, I realized my hands were tied in front of me with something rough that cut into my wrists. Weight pressed on me from all sides and there was movement, a rough jostling. Still, I saw nothing though I knew my eyes were open.

The panic came immediately. It washed over me so strongly I just might have actually screamed despite my previous inability had my mouth not been packed so full and dry. There was the desperate, mindless need to throw my body against the weight and darkness that trapped me, to twist and flail and writhe. My breath stuttered in my lungs, I felt like vomiting.

My years of enforced training in my mother's rooms overrode the instinctive need to react though, froze and locked my body in place through those first few mindless seconds. Strange to find strength in what had always been the forced reaction to being weak before but it saved me from doing something that might have hurt myself, it let my mind find its way back out of the animal panic. The moment went passed and I shut my eyes and forced myself to breathe through my nose. I concentrated on just that and I slowly let go of the unraveling edges of helplessness. I had been helpless before, I reminded myself. I had been panicked before. This situation was new but the feeling was not. I had survived before. I would survive this.

I made it a silent mantra, repeating it over and over again inside my head in the darkness until I believed it. Only then did I open my eyes again.

I still saw nothing but this time, I was prepared better for it and I set my mind to concentrating on questions instead of feelings. Where was I? I moved the fingers of my bound hands even though they were bound too tightly and beginning to throb in time with my heart. They brushed against whatever it was that pressed down on me and I felt fabric. I was surrounded by fabric. The fabric merchant's cart I had seen outside in the courtyard just before I was taken? I had been taken, kidnapped. To smuggle me out, it made sense that they would leave the innocuous way they had come. It explained the jostling as well. It made me feel better being able to form something as simple as a logical thought. Somehow it made me feel just the smallest bit less helpless. I moved on to the next simple puzzle. Was I rolled in one of the bolts of fabric? What if I suffocated? I could not breathe through my mouth thanks to the gag. Buried in fabric, what if something shifted and I found myself smothered? It was not as if I could move to free myself or even alert my captors -- I had to shut my eyes again as the next wave of panic swamped me. Struggling inwardly, I forced myself to breathe, reminding myself of our little red ship of not so long ago, and how it had not fought the waves but simply ridden them out instead. I could do the same. It was not as bad as the first time and when it faded, I opened my eyes again.

I was being abducted. That much was obvious. Strangers had come into my house and trapped me, bound me, carried me away. I remembered the broken cry and felt a sudden clench in my heart. Who had they hurt? Killed? I shut my eyes tightly again. Whatever god it was that had ignored me or sheltered me from the others so long, would it listen to me if I prayed now? Did I want to be heard?

A god would make things worse if they decided to involve themselves. I thought I would still rather face a god. I had no sacrifices to offer but I silently prayed to whatever unknown god it was that would listen. Strangely, as I prayed slowly my heart calmed, just a little. I heard no roar of falling fire or scream of horses in fear but still, I found it easier to breathe and inside me, my mind slowly calmed. In a way, it was a better answer than any crash of lightning would have been and I was grateful.

With a slow exhale, I shifted my wrists, trying to loosen the rope that they had bound me with. I would find a way of escape, I would find a way home, I would find and care for anyone that had been hurt.

Hector.... My heart clenched suddenly. What would Hector think?

Pressing my lips together as best I could around the gag, I narrowed my eyes at the darkness. One step at a time. I was not lost yet.

Timing it as the cart jostled, I carefully moved my feet the smallest bit. Not being able to see, I had no idea if my legs were covered as well or my captors could see them. It didn't seem wise to let them realize I was awake but I wanted to know if my feet were bound. The movement told me they were not but they were encased in fabric as well.

It must have been a long roll of fabric. I was very tall for a woman.

I could not move enough to lift my hands to take away the cloth at my mouth and I thought it would be better to pretend I could not anyway, but I was beginning to hate that cloth even more than the ropes or the stifling fabric. It kept making me want to gag and my mouth was so dry. It hurt and it was somehow more humiliating than anything else. I tried to ignore it, distracting myself with thoughts while I continued to shift my wrists.

I had been taken. And, though I did not know how long I had been in the dark and unconscious, I suspected we were outside the city. The cart was still traveling and I thought, even under the fabric, that I would have at least been able to hear muffled noises if we were in the crowded lower city and town beyond. That we might already be outside the city panicked me again but that wave was even smaller than the last and I survived it.

Outside the city. Who was taking me away? It seemed an even more important question than 'why'. The men had looked like soldiers, built too broad in the shoulders, far too quiet and efficient in the way they had come at me. Soldiers then or thugs. Mercenaries? Enemies of Hector? Of Ilium? Enemies of mine?

Mother?

The thought sent a cold chill through me and I stopped moving for a very long moment. Oh silent god or attentive Fate -- please...

Cassandra had been poisoned. My mother was in her dark tent crouched just outside the city walls. I hadn't recognized the men. Unless my father's house had changed, my present captors weren't from Thebe. I didn't think my father would have condoned this anyway. He had profited by my marriage and at the wedding his blessing and embrace had been sincere. His future was stronger now thanks to his intimate connection with Troy. Even more, he was a warrior. One of my house would have simply challenged Hector to a fight. My mother had other ways about her though and my father had never controlled her or tried to know what she did. Whoever had taken me had needed Hector out of the house and they had poisoned his sister to achieve it. The timing was too close, too perfect. I shivered even in the stifling heat and began to work with my wrists more frantically.

Punishment...

What would my mother do with me in her power? Or would she simply leave me to the mercy of the men that had me now? I knew what that meant for me. Becoming one of the slave women of Pylos was attractive compared to what uses men would find for a woman they had been tossed. By the way I was treated, I guessed that my value was not very high for them. The way I had been kidnapped once before reminded me of the differences in the way a man treated a woman he found of worth and one he did not.

The ropes began to give but not enough. Not at all enough. My pounding head was making me feel sick and so was the stifling heat. My throat was painful thanks to the gag in my mouth and my body ached from the bruises I had no doubt taken in my fight. My hands throbbed painfully. It was hard to not simply give up to that and try to sleep again but that would not help me. I had been in worse pain than this before. I might soon be in worse pain again. I forced myself to ignore what I felt and concentrate on the ropes. My one small consolation -- I did not think they had taken the time to rape me with each second they spent inside the city increasing the danger to them. It was a small consolation only though. We were not in the city anymore and they would not need to speed away for long.

The wagon stopped before I was ready. The ropes had not given enough. Yet. They had not given enough yet. I was not done yet.

My life, at the moment, was balancing on a great deal of *yet*.

Through the fabric, I watched light bloom and I shut my eyes against it, sensitive to the change. Buying myself, coward that I was, one more moment of not having to see what my future held. The stifling weight was lifted from me and I was unrolled as the cloth I had been wrapped in was tipped. It knocked the air from my lungs and made my head spin, made me feel sick again. My body thumped up against more bolts of cloth and I opened my eyes. Perhaps, I should have pretended I was still unconscious but I needed to see. And I thought -- I hoped -- if my eyes were on them, perhaps, just perhaps, the men that had taken me might think just a moment longer before they did anything to me. It was always easier to do evil when no one was watching.

I saw trees above me. I did not hear the sound of Ilium's rivers. A man's face appeared in my vision and I let my eyes widen with the fear I felt. That face withdrew and another came into view. I did not recognize him either but he was smiling as he reached down for me and there was nothing reassuring about that smile. I made a noise in the back of my throat and tried to push away from him. It made him laugh and he caught me up roughly and threw me over his shoulder. All the blood rushed to my head and my sight when dark. I might have vomited then, and been glad to splash it all over the back of my captor, but I was wearing a gag and deathly afraid I would drown. Instead, I whimpered again and shifted as if I were weakly trying to get away from him. Maybe I should have been concerned with pride, been stoic or defiant, but the truth was, stoic and defiant would not help me in the situation I was in. There was no respect to be won, my mind told me, but it would put them on their guard if I fought. People were less on guard against things they perceived as weaker and helpless. So I would be nothing but a helpless female taken from the safety and shelter of her protector. I would seem weak and wounded and terrified, pliable in my fear. It was not what I had shown them in my house but bullies liked to think they were terrifying and they liked their victims subdued. Hopefully they would let what they wanted and what I showed them now influence them more than what I had done within the safe walls of Ilium. I needed them to underestimate me. It was the only advantage I had and it might -- just might -- buy me a chance. At what I wouldn't know until it came but I thought I would rather have the chance than my pride. My priorities were more practical than noble. In shifting, it let me test my captor's balance and my options, but he was steady on his feet and my knee brushed hardened leather. I would need better leverage to damage him with a kick than I had now. Hair in the way, staring upside down at the back of him, I narrowed my eyes as he laughed and slapped the back of my thighs with a blow that stung. I forgot to squeal because I knew it had been meant to hurt but he didn't seem to notice my slip. I was too busy trying to breathe through my nose and keep my stomach from getting sick while still keeping my eyes open so that I could see what was happening around me. I did not think I would have more than one chance at escape if that and I didn't dare let it happen while my eyes were closed and I would miss it.

The man carrying me was walking and the strap of his shoulder bit painfully into my stomach each time he moved. I shuddered once, violently, to make up for the forgotten sound of pain, and heard him laugh again. It was an ugly sound.

"Don't tempt me, girl. Or I may keep you to myself instead of giving you to my little brother."

I remembered to moan in the back of my throat but my mind was sorting desperately through this new information. 'Little brother'? What did that have to do with my mother? Who was his little brother and why was he giving me to him? Was I a war prize then, a lawiaiai? Something he was going to give as a gift to a family member? It seemed a great deal of trouble to go through for a disposable gift. Priam had placed me publicly under his protection. Ilium would not forget my abduction. And as for Hector...

"Nothing like a woman's hair on your thighs," my captor commented and his men reacted as I would expect to the crude comment. Then I was dumped to my feet so fast and hard that it jarred me again and I had to shut my eyes against the darkness. It didn't take a great deal of acting on my part to sway and I didn't have to fake the sound I made to keep from being sick at all. When I opened my eyes, I could finally clearly see who was in front of me.

I still didn't recognize him. Somehow, I always expected to recognize people that meant me harm. I did however recognize the polished black, boiled armor he was wearing. He must have been outside the city waiting for my abductors to come to him. There was no possibility he could have worn it unnoticed in the city. Black armor meant -

Myrmidon. The black ant men.

Phthia?!

It almost knocked the air from my lungs and my eyes went wide enough to satisfy the man smirking in front of me. He caught my aching jaw in his fingers and raised my head from his breastplate to his face. Too old! He was too old! Hector's age. My father had promised me to -

"My little brother has all the luck thanks to that bitch mother of his." The soldier's voice was as ugly as his laugh. What was in his eyes was uglier. I knew him then.

Eurytion. Oldest son of the king of Phthia. King Peleus' son by his second wife. Not even the bards knew what had happened to that unfortunate woman to clear the way for Thetis, the sea witch, and her son to Peleus, younger Achilles. That second son was the boy I had been promised to.

Peleus' heir despite his older son. It was not Achilles I faced now though. And Eurytion had apparently not forgiven the slight to his own mother or himself. All the nightmare things I had heard about the sons of Peleus came rushing over me in a great, horrible wave.

"You know who I am," he sounded surprised but it must have been on my face and in my eyes. I forced tears, they were not that hard, clasping my bound hands in front of me and I nodded, trembling. It made him smile. It was such an ugly, satisfied smile. I felt the cold, clammy fingers of horror wrapping around my stomach and then his fingers tightened on my jaw, hard enough to make it creak and that pain helped pull me back out of the shock of my discovery.

"We will have a great deal of time together, you and I. It's a long sail from here to Phthia. I know. I was without a woman the entire way here. You'll set that right on the way back."

I let the tears slid down my cheeks and my mind twisted into itself while he was distracted with the fake tears. Out. I had to find a way out. I would not survive the trip to Phthia. Who I was inside, what I had become, would not survive it.

"I'm glad you understand." He shook my jaw fiercely and then lifted me roughly into a chariot that waited nearby. Chariots. Because the cart that had carried them into and out of the city would not be fast enough if I was discovered missing and rescue tried to catch up to us. No one knew how long it would be until I was missed and my captors were doing their best to thwart any chance of salvation for me. Eurytion crowded onto the chariot after me and pressed me against the front of it with his body, taking the reins around me. Face to face, it was intimate and filthy and I shuddered again for him so that he laughed. I also pressed my hands against my chest where my loose hair hid them and the ropes that I was loosening on my wrists.

"Soon enough," he promised me and his voice was smug. "It's good to find a woman that knows when to accept her fate. You'll find obedience rewarded."

His type of reward would be no reward at all to me. It would kill me inside. I was a very long way from accepting his predictions about my future though I was careful not to do anything to let him think otherwise. I needed time, I needed them to be careless despite the fact they seem to have planned this far too well. Eurytion snapped the reins with a call to the horses and the weight of his body pinned me in place as the carriage jerked forward.

Lowering my head and letting my shoulders shake as if I were crying silently, I stole looks from the edges of my now dry eyes. I knew where we were. Coming from across the Aegean, he must have a boat nearby, but he could not have harbored it in Ilium's own port. He could never have taken me away from there. He would have hardly been the first merchant to try to sneak extra goods out of

Ilium's market though. He must have ground his shallow bottomed boat on a nearby beach. The forest around, the path -- I was not too familiar with my new homeland yet but Hector had explain it to me, drawn me a map in the dirt of my garden one afternoon when I had asked. He had told me of Besika Bay. Across the river Skamander and down that river path, far enough away from the shelter of Ilium's harbor, it had long, flat sandy beaches and shelter from the winds and waves of the Hellespont. There was a good deal of room for a ship to beach themselves along that bay's shores. Ilium ignored it because it was still not access to or from the Hellespont and that was where their money in trade and tariff came from.

Eurytion was taking me there.

Where there no Trojan guards to stop him.

There were two other light chariots with the one I was in. Three men in each of them, making the baskets over-full and mis-balanced. Eurytion was the only one in light armor. The other men were still dressed like merchants. Phthia -- how had they known to come for me so quickly? News, even as light-footed as it was, could surely not have reached Phthia so soon of my escape from them. Of my marriage. To reach me now, they must have been sailing long before my ship toward their homeland even left Thebe.

It wasn't important. It was a good question but it wasn't a question that mattered at the moment. At the moment I needed my freedom, an escape. And I needed it now -- before we reached the ship. Or ships. Before we reached wherever we were going and the no doubt larger number of men than were surrounding me now.

The chariots moved with a great deal of speed, as they had been meant to. I did not have much time left and I could count on no rescue but one that came from me. Silent god, attentive Fate... give me just long enough. The carriage of the chariot I was in jolted as it went over the uneven road and finally -- *finally* the rope around my wrists was loose enough. I cupped my thumb in the palm of my other hand and braced myself mentally. It was an old trick, one I had learned in my mother's rooms what felt like a lifetime ago. As it was now, my hand would not fit past the slim loosening I had managed with the rope. The joint of my thumb was in the way. I waited until the next jolt of the cart and popped that joint out of its socket.

The pain was nauseating -- again and I went weak a moment with it. I was used to pain but that never made it easy to ignore. My captor reached out with a hand and his fingers closed hard around my upper arm to haul me upward as my knees gave way. He swore in annoyance at me --

and only one of his hands was on the loosely guarded reins.

I jerked my hands, pressed together into a fist, upward. It didn't have a great deal of my weight behind it in the position I was in but it still caught him under his chin and snapped his head back because he wasn't expecting it. With a jerk that tore skin, I twisted my hand downward and free of the noose around my wrists as he roared in surprise and anger. I had a moment in time -- the blink of an eye -- and if I was not fast enough I would lose it all. The chariots were racing and crowded close on the path. I clawed for the reins ahead of where his single hand held them, threading my fingers by instinct. A hundred lessons at my brother's hands and this one moment. With everything that was in me I hauled those reins and drove those horses, and my chariot, exactly where I wanted them to go. Straight into the chariot next to me.

Everything was moving too fast to stop.

The horses collided with the horses next to them. The carriages of the chariots tangled as the driver of the other one instinctively tried to protect his own horses from the wheels of my chariot. The horses panicked as they felt the controlling hands on them loosen. Wood crashed against wood. I threw my arms over my head and ducked as one of the wheels of my chariot locked with the one next to it. The riders in the carriages lost their balance as the tangling wheels fought with the wild horses and the speed that had not stopped yet. The world upended in a scream of abused wood and the screaming of animals. I tried to curl myself into a ball and closed my eyes as everything went mad. A body struck mine. Wood splintered. I was tossed like a hollow pod up against the side of something hard enough to knock the air out of my lungs. I opened an eye to see the earth going by at the wrong angle -- and then I was rolling and it was in dirt and grass. The carriage was still over me and I fought against it as the horses continued to drag it. I freed myself, gasping. There were real tears in my eyes now that I did not even understand the purpose of. My hands clawed in the dirt, terror suddenly strong in me again, heartbeat screaming in my chest.

No. It was horses screaming. Or men.

I didn't even look. There was no room in my mind for anything else but the terror and I did not even try to fight it. I needed it and so I embraced it and the panicked strength and speed it gave me. Desperate, I struggled to my feet, hardly feeling the pain in my body or the throbbing in my head.

I ran.

XXIX.

I ran like a hunted animal, in a burst of speed and strength. The terror, the horror, gave my feet wings as swift as Hermes's and when I heard a voice screaming in fury after me, the blood pulsed through me like fire and I ran even faster, clawing the gag out of my mouth so that I could inhale in great gulps as I fled.

I ran away from the beach. Into the trees. Away from the direction my captors had been going. I ran toward Ilium and safety even though I knew I would never reach it. Even in my unleashed terror, I knew that I did not have the strength or the stamina to keep up my fear wrought flight. I also realized that it could very well be that no one would come in time to save me. If Cassandra had swallowed what I thought she had, Hector could be with her all afternoon - it was a vicious thing to meet the gods in the prison of your own mind. No one else was going to arrive at our house while he was gone either. We were newly married and everyone would leave us our privacy. My only hope of rescue lay in someone having survived the invasion of our house and having found help. I hoped for that because I could not bear the thought of having lost anyone - but my head and heart did not dare offer me a glimmer of expected rescue. I could rely on no one but myself.

The course I ran was angled, to take me away from my captors and toward Ilium but not in a straight line. I hoped it made me harder to follow through the thin trees. I was not even sure of the exact direction of Ilium but I knew enough to run in the opposite direction from the route the chariots had been headed. Already my legs were beginning to burn. My side was on fire and I put my hand with its useless thumb over where it hurt the most and ran on. My body would do whatever I asked it to -- until it could not any more. Then it would simply collapse. I knew, for it had done so before. I needed to stop my mindless flight and I needed to think.

I needed to find a safe place while I still could.

I needed to hide.

Watching where I was going now with a purpose, listening to the sounds behind me because I could not spare the energy to turn my head and look, I, like so many hunted animals before me, found shelter and I hid myself.

Despite myself, I also prayed to my silent, attentive Fate. I prayed a prayer no god had ever listened to. I prayed for mercy.

My breath was loud in my ears and I made myself small where I hid. Like a small animal, I panted through my mouth as silently as I could. I still felt sick and now I felt strangely cold too but I stayed as still as a shadow and slit my eyes against those feelings. I had long ago learned that there were things more important than physical pain. Straining my ears, I tried to hear above the sounds of my own breathing.

"You crazy whore!" It was a roar of fury and my eyes flinched against it even though I was too well trained to let my body react. It was the roar of a monster, of a man mad with anger -- it was the sound of my future if I were found.

I watched from my hiding place as Eurytion burst into view. He walked with a limp and there was blood down the side of his face. I had done that. I had escaped him. I had wounded him. We both knew it.

We also both knew that if he got his hands upon me I would pay for it. And not quickly.

"You'll serve in my bed until I'm tired of you. And my father's. And my brother's." His voice was full of the rot of hatred and I watched as he slowly circled closer. Searching for me. He knew I couldn't have run far. "You'll be nothing more than one of our slaves and when you're not on your back or your knees in front of us, you'll be cleaning the piss tiles. We'll parade you naked in front of our guests at dinners. Just to show them the wife of Hector, Warlord of Troy." The image was too easy to see and I shut my eyes against it and dug my nails into the trunk of the tree that sheltered me. My hunter circled. I heard his voice as he moved and forced my eyes open again so that I could watch him even as my soul flinched in my chest at his words. Humiliation. And -

Hector would hear of it from passing traders and foreigners.

Hector...

"You belong to my family now, slave. And you always will. You know it." He was getting closer. So close. I pressed my lips together and all but stopped breathing. He chuckled and it was like a thick foul liquid bubbling slowly.

"Come out now and I may not use you in front of the Trojan ambassadors your husband will send to try to buy you back from us."

Despite myself, his words had my eyes shutting in reaction. Without a sound, I mouthed one word to my suddenly inattentive Fate.

'Please...'

"You clever little bitch - " his voice was so close and suddenly sure with the knowledge of where I had hidden myself, I knew that he had found me. My eyes snapped open.

And then there was the sound of bodies colliding and the tree I was sheltering with shook from the impact.

I looked down. Yet my mind took a very long time to make sense of what it saw. I saw Eurytion. I saw the bronze of drawn swords. And I saw -

Hector.

My heart stopped in my chest and, in a way that made no sense, suddenly nothing else mattered.

The two men had been in a pile, the result of what must have been Hector bulling into the other man, but they were both on their feet now. Both had their swords free. Neither had shields. Hector had told me before that his great shield slowed him down when he traveled with it slung over his back, tapping at the back of his helmet and his heels whenever he tried to hurry. Eurytion had no shield either -- but he did wear a breastplate and Hector was without armor. Both of their faces were twisted with a dark rage I had never seen before and the sheer power of it made me shudder despite myself. It hardly mattered, neither of the men were paying attention to anything other than who was in front of him.

Hector's sword already had blood on it.

How had he found me?

In the practice and training bouts I had watched as a young girl growing up, there was always a great deal of talk that went on. Taunting before and during the fight. Comments. Even sometimes jokes. There was no talking between Hector and Eurytion. There was not even a pause between the moment they lunged to their feet and the moment they lunged at each other. With no shields to shelter them, their swords served double purpose, and I found myself reacting with small jerks of my own as the bronze blades swung and crashed, hunching closer against the tree. This was a different kind of fear than any I had ever known before. Finally, I understood the difference between what I had seen on the practice fields of my father's training grounds and what I saw before me. It was even different from Hector's challenge on the Island of Chrysa. I saw the difference between men looking to best each other -- and men intent on killing each other.

It was terrifying. So was seeing Hector this way. Seeing, finally, what he had hidden from me, what had only been hinted at in him before. I had never seen Hector's face the way it was now. He was one of Ares' hounds, a creature bent on death and destruction, with no room for mercy or softer emotions. Perhaps there was something wrong with me, broken inside, but as I watched him - I felt suddenly safe. He might be an unleashed nightmare and yet he was *my* nightmare and he fought to keep me safe. No, I did not fear him. Instead, I had a different terror. That terror was that the fight below me would end with Hector's death and not Eurytion's. Someone was going to die today and I felt the bone deep, freezing fear slowly settling in on me, that it might, by cruel intervention, be my new husband.

The best warrior in the world was susceptible to an unexpected patch of uneven ground or a random glance of sunlight in his eyes.

The swords thrust and crashed together. The men wove and dodged, seeking openings and trying to protect themselves. Eurytion was supposed to be one of the best Achaean warriors, training his younger brother in the ways of battle so that the Achaeans bragged that soon they would have two demigods, invincible brothers to fight side by side. But Hector was lawagetas of far reaching Ilium and he had earned that title.

As I watched, Hector's sword slashed

downward to be met and blocked by his opponent's blade and in the same instant those blades were locked, Hector's other hand suddenly came up in a fist. It smashed into the underside of Eurytion's chin and, unlike my blow of earlier, with Hector's full strength behind it, the Achaean's head was jerked back and I heard, even from where I hid, the audible crack of his jaw as his mouth, open in his panting, snapped together. There was blood and a strange, strangled cry and then Hector's knee came up and the other man was knocked backward and off his feet. Hector followed him down. I heard the wet sound of things breaking as both of Hector's knees came down with force on Eurytion's chest and Hector's sword impaled his opponent's sword arm.

For a very long moment, the world seemed to pause. The silence was so loud in my ears it was a roaring like the far off waves. I found myself breathing just as hard as the men in front of my eyes.

Something was wrong with Eurytion's mouth and jaw. Even from where I was, I could see that clearly. Could see the way he was laboring to breathe and the way bright blood spilled from the edges of his lips. His one good arm scrabbled at Hector's chest as my husband knelt over him.

All three of us knew what came next. Surrender and ransom. Peleus would pay well for his son's return, even if the man was damaged. It was a common practice even on the battlefield, much less in single combat. A portion of Hector's own treasure came from ransoms of his past enemies. Hector would ransom Peleus' oldest son and the man would live.

He would live and I would see his promises about my future in his eyes.

Hector's dark head, hair curling in the damp from his exertions, shook. I could not see his face. I heard his voice though, and it was low and hard as he simply said:

"Never again."

His blade flashed upward in both of his hands and he brought it down with the weight of his entire body behind it. Eurytion's body jerked with a cut off cry.

And then Peleus' oldest son fled down to Hades and left his corpse behind.

I pressed the side of my face into the bark of the tree that sheltered me but I did not look away or shut my eyes. I felt again that foul touch and heard that ugly voice in my ears and I let it too, like the soul before it, fly away into darkness and be no more. I exhaled silently and it was then, finally, that I began to tremble. Somewhere away in the woods I heard a call and knew the voice. Knew it was Trojan and it was triumphant.

My enemies were defeated.

All but one.

Slow, Hector stood and it was a great unwinding so that he looked tall and dark and forever. The whisper of what he had been during the fight remained on his face and in his dark eyes. It was as real as the blood that painted him.

I wanted nothing more than to be in his arms.

His eyes moved across the forest in front of him and then he lifted his head to the treetops. I knew he could not see me, because he wasn't looking directly at my hiding spot... but he knew me. He knew where I would hide. His voice was low and sure, and I felt my heart unwind at the safety it promised.

"Andromache - come home."

Without hesitation, as I had so many years ago, I came, carefully slipping down through the branches of my sheltering tree with a whisper of gratitude for its nymph. And, as he had so long ago, Hector was waiting at the foot of it for me still. But this time my feet did not have time to touch the ground before he had me caught and cradled in his arms, pressed tightly close. I wrapped my arms desperately around him and buried my face in his shoulder. His words were murmurs, nonsense sounds but I knew what he meant. I was safe.

He loved me.

And I knew.

In a strange way, my life had now come full circle. And yet – it was not an ending at all but rather a beginning. I was finally home.

I was finally where I belonged.

Epilogue:

I moved across the grass and my bare feet were silent in it as the night air followed me. I wrapped the silence around me like a cloak as I moved through the darkness and the moon shadowed in fickle past the darker shapes I passed.

My husband slept. Finally. All day long, he had held me as if he would hold me forever. He had held me as if I would turn to wind and blow away. Even now the memory of his arms around me and the look on his face, in his eyes, had my throat tightening.

He loved me.

That knowledge, the sudden surety, shook me to my very core.

Hector loved me.

After he had saved me, he had held me all the way back through the city. A city that had cheered my name in a way that still confused me. He had carried me to our bedroom at the top of our house, shutting away the rest of the world outside its door. Even when he had drawn me into the tub, both of us still fully clothed, he had held me. I had found I was not able breathe unless he was holding me and even safe in his arms and surrounded by the warm water it had taken me a very long time to stop shaking. I had fallen asleep in his arms in that tub, resting against his body in that water and when I had woken -- he had still been there. He had kissed the marks on my wrists where my skin was torn. He had lifted me out of the water and kissed the ugly bruises on my arms from rough fingers and, peeling wet cloth away and laying me on the bed, he had kissed the ones on my hip from where I had fallen against something in the kitchen. The scratches on my palms, and even my feet, from the bark of the tree and the wrapped red bruises against my ribs where the rail of the chariot had hit me when I had made it unbalance and tip over, even the edges of my mouth where the gag has torn my skin.

His lips had been too soft to cause pain against the discoloration around my thumb where I had dislocated the joint and he held me while I pushed it back into place. He had kissed away the pain and then gently kissed the throbbing skin around my thumb again.

He had kissed my mouth. My throat. My face and my shoulders. He had not stopped his cleansing kisses at my bruises but had claimed every inch of skin on me. Showing me without words that I was still his, that he was still mine, and that there was no barrier between us.

My husband loved me.

It was almost enough to make me stop what I was doing now, pausing in the dark and looking back over my shoulder toward the towering city walls I now stood outside of. Yet, his love was exactly why I was doing what I was doing now.

He slept now, I knew, deep and at peace in our bed. I went out beyond the safety of the city's walls to make sure he would always be able to sleep that way.

In the deepest shade of night, I went to my father's tents. I knew where they were. I had made it a point to find out when they had first arrived, asking the forgotten servants and slaves that saw everything and feeling better for knowing where my family rested, where my mother laired. I had thought only of my own safety then. Now I thought differently.

My mother was waiting for me in the darkness of her tent's interior as I pushed aside the thick cloth that hide its entrance and stepped inside.

"I knew you would come," she told me and her voice was just as I remembered it to be, dark music and whispered power. I did not hesitate as I approached the chair she sat on.

"Yes." I answered her in the same voice. Her voice... and mine now too. All of my life I had feared this, but today had changed me. It had changed everything. I knew it did not matter – so little mattered about what was between us anymore -- but still, I had to ask.

"Why?"

Her eyes blinked once in the dark, black jewels in an ivory face. For the first time, I realized that they looked like beetle's shells, hard and black and not stars at all the way I had always thought as a child. Threnody crouched at her feet, still and silent, the silver bells in her hair mute. I realized almost abstractly that the dark slave was frightened of me. Clever Threnody. I was not the child I had once been. The pieces of me that had broken today had not fit back together again the way they had before. Something was different now. *I* was different now.

"I deserve better," my mother answered and her voice was sure and sharp. "Achilles is the son of the sea witch, Thetis. The world itself could be ruled by a man that came from that mixed blood, hers and mine."

"They would have used me like a lawiaiai. I would have been a war prize," I found the anger then and it replaced the apathy in me – but it did not replace the calm. Her hand, long and thin like mine, waved the minor discomfort away. Her voice was a hiss.

"A child is a child. What matter how you got it as long as it was gotten."

"You used Cassandra." Pitiful Cassandra. In her delirium she had been triumphant before Hector, so sure of her place without me that she had spoken of it, claimed it as if it were already hers. He had known then -- and rushed home to find me already gone. I did not blame Cassandra though. She was small and helpless in her desires, desperate for what she could not have and too willing to gamble with her empty hands on chances that would never have been. My mother was neither small nor helpless in her desires though and the look she gave me said I was wasting time talking of pointless game pieces who were only made to be broken.

"The child begged to be used. She wants to be you, in the lawagetas' bed and out of it. All I did was open her mind to the gods she claims to have already been visited by." She paused and her voice was smug. "She was grateful to me for it. You should have heard her sobbing thanksgiving at my feet."

It finally broke through my inertia and I stepped forward, bringing my hand down on top of Threnody's head where she crouched. I kept my touch light but I still felt the way she trembled under my fingers. She had taken my first caretaker from me. She had threatened my closest friend all those years. She had found such pleasure in summoning me and in helping my mother with my lessons. She knew what she had helped mold me to be. And she was afraid.

"They hurt my Bithia," my voice was lower, quieter now as I looked down at my mother. My nails trailed against the top of Threnody's scalp as I spoke, light scratches that broke the skin, moving them over and over in the exact same place, making them slim furrows in my repetition. The pain was not enough to move her. "The physicians say it will scar. It will cripple her for life."

My mother looked at me and I wondered if she truly was that detached from everything human. That she did not, could not, understand.

"So find yourself another more beautiful than you to take your place when the danger comes."

I held her eyes with mine.

"I will. But the danger will never come from you again."

I saw it then. The flicker of uncertainty. She had known I would come. She had known I would not let this rest. This was for Bithia.

But even more, what I did, I did for Hector.

I did this for my unborn children by him. She would not have them. She would never touch any daughter of mine.

For the first time in her life, I watched as my mother realized that I might be exactly what she had created me to be.

It scared her.

It scared me.

It served me too tonight however and so I did not turn from it.

Under my hand, Threnody was beginning to tremble. She thought it was from fear and cold. It was from so much more than that but she would not realize it. Yet.

"I have wondered how it was that Eurytion arrived so quickly from Phthia. How he knew where to find me. How he knew when to find me. It was you. Before I even sailed from Thebe you sent for him, didn't you? Not for me. What was he coming to you to receive, mother?"

595

Her smile was smug in the darkness. She did not answer me. She did not need to do anything more than smile to prove me right. My enemy had called to my enemy and it had had nothing to do with me. Had she promised him Thebe? The boat Hector had found waiting for its Achaean prince, the men on it, it had looked like a raiding party he said. It had looked like a raiding party before it had been burned and gutted, its guardians killed.

Had my mother decided Thebe had grown too small for her?

Had she meant to follow me even to Phthia?

Has she meant to take Thetis' place?

"You will not stop." It surprised me how calm my voice was but tonight I was finally the part of me that I had always denied and that part of me knew what needed to be done. "You will see me serving under a man you think will bring your bloodline glory. You are no longer content with the heir of the brightest city in the world."

"No," she said. "I deserve more now."

She had proven she could reach into the very halls of Ilium. My husband was a warrior and the strongest man I knew. Yet poison did not care how noble a man was when it touched him.

It did not care if it touched children...

"When I was small, you used to hold my face like this," I lifted my hands and cupped her beautiful, cold face between my palms. I slid my fingers under the curve of her elegant jaw. My nails, and what was under them, bit into her thin skin, breaking it though barely enough to even draw blood. It was such a small pain, not the type either my mother or myself would consider worth acknowledging. "Do you remember? It used to be one of the only times you would touch me. How I used to hate that gesture."

Her eyes met mine, defiant and perhaps it was only my own fear I imagined I saw in them.

"I am your mother. The gods will curse you and all you love if you harm me."

It made me smile. Too late. She was far, far too late.

"The gods ignore women with blood like ours," I reminded her. "Is that not what you've always told me? But I do not need to kill you to take your sting away, mother."

Threnody's tiny silver bells were beginning to chime quietly as her shakes grew stronger and I saw the whites of her eyes in the darkness near my side. We ignored her, my mother and I, but I saw the understanding flicker in my mother's eyes. Suddenly, now, finally, recognizing the tiny pricks she had felt in her own skin.

"I am taking away your power," I told her calmly. "I am taking away your dark servant. And I am taking away your strength. From this day on you will have to rely on the men in our house for everything you want -- and they will not be kind. I am taking away their fear of you and replacing it with disgust and pity. I cannot kill you. But I will clip your dark wings and you will never again touch me or mine."

My mother's eyes narrowed then and I saw the fury, the hatred, the violence in them. I was already familiar with them all. Her fingers on the arms of her chair tightened as Threnody began to convulse at her feet, choking through a swollen throat. My mother pulled away from me and my nails left long, narrow scratches on her perfect, alabaster skin. In her eyes, I saw what I had become.

I should have mourned that. Instead, I felt only satisfaction.

"You don't have the power to tame me. No one does," she snarled it and her carefully beautiful face convulsed. She lashed out at me with her own long, discolored nails but I stepped back out of the way easily. Already, she was growing clumsy.

"I already have," I told her softly and listened to her howl as she lunged for me over the body of her dying slave. I watched without emotion as her legs refused to support her and she collapsed. The surprise, the shock and fear, bloomed in her eyes at that, still refusing to think that she could ever be brought down, even now. She struggled to rise but I already knew she would never be able to stand on her own again. By the end of the night, there would be very little she would be able to do on her own again.

She had taught me too well. And I was stronger than she was.

She shrieked at me as I turned but I had learned long ago that no one came when you screamed. Not in that family. So I left her there, spitting her curses at me over the cooling body of her only loyal servant and I walked unafraid and undisturbed back out through the tents and into the city, the way lit by moonlight and shadows.

My husband's house was quiet when I returned but the guards standing outside it greeted me when I came back and they did not ask where I had been. On the way home, I had trimmed my nails short and burned them and the bone chips I had hidden under them in a small shrine I had passed in the lower sections of the city, a memorial to an unknown god. Now, in the kitchen I cleansed my hands with vinegar and water to take away the last of what I had brought to my mother's darkness. My darkness now. My hands looked pale and slender in the dim light and I wondered how they could look so clean and pure when I had finally embraced that last dark shard of who I was. I should have felt foul. I should have felt ashamed or afraid. But I had done what I had to save what I loved more fiercely than my own life and all I felt was tired.

Had I lost a future tonight – or won one? Maybe it was too early to tell. I just knew that I wanted my own bed and my own husband and I felt no shame in returning to them even though I knew I should. Quiet, I climbed the stairs.

Bithia slept, calm and untroubled in her bed and Cebriones dozed on a chair nearby. The light from the oil lamp made them golden as I checked them on the way past.

There was no oil lit in my husband's room. Only the moon and the shadows. Yet he was awake in the bed and waiting for me. He asked no questions and I gave no answers. I only came into his arms and found the warmth and safety and comfort I had lived my whole life without. I would have done anything to protect it, to protect him. I *would* do anything. Today, he had saved me with his darkness. Maybe – maybe that was enough to keep from becoming a monster. Maybe it was in how the darkness was bound and used that salvation lay. I did not know. I just knew that we would find out together, he and I.

What price – to save the one we loved most?

He drew me down into the bed with him and his mouth found mine in the night.

I raised my arms and wrapped them around his wide shoulders and my soul returned from the dark tents outside and the unknown future to rest safe with his. Here, in the place where we both belonged.

The little girl that had fled through summer fields was no more. I had grown up. I had found my home.

Acknowledgement

I would like to acknowledge the books that helped me with my research into the exciting era of the late Bronze Age. First on the book shelf was always Homer's *Iliad* for bringing such humanity to an epic about war followed closely by Rosemary Sutcliff's beautiful companion book *Black Ships Before Troy* with its illustrations by Alan Lee. My thanks also to Michael Wood aka Mr. Tightpants for both the mini-series and book *In Search of the Trojan War*. Without these sources, I never would have been able to enter the ancient world in my head or my writing. Thebe is intentionally called Thebe to keep it from being confused with the similar named city in Greece. Mistakes in historical accuracy are mine entirely.

My special thanks to my mother for reading this entire work and always encouraging me to continue. To my father and to my sister for listening to me ramble constantly. To Ethan and Emily for encouraging me to make this story into the very best it could be. To Debbie, Jim and Dave for reading the story and giving me their thoughts as well as their encouragement. To Janna for doing the insurmountable and actually editing this work, each and every wrung out page. And last but never least, to my best beloveds and gentle readers who have read my works down through the years and given me their support and their friendship, a group of whom you too are now a part.